D1448639

Celebrating Katherine Mansfield

Celebrating Katherine Mansfield

A Centenary Volume of Essays

Edited by

Gerri Kimber and Janet Wilson

First published 2011 by
PALGRAVE MACMILLAN

Palgrave Macmillan in the UK is an imprint of Macmillan Publishers Limited,
registered in England, company number 785998, of Houndmills, Basingstoke,
Hampshire RG21 6XS.

Palgrave Macmillan in the US is a division of St Martin's Press LLC,
175 Fifth Avenue, New York, NY 10010.

Palgrave Macmillan is the global academic imprint of the above companies
and has companies and representatives throughout the world.

Palgrave® and Macmillan® are registered trademarks in the United States,
the United Kingdom, Europe and other countries.

ISBN 978–0–230–27773–1   hardback

This book is printed on paper suitable for recycling and made from fully
managed and sustained forest sources. Logging, pulping and manufacturing
processes are expected to conform to the environmental regulations of the
country of origin.

A catalogue record for this book is available from the British Library.

Library of Congress Cataloging-in-Publication Data

Celebrating Katherine Mansfield : a centenary volume of essays /
    edited by Gerri Kimber and Janet Wilson.
        p. cm.
    Includes index.
    ISBN 978–0–230–27773–1 (hardback)
1. Mansfield, Katherine, 1888–1923—Criticism and interpretation.
    I. Kimber, Gerri. II. Wilson, Janet, 1948– III. Title.
    PR9639.3.M258Z589 2011
    823'.912—dc22   2011005249

10 9 8 7 6 5 4 3 2 1
20 19 18 17 16 15 14 13 12 11

Printed and bound in Great Britain by
CPI Antony Rowe, Chippenham and Eastbourne

To Kevin, Ralph and Bella

Contents

Acknowledgements

Sydney Janet Kaplan's essay in this volume comes from a chapter of her book *Circulating Genius: John Middleton Murry, Katherine Mansfield and D. H. Lawrence* published by Edinburgh University Press © Sydney Janet Kaplan, 2010, and is reproduced here (with minor editorial changes) with kind permission of the publishers. Thanks go to Sally Burton the artist, and Jean Allan the owner, for permission to reproduce a detail of the painting entitled 'Double Portrait of Katherine Mansfield' on the front cover. The image of Katherine Mansfield's writing used to illustrate the essay by C. K. Stead (p. 220) is reproduced by kind permission of the Alexander Turnbull Library, Wellington, New Zealand, John Middleton Murry collection, ref. no. qMS-1244.

In addition, the editors would like to thank Paula Kennedy and Ben Doyle at Palgrave Macmillan for their generous support of this project, Kevin Ireland for invaluable editorial assistance, and Ralph and Bella Kimber as always, for their unending patience regarding the 'other' woman in their lives.

Notes on Contributors

Elleke Boehmer is Professor of World Literature in English at the University of Oxford. She has published four widely praised novels, *Screens again the Sky* (short-listed David Higham Prize, 1990), *An Immaculate Figure* (1993), *Bloodlines* (short-listed Sanlam Prize, 2000) and *Nile Baby* (2008). Internationally known for her research in international and postcolonial writing, she is the author of the world bestseller *Colonial and Postcolonial Literature: Migrant Metaphors* (1995, 2005), the monographs *Empire, the National and the Postcolonial, 1890–1920* (2002) and *Stories of Women* (2005), and of *Nelson Mandela* (2008).

Delia da Sousa Correa is Senior Lecturer in English at the Open University and is the editor of *Katherine Mansfield Studies*. She was educated in New Zealand, London and Oxford. Her published research centres on connections between literature and music in the nineteenth-century and modernist periods and includes *George Eliot, Music and Victorian Culture* (2003) and (ed.) *Phrase and Subject: Studies in Literature and Music* (2006).

Clare Hanson is Professor of English at the University of Southampton, UK. She has published extensively on twentieth-century women's writing, her books including *Katherine Mansfield* (1981), *Virginia Woolf* (1994) and *Hysterical Fictions: The Woman's Novel in the Twentieth Century* (2000). Her most recent monograph is *A Cultural History of Pregnancy* (2004) and she is currently completing a study of literature and eugenics in post-war Britain.

Anna Jackson lectures in English Literature at Victoria University of Wellington, New Zealand. Publications include *Diary Poetics: Form and Style in Writers' Diaries, 1915–1962* (2010), *Floating Worlds: Essays on Contemporary New Zealand Fiction*, co-edited with Jane Stafford (2009), and four collections of poetry, most recently *The Gas Leak* (2006).

Sydney Janet Kaplan is Professor of English at the University of Washington. Her most recent book is *Circulating Genius: John Middleton Murry, Katherine Mansfield and D. H. Lawrence* (2010). Her other publications include *Katherine Mansfield and the Origins of Modernist Fiction* (1991) and *Feminine Consciousness in the Modern British Novel* (1975).

Gerri Kimber is an Associate Lecturer at The Open University. She is Chair of the Katherine Mansfield Society and co-editor of *Katherine Mansfield Studies*. She is the author of *Katherine Mansfield: The View from France* (2008) and *A Literary Modernist: Katherine Mansfield and the Art of the Short Story* (2008). She is co-editor of the following volumes: *Framed! Essays in French Studies* (2007) and *Katherine Mansfield and Literary Modernism* (2011).

J. Lawrence Mitchell is Professor of English and Interim Head of the Department of Hispanic Studies at Texas A&M University. His biographical study *T. F. Powys: Aspects of a Life* appeared in 2005, and he is currently working on a book about boxing in literature and art. He has built a comprehensive collection of Mansfield's work in British and American editions including copies of four numbers of the *Queen's College Magazine* while Mansfield was there (one with her cousin Evelyn Payne's signature), copies of *Rhythm*, two variants of the 1911 *In a German Pension*, the rare *Cosmic Anatomy*, and Murry's *Still Life* inscribed 'To Chaddie with love from Jack Murry, December 1916'.

Anne Mounic is maître de conference/lecturer at the University Paris 3 – Sorbonne nouvelle. She is co-editor of the online literary review *Temporel*. Recent publications include *Quand on a marché plusieurs années* (a novel). Among her critical essays are 'Psyché et le secret de Perséphone: Prose en métamorphose, mémoire et création (Katherine Mansfield, Catherine Pozzi, Anna Kavan, Djuna Barnes)' (2004) and 'Jacob ou l'être du possible' (2009).

Vincent O'Sullivan, Professor Emeritus, Victoria University of Wellington, has edited, with Margaret Scott, the five-volume edition of Katherine Mansfield's *Collected Letters*, published by Oxford University Press. He is also widely published as a poet, fiction writer, playwright and biographer. His most recent work is *Further Convictions Pending: Poems 1998–2008* (2009).

Josiane Paccaud-Huguet is Professor of Modern English Literature and Literary Theory at Université Lumière-Lyon 2, where she is also Dean of the Faculty of Languages. She has published extensively on modernist authors (Conrad, Joyce, Woolf, Mansfield, D. H. Lawrence, Malcolm Lowry) both in France and abroad. She is currently working on a translation of Virginia Woolf's *Between the Acts* for Bibliothèque de la Pléiade, and finishing a book on the 'Modernist Moment of Vision', including a chapter on Katherine Mansfield.

Sarah Sandley is CEO of the APN Magazine Group, the publisher of a wide portfolio of titles, including New Zealand's leading current affairs and arts magazine the *NZ Listener*. She was educated at the University of Birmingham, England, and Victoria University of Wellington, New Zealand, where she graduated with a PhD in 1992, having written a thesis entitled 'Epiphany in the Short Stories of Katherine Mansfield'. She has contributed to several publications including 'The Middle of the Note: Mansfield's "Glimpses"', in *Katherine Mansfield: In From the Margin* (1994), and 'Not Epiphanies but Glimpses', in *Worlds of Katherine Mansfield* (1991). She also wrote 22 of the Katherine Mansfield story entries for *The Oxford Companion to New Zealand Literature* (1998).

Angela Smith is an Emeritus Professor in the Department of English Studies, and was a founding member and Director of the Centre of Commonwealth Studies, at the University of Stirling in Scotland. Her books include *East African Writing in English* (1989), *Katherine Mansfield and Virginia Woolf: A Public of Two* (1999) and *Katherine Mansfield: A Literary Life* (Palgrave 2000). She has edited Jean Rhys's *Wide Sargasso Sea* for Penguin (1997) and *Katherine Mansfield Selected Stories* for Oxford World's Classics (2002). She chaired the Europe and South Asia panel of the Commonwealth Writers' Prize for 2006 and 2007. She is a Vice-President of the Katherine Mansfield Society.

Anna Smith teaches children's literature and adolescent fiction at the University of Canterbury. She has completed research on psychoanalysis, especially the work of Julia Kristeva and, more lately, object-relations theory. She writes on New Zealand women artists and in addition has published a novel, *Politics 101* (2006). Her story 'Hesitation Waltz' appeared in *JAAM*, September 2010.

C. K. Stead, Professor Emeritus, University of Auckland, is known as a critic of twentieth-century modernism and of New Zealand literature, including Mansfield. He is the author of a dozen novels, and as many volumes of poems recently gathered in *Collected Poems, 1951–2006*. He was awarded a CBE in 1985, and in 2007 his country's highest award, the ONZ.

Janna K. Stotz completed her MA degree in British and American Literature at Texas Tech University, in which she examined a systems theory approach to various works of fiction. She is the assistant managing editor of the journal *Conradiana* and works as an instructor with TTU's Rhetoric and Composition programme.

Janet Wilson is Professor of English and Postcolonial Studies at the University of Northampton, and in 2010–11 Research Fellow in New Zealand Studies at Birkbeck, University of London. She is also Chair of EACLALS, Vice-Chair of the Katherine Mansfield Society and editor of the *Journal of Postcolonial Writing*. Recent publications include *Fleur Adcock* (2007), the edition *The Gorse Blooms Pale: Dan Davin's Southland Stories* (2007), and the co-edited volumes *Rerouting the Postcolonial: New Directions for the New Millennium* (2010) and *Katherine Mansfield and Literary Modernism* (2011).

Abbreviations

The following abbreviations are standard throughout the volume:

V. O'Sullivan and M. Scott (eds) (1984–2008), *The Collected Letters of Katherine Mansfield*, 5 vols (Oxford: Clarendon Press). Hereafter referred to as *Letters 1*, *Letters 2*, and so on, followed by the page number.

M. Scott (ed.) (1997) *The Katherine Mansfield Notebooks*, 2 vols (Canterbury, New Zealand: Lincoln University Press and Daphne Brasell Associates). Hereafter referred to as *Notebooks 1* and *Notebooks 2*.

Please note that Mansfield frequently omitted conventions regarding punctuation and grammar in her personal writing. Extracts from all of the above volumes are therefore [sic].

Some essays in this volume use John Middleton Murry's 1954 edition of Mansfield's *Journal* rather than the *Notebooks* volumes above. The *Notebooks* are an enormous feat of scholarship and a tribute to the diligence of Margaret Scott who devoted many years to the deciphering of Mansfield's notoriously illegible handwriting. All Mansfield scholars are in her debt. However, it is not always easy to locate specific diary entries, and thus we have allowed the use of the 1954 edition where this was the contributors' preference.

Introduction

Gerri Kimber and Janet Wilson

Celebrating Katherine Mansfield arises out of an international conference held at the former Centre for New Zealand Studies, at Birkbeck, University of London in September 2008, co-organized by Ian Conrich and the editors, which focused on the centenary of the arrival of Katherine Mansfield in London in July 1908 and the start of her professional career as a writer. It brings together new auto/biographical and critical-theoretical approaches to her life and art, in ways that confirm their rich and complex interaction; it features historical and aesthetic studies of her literary modernism, which position her within a post/colonial framework, offers new insights into constructions of voice and self, her handling of genres such as the uncanny, and provides theoretically inflected readings of less well-known stories, most notably the challenging and complex 'Je ne parle pas français'. The volume consolidates the view of Mansfield as an artist constantly concerned with and defined by problems of dislocation, estrangement and displacement, both in her fiction and life and, for the critic, by her somewhat ambiguous reputation as a modernist. It also builds on past criticism, to suggest that as modernism itself is being redefined, and its conceptual and geographical boundaries expanded, so Mansfield's liminality and marginality argue for a recentring of her work. If, as Elleke Boehmer claims in her essay, modernism 'represented an unfolding of different, interacting responses to the predicament of modernity, frequently expressed as a problem of self-alienation', then Mansfield, we claim, is its most iconic, most representative writer.

The essays are arranged into an opening and closing 'frame' (Parts I and IV), which provides biographical and autobiographical perspectives on Mansfield's work, and a central block of two further parts (Parts II and III), which offers theoretical and critical readings of particular stories. This structure foregrounds the socio-historical perspectives that were for many years lacking in Mansfield criticism as framing, critical contexts for the close-grained, theoretically informed readings and analyses of stories which feature in the middle parts. Collectively, however, all the essays in this volume reflect the new impetus in Mansfield studies generated by the publication of the two volumes of *Notebooks* by Margaret Scott and the five volumes of *Letters* edited by Vincent O'Sullivan and Margaret Scott. The importance of this cannot be underestimated. Mansfield was a writer who died young, had a relatively slender output, and worked almost exclusively in a mode of fragmented impressionism. Improved access to her non-fiction, her so-called 'ephemera', greatly advances scholarship, because these writings and jottings shed light onto her thought processes and imagination. As C. K. Stead astutely notes, by being allowed into her studio 'we are able to trace self-discovery becoming literary development and how the two interacted'.[1]

Mansfield's place in the modernist canon has always been marginal if not undervalued;[2] she neither belonged to Bloomsbury, nor was seen in her lifetime as an avatar of high modernism as exemplified by Eliot, Pound and Joyce, although the publication in 1922 of *The Garden Party and Other Stories* coincides with the publication of the movement's high points: *The Waste Land* and *Ulysses*. This eclipse has been due to the general neglect of the influence of women writers on modernism until relatively recently, and in her case she has been overlooked even by some earlier feminist critics. Her chosen genre, the short story, was for many years underestimated in relation to the weightier, more prominent genres of modernism – poetry and the novel – a limitation which is now being rectified by research into modernist little magazines (in which Mansfield herself was so involved) that shows 'the vast hinterland that remains unexplored'.[3] There is also the fact that Mansfield was a colonial expatriate who was not only located in both the provincial margins and the metropolitan centre, but whose life in Europe was itinerant, even nomadic, as she moved about ceaselessly and restlessly for reasons of health and finance. Such complex self-positionings and identities of writers like Mansfield and Virginia Woolf are being reassessed through the perspective of gender, while increased enquiry by postcolonial critics into the hybrid identities of diasporic, exilic writers – often ungrounded and displaced – opens up to new scrutiny the influence of the margins on the construction of the centre. The volume's reoriented perspectives on the origins and nature of Mansfield's modernism come from re-examining the movement's colonial contexts (always less visible than the Anglo-American metropolitan ones), through (post)colonial and transnational theories of place and identity. They too reveal a daring, radical and experimental writer whose complex legacy and reputation are only gradually being disentangled from the web of mythologizing, alternative canonization (in France) and exclusion (in New Zealand in the earlier decades of the twentieth century as C. K. Stead's essay shows), in which they have been enmeshed. For example, a concern with subjectivity and the construction and meaning of voice as a symptom of 'modernist being' in her work in several essays in this volume show Mansfield in a more dynamic and innovative relationship with the experimental modernism of contemporaries such as Virginia Woolf than has previously been realized, while the new light shed on her life in the biographical essays of Part I confirm that only through reading the life back into the art which commemorates it can an understanding of how her fiction developed be acquired. The attention in several essays to the construction of an inauthentic voice in 'Je ne parle pas français' suggests that this story has acquired a special resonance for our age.

*****

This is the first volume of essays devoted to Mansfield and her work since *Katherine Mansfield: In from the Margin* (1994), the proceedings of two centennial events held in 1988 to honour her birth. The editor, Roger Robinson, celebrates the expansion in Mansfield's reputation that the commemoration made visible: her centrality to twentieth-century literary culture, due to her transformation of the short story in English and essential contributions to modernism.[4] Recent work such as Angela Smith's *Katherine Mansfield: A Literary Life* (2000) and Sydney Janet Kaplan's *Circulating Genius: John Middleton Murry, Katherine Mansfield, D. H. Lawrence* (2010) substantiates these claims. The revived interest in her life and times following the publication of the *Notebooks* and *Letters* builds on the momentum generated by Claire Tomalin's landmark biography *Katherine Mansfield: A Secret Life* (1987), and examinations of her representations of gender, notably Kate Fullbrook's *Katherine Mansfield* (1986), Kaplan's *Katherine Mansfield and the Origins of Feminist Fiction* (1991), Mary Burgan's *Illness, Gender and Writing: The Case of Katherine Mansfield* (1994) and Pamela Dunbar's *Radical Mansfield: Double Discourse in Katherine Mansfield's Short Stories* (1997). A new biography by Kathleen Jones, *Katherine Mansfield: The Storyteller*, was published in 2010. Mansfield studies currently benefit from new scholarly interests in modernism, remappings of socio-historical contexts and interdisciplinary approaches. Her friendships with contemporaries like D. H. Lawrence and Virginia Woolf have been re-examined;

archival research underpins reassessments of the relationship with John Middleton Murry; her work as a magazine editor with Murry on *Rhythm* and *Blue Review*, and the impact of these journals more generally has been subject to new scrutiny; and Mansfield's relationship in her work to musical form and the visual arts, the post-Impressionists and the Fauvists, as well as her many friendships with artists, are now identified as vital components of her modernist aesthetics.[5]

Many essays in this collection build on recent research, extending the feminist approaches of the 1980s and 1990s, by reading her, for example, in terms of the Freudian uncanny, the Lacanian 'real' and (post)colonialism, while others reach into new areas such as the influence of Dickens on her work. A concern, for example, with the effects of sound and rhythm in her writing, is explored through the psychoanalytic, philosophical approaches of Josiane Paccaud-Huguet and Anne Mounic. Its synaesthesia – the use of techniques associated with cinema and the musical dimensions of her prose, as discussed by Delia da Sousa Correa and Sarah Sandley – fill out the picture of her artistic multidimensionality. Mansfield's experimental techniques of impersonation and strategies for alienating the reader show how her practice converges with Middleton Murry's definition of art in *Rhythm*: 'Modernism [...] penetrates beneath the outward surface of the world, and disengages the rhythms that lie at the heart of things, rhythms strange to the eye, unaccustomed to the ear, primitive harmonies of the world that is and lives.'[6] Her use of tropes of doubling, the transgression of boundaries, images of splitting, rupture and self-objectification, all symptoms of the divided colonial subject, point to the deep uncanniness of her writing, as Clare Hanson argues.

Mansfield was called by Elizabeth Bowen in 1957 'our missing contemporary', and her continuing relevance suggests this comment still rings true.[7] The essays in this volume offer an outline of a twenty-first-century image of Mansfield. Contemporary theories of textual practice, self and identity, when applied to her work, position her as a colonial modernist, an emancipated woman writer-traveller (Wilson and Boehmer), and avid letter writer and diarist (Jackson), who constructs her reader as collaborator in the fiction-making process (Stotz); a writer who 'enacts' femininity in her fiction through models and stereotypes which stress the arbitrariness of gender; who produces self, being and voice performatively, in ways inevitably linked to the anxiety of other female writers of the time, like Virginia Woolf, who feared that their voice might not be heard (Mounic); who manipulates different genres within single fictions (Hanson), whose affinity with Dickens extends to appropriations and adaptations of voice and style (Smith), and who aware of 'this sadness in life' and 'darkly illumined' by the tragic experience of death, creates a sense of wonder through a resonance of being (Mounic). In short, here is a repositioning of Mansfield as a modernist who was ahead of her time, whose formal experimentation can also be seen as anticipating postmodern metafictional practice such as play with genre, consciousness of the text as artifice, performances of gender and voice, and the awareness of and appeal to popular culture. This contemporaneity is revealed, for example, in Paccaud-Huguet's essay which uses Lacanian psychoanalysis to illuminate theories behind concepts (such as the 'symptom' and 'transfer') which Mansfield articulates in the only discourses available to her.

*****

The first part of *Celebrating Katherine Mansfield*, 'Biographical Readings and Fiction', opens with an important study by Vincent O'Sullivan of the last year of her life; its focus is the book *Cosmic Anatomy*, the major intellectual and literary influence upon her when she entered the Gurdjieff Institute at Fontainebleau. O'Sullivan maps Mansfield's attitudes towards her impending death in her last year in relation to the loss of certainty that permeated European culture and thought in the post-war milieu; he re-evaluates the alternative system that Gurdjieff's theories and the *Cosmic Anatomy* represented at a time when Mansfield was seeking unity and personal harmony. Essays by J. Lawrence Mitchell and Sydney Janet Kaplan which follow, introduce recent scholarship on Mansfield's relationship to her brother Leslie and her marriage to John Middleton Murry. Mitchell adopts a biographical, historical approach in examining Mansfield's reactions to Leslie Beauchamp's death in 1915, drawing on the New Zealand National Archives, eyewitness reports and published letters to differentiate from the facts (as far as they can be ascertained) the myth that Mansfield (and Murry) constructed. Mitchell reworks the biographical-critical framework which has hitherto informed several of Mansfield's key stories that allude to the brother–sister relationship, notably 'The Garden Party'. Kaplan also draws from biographical accounts to examine the relationships and activities of Middleton Murry and Mansfield, as well as their correspondence during their long separation in the crucial year 1918 when Mansfield was in France. In an exemplary scholarly-textual analysis she demonstrates intertextual links between the letters, Murry's novel *Still Life* (1916) and 'Je ne parle pas français' (written in 1916), suggesting that the texts vitally reflect their turbulent relationship. This includes the replication in both plots of the homosocial bonds and triangulated relationships that developed between Lawrence, Murry and Mansfield, and between Murry, Mansfield and Ottoline Morrell: evidence of art imitating life. All three essays in Part I challenge or overturn earlier views of Mansfield's most intimate relationships, and are therefore crucial for understanding how she both identified herself through others and dealt with the difficulties and losses that these relationships entailed.

Part II introduces Mansfield's work from relatively broad-angled views on modernist writing. It opens with Elleke Boehmer's politico-critical reorientation of Mansfield as a modernist writer through questioning the reasons for the omission of her name from contemporary accounts of canonical modernism. Boehmer makes the case for expanding the largely metropolitan, male-dominated modernist canon, and reintroducing Mansfield as a colonial modernist, a concept which she illustrates in relation to the African laundress in 'Je ne parle pas français'. Delia da Sousa Correa addresses the impact of music upon Mansfield's modernist aesthetic by analysing the relationship between musical form in her rhythmically attuned writing, and her use of musical allusion in particular with reference to the music of Wagner and Chopin, in ways that can be traced to Victorian literary models. Similarly, Sarah Sandley examines Mansfield as a cinematic writer, who was attracted by the new modes of visual entertainment (acting as an extra in movies made in London), and who in her desire to make her country 'leap into the eyes of the old world', introduced into her work key visual and filmic devices such as flashback and close-ups. This part concludes with Janna Stotz who introduces the concept of the 'play frame', pointing out how, in Mansfield's work, objects are presented within a boundary, border or frame – for example, mirrors, photographs and paintings as 'bounded artefacts' – by which messages are echoed both within and outside the narrative frame. Drawing on Gregory Bateson's essay, 'A Theory of Play and Fantasy', Stotz constructs a reading process for Mansfield's narratives whereby readers move between the outer and inner frames to complete the message included within the frame, thereby collaborating in the process from narrative consciousness to narrative creating.

Part III provides new methods of reading Mansfield which draw upon theoretical perspectives from Lacanian and Freudian psychoanalysis, as well as Kierkegaardian existentialism. All are concerned with the relationship between narrative form, consciousness and the self, and variously suggest that the act of creating involves some displacement or renegotiation of the subject/narrator's sense of being. Clare Hanson, in a groundbreaking essay, examines Mansfield's use of the uncanny, taking as her starting point Freud's essay 'Beyond the Pleasure Principle' (1920), in which he defines the concept as something repressed or hidden that comes out into the open. Doubling, blurred boundaries between the animate and inanimate, and the presence of the ghostly and alienating as mechanisms of repression which function to 'undo the logic of identity' occur in 'The Stranger', just one story that shows a deeper doubleness and uncanniness in Mansfield's writing than has yet been realized. Hanson draws on Freud's notion of the death drive – a desire to return 'to an old state of things' – and, linking this to Roland Barthes's theories about the aesthetic effect of the photograph as spectral, applies it to 'The Daughters of the Late Colonel' and 'The Fly'. Anne Mounic and Josiane Paccaud-Huguet provide nuanced analyses of the ways in which voice, selfhood and being are constructed in Mansfield's work. 'Voice' and the intensity of affect in Mansfield's goes beyond the natural voice or oral effect, as Mansfield aims to 'give voice to' or to perform her experience of the lapse of confidence in the voice's reality. Mounic argues that Mansfield captures figures of being in the flow of becoming, appropriating 'time as the inner pulsation of subjective achievement', and creating presence through the features of reciprocity and rhythm. Figures of wonder in her work (the aloe, the pear tree), she claims, come from a merging of self and object; so 'vital breath' becomes a way of approaching the sphere of unknowing. Paccaud-Huguet, drawing on Lacan's concept of *feminine jouissance* (female sensual pleasure), examines the 'economy of the [subjectless] voice' in terms of Mansfield's challenge to the socio-symbolic system of gender relations; and argues that Mansfield, like Lacan, shows that the 'symptom' is the most 'real' and, when transferred into writing, the most enduring part of 'ourselves'. Anna Smith focuses on how writing the consciousness, inscribing it in language, constitutes the Mansfield text. In her analysis of the first-person narrative voice of Raoul Duquette in 'Je ne parle pas français', she also examines the complexities of the self that is written out of experience even while being constructed in the writing process. Referring to Lacan's comment on the case of a patient who had plagiarized – 'an instance of Being which like the anorexic bites on nothing' – she argues that the narrative links plagiarism and writing. Duquette mobilizes himself into speech by imitation and borrowing, and in faking the words of those whom he has borrowed from (or eaten, or consumed), he literally disappears. In this story about appetite, writing – using the words of another to produce a voice – therefore becomes an 'evacuation of the self'.

The final part returns to life writing and its relationship to the writing of fiction, so providing a parallel to the biographical approach of the essays in Part I. Janet Wilson claims that Mansfield, conscious of shades of belonging and not belonging, reconfigures the dialectic between home and abroad in her New Zealand stories. Early sketches and vignettes show representations of the divided self which made her, as a colonial subject with plural identity structures, seek identification with both English culture and the Maori 'Other'. Using postcolonial theory, and with reference to Mansfield's early New Zealand stories written for *Rhythm*, Wilson argues, like Elleke Boehmer, that Mansfield is a liminal, colonial modernist writer, notably in her representations of the ambivalent locatedness of the 'unsettled settler'. Vincent O'Sullivan has noted how Victorian literary culture filtered into the very fabric of the colonial city of Wellington, and became known to Mansfield partly through the locations of the socially aspiring Beauchamp family; the childhood home in Karori, for example, where she spent her happiest years, was called 'Chesney Wold', the name of which, as O'Sullivan comments, was 'taken from the grand house of the coldly aristocratic Dedlocks in *Bleak House*'. He further notes how 'out of Chesney Wold and its neighbouring paddocks and streets [came] stories written by a young woman who so deeply admired the man who named the house that so haunted her memories'.[8] This colonial coincidence is a suggestive symbol of Mansfield's affinity with her famous predecessor, the focus of Angela Smith's essay on how Dickens influenced her creativity. With particular reference to *Our Mutual Friend* and Mansfield's story, 'Je ne parle pas français', Smith demonstrates that Mansfield responded imaginatively to Dickens's teeming universe, finding inspiration in his satirical sketches, his representations of voice through distinctive idiolects and his poignant images of childhood. Her argument reinforces the strength of Mansfield's own claim that, throughout her life, she was indeed 'not reading Dicken's *idly*'.

Smith's evidence for Mansfield's attraction to Dickens comes mainly from her letters and, in turn, Anna Jackson in her essay examines Mansfield's epistolary art, invoking Tom Paulin's letter-writing poetics, the 'rejection of the written for the writing, and the rejection of the mind in rest for the mind in action'. While exploring the relationship of 'sharing' (Mansfield's term) between the writer of the letters and the reader, Jackson also identifies Mansfield's retreat from the 'newness and nowness' (Paulin's term) of her letter writing, and with the help of memory over time begins to establish depth in her epistolary relationships. Finally, there is C. K. Stead's 'autobiographical fragment' in which he talks about his own encounter with Mansfield, first through the reception of her work in New Zealand as a modernist and hence an outsider to the realist-dominated tradition of cultural nationalism that sprang up in the 1930s and 1940s; then in many forms over the decades as editor, critic, poet and novelist, and most recently in his novel *Mansfield* (2004), testifying to the different ways Mansfield has inspired him and continues to hold a central place in his literary life. This essay, which was delivered as the opening address of the conference, signals both a terminus and a new departure, in that it raises questions about Mansfield's debts and legacies and the reception of her work more generally, which have not otherwise been addressed in this selection.

*****

Celebrating Katherine Mansfield defines new directions in Mansfield studies, with interpretations of her work and explorations of her literary legacy offered in essays covering areas as diverse as musicology, (post)colonial theory, and epistolary and biographical studies. Current developments in modernist studies, which this interdisciplinarity represents, reinforce this momentum. Landmarks since the 2008 conference – the founding of the international Katherine Mansfield Society, the new journal *Katherine Mansfield Studies* and annual conferences (notably the celebration in Menton in September 2009 of 40 years of the New Zealand Post Winn-Manson Mansfield Menton Fellowship for creative writing, and the Cambridge conference in March 2011 on Mansfield and her contemporaries) – attest to her growing importance for new generations of scholars. The editors intend that *Celebrating Katherine Mansfield*, along with our other collection, *Katherine Mansfield and Literary Modernism*, in bringing together and extending the flow of scholarship and criticism of her work over the past two decades, will confirm and reposition Mansfield's reputation as a foremost practitioner of the short story, and so expand contemporary knowledge of literary modernism.[9]

Notes

1. C. K. Stead (2010) 'Foreword', *Katherine Mansfield Studies*, 2, vii–viii.
2. In M. Levenson's *The Cambridge Companion to Modernism*, published as recently as 1999, Mansfield is not mentioned once, though her novelist friend Virginia Woolf merits detailed discussion. This is an inexplicable oversight which demonstrates how short story writers are frequently marginalized. See G. Kimber (2008) *Katherine Mansfield: The View from France* (Oxford: Peter Lang), p. 51.
3. See P. Brooker and A. Thacker (eds) (2009) *The Oxford Critical and Cultural History of Modernist Magazines*. Vol. 1, *Britain and Ireland 1880–1955* (Oxford University Press), p. 4; R. Scholes (2010) *Modernism in the Magazines: An Introduction* (New Haven, CT: Yale University Press).

4. R. Robinson (ed.) (1994) 'Introduction', in *Katherine Mansfield: In from the Margin* (Baton Rouge and London: Louisiana State University Press), pp. 1–8 (p. 2).
5. *Katherine Mansfield Studies*, 3 (2011) will be devoted to Mansfield and the visual arts. See also J. McDonnell (2010) *Katherine Mansfield and the Modernist Marketplace: At the Mercy of the Public* (Basingstoke: Palgrave Macmillan).
6. *Rhythm*, 1: 1 (1911).
7. E. Bowen (1996 [1956–57]) 'A Living Writer', in J. Pilditch (ed.) *The Critical Response to Katherine Mansfield* (Westport, CT: Greenwood Press), pp. 70–6.
8. Taken from Vincent O'Sullivan's unpublished address to the audience at the Katherine Mansfield Society's inaugural 'Birthday Lecture', at New Zealand House in London, 15 October 2010.
9. J. Wilson, G. Kimber and S. Reid (eds) (2011) *Katherine Mansfield and Literary Modernism* (London: Continuum).

Part I

Biographical Readings and Fiction

1
Signing Off: Katherine Mansfield's Last Year

Vincent O'Sullivan

Mansfield begins her first letter in 1922, written to her brother-in-law Richard Murry, with the jaunty claim, 'I suppose I am one of those optimists.' It is a word that places her at once, deliberately, and yet again, at a remove from the temperament of the man she had lived with off and on for the past ten years, and whose own disposition was crucial to what she would decide later in the year. She had noted, time and again, how to be in love does not necessarily prevent lovers being poles apart. 'And who could not feel it who lives with a pessimist.' But my interest is not in adding to those many discussions that tend to condescend to Mansfield by assuming she should really have married someone else. The question that for the moment I would most like to ask is why she was so drawn to the book she first mentions when she tells Richard in that same letter: 'Furious reading consisted of 1) Shakespeare 2) Cosmic Anatomy 3) the Bible.'[1]

We know from a notebook kept precisely for that reason how she responded to reading Shakespeare, and the plays are often there in her letters. Surely one of the more self-scrutinizing remarks in her correspondence is when, early in February 1922, just after she has settled in Paris and begun her sessions with Manoukhine, she tells Murry how in reading the plays 'I began to see those marvelous short stories asleep in an image as it were.' She quotes Caesar's lines in Act I from *Antony and Cleopatra:*

> Like to a vagabond flag upon the stream
> Goes to and back, lackeying the varying tide
> To rot itself with motion (I, iv, 42).

That is terrible, and it contains such a terribly deep psychological truth. That *'rots* itself' . . . And the idea of 'it' returning and returning, never swept out to sea finally. You may think you have done with it for ever but comes a change of tide and there is that dark streak reappeared, more sickeningly rotten still. I understand that better than I care to. I mean – alas! – I have proof of it in my own being.[2]

Mansfield kept a copy of the Bible with her always: her letters and stories and notebooks have dozens of references to it; and between Shakespeare and the Bible another book now becomes essential reading – *Cosmic Anatomy*.[3] James Moore, who knows far more about Gurdjieff, Ouspensky and the traditions they derive from than any other commentator on Mansfield, has a chapter in his study *Gurdjieff and Mansfield* called 'Cosmic Anatomy'.[4] Yet he does not attempt to come to grips with what it was in that book that so attracted her. And 'attract' is far too moderate a word. As she told her friend Violet Schiff (whose husband Stephen Hudson completed the Scott-Moncrieff translation of Proust, and arranged Mansfield's meeting with James Joyce), she had 'passed through a state of *awful* depression' in the last months of 1921. 'But I see my way now, I think. What saved me finally was reading a book called *Cosmic Anatomy*, and reflecting on it.'[5]

A. R. Orage, that 'desperado of genius' as Bernard Shaw called him,[6] was Mansfield's old editor from the *New Age*, and had published her first German stories. Their friendship was a long, and at times rocky one. T. S. Eliot thought him 'the best literary critic of that time in London',[7] and he was a man for enthusiasms. At different times deeply committed to Theosophy, then Socialism, then Nietzsche, he was now swept away by eastern and esoteric texts. Mansfield had written him a warm, admiring letter from Menton exactly a year before. It is not clear why she wrote at that time, but she effusively complimented him: 'you taught me to write, you taught me to think; you showed me what there was to be done and what not to do'.[8] There are other letters that don't survive. But certainly in late 1921 he posted a book to Switzerland, not to Mansfield, but to Murry for review.

In fact Murry, for several years, had carried what might be called a cautious enthusiasm for mysticism, yoga and the vague attractions of 'eastern thought'. Mansfield had practically none, but she liked the man who instructed Murry. His name was Millar Dunning, who had come from Devonport in Auckland, never returned home, and in 1920 published his one book, *The Earth Spirit*, described as containing 'a series of meditations on natural landscapes interspersed with prophecies of a coming New Age'.[9] It seems they had met at Garsington, and they got on well enough for Mansfield and Murry to stay with him in 1917 (Murry would later return to live near him when Mansfield decided on Fontainebleau). But the friendship with Mansfield seems both important and shadowy. There is a still unpublished notebook from the time of that early visit, but it is mostly fairly lugubrious poems by Murry, one of which imagines Mansfield as already dead, and drew the rather tart assessment from her:

> I don't like the poem. I don't think one ought to cultivate these flowers. The final page has lovely things in it but Sir why waste such flowers on funerals? Oh, I *do* think it is so wrong. Please *don't* lay me out. How can you?[10]

But whatever mild interest had been stirred by Dunning, it was a far cry from the book that now turned up in the post. When Murry opened *Cosmic Anatomy* he was appalled. Years later he would write rather cagily, his opinion obviously tempered by what it had meant to his wife:

> To such speculations I have since learned to attach a meaning, as a sometimes useful method (if used warily) of making the borderlands of psychology accessible to thought; but at that time they meant nothing – less than nothing; they were positively repellent. I put the book aside. K. M. picked it up.[11]

No doubt there was a touch of intended log-rolling to explain why it was sent to Murry at all. At that time he was one of the busiest and most respected critics writing in England – although Ezra Pound a month or so later in the *Dial* would give him a fair trouncing for not understanding French literature as he himself did. (A word in passing on literary malice. Pound disliked Mansfield, and I think it unlikely that there isn't a carefully chosen image when he writes 'Murry's article [on Flaubert] lacked only one thing: an editorial note to the effect that the article was given in order that the reader might understand for himself, at first hand, with the bacilli of the disease under his own eye and microscope').[12] But Pound's opinion aside, it was in Orage's interest to get a top reviewer for *Cosmic Anatomy and the Structure of the Ego*. The title page identified the author simply as 'M. B. Oxon'. The man behind the degree was Louey (as he insisted on pronouncing Lewis) Wallace, described by a contemporary as a Scot with 'a rosy face and a general air of self-depreciation, no matter whom he was talking to'.[13] Wallace had made his money as a sheep farmer in New Zealand, and was then connected with merchant banking. He had put up 500 pounds when Orage took over the *New Age* in 1907. He wrote rambling, quasi-scientific articles for the journal, promoting Social Credit economics, and challenging Freud from the perspective of Egyptology. Until the war in 1914 he continued to put in 100 pounds a year. And *Cosmic Anatomy* was his opus. By the end of January 1921, as Mansfield was about to begin her X-ray course with the Russian doctor who had once treated Gorky, and with her new enthusiasm for Wallace's book, 'she seemed presented', as Moore wrote, 'with not one but two escape routes: by licensed, attested, copper-bottomed Western science, and by spiritual revitalization'.[14]

Although Mansfield later in the year would hear the Russian Ouspensky explain Gurdjieff in his London lectures, her first enthusiasm for what eventually led her to Fontainebleau, and the Institute for the Harmonious Development of Man, derived from a book which was considered eccentric even by the author's own circle. The question of why it so attracted her is usually sidestepped by those who write on her. After all, nothing could seem further from what we know of her up to this point. It has none of the clarity of her own writing, or the precision and control she admired in others. As one reads it today, one is provoked on almost every page to describe it as either cranky or confused. To suspend disbelief is a tall order, yet to some extent that is what we must try for a time to do, to approach why it was so important to Mansfield; why reading it over the New Year so changed her life.

*****

The book opens with a mild enough generalization that almost everyone she knew would have agreed with. 'Before the war men were growing less sure that all was for the best in the best of worlds, but they were much too busy to realize the fact. The check resulting from the war has allowed them to do so.'[15] As Freud put it, the Great War put an end to what he called 'this once lovely and congenial world', as it withdrew access to 'the treasures of [...] civilized humanity'.[16] We remember how, at the end of 1919, Mansfield castigated Virginia Woolf for not taking this on board, when she reviewed *Night and Day*, and compared the novel to a stately ocean liner – majestic but outmoded.[17] As she put it more strongly in a letter to Murry:

> My private opinion is that it is a lie in the soul. The war never has been, that is what its message is. [...] I feel in the *profoundest* sense that nothing can ever be the same that as artists we are traitors if we feel otherwise.[18]

As so many of her contemporaries would have agreed, the West was shot. At that very moment, Heidegger was elaborating the groundwork for Existentialism,[19] with which Mansfield's own thinking soon enough would have more than a little in common. Less rigorously, such friends as Dunning and Orage moved away from European traditions. If western civilization had, in a sense, run out with the war, so too had its celebrated Enlightenment, so too had our arid intellectualism. Not that Mansfield needed the war, nor anyone else, to tell her about the limitations of *that*. Back in 1915, she had put to Murry:

> Whose fault is it that we are so isolated – that we have no real life – that everything apart from writing and reading is 'felt' to be a waste of time. [...] Why haven't I got a real 'home', a real life – [...] Im not a girl. Im a woman. I *want* things. [...] To write all the morning and then to get lunch over quickly and to write again in the afternoon & have supper and *one* cigarette together and then to be alone again until bed-time – and all this love and joy that fights for outlet – and all this life drying up, like milk, in an old breast. Oh I want life – I want friends and people and a house.[20]

She will say much the same thing, in different ways, for the next seven years.

She put her discontent far more sharply when in Randogne she made a note as she read Diderot's fortuitously named 'Jacques le Fataliste': 'I do not want to be a book *worm*. A worm burrows everlastingly. If its book is taken away from it the little blind head is raised, it wags, hovers, terribly uneasy, in a void until it begins to burrow again.'[21] When she read in Wallace's early pages that 'Mankind is now moving from Reason and Intellect towards Feeling and Emotion, and needs Instruction therein,'[22] one can catch at least what may first have appealed to her.

*****

And so the reader begins an initiation into often unspecified eastern texts, cosmic and astrological imagery, a bewildering amalgam of mythologies and philological unravelling that presumably dovetails with a range of scientific data for a vast depiction of what is called 'Cosmic Man'. Although, as the author insists, his book

> is not concerned with proving any facts or demonstrating any theories, and all the facts and theories are used merely as symbols, by the manipulation of which I am trying my best to put my readers in a

position of mind from which they may, if they will, see all that does and does not exist in a new light, which nevertheless is the oldest that is, and in what we call ancient days, was formulated, 'All is Vishnu'.[23]

From then on, the book makes difficult reading. What it defines near the beginning as a primary concern with 'the transference of energy' involves complicated cross-referencing, suspensions of logic and diagrams that to me, at any rate, are indecipherably complex. However one allows for metaphor or dramatization, almost always I was against a blank wall, my own incomprehension bafflingly on one side, the book's insistent 'truths' on the other, although as Wallace encouragingly says, it does not matter whether 'we are in England or New Zealand', the argument will hold. (I know my own reaction to the book is of little interest. I mention it to be up front about what is perhaps an impediment in discussing Mansfield's reading of it.)

In a notebook she began to use in the New Year, she enters a few teasing sentences that respond to what strikes her in *Cosmic Anatomy*:

1. To escape from the prison of the flesh – of matter. To make the body an instrument, a servant.
2. To act and not to dream. [...] What is the universal mind?[24]

She then transcribes a sentence in Sanskrit from the Isha Upanishad. When Murry glossed it in his 1954 edition of the *Journal* he quotes from what Wallace calls 'the translation': 'OM (my) mind, remember (thy) acts, remember (O) mind, remember (thy acts), remember'.[25] Wallace adds, but Murry does not, 'There is a great deal more in it than this.' His own reading of the line expands on love and death and memory, and the notion of uniting what he calls 'the reunion of freewill and fate'.[26] We cannot of course guess at what configurations so appealed to Mansfield, beyond saying that several of the words Wallace insists on, she too returns to time and again in both letters and notebooks. In the same week as she was again reading *The Tempest*, she makes the fullest note on the other book she is reading slowly and carefully, as she continues to reprimand herself for her lack of focus and will:

I have read a good deal of Cosmic Anatomy – understood it far better. Yes, such a book does fascinate me. Why does Jack hate it so? To get even a glimpse of the relation of things, to follow that relation & find it remains true through the ages enlarges my little mind as nothing else does.[27]

She rather simplifies a Wallace paragraph that mixes mythology and etymology as Robert Graves will later do, with far deeper scholarship and conviction, in the notes to his Greek myths. What excites her is the way this proposes an extension of meaning and possibility that would not otherwise have occurred to her. 'Its only a greater view of psychology,' she writes. 'It helps me with my writing for instance to know that hot + cross bun may mean Taurus, Pradhana, substance. No, that's not really what absorbs me, its that reactions to certain causes & effects always have been the same.' She remembers episodes in 'The Daughters of the Late Colonel', and writes, 'It wasn't for nothing Constantia chose the moon & water – for instance.'[28]

For a woman who, as she said, thought of death every day, and so often returned to a sense of division in her own personality, Wallace's reassurances of the unity underlying casual phenomena must have been appealing, as must the possibilities he offered of rescuing time from mere mechanical process. If one cares to trace them out, there are links with both that Bergsonian conception of personal time that Mansfield certainly was familiar with during her early days with Murry, co-editing *Rhythm*, and with what later would become the common currency of Existentialism – the notions Wallace touches on as he insists on 'the particular moment of time in which [one] happens to be', and what he calls 'the personal time equation'.[29] Time is not what one resists; it is what one collaborates with to give experience meaning. Whatever obscurities intervene, there is a direct line from Wallace to her recording, the day she meets Ouspensky at the end of September, what presumably was a snippet of conversation:

Do you know what individuality is?
No.
Consciousness of will. Conscious that you have a will and can act.[30]

Yet apart from these instances, there is little other direct mention of the book that so mattered to her. She does not show any apparent interest in what it says about reincarnation or immortality. Clearly what it did encourage was the self-examining that had always, to some extent, been a part of her notebooks. If you asked that *almost* impossible question, 'What is *Cosmic Anatomy*'s appeal?' at least one hesitant answer could be something like this: 'it brings home to a sympathetic reader that what we usually think of as reality is only one, small aspect of it. And there is something we can do about that.' This is how Wallace puts it, stripped of its elaborate schema: 'In fact, the real expression of consciousness is this taking up of possession within our reach [...] that yearning towards unity which we feel to be inseparable from a real universe.'[31] Whether it was direct influence, or merely the coinciding of similar concerns, it is certainly the case that a close reading of Mansfield's last letters and notebooks brings home how similar her vocabulary so often is, how much it shares with the language of Wallace, Gurdjieff and Ouspensky.

There is the case of course to be made that a book most of us feel awkward with nudged her along rather than turned her round. It gave her confidence to trust herself, to break with 'conventional wisdom', to 'Risk anything',[32] that phrase Mansfieldians like to quote with approval, but not always in context, where it means taking on what most of them would have little rapport with. When she spent August in London, heard Ouspensky lecture on Gurdjieff and learned from Orage especially more of the Institute that was soon to be set up in France, a good deal of what she was told she already was familiar with from *Cosmic Anatomy* – there was that favourite Gurdjieffian image of human beings as machines; our reluctance to risk the unknown; the spiritual significance of eurhythmic dance; the need for physical work to balance our emotional and intellectual 'centres'; the 'unity in being' that we aspire to in fact being achievable. I suppose what I am insisting on, while admitting that there is only so much, after all, that we can hope to know about Mansfield's thinking in these last months, is that she was excited and challenged by the vast intricacy of esoteric theory, and by the possibility of knowledge that she knew nothing about, that so often went *against* the grain of what she did know – or that Murry knew. But it was the practical, demonstrable results that derive from it that interested her far more. She did not need astral planes and mythic survivals to accept that here was her chance – her last-ditch chance – to find the circumstances, the setting, where more than anywhere else she could work towards utter honesty, towards an escape from isolation and to reach a sense of coherence. Those friends who most supported her were far more fully committed than she to the full Gurdjieffian programme. As she told Murry, 'I don t *feel* influenced by Youspensky or Dunning. I merely feel Ive heard ideas like my ideas but bigger ones, far more definite ones.'[33] What she shared with them had been put straightforwardly for once by Wallace: 'In essence it is so simple [...] to accord with that yearning towards what we feel to be inseparable from a *real* universe.'[34]

You have only to think how often Mansfield comes back to that, and how elusive it had seemed for her. She put the problem very directly when she wrote to Koteliansky, a few days after going to Fontainebleau, and told him why she had decided on it. She takes up a conversation they had in London a few weeks before. She reminds him how she believes in individual strength and growth, but does not seem up to managing it:

> Circumstances still hypnotize me. I am a divided being with a bias towards what I wish to be, but no more. [...] So I am always conscious of this secret disruption in me – and at last (thank Heaven!) it has ended in a complete revolution. [...] I have known just instances of waking but that is all. I want to find a world in which these instances are united.[35]

As she tells Murry two days later, she knows that after she had written 'The Fly' there are only a few 'scraps', as she calls them. 'If I had gone on with my old life I never would have written again, for I was dying of poverty of life.'[36] (Only Claire Tomalin, as far as I know, has taken seriously Mansfield's reportedly telling Orage about the kind of story she would like to write, once that poverty had been escaped:[37] a story less dependent on that glancing, associative flow we think of as so characteristic of her, or the flicker of isolated perception – all that she took on board from Impressionism. The new story would be more extensive, the sum of a personality rather than the glinting revelation.)

*****

But back to the short story writer who is more familiar to us. Once she was in Paris, in early February, Mansfield had noted:

> I begin to see it [her leaving Switzerland and Murry] as the result, the ending to all that reading. I mean that even Cosmic Anatomy is involved. Something has been built – a raft, frail and not very seaworthy but it will serve. Before I was cast into the water when I was 'alone'. [...] and now something supports me.[38]

There is an image there that takes us straight into the story she began to write the next week.

None of her stories have come in for so much commentary as 'The Fly'. We know how the image fascinated her, how it served its turn for such devastating news as on the day in 1918 when her doctor told her that what she had thought rheumatism was in fact gonorrhoea:

> Oh, the times when she had walked upside down on the ceiling, run up glittering panes, floated on a lake of light, flashed through

a shining beam! And God looked upon the fly fallen into the jug of milk and saw that it was good. And the smallest Cherubims & Seraphims of all who delight in misfortune [...] shrilled 'How is the fly fallen fallen'.[39]

It is difficult not to read 'The Fly' biographically, regardless of how earnestly Theory advises against such old humanist practice; hard not to see the Boss as God, as Harold Beauchamp, as Fate, as the stopping and starting of disease, even as medical 'bombardment', that phrase used by Manoukhine for what his X-rays did to the spleen. Or not to read the story as a descant on false hopes, with the fly's optimistic belief that 'the horrible danger' was over, that it was 'ready for life again', until the next drop fell. (To be drowned in ink – a sardonic note too from a writer who thought writing, pure and simple, so diminished life.) Mansfield may – or may not – have been struck as she went over *Cosmic Anatomy* a few days before by the metaphor it finds for trying to escape death: 'The flood follows; on he climbs, throwing away his possessions, till at last, almost naked, he reaches a place of safety, where he stops till the little deluge is over.'[40] Whatever, it is a story of unrelenting grimness, a story that supposes, 'What if nothing can be done?' While somewhere in the background frolic the 'wanton boys' from *King Lear*, and Hardy's President of the Immortals.

*****

Mansfield was not much interested in the short story once she finished 'The Fly'. She was half-hearted about those she had been commissioned to write, and let them lapse, even as she led her publishers on with assurances they were on the way. She talked of a long story about a wedding that would form a triptych with 'Prelude' and 'At the Bay', but left only a few pages. In the second half of the year she seems to have found it more rewarding to work with her Ukrainian friend Koteliansky on translations of Dostoevsky's letters, and on Gorky's *Reminiscences*, than to press on with her own writing. As she told her cousin Elizabeth Russell in almost her last letter, 'I am tired of my little stories like birds bred in cages'[41] – a sentence written with her last and almost shortest story in mind, a keepsake for Dorothy Brett when her friend stayed with her in Switzerland in July.

There is no puzzling about where the idea for 'The Canary' came from. Looking out from the sixth-floor window of her Paris hotel early in the year she noted, 'It's so nice to watch la belle dame opposite bring her canary *in* when it rains and put her hyacinth *out*.'[42] A few weeks later she came back to it:

The woman in the room opposite has a wicker cage full of canaries. How can one possibly express in words the beauty of their quick little song rising, as it were, out of the very stones ... I wonder what they dream about when she covers them at night, and what does that rapid flutter really mean?[43]

She told Brett how they 'fascinated me completely. I think & think about them'.[44] As she had done with the fly, she now took up canaries as an analogy for herself:

[T]he truth is some people live in cages and some are free. One had better accept one's cage and say no more about it. I *can*. I *will*. And I do think its simply unpardonable to bore one's friends with 'I can't get out'.[45]

Those caged birds neatly paralleled her own confinement, much as during the war 'the battlefield' had become a way to speak about her lungs.

*****

It was back in Switzerland in June, after four months of treatment, that it came in on her with certainty that conventional medicine had nothing more to offer. You could say a yearning for *being*, a way to touch that elusive 'extended consciousness' as *Cosmic Anatomy* called it, is at least part of her last story. The birds she watched from her hotel window are moved back to the Thorndon suburb where she grew up. As she had recently told a South African writer she corresponded with, warning her against metropolitan enticements, it was only Tinakori Road she now wanted to think about. It is a celebration and a lament, a story too about *breathing*, a topic that preoccupied her (Wallace had something to say about that too, incidentally, relating it to mythical birds). The story's rather sentimental narrator puzzles about death, about what the bird's song may have meant: 'It is there, deep down, deep down, part of one, like one's breathing. [...] One can never know. But isn't it extraordinary that under his sweet, joyful little singing it was just this – sadness? – Ah, what is it? – that I heard.'[46] One might reasonably take those contrasting images of the entrapped and dying and defiant fly, and the struggle towards clarity and 'voice', as it were, from the caged singing bird, as bracketing so much of Mansfield's thinking in her last year. The steady gaze as she looked at finality and fact, yet set against it, even deriving from it, a stand to declare herself on her own terms.

There is one final literary work, not as fine as the stories, but as biographically pertinent. At the same time as 'The Canary', Mansfield wrote a poem she called 'The Wounded Bird'.[47] It is the kind of poem she had often written – metrically loose, touching on what she often did better in stories, more sentimental than her prose, more Georgian than modern – the kind of poem that Murry would have liked. It begins:

> In the wide bed
> Under the green embroidered quilt
> With flowers and leaves always in soft motion
> She is like a wounded bird resting on a pool.

The same lines come back towards the end of the poem, with the fear of inundation and loss:

> Oh waters – do not cover me.
> I would look long and long and long at these beautiful stars!
> Oh my wings – lift me – lift me –
> I am not so dreadfully hurt.

A fortnight before she died, in defence of her decision to go to Fontainebleau, she told Murry, 'But this place [...]. [...] has taken from me one thing after another (the things never were mine) until at this present moment all I know really really is that I am not annihilated.'[48] The story and the poem, their images that she manipulates to speak about herself, yet to distance herself from what they imply – were the last *literary* things, one might say, that needed to be got rid of before the stark existential purity of that last remark.

The story of those last few months has been well told. Mansfield herself says little of quite how unusually severe those early winter months were, or quite how tough the going at times must have been. Certainly it was the least comfort, in some respects, that she had ever known. But the steady note of her letters – apart when she is ticking Ida off – is a cool alertness to what is going on, a detailed delight in the simplicity and routine and effort she feels she is part of; her certainty that this is where she has *chosen* to be. There is no hyped optimism. There is no looking too far ahead. These last months are well told too in the two biographies that matter. I think Alpers is mostly correct when he says that Gurdjieff's theories need scarcely concern us when we look at those months, and that the man himself was remarkably kind to a woman whom he knew – everyone there knew – was dying. But I don't think Alpers was just in his assessment of those who were close to her in

Fontainebleau, when he claims that Gurdjieff's appeal was 'mainly suitable for persons not well read'.[49] In fact those she had most to do with, from Orage to the gifted musicians the de Hartmanns, the Salzmanns, with their extensive experience in the theatre, to eminent medical figures and those sympathetic Russian women she grew close to, are the ones she has in mind when she writes, 'they are my own people at last'.[50] For the first time since leaving Wellington she felt herself part of a *living* community as she pressed on with what she called 'healing myself'. What she shared with both the men and women she was close to – and it surprised her, a little, how well she got on with both – was what she called 'warm, eager living life'.[51] I suspect there is still a reluctance to give those people their due, to take what Orage, for example, says about his talks with her, or what was remembered by Olga Livanoff, later the wife of Frank Lloyd Wright, with the same seriousness as anything said by Lytton Strachey, shall we say, or Clive Bell.

Mansfield now preferred to use 'dying' as a metaphor for getting on with life. 'I have to die to so much; I have to make such *big* changes. I feel the only thing to do is to get the dying over – to court it, almost (Fearfully hard, that) and then all hands to the business of being reborn again.'[52] As I suggested in the Introduction to volume 4 of the *Letters*, using a word that post-modernism is almost as embarrassed by as it is by 'aesthetics': 'Mansfield's dying is heroic not only because she did it so bravely, but because she refused to accept that her entire being must be dominated by how close finality was.'[53] It was a matter, as she said, of seeing 'where I stand – what *remains*'.[54] What is most insistent about those few months at Fontainebleau, is that *they were on her own terms* – a matter of asserted will, rather than compelling circumstances.

*****

I conclude with what always has struck me as so poignantly part of that 'reality' she believed she had come to, and so indicative of the life she was refashioning. It is that list of those words and phrases she was trying to learn in Russian, phrases like:

> I was late because my fire did not burn. [...]
> The sky was blue as in summer. [...]
> The trees still have apples. [...]
> I fed the goats. [...]
> I go for a walk.
> What is the time. Time.[55]

Yet the pathos is what *we* put there. For Mansfield it was a matter of getting on with what the occasion required. Time and circumstance deriving their value from an act of will, a commitment to her decision that *this is how things must be*. As that book which 'saved me finally' had put it, and encouraged her to accept, 'our creation is a reality'.[56]

Notes

1. *Letters* 5, p. 4.
2. *Ibid.*, p. 51.
3. 'M. B. Oxon' (1921) *Cosmic Anatomy and the Structure of the Ego* (London: John M. Watkins). Hereafter referenced as *Cosmic Anatomy*.
4. J. Moore (1980) *Gurdjieff and Mansfield* (London: Routledge & Kegan Paul), pp. 125–42.
5. *Letters* 5, p. 8.
6. Moore, p. 86.
7. Cited in J. Webb (1980) *The Harmonious Circle: The Lives and Work of G. I. Gurdjieff, P. D. Ouspensky, and Their Followers* (London: Thames and Hudson), p. 196.
8. *Letters* 4, p. 177.
9. Webb, p. 248.
10. Unpublished notebook, Alexander Turnbull Library, Wellington.
11. Webb, p. 228.
12. E. Pound (1922) 'Paris Letter', *Dial*, April 1922, p. 405.
13. Webb, p. 207.
14. Moore, pp. 130–1.
15. *Cosmic Anatomy*, p. 1.
16. S. Freud (1980 [1915]) 'Thoughts for the Times on War and Death', J. Strachey (trans.), A. Dickson (ed.) in *Civilization, Society and Religion*, Pelican Freud Library, 12 (Harmondsworth: Penguin), p. 63.
17. K. Mansfield (1919) 'A Ship Comes into the Harbour', *Athenaeum*, 21 November.
18. *Letters* 3, p. 82.
19. M. Heidegger (1927 [1962]) *Time and Being* (New York: Harper and Row).
20. *Letters* 1, p. 177.
21. *Notebooks* 2, p. 332.
22. *Cosmic Anatomy*, p. 1.
23. *Ibid.*, pp. 10–11.
24. *Notebooks* 2, p. 311.
25. J. M. Murry (ed.) (1954) *Journal of Katherine Mansfield* (London: Constable), p. 292.
26. *Cosmic Anatomy*, pp. 106–7.
27. *Notebooks* 2, p. 313.
28. See *Cosmic Anatomy*, p. 206.
29. *Ibid.*, p. 21.
30. *Notebooks* 2, p. 309.
31. *Cosmic Anatomy*, p. 21.
32. *Notebooks* 2, p. 286.

33. *Letters* 5, p. 285.
34. *Cosmic Anatomy*, p. 91.
35. *Letters* 5, p. 304.
36. *Ibid.*, p. 305.
37. C. Tomalin (1987) *Katherine Mansfield: A Secret Life* (London: Viking), p. 235.
38. *Notebooks* 2, pp. 323–4.
39. *Ibid.*, pp. 153–4.
40. *Cosmic Anatomy*, p. 30.
41. *Letters* 5, p. 346.
42. *Ibid.*, pp. 43–4.
43. *Ibid.*, p. 70.
44. *Ibid.*, p. 76.
45. *Ibid.*, p. 196.
46. From 'The Canary'. K. Mansfield (2007) *Collected Stories* (London: Penguin), p. 422.
47. V. O'Sullivan (ed.) (1988) *Poems of Katherine Mansfield* (Oxford University Press), p. 82.
48. *Letters* 5, p. 341.
49. A. Alpers (1980) *The Life of Katherine Mansfield* (London: Jonathan Cape), p. 378.
50. *Letters* 5, p. 309.
51. *Notebooks* 2, p. 287.
52. *Letters* 5, p. 294.
53. *Ibid.*, p. x.
54. *Ibid.*, p. 294.
55. *Notebooks* 2, p. 341.
56. *Cosmic Anatomy*, p. 182.

2
Katie and Chummie: Death in the Family

J. Lawrence Mitchell

> But how death has changed everything!
> ('Sympathy', Virginia Woolf)[1]

Throughout the First World War *The Times* published daily casualty lists – 'Rolls of Honour' – that reflected the terrible toll the war was taking on the young men of Britain. At the end of October 1915, Prime Minister Herbert Asquith reported to Parliament that there had been nearly half-a-million casualties.[2] Among the dead and missing officers listed on 26 October of that year appeared the following:

ACCIDENTALLY KILLED.
Beauchamp, Sec. Lt. L. H. 8th S. Lancs Regt.[3]

Leslie Heron Beauchamp was, of course, Katherine Mansfield's brother, and it was his death that is widely acknowledged to have been the catalyst that precipitated a fundamental shift in the nature of her work. As she impressed upon her father in a letter, 'the loss of our darling one [...] has changed the course of my life *for ever*'.[4] There have been those who feel that Mansfield's reaction bordered on the histrionic, given what they see as the very limited contact between the siblings over the years. Margaret Scott observes, however: 'There are evidences – unpublished until now – that Leslie was always important to KM. [...] All the pain and grief she felt were truly felt.'[5] In this essay the nature and extent of this brother–sister relationship will be explored, with particular reference to relevant correspondence in the Alexander Turnbull Library (ATL) and to hitherto unexamined War Office records in the National Archives. For without careful scrutiny of the dates, locales and obligations associated with Leslie's military training, we cannot confidently assess their relationship during his eight months in England.

Leslie – often called 'Chummie' and sometimes 'Bogey' – had more contact with his sister, despite their long periods of separation, than is generally realized. He spent four months back 'Home' (as they called England) with his parents and sisters in 1903 and his childish signature appears in Kathleen's autograph book on 4 April 1903, while they were all in a residential hotel in Bayswater,[6] and they were in London again for a similar period in 1906.[7] By 1908, Kathleen was already claiming a special bond in a letter to her cousin Sylvia Payne: 'I have never dreamed of loving a child as I love this boy. Do not laugh when I tell you I feel so maternal towards him.'[8] Later that year he has become 'the brother of brothers' in a letter to her sisters, Vera and Jeanne.[9] When he reappeared with the family in London in 1911 for the coronation of George V, he was old enough at 17 to be impressed by his sister's literary achievements and connections and to be entrusted with a key to her flat at 69 Clovelly Mansions. For a while, he contemplated remaining in England and attending Oxford or Cambridge. But his father dissuaded him, allowing him, as a consolation prize of sorts, to buy a car to take back home.[10] It is also worth noting that Ruth Elvish Mantz claims that Chummie 'stayed behind in London after the family had left' (on 8 March 1912), and that brother and sister 'became closer friends than before'.[11] Upon his return to Wellington, Leslie joined the New Zealand Territorial Force and was only discharged on the day he sailed for England.[12] Why did he opt for the British Army instead of following his initial plan to join the New Zealand Expeditionary Force? Perhaps the deciding factor was that he knew England quite well and had family there – his Aunt Belle in Surrey and his sister Kathleen in London.

Leslie sailed on the SS *Indrabarah*, on Christmas Eve, travelling first-class, and arrived in England on 5 February 1915.[13] He 'made a bee line for Tadworth' (Surrey) to stay with Aunt Belle and her wealthy husband, Harry Trinder. He was met at the train station by their 'beautiful new Wolseley', and driven to their palatial home in Surrey where he was 'treated like a Duke' – all 'rather different from the trenches', he recognized. From this home base he made the social rounds, visiting relatives in Malvern and hobnobbing with various locals, among them 'a charming wealthy widow'. On 11 February 1915, at the Bank of New Zealand, he unexpectedly ran into his sister Kathleen, whom he had not seen for some four years:

On coming out of Kay's room [...] who should I run into but Kathleen who had come to draw her money. Considering that she has had the 'flu [...] I thought she was looking wonderfully fit – quite pink cheeks, which she has gained since living in a cottage near Harrow. We went off to lunch together and picture her happiness at seeing one of the family, not having the faintest idea that I was coming over – She is more in love than ever with Mr. Murray [sic] which is a thing to be thankful for and with a new contract with one of the monthlies for a series of war sketches, they have prospects of a little money coming in [...] I do not expect to see K. again for some time.[14]

Her unawareness of his presence in England is puzzling. It would seem to suggest how out of touch she was with her family, were it not for the existence of two very long loving letters she had written to them in mid-December 1914. There is also Leslie's letter from 47 Fitzherbert Terrace, dated 6 December 1914 ('Off at last! Father gave in this morning'),[15] suggesting that he was on his way to Egypt – which would explain her surprise at seeing him. We only have Murry's word that Leslie gave her £10 for what was ostensibly a trip to Paris to collect materials. We do know that Leslie's report that Katie was 'more in love than ever with Mr. Murray' was simply not true. Whether he was misled by his sister – as most commentators assume – or whether he knew better and wished to protect her, we simply cannot be sure. In any case, she left for Paris on 15 February, embarking upon that 'indiscreet journey' about which she would later write so vividly. Leslie and/or Murry were at Victoria Station to bid her farewell.[16] In prospect, Francis Carco may have seemed a welcome change from the 'pusillanimous' Murry,[17] but he did not live up to Mansfield's – no doubt unrealistic – expectations. She was soon back in England, returning to Murry only reluctantly. John Carswell is probably right in his speculation that 'the inducement to return was her brother'.[18] Certainly she had seen enough of the world at war to have her anxiety raised about what lay in store for her beloved brother.

At the suggestion of Uncle Harry (Trinder), Leslie met with a member of Lord Kitchener's staff in the War Office, flourished his discharge papers from New Zealand and within 24 hours had secured a commission in the South Lancashire Regiment. By the beginning of March he was already at Balliol College Oxford for an 'instructional course'.[19] By now he had seen 'Katie', as he called her, two or three times. On 11 March he wrote Katie a very exuberant letter from Oxford:

Today I had charge of about forty men in field manoeuvres and was congratulated on my work – consequently I am feeling fearfully bucked. Being in command of men is a wonderful sensation – one feels absolutely Napoleonic – and to lead a bayonet charge must be glorious![20]

This letter was rerouted from Rose Tree Cottage to D. H. Lawrence's current residence in Sussex, where the inhabitants would hardly have shared Leslie's bellicose sentiments; it is therefore unlikely that Mansfield read this letter aloud.

Leslie's next stop was Bournemouth where he briefly shared a billet with Edward Shanks, the Georgian poet, who was in the same regiment. Shanks characterized Leslie for Antony Alpers in 1949 as 'a pleasantly intelligent young man of no pronounced interests', who 'never mentioned Kathleen, though it came out that he knew Orage'.[21] Somehow this statement does not ring true. To begin with, Leslie had quite well-developed literary and artistic interests;[22] and he was *so* proud of his sister that it is hard to believe he managed to mention the editor of the *New Age* without explaining that his sister wrote for the magazine too and had introduced them. His own letter from his Bournemouth lodgings must raise further doubts about the reliability of Shanks's recollections. Leslie had sent a telegram inviting Kathleen to visit him in Bournemouth, an invitation she evidently declined, citing her health. Nonetheless, Leslie was eager to share his news in his follow-up letter: 'Who do you think has been staying with me? Edward Shanks who knows you, JM[urry], Beatrice H[asting], Orage and many others. He, as you know, wrote for the *New Age.'*[23] It is not impossible that Shanks knew, or knew of, Mansfield – possibly through common acquaintance with Eddie Marsh who had generously helped with the financing of *Rhythm* and the *Blue Review*. Yet he is not mentioned by any of Mansfield's biographers, nor in any of her letters, and, most importantly here, never seems to have written for the *New Age*.[24]

By the end of May 1915, Leslie anticipated no more weekend leaves, so he was understandably upset when he somehow made a mistake and presented himself at 25 Elgin Crescent instead of 95, the latest address of his compulsively itinerant sister. In his subsequent letter to Kathleen, he explained why he failed to show up and suggested meeting her in Reading: 'I must see you soon – Could I possibly see you in Reading on Saturday afternoon or evening? [...] we must meet somehow – I have thousands of things to tell you.'[25]

The last extended phase of training at Aldershot under the command of Colonel A. G. B. Lang was meant to give 'final polish' to the battalion.

Leslie reported to his parents, 'my bombers have been congratulated several times on their efficiency',[26] but his life was not all work. Leslie was staying at the Strand Palace Hotel in London in mid-August when he wrote to his parents about some of his earlier social jaunts, and boasted that he was spending that weekend at a big house party for shooting and tennis. Life for a junior officer appeared to be very full and rewarding. No wonder his fellow officers in the mess ragged him 'fearfully' about his 'distinguished pals and connections'.[27] When he mentioned, for example, that 'dear old Lady Roberts was most charming' during his trip to Englemere, he was referring to the recently widowed wife of Field Marshall Lord Roberts, former Commander-in-Chief of the British Army.[28] Towards the end of July he travelled north to Brantwood, the art-filled former home of John Ruskin with a view over Coniston Water, to stay with the current owner, artist Arthur Severn and his wife who had been Ruskin's 'devoted niece'.[29] Neither his sister nor the literary circles in which she moved could compete with weekends at 'a magnificent house and garden [...] containing magnificent pictures and *objets d'art* from all parts of the world', the description of the home of Lady Roberts he sent to his parents.

It was from Aldershot Barracks that Leslie was sent for a six-day course (19–24 August 1915) of specialized training as a bombing officer on Clapham Common. The location of this course enabled him to spend almost a week with Kathleen.[30] Enthusiastic as he was about his job, Leslie was also well aware of the dangerous assignment he had undertaken. In fact, he wrote to his parents the day after his course ended in terms that could hardly have been reassuring:

> These bombs are frightfully deadly and very tricky to handle so it is imperative for every man before he goes into action to know all about their interior and external workings. [...] Now I have to instruct the whole battalion – officers and men.[31]

There is no evidence that he painted any such alarming picture for his sister when he visited her 'dear little house in Acacia Road, St. Johns Wood'. In his first letter home, he deemed 'Jacky Murray' [sic] to be 'a very kind quiet soul' and thought 'he and Kathleen are perfectly sweet to each other'.[32] There is a slightly patronizing tone, *de haut en bas*, about these comments from a young man accustomed to more palatial accommodation. Nonetheless, Leslie and Kathleen spent their time reminiscing – playing the 'Do you remember game' they both so enjoyed. Her last and only surviving letter to him is of special interest.

If the dating in the *Collected Letters* is correct, the hasty note to him on Selfridges stationery was written the day he left Acacia Road, that is to say on 25 August.[33] In fact, Mansfield only wrote '*Wednesday 1915*' and her comment 'Ever since last Sunday you are close in my thoughts' does not make much sense if he had been staying with her at the time (that is, on Sunday, 22 August). It would also seem unlikely that she failed to write to him again in his last month in England. Yet the letter reads like a farewell letter, prompted by a final brief visit before leaving for the front: 'It meant a tremendous lot, seeing you and being with you again and I was so frightfully proud of you.' The contents of the letter make more sense if it dates from Wednesday, 22 September, after a final get-together on the previous Saturday or Sunday.

Early in September Leslie found time to visit friends in Camberley, Surrey and mentioned for the first time a young woman: 'Maureen was too adorable for anything but, poor child, was terribly cut up just before I left.'[34] In a letter the night before the revised departure date of 22 September (the date Alpers cites),[35] he wrote lovingly to his mother and mentioned a second female acquaintance: 'The other evening Lydia gave me a little *tête à tête* dinner at The Piccadilly and afterwards I took her to The Empire where we saw the most amusing review, *Watch Your Step*.'[36] The 'other evening' would have to be 18 or 19 September – so we *know* he was in London on leave and must have paid a visit to his sister before his night on the town.

After frustrating delays, his battalion – 30 officers and 920 other ranks – finally left barracks in two trains at 6:45 pm on 26 September 1915 via Boulogne. Leslie managed to send a telegram to Kathleen: 'Off at last – the goodbye would have been too awful. Au revoir. Leslie.'[37] They arrived at their final destination, Haute Farm, Ploegsteert, on 3 October 1915 to relieve the 16th Canadians in the fire trenches of Ploegsteert Wood.[38] For the most part, this was a relatively quiet sector, but enemy machineguns were active south of the farm and they were close enough to the front lines to be threatened by 'tired' (stray) bullets. The day after their arrival Leslie wrote to his family to say: 'I am in top-hole condition physically and mentally' and added: 'I nearly lost my heart (I must confess) to the most charming little French girl in a certain café.'[39] His brief pencil note to Katie headed '5th Oct. Somewhere in Flanders' said 'No time for a letter – Am frightfully fit and full of beans! We are up and doing at last [...] the trenches are beastly wet owing to big bombardment going on.'[40] This would prove to be his last letter.

The next day, 6 October, Colonel Lang's War Diary noted: 'We lost 2 Lt. L. Beauchamp & No 15000 Sergt. Holden – bombing officer and

Sergt. by the premature explosion of a bomb while instructing a class of officers & NCOs.' Details of the accident are to be found in the required incident report.[41] It shows that Leslie and his 24-year-old sergeant, James Holden of Salford,[42] were demonstrating 'Nobel Lighter' hand grenades for another company – that is, grenades with a Nobel detonator.[43] This type of grenade must have been somewhat unfamiliar because Colonel Lang asked several questions about lighting it – it was one of a type that required two men. Leslie and his sergeant then moved away from the assembled group towards a pond but within a few seconds the grenade exploded prematurely. Holden died within ten minutes and Leslie within 45 minutes. He was the first officer in his battalion to be killed, and, in fact, the only one in the three months (22 September–31 December) of 1915 that the battalion spent in Ploegsteert Wood.[44] He had spent a total of 124 days in the army, but only three at the front.[45]

The official notification by telegram was first delivered to 'A[lexander] Kay', manager of the Bank of New Zealand in London on 10 October 1915. It read: 'Deeply regret to inform 2 Lt. L. H. Beauchamp 8th South Lancs. Reg. was killed accidentally on 7th Oct. Lord Kitchener expresses his sympathy.' In fact, the reported date was an error. Kay sent his telegram to Mansfield the next day.[46] Murry recorded Mansfield's reaction in an exercise book as soon as she had rushed off to visit Kay:

> Three minutes ago Tig had a telegram to say her brother is dead [...] I cannot believe it yet; and she cannot. That is the most terrible of all. She did not cry. She was white and said: 'I don't believe it; he was not the kind to die'.[47]

Back in New Zealand, the bad news did not arrive until 12 October. Annie Beauchamp had just finished a letter to her son when his father 'walked into my room with the tidings of his death'.[48] In the unposted letter she had complained about Kathleen's failure to write, but added: 'I am very glad Kathleen was good to you & I am sure it gave her great pleasure.'

In his *Reminiscences and Recollections* (1937), her father's analysis is revealing in a variety of ways and merits citation:

> My wife was sadly shaken by the loss of her youngest child and her only boy. If possible Kathleen felt it even more deeply. Leslie and she had been inseparable whenever they were living together. Lonely and absorbed in her intellectual work, she welcomed the arrival of Leslie in England. It was her one bond with the life in which she had been brought up and which now was meaning more and more to

her. She lived for the fugitive hours that she was able to spend with him, and when the news came of his death the shock was almost unbearable.[49]

'What You Please', one of the earliest of Mansfield's compositions to include Leslie, was probably written while the family was in London in 1906. It is an oddly prescient story (given Leslie's future area of expertise in the army and his eventual fate), in which Leslie buys fireworks and instructs 'Kathie' how to use them: 'You hold this big one in your hand & then light it and throw it away.'[50] It also shows Mansfield's keen observation of her 'little brother'. She notes, for example, 'the light in Leslie's eyes – the way his little hand had trembled when he showed her the great beautiful packet'. Equally prescient – or perhaps written with a sense of dread – is her story 'The Wind Blows', which celebrates the brother–sister bond and their shared nostalgia for *le temps perdu*. It was published in the short-lived magazine *Signature*, just two days before his death.

Soon after, as she struggled to come to terms with the loss she had suffered, Mansfield reconstructed their conversation at 5 Acacia Road. Memories of the commonplace (in which she always invested heavily) – here fallen pears at 47 Fitzherbert Terrace, and a pink garden seat at 75 Tinakori Road – become sacralized merely by association with her dead brother. Above all, there is the memory of his reassuring familial presence and his 'absolute confidence that I'll come back' – a confidence the reader is retrospectively shown to be misplaced by his impulsive 'goodbye darling', and by the strange wind (characteristically a negative force in Mansfield's work) that blows through the garden.[51]

When she wrote to Samuel Koteliansky, now resident at 5 Acacia Road, from Marseilles, her brother and the war were still very much on her mind. She asked about one of her brother's caps in an upstairs drawer, and mentioned his photograph on her mantelpiece and a second letter from Leslie's friend (James E. Hibbert). 'He told me that after it happened he [Leslie] said over and over – "God forgive me for all I have done" and just before he died he said "Lift my head, Katy, I can't breathe."'[52] In 1984 the editors of the *Collected Letters* stated: 'The friend's letter has not survived' and thus Mansfield's second-hand account understandably became the basis for all subsequent accounts.[53] In fact, both letters from Hibbert were in Murry's possession all along, though he evidently did not want them made public in his lifetime.

The first letter from Hibbert explained that Leslie was 'conscious for a very short time [...] & cannot have suffered'. He also described his grave 'in a quiet part of the wood' and added: 'After the war you will undoubtedly be able to find out where the place is & visit it.'[54] But Mansfield needed more details, in particular whether he spoke before he died and whether he knew he was going to die. Hibbert responded: 'I can answer yes to each question. He was heard to say several times "God forgive me for all I have done", and then just before he died he asked that his head might be raised as he could not breathe.' Hibbert also thoughtfully enclosed 'a small piece of moss growing beside the grave'.[55]

Some may be shocked at Mansfield's intrusion of herself and see it as just another example of her 'flagrant fibbing' (Alpers's phrase).[56] Yet her behaviour should not surprise us, given her unusually strong identification with her brother, even if Murry seems to have found it uncomfortably inconsistent with his portrait of 'Saint' Katherine. Clearly, she very much needed to believe that she had a role in the final drama of her brother's life – that *she* was in Chummie's thoughts even as he lay dying.[57]

But C. K. Stead rooted out this little white lie and constructed yet another version of the 'truth' in his novel *Mansfield* (2004). Here Hibbert himself is placed centre stage – so the line becomes '"I can't breathe," he said. "Lift my head, Jamie".'[58] This, of course, is really no truer than Mansfield's version. There is no evidence Hibbert was at the scene of the accident – he is not mentioned in the incident report and Leslie was instructing another company. Nevertheless, Stead's imaginative reconstruction of Leslie's dying moments is a powerful *tour de force*.[59]

We need not flinch from admitting that Mansfield made creative use of Leslie's death just as she had made creative use of his life, and the lives of other members of her family. Alpers long ago registered Vera's resentment of her sister for playing fast and loose with the facts of the real-life garden party. '*I* was the one who went down with the things' for the carter's family, she told him.[60] In the story, Leslie is given a privileged place as 'Laurie', Laura's younger brother and boon companion. When the actual event took place in 1907 Katie was an unhappy 18-year-old – going through a phase of 'unremitting self-absorption'[61] – and Leslie a mere 13. Within the framework of 'The Garden Party', however, Laurie is old enough to be going off to the office with his father. He shows his appreciation of his sister, Laura, 'the artistic one', by asking her to 'just give a squiz at my coat'.[62] She, of course, is distracted by his admiration for her 'absolutely topping hat' (495) – language that, on evidence of his letters, authentically captures Leslie's superlative-laced colloquialisms.[63]

Christine Darrohn makes an intriguing case for 'The Garden Party' as a war-story of sorts, but her claim that 'by the end of the story Laurie no longer understands Laura because she has been irrevocably changed by her encounter with Scott', is surely mistaken.[64] It ignores the carefully developed signals of their importance to one another and it fails to recognize the significant symmetry of the names 'Laura' and 'Laurie'. Mansfield's Sheridan family includes sisters 'Meg' and 'Jose', names obviously borrowed from Louisa May Alcott's *Little Women*. But there *had* to be a place for 'little brother', in Mansfield's schema; so 'Laurie', the boy next door in Alcott's novel, is ushered into the family at the expense of a sister. The name 'Laura' was selected to mirror 'Laurie', and to suggest a special bond between the siblings, indeed the kind of bond characteristic of twins. Thus, when Laura, overwhelmed by Death, is lost for words to describe Life, Laurie intuitively 'quite understood' (499). Mansfield was giving fictive form to a conviction that certainly predated Leslie's death: that 'we were almost like one child. I always see us walking about together, looking at things together with the same eyes'.[65] A letter to her sister Vera in 1916 says much the same thing: 'we understood each other so wonderfully – When we talked together we were like "one being"'.[66] And the idea is central to 'The Wind Blows' as well, where 'Bogey's ulster is just like hers' and 'they stride like one eager person through the town' (193–4).

The evidence here assembled shows that Leslie was fully engaged most of the time in the business of preparing for war – at Balliol and in Bournemouth, in Winchester and in Aldershot. When on leave, the social circles in which he mingled were those of his parents and relatives in England – people of wealth and influence, who could provide the material comforts and admiration he so obviously enjoyed. He also mentions two young women (Maureen and Lydia) in England and one in France, in whom he appears to have taken some mildly romantic interest. His trips took him to such places as Englemere (near Ascot, Berkshire), Camberley (Surrey), Malvern (Worcestershire) and to Ruskin's former home in the Lake District. His sister Kathleen was not just an obligation – he loved her deeply and expressed his love in disconcertingly strong terms – but she was hardly his first priority and, save for the one week-long stay at 5 Acacia Road, he only visited occasionally. In May 1919 she recalled those visits tenderly:

> I hear his hat & stick thrown on to the hall table. He runs up the stairs, three at a time [...] he puts his arm around me, holding me tightly & we kiss – a long, firm family kiss. And the kiss means: We are of the same blood; we have absolute confidence in each other; we are proud of each other; we love; all is well.[67]

Thus when she wrote 'To you only do I belong, just as *you* belong to me,'[68] we do well to remember that this is a dialogue with the dead, that the disembodied Leslie whose voice still echoes for her 'in trees and flowers, in scents and light and shadow', is in fact being summoned, invoked as a muse.[69] Leslie was never safer as an object of affection than when dead, but he was also never more useful to her as a writer.

Postscript

Remarkably, despite the fuss over details of its location, neither Mansfield nor her father seems to have visited Leslie's grave. She retained only a mental image[70] – 'the wretched little picture I have of my brother's grave',[71] as she described it for Ottoline Morrell at the time of the Versailles Peace Treaty – and that small piece of moss. Perhaps some trace of guilt about her failure to visit can be discerned in her story 'The Fly', wherein 'For various reasons the boss had not been across' (531) to visit his son's grave in Belgium. Yet Katie had her own way of saying, in the spirit of Catullus: 'Frater, ave atque vale'.

Notes

1. S. Dick (ed.) (1985) *The Complete Shorter Fiction of Virginia Woolf* (San Diego: Harcourt Brace Jovanovich), p. 103.
2. See *The Times*, 30 October 1915, p. 8 col. B.
3. 'Roll of Honour', *The Times*, 26 October 1915, p. 6.
4. *Letters* 1, p. 251.
5. *Notebooks* 1, p. xxi.
6. Autograph book, ATL MSX 5969. A birthday gift from 'grandmama', 1901. The hotel was at 27 St Stephen's Square, Bayswater W. (*Letters* 1, p. 4).
7. Katherine Mansfield's real name was Kathleen Mansfield Beauchamp.
8. Mansfield to Sylvia Payne, 4 March 1908, ATL; cited in J. Meyers (1978) *Katherine Mansfield: A Biography* (New York: New Directions), pp. 119–20.
9. *Letters* 1, p. 87.
10. F. A. Lea (1960) *The Life of John Middleton Murry* (Oxford University Press), p. 30, citing Murry's diary, writes: 'there he [Murry] caught his first glimpse of her young brother, Leslie, who had just been buying a car to take back to New Zealand, very impressive to me – a denizen of the strange and inaccessible world of wealth'.
11. R. E. Mantz and J. M. Murry (1933) *The Life of Katherine Mansfield* (London: Constable), p. 332. Meyers, p. 120 repeats this claim, but Claire Tomalin explicitly states that Leslie went home with the rest of the family (on 8 March 1912). C. Tomalin (1988) *Katherine Mansfield: A Secret Life* (New York: Alfred Knopf), p. 102.

12. Details from his *Personal Record Book Showing Military Training and Service.* ATL MS-Papers-7224-05.
13. He kept a diary on the trip – now in the ATL MS-Papers-2063-11. The date of his arrival is from the 'Incoming Passengers' list in the National Archives. Copy received 8 November 2008 via Documents Online.
14. LHB to parents, 11 February 1915, ATL MS-Papers-2063-01.
15. LHB to [KM?] 6 December 1914, ATL-MS-Papers-2063-01.
16. J. Carswell (1978) *Lives and Letters: A. R. Orage, Katherine Mansfield, Beatrice Hastings, John Middleton Murry, S. S. Koteliansky, 1906–1957* (London and Boston: Faber and Faber), p. 103. Carswell only mentions Leslie; Antony Alpers only mentions Murry. A. Alpers (1980) *The Life of Katherine Mansfield* (New York: The Viking Press), p. 178.
17. An epithet used by his biographer, Lea, p. 47.
18. Carswell, p. 106.
19. LHB to James Mackintosh Bell, 7 March 1915, ATL MS-Papers-2063-02.
20. LHB to KM, 11 March 1915, ATL MS-Papers-2063-03.
21. Edward Shanks to Alpers, 2 September 1949; cited in Alpers, *Life*, p. 182.
22. His school magazine, for example, said: 'He distinguished himself by his aptitude for Classics and by his literary work.' *The Waitakian*, 16 April 1915, 108.
23. LHB to KM, 6 April 1915, ATL MS-Papers-2063-03.
24. Edward Shanks does not appear in any of the lists of contributors at the end of the complete run of the *New Age* in the Brown University online collection of modernist journals. See: http://dl.lib.brown.edu/mjp/ (accessed 15 May 2010).
25. LHB to KM, 26 May 1915, ATL MS-Papers-2063-04.
26. LHB to parents, 13 August 1915, ATL MS-Papers-2063-05.
27. *Ibid.*
28. *Ibid.*
29. Leslie's account of the visit to Brantwood, the only example of his skills as a writer, was published in *The Waitakian*, 12 September 1915, pp. 163–5 under the title 'A Trip to Ruskin's Home'.
30. Murry's account gives a somewhat misleading impression. He writes, with an almost wilful imprecision: 'Katherine's brother, who had finished his training, came there often. From there he left for France, and thither a few days afterwards came the news of his death.' J. M. Murry (1935) *Between Two Worlds: An Autobiography* (London: Jonathan Cape), p. 350. Of course, Leslie was in Flanders, not France.
31. LHB to parents, 25 August 1915, ATL MS-Papers-2063-05.
32. *Ibid.*
33. *Letters* 1, p. 197. Curiously, the ATL (MS-Papers-2413) dates the letter as of Saturday, September 25th.
34. LHB to parents, 9 September 1915, ATL MS-Papers-2063-05.
35. On the basis of this letter, Alpers used '6 a.m. on 22 September' as the date of Leslie's departure for Flanders. In fact, the War Office records show that the battalion's departure was delayed again until 26 September 1915.
36. LHB to Annie Beauchamp, 21 September [1915], ATL MS-Papers-2063-05. The play opened on 4 May 1915 and ran for well over 200 performances. The theatre was demolished in 1927.

37. LHB to KM, 25 September 1915, ATL MS-Papers-2063-05.
38. Details from Lieutenant-Colonel A. G. Lang's official War Diary for September and October, 1915, WO95/2250/281863.
39. LHB to parents, 4 October 1915, ATL MS-Papers-2063-05.
40. LHB to KM, 5 October 1915, ATL MS-Papers-2063-05.
41. WO/339/35941. The report is dated 9/10/15 and is signed by Lieutenant-Colonel Lang. Two doctors were quickly on the scene.
42. Holden was a married man and left a widow, Mary Holden, of 32 New Park Rd, Salford. Official notice of his death did not appear in the local (Salford) newspaper until December 1915. It is unclear whether this time-lag indicates that priority was given to the cases of officers versus other ranks or that Leslie Beauchamp's case got especially prompt attention because of his father's status. Some of the later correspondence suggests the latter explanation is the more likely.
43. The original 'Nobel Lighter' was a method of discharging nitroglycerine with a percussion spark for which Alfred Nobel received a Swedish patent in 1863. 'I do not believe that "Nobel Lighter" is the formal name of a grenade – just a reference to the ignition system, so I am not sure whether we are talking about an improvisation that happens to use a Nobel Lighter or whether this is a bomb in the numbered series which has that device.' Personal communication (4 April 2005) with Dr Stephen Bull, Curator of Military History, Museum of Lancashire.
44. He was 'our first loss' according to Company Commander Captain J. G. Harding, in a letter to Mrs Beauchamp dated 6 October 1915. Perusal of *The Times* 'Roll of Honour' for 1 September through to 31 December 1915 reveals no other fatalities among the officers.
45. The precise number of days of service is specified on the War Office form used to calculate his pay due at seven shillings and sixpence per day (WO/339/35941).
46. For the War Office telegram, see WO/339/35941; Kay's telegram read 'Deeply regret inform you Leslie killed 7th Oct. Come and see me.' ATL MS-Papers-7224-05.
47. Cited in Carswell, pp. 111–12, from an exercise book apparently left behind in Acacia Road and discovered among the papers of Samuel Koteliansky after his death in 1955.
48. Note on envelope of letter from AB to Leslie, 12 October 1915, ATL MS-Papers-2063-08.
49. H. Beauchamp (1937) *Reminiscences and Recollections* (New Plymouth, New Zealand: Thomas Avery & Sons), p. 94.
50. *Notebooks* 1, p. 72.
51. *Notebooks* 2, pp. 14–15.
52. *Letters* 1, pp. 199–200.
53. See, for example, Meyers, p. 120 and Alpers, *Life*, p. 183.
54. JH to KM, 26 October 1915, ATL MS-Papers-7224-05.
55. JH to KM, 13 November 1915, ATL MS-Papers-7224-05.
56. Alpers, *Life*, p. 175.
57. 1n 1919 Leslie's dying words are still very much in her thoughts. Writing to Murry on 1 December, urging him not to visit her in Ospedaletti, she writes:

'God forgive me for what I have done. Those words Chummie spoke as he died. Ever since I've had your telegram they seem *mine*' (*Letters* 3, p. 154).

58. C. K. Stead (2004) *Mansfield: A Novel* (London: Vintage), p. 71.
59. In the following chapter (four), Stead has Jack (Murry) realize that 'Leslie had *not* named her. [...] The "Katie" was invention' (p. 80).
60. Alpers, *Life*, p. 46.
61. *Ibid.*
62. 'The Garden Party', in A. Alpers (1984) *The Stories of Katherine Mansfield* (Oxford University Press), p. 489. All page references to Mansfield's stories are to this edition and are included in the text.
63. Leslie uses phrases like 'frightfully fit', 'frightfully proud', 'fearfully bucked', 'fearfully keen', 'splendidly well' and 'in top-hole condition'. Twice in letters Mansfield mentions his use of 'absolutely'.
64. C. Darrohn (1998) '"Blown to Bits": Katherine Mansfield's "The Garden-Party" and the Great War', *Modern Fiction Studies*, 44: 3, 513–39.
65. *Notebooks* 2, p. 15.
66. *Letters* 1, p. 246.
67. *Notebooks* 2, p. 166.
68. *Ibid.*, p. 16.
69. *Ibid.*
70. It is not clear whether she is referring to the photograph now in the ATL. MS ref. not available.
71. *Letters* 2, p. 339.

3
'A Furious Bliss': Katherine Mansfield and John Middleton Murry 1916–1918

Sydney Janet Kaplan

From its inception, Katherine Mansfield's relationship with John Middleton Murry had relied on a delicate balance, dependent upon her maintenance of individual freedom. Murry later wrote about his disinclination 'to urge any claim' on her. He declared that he 'always was, and always would be, man enough to ask nothing of a woman but what of her own motion she could not help giving'.[1] This concept of personal freedom had first been tested in 1915, during Mansfield's brief romance with Francis Carco, and again, late in 1916, when both she and Murry were swept into the intrigues and gossip of Garsington. Murry was then preoccupied with his work at the War Office and with his attraction to Lady Ottoline Morrell, while Mansfield was unsettled, unfocused and longing to be alone. She too seemed to need an outlet for her emotions and an epistolary flirtation with Bertrand Russell – who had been Ottoline's lover – appears to have briefly served that purpose.

Mansfield's letters to Russell during November and December of 1916 are filled with exultant exclamations about the art of writing, but she actually had not been able to do much of it during those months while she and Murry were living at 'The Ark', along with Brett and Carrington in Keynes's house on Gower Street. She wrote to Russell on 1 December about 'so many interruptions. Life seemed to rush in and out of my door like the teller of the tale in a Dostoievsky novel.'[2] Those interruptions must have included Murry, who also intrudes – at least subconsciously – in her allusion to Dostoevsky, for Murry's book on him had just been published. In fact, Mansfield had not been able to detach herself from her personal life enough to devote herself to her writing ever since the failure of the experiment in communal living with the Lawrences in Cornwall earlier that year. Since then, everything she wrote remained sketchy or unfinished.

She hoped to remedy that problem by taking a studio in Chelsea. By February 1917 she and Murry had moved out of 'The Ark' and were living separately, she in her studio and he in rooms not far from it, but they saw each other every evening for supper. To complicate matters, L. M. (Ida Baker), back from a two-year stay in Rhodesia, was now working as 'a tool setter in an aeroplane factory',[3] and had moved into Mansfield's studio, where she slept behind a screen. What this peculiar arrangement meant to the sexual life of Mansfield and Murry is not precisely known, but it can be surmised.[4]

During this period, Murry felt he had been condemned to 'hack-work', yet longed to elevate the status of criticism. He published *30* unsigned reviews of French literature for the *TLS* in 1917.[5] These demanded an enormous amount of reading, and all this work was additional to his full-time job at the War Office, where he was translating German newspapers. Murry later said that he was 'near the verge of madness',[6] and insisted that 'every faculty of mine was now strained upon the war. I was not.'[7] But read against his journal entries, these later statements are questionable. The clarity of his journal comments on the art of writing, his gossipy interest in L. M.'s behaviour in Mansfield's studio and his astute observations about the war do not suggest a man on the 'verge of madness'. They also suggest that he might not have been miserable *all* the time. An entry written on 9 April 1917 provides an antidote: 'This has been one of those strange things that I must call "a happy day".' He then writes a description of himself and Mansfield waking up, 'sleepy and warm in each other's arms'. In the afternoon they go to the National Gallery and look closely 'only at the pictures we wanted to look at'. Clarifying their artistic preferences, Murry exclaims: 'We wouldn't have Rembrandt's "Saskia as Flora", because we didn't like her, even though she was Rembrandt's woman & Rembrandt did her. We basked in the clear light of Poussin's grave and deliberate masterpieces because we loved them.'[8]

The return of spring appears to have remained true to its traditional associations with love and romance in the relationship between Murry and Mansfield. Murry's pleasure in waking with Mansfield in his arms is paralleled by a love letter Mansfield wrote to him in his 'private book' on 19 May 1917:

Last night, there was a moment before you got into bed. You stood, quite naked, bending forward a little – talking. It was only for an instant. I saw you – I loved you so – loved your body with such tenderness – Ah my dear – And I am not thinking now of 'passion'.

No, of that other thing that makes me feel that every inch of you is so precious to me.

She describes then his 'creamy warm skin', his 'ears, cold like shells are cold', his 'thin young back' and her hopes that the two of them 'shall do very great things'. But at the end of the letter Mansfield makes this claim: 'I want nobody but you for my lover and my friend and to nobody but you shall I be *faithful*,' which sounds very much like a disavowal of the 'freedom' she was accustomed to claim.[9] Yet it might well have been a ploy in her continuing wariness of the threat posed by Garsington. An editorial footnote to this letter to Murry points out that he was on his way to spend the weekend at Garsington just at the moment Mansfield was writing it.[10]

Ambiguous motivations notwithstanding, the sensual blossoming of the spring was accompanied by a creative blossoming as well for Mansfield, who was now energetically writing – and publishing – stories and 'Fragments' in the *New Age*. While she appears to have been basking in the pleasure of this renewed creativity and the enticements of new social possibilities, Murry was slowly sinking into depression. His only relief from his work at the War Office and his unrelenting journalism was, as he put it, 'an intensity of speculation – using the word in Keats's sense – far more consuming than ordinary work could ever be'.[11] This completely mental activity at first shielded him from realizing the onset of a breakdown, both physical and emotional. The doctor who examined him feared he might develop tuberculosis and wanted him to take a recuperative rest in the country. His condition was serious enough for the War Office to give him sick leave and continue his salary.

A far more socially conscientious Murry of the 1930s remarked that this was his 'one authentic taste of the condition of a future society in which there is economic security for all'.[12] Yet there is quite a bit of irony in the fact that Murry would spend that sick leave at Garsington, under the care not of a beneficent welfare state, but of an aristocratic patron. Regardless of Lady Ottoline's disappointment with Murry, she nonetheless quite graciously invited him to stay at Garsington after Mansfield begged her to do so.

A much darker irony, of course, is that Murry recovered and Mansfield fell ill during this – retrospectively ominous – Garsington sojourn. She was chilled on the way from the station to visit him there and when she returned to London the chill developed into fever, perhaps – as the doctor diagnosed at first – an attack of pleurisy. And then shortly afterwards he discovered a spot on her right lung.

On 13 December, Mansfield had written to Murry: 'I cant sleep for a nut. I lie in a kind of *furious bliss!*'[13] And Murry later remarked that 'the fury of the bliss would suddenly change into a fury of irritation'.[14] He began to see in her 'a quite unfamiliar note of exasperation'. Whether Murry really experienced then 'the grim sense of foreboding' that he describes in *Between Two Worlds* is not possible to know, but it dramatically enhances his construction of his life's tragedy:

I was engulfed in a black wave of unfaith. And such was the state of mind which lay in wait for me that the sudden reversal of our roles – my illness as it were in a moment transferred to her – was sinister with destiny. That possibility had never entered my mind; but now that it was a reality, it seemed to be self-evident. That was precisely how Necessity – the Beauty of Necessity – would reveal itself in us![15]

Murry's reference to 'Necessity' also suggests a new paradigm for his interpretation of experience. For Murry, Garsington at the end of 1917 had provided his own symbolic *intellectual* turning point. It was during his stay there that he read Colvin's *Life of Keats*, and 'began to read the poetry with a new understanding'.[16] The shift from the influence of Dostoevsky to that of Keats would have significant consequences for Murry's career as a literary critic. But more personally, it demarcates a point beyond which everything would be dominated by the subject of tuberculosis. Murry sensed that its intrusion had 'suddenly' made Mansfield 'become a different person. Her "furious bliss" and her furious exasperation belonged to another Katherine than [he] had known.'[17]

Mansfield's exhausting journey to Bandol, where she had been so happy with Murry in 1916, only weakened her further and intensified her emotional volatility. She wrote to Murry on 11 January 1918 that she felt 'like a fly who has been dropped into the milk jug & fished out again but is still too milky & drowned to start cleaning up yet'.[18] Although her doctor had discovered tuberculosis in her right lung, she complained to Murry on 18 January that now she had pain in her left lung too. She definitely was not improving. She began writing 'Je ne parle pas français' on 29 January, a day when she was upset that she had not received any letters from Murry and was not ready to believe that hers were being delayed in the mail. She did not yet realize how much the intensification of the war had affected the delivery of mail, nor did she know until the next day that the Germans had bombed London, killing 47 people on the night of the 28th. Did this momentary disruption in the frantic pace of the couple's intense letter writing elicit intimations of duplicity again? Despite her constant expressions of love for him in her correspondence, even on the *same* day that she began writing 'Je ne parle pas français', she must have felt an undertow pulling her towards submerged resentments and suspicions. Only two days earlier, in a letter to Murry full of depressed anger, she referred to Ottoline Morrell as *'corrupt – corrupt'*.[19]

When she tried to explain the origin of the story to Murry, she suggested that it 'is of course taken from – Carco & Gertler & God knows who'.[20] Her lonely return to France seems to have brought back the memory of that earlier escapade there with Francis Carco in 1915. Now, he would be added to her growing list of the 'corrupt' and her new story could not repeat the pattern of her affair with him, for that would have situated *her* as the duplicitous partner to Murry. Instead it harks back to Murry's initial friendship with Carco in 1911, and also to her own first meeting with him in 1912 when she supposedly said: 'Je ne parle pas français.'[21] (There was also her second encounter with Carco in the winter of 1913–14, when he took Murry 'on a strange journey into the underworld' to sell their furniture in the brothels of Paris.)[22]

But why does she also mention Mark Gertler here? Mansfield's imaginative linking of the two men, who never knew each other, appears to date back to that famous Christmas Eve party of 1914 at Gilbert Cannan's windmill, when Mansfield performed the skit in which she left Murry for Gertler, who represented Carco. There is an entry in Murry's journal on 29 December 1914 that suggests an additional reason Mansfield might have mentioned Gertler. Murry describes a conversation he had with him soon after the Cannan's party, in which Gertler recounted his sexual history. Murry seems amazed by the details Gertler revealed, such as the fact that by the age of eight he had become completely developed physically and was sexually active. Murry also writes down some of Gertler's anecdotes, including one about a sexual encounter with a girl of only 14, and then compares his own naivety with Gertler's sexual sophistication.[23]

Given their mutual delight in gossip, it is likely that Murry went over the details of this conversation with Mansfield, and now, three years later, she found herself combining Gertler's precocious and promiscuous sexuality with that of Carco, to bolster her now seemingly obsessive focus on 'corruption'. Her letter to Murry about the story's origin continues with:

> I read the fair copy just now and couldn't think where the devil I had got the bloody thing from – I cant even now. Its a mystery. Theres

so much less taken from life than anybody would credit. The african laundress I had a bone of – but only a bone – Dick Harmon of course is partly is[24]

(The reference to the 'african laundress' who seduced the ten-year-old Duquette seems to be derived from an incident in Carco's childhood.) Yet, Mansfield's paragraph drops off here unfinished. Dick Harmon, the man who brings his lover, 'Mouse', to Paris and then abandons her there, is, obviously, 'partly' Murry.

The 'plot' of the story, as Alpers suggests, links Mouse 'partly' with 'the Marguéritte whom [Murry] deserted in 1911 and allowed to think his mother was to blame'.[25] Mansfield would have known about Murry's love affair with Marguéritte because he had told her about it at the very beginning of their relationship, when they used to talk for hours about his troubled past. Whether he confessed his lingering guilt then, or whether he even told Mansfield that he had *abandoned* Marguéritte, is uncertain. Nonetheless, she would have more recently discovered the persistence of Murry's unresolved feelings through reading *Still Life*. There, his fictional reconstruction of the situation sets it firmly within the context of its protagonist's *current* relationship with a woman very similar to herself. In her now vulnerable condition, alone and very sick, did she begin to worry about Murry abandoning her?

The parallels with the Murry/Marguéritte situation, however, need to be put into perspective by considering some more recent history: the pattern of triangular relationships that had affected Mansfield's feelings for Murry over the past few years. In this way, 'Je ne parle pas français' is a counterpart to 'Bliss', which she would write only two weeks later. In 'Bliss' the triangle is composed of two women and one man; the erotic energy of the story is bisexual. In 'Je ne parle pas français' the triangle is composed of two men and one woman, and again, bisexuality infiltrates the story's emotional core.[26] Both stories reveal betrayal and disillusionment, but the latter depicts rejection and abandonment as well. If 'Bliss' draws some of its emotional complexity from the triangular relationship between Murry, Ottoline Morrell and Mansfield, 'Je ne parle pas français' reprises the homosocial triangle of Murry, Lawrence and Mansfield (or the earlier one of Murry, Gordon Campbell and Mansfield).

In Murry's *Still Life* there are two interlocking romantic triangles. The first consists of Maurice Temple, Dennis Beauchamp and Anne Cradock. The second, more submerged triangle, is that of Maurice, Anne and the *memory* of the French woman, Madeleine. That memory, and the guilt it elicits from Maurice, undermines – and eventually destroys – his relationship with Anne, who turns to Dennis and leaves with him at the novel's end. Additionally, the novel actually duplicates two subtexts of 'Je ne parle pas français'. The first is Maurice's use of his mother as an excuse for abandoning Madeleine, which is reprised in Dick Harmon's abandonment of Mouse for the same reason. The second is the intensity of the male friendships, which in both stories position the Murry-like characters in the passive role.

Along these lines it may be useful to read some details intertextually. There is, for example, the letter Dick Harmon leaves for 'Mouse, My Little Mouse':

> It's no good. It's impossible. I can't see it through. Oh, I do love you. I do love you, Mouse, but I can't hurt her. People have been hurting her all her life. I simply dare not give her this final blow. [...] It would kill her – kill her, Mouse. And, oh God, I can't kill my mother! Not even for you. Not even for us.[27]

The letter almost seems like a commentary on Murry's own use of a letter from Maurice's mother, to suggest her role in destroying his love affair with Madeleine:

> You promised me that you would never write to her again [...]. But I can't see that it would matter now when you don't even care enough for me to let me know where you are living. [...] – this could be the same. I don't even know if you are alive. If you only knew what I have had to suffer in the nights thinking of you.[28]

In the same envelope, Maurice's mother encloses another letter, a painful one from the abandoned Madeleine, who bemoans his long silence, and melodramatically tells him she will not write again: 'Je serais morte.'[29] Madeleine's final desperate attempt to contact Maurice through his mother will not be Mouse's response to Dick. When Dick begs her at the end of his letter: 'And don't write. I should not have the courage to answer your letters and the sight of your spidery handwriting –' (88), her response to his desertion is far more stoical than Madeleine's. She tells Duquette when he asks if she would try to see Harmon again: '"What an extraordinary idea!" she said, more coldly than ever. "Of course I shall not dream of seeing him. As for going back – that is quite out of the question. I can't go back"' (89).

Dick Harmon's letter, with its emphasis on 'hurting' and its equivocation is highly reminiscent of Maurice's self-excoriation in *Still Life*:

Here I am twenty-four, absolutely tortured by the thought of all the people there are roaming about the world, whom I've hurt in some way or in another. [...] The funniest part of it is that the reason why I hurt all these people is that I haven't got the courage not to. If I'd just told them I was – well, just what I am – quite early on, it would have been all right. [...] I can see myself telling my mother that I knew I was going to make a mess of everything.[30]

These words of Maurice's are said to Dennis in reference to his problems with Anne, as well as alluding to his past mistreatment of Madeleine. But the significance of the conversation is in its revelation of the intensity of Maurice's feelings for *Dennis*, as when Maurice says:

If I once begin to think about myself really, I can't see where my sentimentality stops. It's mixed up with everything I do, somehow. It's not only that I can't end anything, but I can't even believe that anything is going to end. [...] For instance, when you go away again. You'll have to sometimes, I suppose? I simply can't face the idea of saying good-bye to you, and yet I can't get it out of the back of my mind. That a thing should be over and done with for ever – it almost makes me freeze with horror.[31]

Although Maurice slides the discussion back to Anne, more safely maintaining the aura of homosocial rivalry, the strongest emotion in the conversation is his fear of Dennis's leaving. But that fear is in itself ambivalent, for his unconscious rivalry over Anne is what makes the idea of that leaving almost a wish that it happen. It is the same kind of ambivalence that marks Raoul's reaction to Dick Harmon's letter to Mouse. Although he had been imagining that Dick had 'shot himself', he recovers quickly from his fantasy after reading Dick's letter: 'My relief at his not having shot himself was mixed with a wonderful sense of elation. I was even – more than even with my "that's very curious and interesting" Englishman' (88). That Mouse, the rejected woman – whom Dick rather hysterically asks at the end of his letter to 'forgive' him: 'Don't love me any more. Yes. Love me. Love me' – is used primarily as the locus for two men's relations with each other might well be Mansfield's point.

Dick Harmon appears to be the passive partner in his friendship with Duquette despite Duquette's claim that 'Even with Dick. It was he who made the first advances' (70). Since Duquette's first-person narration never allows (except in the case of Dick's letter) the reader to penetrate the thoughts of other characters, Dick's feelings for Duquette remain unclear. It is Duquette who describes his own pleasure in being invited to dinner by Dick: 'I was so deeply, deeply flattered that I had to leave him then and there to preen and preen myself before the cubist sofas. What a catch! An Englishman, reserved, serious, making a special study of French literature . . . .' (71).

When Duquette catches a glimpse of a photograph of Dick's mother, he imagines her saying to him: 'Out of my sight, you little perfumed fox-terrier of a Frenchman' (72). And the fox-terrier image thus becomes an extended metaphor for Duquette's sense of his role with regard to Dick. When Dick suddenly decides to return to England, Raoul 'stood on the shore alone, more like a little fox-terrier than ever . . . .', and thinks how

> after all it was you who whistled to me, you who asked me to come! What a spectacle I've cut wagging my tail and leaping round you, only to be left like this while the boat sails off in its slow, dreamy way . . . .

His romantic feelings change rapidly to anger:

> Curse these English! No, this is too insolent altogether. Who do you imagine I am? A little paid guide to the night pleasures of Paris? ... No, Monsieur. I am a young writer, very serious, and extremely interested in modern English literature. And I have been insulted – insulted. (73–4)

Mansfield captures here a not atypical reaction of people to Murry, who himself recognized that

> time and time again, both men and women, whom I thought to be my friends, have made it a capital charge against me that I possess some mysterious 'personal charm': to which they succumb, and then cherish resentment against me for my behaviour to them.[32]

Murry's response to 'Je ne parle pas français' was – not surprisingly – complex and ambiguous. He had no idea at first that any hostility towards himself might have contributed to Mansfield's 'furious' creative energy during its composition. When she had told him she was working on it and believed that it was 'the real thing',[33] he responded with genuine enthusiasm and respect for her creative powers. She had only sent him the first 'chapter' of the story on 4 February, however, and suggested – perhaps as a way to adjust his reading of it – its connection to 'Carco & Gertler & God knows who'. That letter reveals how anxious she was that Murry read the story in the right way: 'Oh God – is it good? I am frightened. [...] Tell me – dont spare me. Is it the long breathe as I feel to my soul it is – or is it a false alarm?'[34] Mansfield here seems to appeal to Murry for a *diagnosis*. Her reference to 'the long breathe' and the 'false alarm' belongs to the discourse of medicine, a reminder of the predominant issue of her life now.

Murry's response on 8 February was everything she could have wished for: 'not only first rate; it's overwhelming. The description, no, not description, creation, of that café is extraordinary.' He did not simply offer praise, however, he analysed his impressions as seriously as he would do in one of his literary critiques. Making a significant observation about the story's echoing of Dostoevsky's *Letters from the Underworld*, he told her that it affected him in a way no other writing has 'except D's'. He was intrigued by the character of Raoul Duquette, and remarked that Duquette

> isn't what he would be if it were either Dostoevsky (or me) writing, for then he would be Dostoevsky thinking aloud. But instead of this, you have got this strange person, who's strange, not, as D's man would be, because he has thought everything to a standstill, but because he is conscious of a piece out of him. [...] Yes, he's conscious of having no roots. He sees a person like Dick who has roots and he realises the difference. But what it is he hasn't got, he doesn't know. Nor do I.[35]

Murry's analysis here is characteristically self-reflexive. There is his linking of himself and Dostoevsky, most obviously, especially his reference to thinking 'everything to a standstill'. There is also his initial identification with Dick – 'who has roots' – and that puffs him up considerably. But Duquette's awareness of 'a piece out of him' is one of Murry's continuing fears about himself.

At this stage of his reading then, Murry was definitely perplexed: 'What you are going to do with them I haven't the faintest idea. But I am ravenous to know.' He struggled to define what it was about the story that distinguished it from her others:

> This is the only writing of yours I know that seems to be *dangerous*. Do you understand what I mean – by the adjective? Its *dangerous* to stop the world for a timeless moment.

To put it another way. Here you seem to have begun to drag the depths of your *consciousness*.[36]

Of course Mansfield was delighted with Murry's response, but she must have felt uneasy by the time she received it, since she had, by then, shown that Dick's 'roots' were in very thin soil indeed: 'I read it & I wept with joy. How can you so marvellously understand – and so receive my love offering. Ah, it will take all of the longest life I can live to repay you.' Yet despite her pleasure in his response, she adds: 'But Christ! A devil about the size of a flea nips in my ear "suppose he's disappointed with the 2nd half?"'[37] Mansfield's light-hearted concession to doubt ('the size of a flea') belies her anxiety. She must have known that as astute a reader as Murry would recognize the animus mixed into the ingredients of her brew. And she was not finished working through it either. She closes her letter with a brief remark: 'My new story is signalled.' That story would be 'Bliss'.

It took Murry a while to react to the second half. When he received it on 15 February, he telegraphed her and then wrote that he 'wasn't prepared for the tragic turn of *Je ne parle pas*, and it upset me – I'm an awful child.'[38] His letter reveals his ambivalence, although he tries to cover it up by praising Mansfield's artistic delineation of 'Mouse'. He then quickly veers to the other story she had sent him at the same time, 'Sun and Moon', which clearly seemed to garner his emotional energies more fully by allowing him an unambiguous avenue for identification. Its central character, the little boy, 'Sun', evokes the image of the sensitive child-self that Murry liked to believe he still held inside himself.

It would not be until 23 February, after Mansfield had written to express her concern that he was dissatisfied with her story and asked him to explain his reactions, that Murry finally tried to analyse his feelings about it. He insisted that he was not 'disappointed' with it, but rather 'utterly bowled out by it', that he was 'so passionately fond of the Mouse' that he was devastated by what happened to her.

> Look here, you must see that what you call my disappointment [...] was just my confession that you had done it – done it absolutely. My disappointment as a child was my satisfaction as an artist [...] 'Sun & Moon' were really tinies. His tragedy would be put right. But Mouse & Dick, they were too much like us. If they had been exactly like it wouldn't have upset me because I know we're alright. But they were different, our brothers & sisters spiritually.[39]

Murry cannot admit to his recognition of the attack on his relationship with Mansfield hidden within 'Je ne parle pas français'. He has to insist that he knows *they* are 'alright'. To go any further would damage the love story they were carefully constructing in their letters during these months of separation. That separation, although it made them miserable, was having a remarkably energizing effect on their writing. In fact, their entire correspondence until Mansfield's return on 11 April 1918 might well be read as a collaborative text in which each participant engages in the construction of a writing self. That text has a narrative structure – teleological from its inception – in which the story it depicts is the heroic struggle of two lovers separated by fate in the forms of war and illness. The story's climax is the bombardment of Paris, and its dénouement will be the wedding of its two lovers.

Notes

1. J. M. Murry (1935) *Between Two Worlds: An Autobiography* (London: Cape), p. 320.
2. *Letters* 1, p. 285.
3. I. Baker (1972) *Katherine Mansfield: The Memories of LM* (New York: Taplinger), p. 100.
4. See Antony Alpers for a vivid description of the complex situation between Mansfield and L. M. in the small studio. He quotes a passage from Murry's journal describing L. M. standing naked in front of Mansfield's door, hoping for her admiration. A. Alpers (1980) *The Life of Katherine Mansfield* (London: Jonathan Cape), pp. 240–2.
5. For a listing of all Murry's unsigned pieces in the *TLS* see D. Bradshaw (1991) 'John Middleton Murry and the *Times Literary Supplement*: The Importance and Usage of a Modern Literary Archive', *Bulletin of Bibliography*, 48: 4, 199–212.
6. Murry, *Between Two Worlds*, p. 429.
7. *Ibid.*, p. 432.
8. J. M. Murry, 'Diaries and Notebooks' [unpublished], The Alexander Turnbull Library, MS 4147. In her letter to Ottoline Morrell on 24 April, Mansfield noted the 'little Poussin cherubs climbing up & down the budding tree outside my window' (*Letters* 1, p. 305).
9. *Letters* 1, pp. 307–8.
10. *Ibid.*, p. 308.
11. Murry, *Between Two Worlds*, p. 443.
12. *Ibid.*, p. 444.
13. *Letters* 1, p. 344.
14. Murry, *Between Two Worlds*, p. 444.
15. *Ibid.*, p. 450.
16. *Ibid.*, p. 446.
17. *Ibid.*, p. 450.
18. *Letters* 2, p. 8.

19. *Ibid.*, p. 42. On 29 January Woolf remarked about Ottoline to Vanessa Bell: 'But she's got Murry back.' N. Nicolson with J. Trautmann (eds) (1976) *The Letters of Virginia Woolf*, vol. 2 (New York: Harcourt), p. 214.
20. *Letters* 2, p. 56.
21. The evidence for this is not certain, since it is only recorded in Carco's memoir of 1940, *Bohème d'Artiste*, and could have been constructed out of his reading of her story.
22. Murry, *Between Two Worlds*, p. 276.
23. Murry, MS 4147, pp. 52–4.
24. *Letters* 2, p. 56.
25. Alpers, p. 273.
26. In a formal analysis, W. H. New draws attention to 'the triangular pattern' of the story, 'one that is conventionally associated with a corrupted love'. The pattern involves more than one triangle; the first consists of Duquette, Dick and Mouse; the second of Dick, Mouse and Dick's mother; yet another of 'Raoul, Dick, and their sexual ambivalence'. W. H. New (1999) *Reading Mansfield and Metaphors of Form* (Quebec: McGill-Queen's University Press), p. 93.
27. K. Mansfield (1945) *Collected Stories of Katherine Mansfield* (London: Constable), p. 87. All further references to Mansfield's stories are to this edition and are placed directly after each quotation.
28. J. M. Murry (1916) *Still Life* (London: Constable), p. 239.
29. *Ibid.*, pp. 240–1.
30. *Ibid.*, pp. 326–7.
31. *Ibid.*, p. 327.
32. Murry, *Between Two Worlds*, p. 209.
33. *Letters* 2, p. 51.
34. *Ibid.*, p. 56.
35. C. A. Hankin (ed.) (1983) *The Letters of John Middleton Murry to Katherine Mansfield* (London: Constable), p. 115.
36. *Ibid.*
37. *Letters* 2, p. 68.
38. Hankin, p. 121.
39. *Ibid.*, p. 127.

Part II
Mansfield and Modernity

4
Mansfield as Colonial Modernist: Difference Within

Elleke Boehmer

A constellated aesthetic

Although modernism involved a series of movements that were animated by, and shaped within, cosmopolitan and transnational cultural arenas, modernism's dominant methodological and critical co-ordinates generally, and in some ways quite remarkably, remain transatlantic, even in the twenty-first century. The cross-cultural and international exchanges that took place between writers and artists, and the various cross-border journeys they undertook, all centrally formative to what we now understand to be modernism, are perceived to be in the main exchanges and journeys between Britain, the rest of Europe and America. Despite the heterogeneous cultural and national make-up of many of modernism's key figures, including Jacob Epstein, William Plomer, Claude McKay and, not least among them, Katherine Mansfield, the Anglo-American axis built on the cultural and educational pilgrimages and pathways of influence traced by major modernists, such as T. S. Eliot and Ezra Pound, continues by and large to dominate the field. Even Richard Begam and Michael Valdez Moses's *Modernism and Colonialism* (2007), a path-breaking collection investigating how 'the modernist revolution can be understood as a critical and artistic engagement with the [...] European quest for empire', ultimately circumscribes or corrals the investigation it wishes to pursue by focusing, the introduction emphasizes, on 'traditional' modernism, by which is meant the predictable canonical modernist writers, including Eliot, James Joyce, D. H. Lawrence and Virginia Woolf.[1]

Against this approach, I want to contend in this essay that modernism – especially here the art of the New Zealand-born modernist traveller Katherine Mansfield – was moulded and informed within a colonial geography, and that it was accompanied by a keen awareness of cultural and racial difference: indeed, the more colonial or provincial the writer the keener the awareness. The case for a definitive networked colonial modernism could, I believe, be persuasively demonstrated by setting the early twentieth century's mainstream figures – Eliot, Pound, Woolf, Joyce, Yeats – in relation to, or in dialogue with, modernism's expanded or constellated cosmopolitan, colonial or colonial-metropolitan (for example, Irish) contexts – though this will not be the burden of this essay. But the case can also be made, as persuasively, by examining more closely the ways in which modernists of colonial provenance – here Mansfield (but also, arguably, Claude McKay, William Plomer, Mulk Raj Anand, Jean Rhys and others) – shaped their modernist techniques within the crucible of their outsider colonial experience, or from their perspective as colonial others who felt themselves to be both players within, yet to some degree alienated from, the metropolitan city.

The task of what follows therefore will be to read two Mansfield stories side by side as presenting a case-in-point for a colonial outsider's articulation of what Homi Bhabha calls 'difference within', that is, for their encoding of colonial otherness as embedded, at times almost imperceptibly or in hidden ways, yet still palpably, within the metropolis, even within the metropolitan self.[2] *Worldwide*, both in the imperial centre *and* from the vantage point of the colonial periphery, this reading of Mansfield suggests, modernism represented an unfolding of different, interacting responses to the predicament of modernity, frequently expressed as a problem of self-alienation.[3] Or, put another way, the troubled yet also creative, and even at times collaborative, interactions that colonialism as both system and practice produced, especially in transnational and cross-cultural domains, contributed to the making of modernist perceptions and techniques centred on experiences of anomie, hallucination, rupture, splitting and other modes of self-objectification.

In the essay I will first expand further these contentions about modernism as being in significant ways, and at different representational levels, generated and honed by empire, and then relate these observations to Mansfield's mode of seeing Europe as a young, self-consciously modern writer. I will track her sharp if highly inflected awareness of disruptive colonial 'difference within' in two stories, briefly in 'The Luft Bad' from *In a German Pension* (1911), an early, curiously cryptic sketch about social and physical ostracism, and then, more extensively, in one of her more capricious, epistemologically uncertain, eminently modernist stories, 'Je ne parle pas français' from *Bliss* (1920). As an aside, Mansfield in 'The Luft Bad' offers her readers a marvellously oblique and off-hand riposte, which critical hindsight charges with significance, to the hegemony of the Anglo-American axis in modernist critical discourse (as of course in western politics also). Following the I-narrator's prevarication in the story in response to the question as to whether she is an American or an Englishwoman, her interlocutor comments: 'You must be one of the two; you cannot help it' (732).[4] As against the seemingly international make-up of the 'Luft Bad's' clientele, the white colonial would appear to be the inadmissible third term within its configuration of possible western Anglophone identities.

As is becoming more widely acknowledged, Mansfield is the pre-eminent figure towering at once over colonial and metropolitan fields of writing at the beginning of the twentieth century, chiselling her fine, self-consciously modernist aesthetic in both arenas, interacting with both as imaginative domains.[5] Along with Anand, Plomer, Slessor, McKay, though perhaps more influentially than they, it is Mansfield who demonstrates par excellence how aspects of what we now term modernism crystallized around certain colonial experiences (in particular, of exile and cultural alienation), and colonial and nascent national energies (especially of making new). It is her work, in many cases preceding that of the others named, which allows us to detach ourselves from the assumption that creative production elsewhere across the world in this period was merely reflective and derivative of Euro-American modernism; or masked as either the one or the other, American or European, without alternative interpretations.[6]

The colonial landscape of modernism

It is important to recognize that the broader colonial landscape of modernism is not only a methodological or ideological construct but is licensed by the late nineteenth- and early twentieth-century history of colonialism, in particular that of the British Empire. Modernism – defined as a self-reflexive concern with formal innovation in the face of the perceived historical and moral crises besetting the West – was perhaps the first global development in literature and the arts, as new research on the responses to empire of the mainstream modernists suggests.[7] It was a development enabled first and foremost by the communication channels, and the travellers' and migrant pathways that empire put in place.[8] But, in so far as modernism represents a serious – fascinated yet also frightened – confrontation with the other, it was also enabled by the contacts between mutually unfamiliar cultures that empire brought about, unequal and unjust as these often were. In similar ways to how modernity in the colonial context constitutes for historian Dipesh Chakrabarty not a continuous line of progress but a layering of disjointed temporalities, modernism in the context of a world-embracing Anglophone empire emerged out of that empire's concatenation of discontinuous cultural perceptions of time and space.[9] As Jed Esty justly writes in *Modernism and Colonialism*, 'the modernist [novel] assimilates the temporality of a global and imperial era when nations spilled beyond their borders and when the accelerating yet uneven pace of development seemed to have thrown the time of modernity out of joint'.[10]

Modernism famously acknowledged the epistemological challenge and stimulation represented by the distant and the other: think only of Picasso's *Les Demoiselles d'Avignon* (1907); the ambivalent physicality of the West African fetish figures in D. H. Lawrence's *Women in Love* (1920); or Jacob Epstein's referencing of Indian temple art in his erotically charged sculptures leading up to 'Rock Drill' (1915).[11] Modernism was also perhaps the first multi-stranded movement in the arts that could claim participation worldwide, not only on the part of writers and artists, but also in its implicit appeal to audiences and readers across the globe, *and* in its concomitant response to them. The situation arose where colonial and native writers were deploying the so-called modernist devices of defamiliarization and dissociation to give expression to their decentred, culturally disrupted realities, at around the same time that metropolitan modernists were turning to other cultures to transform their society and the western self.[12] To say it more strongly, cross-border dialogues facilitated by colonialism's globalizing forces encouraged at various different levels the process of giving the other voice – as well as of investigating who the other was in the first place. So, as metropolitan modernist writing formed a counterpoint to, and a correlate for, what was happening away from the centre, colonials – citizens of the empire – were transfiguring European representation by introducing to it, as Mary Lou Emery writes of Caribbean modernism, their 'unique', transcontinental 'crossroads of styles, forms and cultures'.[13]

A related development was that, with the vast expansion of the imperial metropolises, colonial writers like Mansfield, Claude McKay, Mulk Raj Anand, Jean Rhys, C. L. R. James (to draw names only from the English-speaking world), gravitated to these cities' cultural, aesthetic, class and sexual freedoms. They themselves constituted part of their experimental hubbub, and their exilic and migrant perspectives contributed to the living collage that was the urban avant-garde. Moreover, the preoccupation with alienation and disoriented or displaced identity shared by the new colonial writers, related to and interacted with the breakdown in transcendent or universal systems of understanding that also preoccupied the metropolitan modernists. As this suggests, the creative involvement of other cultural and national players inevitably intensified those experiences characteristically associated with modernism: 'making new', the fragmentation of absolutes, the sense of occupying the fringes of history, interests in subjective and multiple perspectives, and in the fluidity of consciousness. As her notebooks attest, Mansfield felt particularly drawn to, and inspired to write by, the spectacle of diverse figures from different cultures and nationalities moving through the streets of London. The signs of differences *within* the city became for her signs of the difference *of* the modern city, and of her own translated status within it. The colonials' culturally and nationally trans-migrated art also provided models, or, at least, analogues, for the multilingual, discontinuous and generically mixed utterance that modernism increasingly began to favour, as is demonstrated by the teasingly innovative jump-cuts that characterize the colonial Mansfield's short stories.

It is true of course that the participation of colonial writers and artists in the expanding modernist movement or movements was not as frequent, intensive or, in many cases, as involving as it was for the Anglo-American metropolitans: their status was simply not equivalent. Especially for black writers like McKay, but also for white colonials marked, as Mansfield said, by 'the taint of the pioneer in my blood', their sense of place in Britain and the rest of Europe was not comparable with that of the British and the Americans.[14] Yet the mere fact that there were prominent colonial participants in metropolitan modernism – Mansfield and Yeats, Plomer and McKay, Anand and Rhys – testifies to the importance of their contribution and the significance of their insights, as against the ongoing emphases within modernist criticism. Their 'political and artistic movements across [the] exclusionary and shifting boundaries' they encountered, produced in them, to different degrees, an energetic 'aesthetics of trans-figuration', to cite Emery once again. Far from their relationship to the centre being belated, as has been suggested in relation to Anand and Rhys for example, the vigorous and heterogeneous modernity they represented cannot but have informed or impinged on metropolitan modernist interests in the inverse, the miscellaneous, the disjointed. In corresponding terms, Paul Gilroy designates the African slaves of the New World the first moderns on the basis of their painful but ultimately transformational interaction with, and adaptation to, a variety of transatlantic cultural developments.[15] Empire (alongside war, urbanization and modernity itself) made modernism possible, which is to say, powered its developments, even if at times obliquely, or in contrapuntal forms.

Katherine Mansfield, colonial modernist in metropolitan London

Born in Wellington, New Zealand, Mansfield's complex 'voyage in', her creative trajectory from her 'little land' to the metropolis, maps a restless striving away from the bourgeois provinciality of the colonial backwater she came from. Her permanent move to Europe in 1908 was followed by ceaseless and often fretful travel within Europe. Yet in her work this restlessness is offset by the travelling colonial's strong preoccupation with self-alienation and a related yearning for her lost homeland, what Bhabha following Freud terms the postcolonial *unheimlich*, the sense of viewing the world as a permanent outsider.[16]

As Angela Smith amongst others observes, Mansfield's short stories ceaselessly explore sites of liminality and estrangement.[17] In particular her more trademark and influential modernist tales, like 'Prelude' or 'The Garden Party', generate moments of rupture and fission provoked by moral and emotional crises connected to feelings of being unable to conform or to fit in. In story after story, Mansfield's view of the unstable, multifaceted self, which her vagrant experience arguably fostered in her, comes up against not only the limitations imposed by bourgeois provinciality, but also the violations and betrayals foisted on her by the modernist city. Both city and colony are places of discomposure and disruption: something that powerfully suggests the extent to which Mansfield's bifurcated colonial/metropolitan positioning is integral to her modernism and, in particular here, to the ways in which she visually encoded London. As a double- or reverse-image study to the present essay, Mansfield's perspective as colonial modernist, with the emphasis on her colonial aspect, could be persuasively traced through the short stories visibly set in New Zealand ('At the Bay', 'The Garden Party', 'Prelude'), where the presence of the alien, what Spivak describes as 'the wholly other', in the form of death, violence, weird botany, irrupts into the orderly and apparently secure pastoral landscape of her lost homeland.[18] Here however the focus is on a pair of Mansfield's stories that explore the converse to this antipodean landscape painting, by looking at instances of how racial and colonial others manifest in the interstices, if not indeed at the heart, of the colonial metropolis.

An indication of the mutually reinforcing 'fit' between Mansfield's cold colonial eye – maddened by the tedium of her 'new world', feverish with metropolitan excitement – and her modernist aesthetic, can be read off from her almost ready-made responses to London, following her return there as an aspirant artist. These suggest that her artistic vision as an alienated colonial, self-hating, precociously jaded and disillusioned, had already begun to constitute the ground of her aesthetic *before* she arrived back in the metropolis as an experimental young writer. She approached the city not merely as her self-appointed environment as a modern artist, but with a distancing, decentring aesthetic already largely in place, a vision primed to seek and find signs of difference even if encrypted or obscured. This aesthetic had arguably been in formation from the time a year or so earlier that she copied from Oscar Wilde's *Dorian Gray* into her reading notes the words: 'Being natural is simply a pose – and the most irritating pose I know.'[19] Her aesthetic vision certainly was in place when, in September 1907, she wrote these provocative lines from Wellington in response to E. J. Brady, the editor of the *Native Companion*, a Melbourne journal:

> I send you some more work – practically there is nothing local – except the 'Botanical Gardens' Vignette – The reason is that for the last few years London has held me – very tightly indeed – and I've not yet escaped. You ask for some details as to myself. I am poor – obscure – just eighteen years of age – with a rapacious appetite for everything and principles as light as my purse.[20]

If the colonies to Mansfield were raw, unsophisticated and desperately confining, then, as these lines suggest, London by contrast was the space in which her intense, highly wrought *yet* New Zealand-inspired symbolist language might find its referent and appropriate context. Her envisioning of London shows evidence of an intercalation of *both* colonial *and* modernist elements, or of a concatenation of various differences, difficult to prise apart.

That fit between Mansfield's colonial eye and her modernist aesthetic comes through clearly when her responses to the imperial metropolis are compared to those of other colonial travellers, for example the reformist Indians who visited the city in growing numbers in the turn-of-the-century decades. For the latter, as their travel writings show, London was mapped through anticipated, even familiar, images of rushing crowds and cosmopolitan streets, indices they registered as familiar in order to vouch for their own worldliness and sophistication. For a journalist-writer and campaigner such as B. M. Malabari in the 1890s, for example, the enigma of arrival was registered in his travelogues and letters not only through evoking the wheeling activity and teeming noise of the populous metropolis, but also, paradoxically, by noting its predictability.[21] London with its crowded streets, rampant commercialism and its St Paul's was as it was expected to be. The metropolis was sometimes alarming in its foreignness, but it also offered perspectives on the speeded-up, crowded modern world that the Indians could relate to, often from the vantage point of their urban upbringing, and which they could read according to the cultural codes acquired as part of their education.

For Mansfield, by contrast, judging from her letters and notebooks of this period, London comes in ready-sculpted, aestheticized form, as peopled by displaced, enervated individuals, locked into their secret capsules of subjectivity, touched with an intense expressionist colour and with a certain typicality, who bear the signs of their modern alienation on their faces and person. The city, so long hankered for from the distance of Wellington, projected from afar, is already modernist in Mansfield's representation, déjà vu in its garishly lit artificiality, its spectacle and its anomie. Consider for example the following, from a Murry-edited notebook entry for 1910:

> Over an opaque sky grey clouds moving heavily like the wings of tired birds. Wind blowing: in the naked light buildings and people appear suddenly grotesque, too sharply modelled, maliciously tweaked into being.
>
> A little procession wending its way up the Gray's Inn Road. In front, a man between the shafts of a hand-barrow that creaks under the weight of a piano-organ and two bundles. The man is small and greenish brown, head lolling forward, face covered with sweat. The piano-organ is bright red, with a blue and gold 'dancing picture' on either side. The bundle is a woman. You see only a black mackintosh topped with a sailor hat; the little bundle she holds has chalkwhite legs and yellow boots dangling from the loose ends of the shawl. Followed by two small boys, who walk with short steps, staring intensely at the ground, as though afraid of stumbling over their feet.
>
> No word is spoken; they never raise their eyes. And this silence and preoccupation gives to their progress a strange dignity.
>
> They are like pilgrims straining forward to Nowhere, dragging and holding to, and following after that bright red, triumphant thing with the blue and gold 'dancing picture' on either side.[22]

Some years later, related impressions of the shock of the strange the city brings, and of the restless coming and going of disassociated individuals, are extended and further sharpened. In this letter to Murry of 25 November 1917, the introduction to the perception is framed by parentheses, as an aside, as an already self-contained vignette capturing a certain emotion, a city 'veine', the terror of the anonymous encounter, as well as the distancing effects of watching and being watched:

> (By the way – isn't *Furnished Rooms* a good title for a story which plays in the Redcliffe Road – I cant resist it. Come & look over my shoulder – – The meeting on the dark stairs – you know, someone is coming down & someone is coming up – IS someone there? The fright – the pause – the unknown in each other glaring through the dark & then passing (which is almost too terrifying to be borne). Then the whole Street – And for back cloth the whole line of the street – and the dressmakers calling to the cat, the chinamen, the dark gentlemen, the babies playing, the coal cart, the line of the sky above the houses, the little stone figure in one of the gardens who carries a stone tray on his head, which, in summer is filled with flowers & in winter is heaped with snows, the lamenting piano, and all those faces hiding behind the windows – & the *one* who is always on the watch.[23]

It is worth observing how formally composed this is as a scene, with the horizontal lines of the street and the windows outlining the street-level bustle, and the whole pregnant with some nameless and frightening import. The 'chinamen', the 'dark gentlemen' – note that they are distinguished – form part of the scene, the everyday 'back cloth', yet are at the same time picked out by 'the *one*' always on the watch, imbued at one and the same time with a picture-book local-colour quality, yet also with the nameless sense of terror she communicates at the sight of the passing spectacle.

As her evocative, intensely symbolist compositions suggest, Mansfield is no urban scene-painter, reading London in terms of a received vocabulary. Instead she is interested in how the disaggregated bits, parts and colours of the modern metropolis, when placed in relation to one another, can be interpreted as signs of their own and the city's wider circumambient strangeness. Throughout her mature work we see her pondering how, by using these signs, she might develop an expressionist visual vocabulary with which to represent the city from within, as if for the first time. Her colonial position and perspective enter the compositions at those points where she can be seen to key her own sense of marginality as a colonial artist, her decentredness and duality, into the passing and random urban phenomena. She translates the symbols of the city – the stochastic flow, the intense colour and brief clustering of the crowd, the people going up and down, the solitary individual at the window – to conform to her own distant and distancing vision.

Mansfield's emergent modernist perspective therefore becomes an ironic articulation of her colonial position, and not a refutation of it. As if underscoring this close fit, at certain points in her early notebooks, such as in her first novel draft 'Juliet', collected as part of the Margaret Scott *Notebooks*, marginal or colonial and modern or metropolitan spaces symptomatically blend into one another. Both spaces are beset by 'climactic disturbance', illuminated by half-lights or a strange exposing light, transfixed by 'the strange longing for the artificial'.[24] The same might also be said of the following vignette from 1914: the scene is London, but it could also be Wellington, with its equally barren shapes and 'strange longings':

> It was evening, with little light, and what was there was very soft – the Freak Hour when people never seem to be quite in focus. I watched a man walking up and down the road – and he looked like a fly walking up a wall – and some men straining up with a barrow – all bottoms and feet. In the house opposite, at a ground-floor window, heavily barred, sat a little dark girl in a grey shawl reading a book. Her hair was parted down the middle; she had a small oval face. [...] I felt a sort of Spanish infatuation....[25]

It is reminiscent of Mansfield's evocations of strangeness through figures of cultural difference, be they 'chinamen' or Spanish-looking women present within ordinary street-side scenes, that 'The Luft Bad' opens with an at-first-bizarre 'Black Sambo' reference, that, in juxtaposition with 'Je ne parle pas français', can be seen as pointing on to the latter's more complex if still stereotyped representation of the African laundress. The umbrellas carried by the half-naked German women taking their air bath in the sunshine in 'The Luft Bad' convey a sense of 'ridiculous dignity', of a vain clutching for civilization in a state of nakedness – in Mansfield's phrase, they add 'a distinctly "Little Black Sambo" touch' (729). Whether 'brown' or untanned, the air-bathing women's partially unclothed appearance, set off by their flamboyant pieces of coloured cover, both of umbrella and of abbreviated bath-costume, appears to invite the analogy to the near-naked black child caricature.

Mansfield presumably derived the Black Sambo stereotype either from a general pool of representations of African Americans in popular journalism and music-hall culture of the first decade of the twentieth century, or, more probably, from a specific source, the illustrated children's book *The Story of Little Black Sambo*, published by the Anglo-Indian Helen Bannerman in 1899, set not in Africa but in India.[26] Bannerman's Black Sambo, who has marked African American features despite his

Indianness, carries, significantly, a 'beautiful' 'Green Umbrella' as part of his extravagant get up, which the tigers in the tale steal. The narrator's first umbrella in 'The Luft Bad' is 'a green cotton thing': the colour reference in common suggests an intertextual link. Yet, while the racist and jingoist connotations of the Black Sambo figure are unmistakeable, whatever their source, it is significant that across the run of this brief sketch of a short story, the extreme self-consciousness of the I-observer that at first distances and disparages her fellow bathers with the Black Sambo tag, by the story's end produces a partial identification with it.

Ironically for a story concerned with air-bathing, with indulging in the freedoms of nudity, air and light, 'The Luft Bad' is preoccupied with a variety of forms of bodily confinement if not entombment, with habits surrounding the consumption of food, with 'superfluous flesh', with the 'ills that flesh is heir to' (731, 730: a writer as aware of wording and rhythm as Mansfield surely intended the pun). From the Hungarian lady's description of the 'beautiful tomb' she has had built for her second husband through to the man in the male section of the 'bad' buried in mud, each one of the identified figures, the Russian, the 'brownest' woman, are physically tethered or restricted, if only by the mortification of the flesh through starvation and diet. The I-narrator too feels thus confined, her consciousness of her own proportions aggravated not only by the other women's stares and her own painful self-consciousness, but also by her sense of indefinable difference from them which underlies this self-consciousness. Cosmopolitan as the clientele may be, 'Hungarian', 'Russian' or German as their habits are, they are pointed in their references to the narrator's ambiguous national status, her being neither English nor American. By the story's end their exercise in labelling her prompts her to withdraw from the bathing group and take to the swings, a seemingly temporary move which then has consequences for her air-bathing. The experience which she has while swinging, a near-ecstatic moment of communion with the blue sky, an unanticipated true air bath, confirms the virtues of isolation, of willed separateness.[27] Henceforth, she makes it known, her husband's large umbrella, his '"storm" gamp', presumably black, becomes her indispensable bathing accoutrement and screen against all social heavy weather, behind which she hides in a corner even though she is not, or no longer, 'ashamed of her legs'. She has opted for the guise of Little Black Sambo, as the outward figure of her inner difference, down to her choice to carry the unmistakeable cheap black umbrella of the tropics. Her exposure to a different intensity of bodily experience on the swings, self-pleasing and freeing, breaks down her self-consciousness with respect both to her physical body, and to what might be termed her body-image.

'Je ne parle pas français'

'Je ne parle pas français' (1919/20), one of Mansfield's more sexually dissident stories, condenses and refines the provisional and glancing visual codes of her notebooks and letters.[28] The story, which presents as the preening, self-regarding commentary on his languid café life of the I-narrator Raoul Duquette (a Parisian male prostitute and would-be artist), was considered transgressive at its very first appearance. To publish it, 'a reluctant' Mansfield was pressed to make cuts to the sexually explicit content. With its metaphors of 'submerged' unconscious worlds, the story indeed announces itself as interested in discovering through the medium of its deluded first-person narrative, how the self – that constant subject of modernist interest – both subtends and exceeds conventional characterization.[29] And this is no matter how overweening, pretentious, or degraded that self. Throughout, the scene-composition is self-consciously cinematic: 'the direct result of the American cinema acting upon a weak mind'.

Empire, whether in ideological form or as a material force that shaped Mansfield's own reality, does not noticeably interfere in Duquette's recollection of the passing encounters with women and men from which he aspires to make his art, except once: in a generative ur-encounter with an 'African laundress'. His recollection of this encounter, the single memory he retains from childhood, introduces a hyper-disruptive moment into what is already a self-consciously perverse narrative. The 'very big, very dark' African laundress was inclined to play with him as a child, Duquette recalls, to make him scream for 'joy and fright', and to shower deafening kisses upon his ears. Finally, in what became a repeat-performance that has, it appears, moulded his parasitic relations with others since, she would put him to her breast. He now surmises that he has inherited from this experience an enervating languor and succubus-like emotional greed.

The unexpected encounter Mansfield offers between the 'little and light' man-child and the voluminous African laundress in 'Je ne parle pas français' is not innocent of Lawrentian-type colonialist connotations linking black Africanness to visceral knowledge and intuition. Even taken along with the more positive, yet no less stereotyped, associations of the black woman with fecundity and the elemental, this much is evident. However, there is something more interesting at work in the story than a mere recognition, in conventional terms, of an African physicality residing at the very heart of France (and at the centre of the small Parisian's psychic make-up), even if that recognition of an irruptive Africanness is in fact uncannily prescient of the emergence of *négritude* and its reversed aesthetic binaries in Paris some five or six years later.

Perhaps the most striking feature of the story is the undeniable agency of the laundress herself. In this aspect of her characterization, above others, Mansfield moves beyond stereotype. The laundress may be predatory and corrupting, even abusive and dangerous – a poisoning well – yet she is also represented as both self-pleasuring and attentive, and she is concerned to mother a child who seems to lack alternative parental support. Here the reader may recall that we are reliant upon Duquette's already suspect self-rationalizing memory-work for our account of the woman. Yet, quite separate from his portrait of her as an abusive domestic, it is equally possible that the woman was a laundress who doubled as a paid wet-nurse – as such, the mechanics of Duquette's memory would have manifested no differently. As a wet-nurse, the African woman is of a kind with numerous other replacement mothers in Mansfield's stories, who stand in for yet can never fully embody the lost centre and what it represents: aesthetic tradition, primal connectivity.

In her ambivalent vitality, and in contrast to the African woman's despairing appeal in Conrad's *Heart of Darkness*, the laundress reflects Mansfield's provocative understanding, as a metropolitan outsider, of the transgressive force of the stranger – of the one from elsewhere who positions herself so as to become closer even than a mother. In other words, if we read Duquette's story slant, as it must surely be read, and consider the African woman figure as more used than using, more possessed than possessor, the apparently abusive and also colonialist situation of white child vis-à-vis its exotic molester is disrupted. A very different though equally disturbing predatory situation is laid bare in which, as so often in Mansfield, margin and centre, victim and victimizer, the stranger without and the stranger within, are inextricably intertwined.

As in 'The Luft Bad', though more transgressively so, in 'Je ne parle pas français' an accommodation of the signs of the other, though it is an experience marked by sensations of scorn and revulsion, becomes for the colonial-and-modernist Mansfield an expression of inner difference, if not of perversity. Blackness in both stories is a figure of the strange, yet it is also the figure which most narrowly approaches that most familiar of strangenesses, the neither-nor (neither insider nor outsider) of otherness within.

Notes

1. See R. Begam and M. Valdez Moses (eds) (2007) *Modernism and Colonialism* (Durham, NC and London: Duke University Press), pp. 7 and 5.
2. H. Bhabha (1995) *The Location of Culture* (London: Routledge), especially pp. 109–10.
3. See P. Mitter (2007) *The Triumph of Modernism: India's Artists and the Avant-garde 1922–47* (London: Reaktion), pp. 9, 11. For a recasting of the canonical self–other relationship of empire as a relationship that can be seen as taking place 'between others' or between various different 'centres', see E. Boehmer (2002) *Empire, the National and the Postcolonial: Resistance in Interaction* (Oxford University Press). See also chapters 3–5 in E. Boehmer (2005) *Colonial and Postcolonial Literature: Migrant Metaphors* (Oxford University Press).
4. K. Mansfield (1981) 'The Luft Bad', in *The Collected Short Stories* (Harmondsworth: Penguin), pp. 729–32.
5. As for example does Jahan Ramazani in various essays, one concluding the Richard Begam and Michael Valdez Moses collection ('Modernist Bricolage, Postcolonial Hybridity', Begam and Moses, pp. 288–314), which investigate the modernist ramifications of bricolage, juxtaposition, polyglossia and astringency in the postcolonial work of Brathwaite, Ramanujan, Okigbo and others. Yet even Ramazani at times prefers to see the travelling of poetic influence as emanating largely from the traditional centres in the modernist period. See, for example, his (2007) 'Travelling Poetry', *Modern Language Quarterly*, 68: 2, 281–303.
6. L. Doyle and L. Finkiel (eds) (2005) *Geo-modernisms: Race, Modernism, Modernity* (Bloomington: Indiana University Press); see also H. Booth and N. Rigby (eds) (2000) *Modernism and Empire* (Manchester University Press, 2000).
7. See, for example, J. Berman (2001) *Modernist Fiction, Cosmopolitanism, and the Politics of Community* (Cambridge University Press); S. Gikandi (1996) *Maps of Englishness: Writing Identity in the Culture of Colonialism* (New York: Columbia University Press), especially his remarks on Eliot; K. Phillips (1994) *Virginia Woolf Against Empire* (Knoxville: University of Tennessee Press).
8. See D. Lambert and A. Lester (eds) (2006) *Colonial Lives Across the British Empire: Imperial Careering in the Long Nineteenth Century* (Cambridge University Press); E. Boehmer (2004) 'Global Nets, Textual Webs; or What isn't New about Empire?', *Postcolonial Studies*, 7: 1, 11–26.
9. D. Chakrabarty (2000) *Provincialising Europe: Postcolonial Thought and Historical Difference* (Princeton University Press). As Edward Said (1993) *Culture and Imperialism* (London: Cape), p. 276, also recognized, modernism *was* in a sense the release of energy produced by that intersection of different timeframes. If, as Johannes Fabian suggests, colonialism imposed on other cultures 'a stream of Time' – the time of European history, the time of the modern – in and through modernism those other cultures asserted their simultaneity. See J. Fabian (1983) *Time and the Other: How Anthropology Makes its Object* (New York: Columbia University Press).
10. J. Esty (2007) 'Virginia Woolf's Colony', in Begam and Moses, pp. 70–90.
11. R. R. Arrowsmith (2010) *Modernism and the Museum: Asian, African and Pacific Art and the London Avant-Garde* (Oxford University Press).

12. See A. Gasiorek (2007) 'War, "Primitivism", and the Future of the West: Reflections on D. H. Lawrence and Wyndham Lewis', in Begam and Moses, pp. 90–110.
13. See M. L. Emery (2007) *Modernism, the Visual and Caribbean Culture* (Cambridge University Press), p. 62. See also S. Gikandi (2003) 'Picasso, Africa and the Schemata of Difference', *Modernism/Modernity*, 10: 3, 455–80.
14. 'To Stanislaw Wyspianski', in V. O'Sullivan (ed.) (1988) *The Poems of Katherine Mansfield* (Oxford University Press), p. 30.
15. P. Gilroy (1993) *The Black Atlantic: Modernity and Double Consciousness* (London: Verso).
16. Bhabha, pp. 136–7; see also J. Kristeva (1991) *Strangers to Ourselves*, Leon Roudiez (trans.) (London: Harvester Wheatsheaf), p. 181.
17. A. Smith (1999) *Katherine Mansfield and Virginia Woolf: A Public of Two* (Oxford: Clarendon Press).
18. G. Spivak (1999) *A Critique of Postcolonial Reason: Towards a History of the Vanishing Present* (Cambridge, MA: Harvard University Press), pp. 169–97.
19. J. M. Murry (ed.) (1954) *The Journal of Katherine Mansfield* (London: Constable), pp. 11, 18. Hereafter referred to as *Journal*.
20. *Letters* 1, p. 45.
21. See B. M. Malabari (1895 [1891]) *The Indian Eye on English Life*, 3rd edn (Bombay: Apollo Printing Works).
22. *Journal*, p. 45.
23. *Letters* 1, p. 339.
24. *Journal*, pp. 37–8.
25. *Ibid.*, p. 51.
26. H. Bannerman (1899) *The Story of Little Black Sambo* (London: Grant Richards). Prior to Bannerman, and no doubt an influence upon her, the Victorian children's illustrator Florence Kate Upton invented the golliwog, inspired by a minstrel doll she had had as a child.
27. P. Dunbar (1997) *Radical Mansfield: Double Discourse in Katherine Mansfield's Short Stories* (Basingstoke: Macmillan), pp. 17–20.
28. 'Je ne parle pas français', in A. Smith (ed.) (2002) *Selected Stories* (Oxford World's Classics), pp. 142–67. Citations are from pp. 143 and 146–7.
29. For a reading of the story as a Freud-influenced investigation of a Dostoevsky-like 'underground' which however does not discuss the Africanness of the laundress, see Dunbar, pp. 73–83.

5
Leaping into the Eyes: Mansfield as a Cinematic Writer

Sarah Sandley

The earliest evidence of Mansfield as 'movie'-goer is in a short letter from John Middleton Murry written in March 1912, in which he asks her on their first formal date: 'Will you suggest the day for the visit to the pictures? They're all the same to me.'[1] The 'pictures' or 'movies' as they were also popularly referred to: the very word captures the main objection that many writers and intellectuals raised against early silent film. Movement without inner motive; the life of the body, not the life of the mind; the flat, mechanized exterior opposed to the rich psychological interior. Throughout most of the 1910s the established press largely ignored the new medium: they carried no reviews, and no listings. The *Daily News* was the first newspaper to run a regular film column, but this was not until 1919, and according to Laura Marcus in *The Tenth Muse*, 'The established monthlies and reviews such as *The English Review*, *The Fortnightly Review*, *The Quarterly Review* and *The Nineteenth Century* [...] covered the topic of the cinema no more than half a dozen or so times each between the late 1910s and the 1920s.'[2]

When not ignored by writers, the new medium was frequently derided by them. In 1918 Virginia Woolf wrote in a review of Compton Mackenzie's novel, *The Early Life and Adventures of Sylvia Scarlett*, 'the cyclist runs over a hen, knocks an old woman into the gutter, and has a hose turned upon him. But we never care whether he is wet or hurt or dead. So it is with Sylvia Scarlett and her troupe,' reserving her killer blow for the conclusion: 'it is not a book of adventures; it is a book of cinema'.[3] D. H. Lawrence deplored the new medium, thundering in his 1930 essay 'Pornography and Obscenity' of 'the close-up kisses on the film, which excite men and women to secret and separate masturbation',[4] a response which Mansfield seemed to have anticipated in a letter to Beatrice Campbell in 1916, in which she wrote of Lawrence: 'I shall <u>never</u> see sex in trees, sex in the running brooks, sex in stones & sex in everything.'[5]

And yet, for all this condemnation, which persisted from the birth of movies in 1895 until the 1930s, there was, from the beginning, a small group of writers who understood what Marcus has said, that 'The repeated verbal play on "moving" as pertaining to both motion and emotion is a crucial reminder that both these terms are connoted by the Greek word kinema',[6] and who embraced the new art form, both as entertainment, and as artistic inspiration. Amongst them can be counted H. G. Wells, James Joyce and Katherine Mansfield.

Murry, reputedly a diffident young man, would surely not have invited Mansfield out to the movies in 1912 unless he had been confident of her accepting it had been a safe bet, so we can assume not only that she was a film-goer before then, but also that she was vocal in her admiration for the medium. It is perhaps no surprise that Mansfield was fascinated by film. Her letters and notebooks attest to the fact that she had an acutely visual imagination, and was creatively energized by art and by nature:

When one has been working for a long stretch one begins to narrow ones vision a bit, to fine things down too much. And its only when something else breaks through, a picture, or something seen out of doors that one realizes it.[7]

The *Journal* also shows that she often had to ensure she was not distracted from writing by outdoor views: 'I have changed the position of my desk into a corner. Perhaps I shall be able to write far more easily here. Yes, this is a good place for a desk, because I cannot see out of the stupid window.'[8] Small wonder then that this most visual of modern art forms appealed to her.

It is unlikely that Mansfield was introduced to film in New Zealand before she left for good in 1908. Although Wellington had its first screening in 1896, either films were shown by itinerant exhibitors who set up in a hall for a few days, or they were on the bill of vaudeville shows. The rebellious young Kathleen Beauchamp – daughter of the Chairman of the Bank of New Zealand – may, like Matilda in 'The Wind Blows', have had the temerity to slam out of the house yelling to her mother 'Go to hell!',[9] but it is unlikely that she would have risked provoking her parents' censure by being seen in the audience of a vaudeville show. Nor is there any reference to film in either her journals or her letters of the time. It seems most likely that she first started watching films in London around 1911, when she settled at 69 Clovelly Mansions on Gray's Inn Road after a turbulent couple of years which on a personal level included her marriage to George Bowden and a miscarriage, and on a professional level saw her work first published in the *New Age*.

A picture-theatre boom ran in Britain from 1908 to 1914, by which time there were about 500 cinemas in London alone. Clovelly Mansions was surrounded by them: the Athenaeum Cinema at 198–212 Gray's Inn Road was practically next door and there were at least six on Tottenham Court Road. The 1500-seat capacity Holborn Empire was a short walk away at High Holborn, as was the Holborn Cinema on Chancery Lane. In turn this was just around the corner from Cursitor Street – home of the *New Age* and the meeting place of the *New Age* group, where Mansfield was a frequent visitor in the early 1910s.

Around 1911, then, was the start of Mansfield's enduring interest in films. For the rest of her life, unless bedridden, she went to the movies on a regular basis. From 1912, until a few months before her death, she peppered her letters and notebooks with references to movies she had seen, she played with cinema as a figurative device, invented fictional film scenes involving her intimate friends and wrote 'Pictures' (a short story about the experience of a movie extra). She named one of her cats 'Charlie Chaplin' after the actor whom she described admiringly as 'a marvellous artist',[10] and, according to Brownlee Kirkpatrick, in 1920 she wrote an unsigned leader for the *Athenaeum* about Mary Pickford and Douglas Fairbanks's arrival in London, which gives us some insight into the pleasure she derived from cinema-going:

> We are not those who think shame to be seen flitting into the plush darkness of a cinema; we confess to a taste for it. And so it were idle to pretend that these eminent people are unknown to us. Have we not seen Mr. Fairbanks leap over the railway train on to the roof through the skylight into the cellar, at a breath?[11]

None of which is to say that she was unaware that movie-going was considered a pastime for the 'lower orders' – this leader, whilst attributed to Mansfield, was unsigned, and she never mentioned movies in letters to her family.

Mansfield's movie-going and experimentation with film

So what did Mansfield see? She died in 1923, before the advent of 'talkies' in the late 1920s, and only ever saw silent movies. In the 1910s this typically consisted of a two-hour continuous programme of what Tom Gunning called 'the cinema of attractions': a mixture of short films, with one longer one, covering the most diverse range of genres – comedy, drama, travel, vaudeville (gymnastics, tricks, tableaux) – and a broad category of 'interest films' which ranged from flower and bird studies, to zoological, industrial and sociological films, as well as microcinematography and newsreels (including war footage from 1914).[12] Silent movies made quite high demands on the audience, who had to interpret both dialogue and visual clues so they could follow the narrative and infill emotional content. This was helped along by continuous musical accompaniment. Mansfield was a capable cellist who loved music, and who would habitually divide sections of manuscripts by doodling treble clefs. Her near contemporary Dorothy Richardson published a column on the co-creative aspect of 'Musical Accompaniment' at the movies in the journal *Close Up*:

> Our first musician was a pianist who sat in the gloom beyond the barrier and played without notes. His playing was a continuous improvisation varying in tone and tempo according to what was going forward on the screen. [...] For the Gazette he had martial airs ... [...] Jigs accompanied the comic interludes and devout low-toned nocturnes the newest creations of fashion. For drama he usually had a leitmotif, borrowed or invented, set within his pattern of sound moving suitably from pianissimo to fortissimo. [...] music is needed and generally liked even by those who are not aware that it helps them to create the film and gives the film both colour and sound.[13]

One of the most notable features of the time was the sheer volume of films shown – about 5000 a year – with the programme in most places changing twice a week. The longest single film was still only 15 minutes. Multi-reel features, with a new focus on narrative storytelling, emerged around 1912 and were becoming the norm by 1915 – the year in which Charlie Chaplin's *Tramp* made its first appearance, and D. W. Griffith's *The Birth of a Nation* and Louis Feuillade's crime serial *Fantômas* were released in England. But of these now-famous individuals and films, only *Tramp* and *The Birth of a Nation* hit the public consciousness. Consequently, Mansfield very rarely mentioned *specific* films that she had seen. Certainly, though, we can be confident that she saw every Chaplin movie then available (indeed the last movie she saw, six months before she died, was *The Kid*), and in Paris in 1915 she saw episode nine of Feuillade's *Fantômas*.

By the mid-1910s the majority of modern film-editing strategies, designed as tools to build narrative understanding and emotional response in the spectator, were in place. These included cross-cutting between parallel actions (which creates discontinuity and builds narrative tension), point of view shots, symbolism, atmospheric insert shots and lighting effects. Most significant of all, though, was the close-up and the related technique of reverse angle cutting (successive close-ups from different perspectives). Close-ups control the attention and emotional response of the spectator. Whilst modern eyes are almost inured to the power of the technique, there is ample evidence that it had a significant impact at the time of its introduction in the mid-1910s. Anne Friedberg writes:

> To many the close-up played a critical role in a wholly new visual rhetoric. [...] it limited and directed attention, indicated emotion, magnified aesthetic import. [...] the close-up produced revelations of a new emotional and dramatic magnitude in showing the 'micro-physiognomy' of the human face.[14]

As will be discussed in detail later in this essay, filmic techniques are evident in Mansfield's fiction from 1915 and play a crucial role in the innovation that positions her at the forefront of modernist developments in narrative.

The final episode of the *Fantômas* serial, which Mansfield saw in 1915, was the only movie that she commented on in any detail, writing to Murry from Paris:

> Instead of having dinner today I ate some bread & drank some wine at home & went to a cinema. It was almost too good. A detective drama, so well acted and so sharp and cruel with a horrible décor – the environs of Calais – Wickedness triumphed to everyone's great relief, for the hero, an apache called L'Fantôme was an admirable actor.[15]

Feuillade is not known as a technical innovator, but his plots are deftly constructed. The *Fantômas* serial moves across three countries, tracking the exploits of an elusive master criminal, Fantômas, and keeping the viewer in suspense until the dénouement. Even at that point the viewer cannot be certain about Fantômas's fate, as his capture is immediately followed by escape. This fluidity and uncertainty would no doubt have appealed to Mansfield – who rarely provided any form of orthodox start and finish to her narratives – as would the prominent role of disguise: the main character slips into and out of assumed identities with an ease that resonates with many of Mansfield's own characters, not least the character of Raoul Duquette in 'Je ne parle pas français': 'How can one look the part and not be the part? Or be the part and not look it? Isn't looking – being? Or being – looking?' (288).

Mansfield's experimentation with film was most intense between 1915 and 1917 when she acted as an extra and also tried her hand at script-writing. There is a certain amount of mystery that surrounds Mansfield's escapade as an extra in January 1917. In letters to Bertrand Russell she described herself as acting in an 'exterior scene in walking dress' and 'what the American producer calls "slap up evening dress"'.[16] It was an inauspicious time to try and 'get a break' in the movies. The war had had a severe impact on the film industry in Britain: two of the largest local companies closed in 1916, and American directors also retreated that year. According to checks of the trade journals *Bioscope* and *Kine Weekly*, as well as the fan magazine *Picturegoer* and the cinema-friendly *Evening News*, there were only four films made in January 1917. None of them had American producers – although the terms 'producer' and 'director' were almost interchangeable at that time – nor was D. W. Griffith in the UK. Mansfield's story 'Pictures', in which a down-at-heel but aspiring actress and contralto singer Ada Moss moves between casting agencies and film companies, enduring successive humiliations and rejections that result in her turning to prostitution, is undoubtedly an accurate depiction of the fate that befell some would-be actresses at that time. For Mansfield to have secured any work at all we have to assume that she had a contact who helped her. It is probable that she made this contact when she was writing for the *New Age* which was just around the corner from the Holborn Restaurant, the informal headquarters of the activist part of the British film industry which had started to fight the government over matters that affected the business, such as censorship. Of the four films made at that time, by far the most likely candidate is *Masks and Faces*,[17] based on an 1852 play of that name, and described at the time as 'the biggest film, so far as stage stars are concerned, that has ever been screened',[18] in which George Bernard Shaw made a cameo appearance. The editor of *Kine Weekly* visited the Elstree studio where it was made on 17 January 1917 – the day after Mansfield may have been there – and wrote of the experience: 'I seemed to have been switched back a century or so. All around me wandered ladies in brocades, gowns and powdered wigs, knee-breeches and buckled shoes.' He also wrote that 'Nearly everyone in the audience was a celebrity.'[19] If it seems odd that Mansfield did not write more about this experience in her letters, it can perhaps be explained by the fact she was living in 'The Ark' in Gower Street at that time with Murry and Dorothy Brett, the very people to whom she most often expressed her interest in film.

The scriptwriting she engaged with is alluded to in January 1915 when she wrote in her journal, 'Got on slowly with "Cinema", but badly.'[20] No remnant of 'Cinema' remains, so what can it mean? What she was working on then appears to anticipate the five so-called experiments in dialogue in 1917 (remembering that silent movies did have dialogue), which read like film scripts. And, as Vincent O'Sullivan writes, 'The parentheses in "A Pic-nic" are actually instructions for the camera, the visual images we are to have in mind as the dialogue proceeds':[21]

A PIC-NIC
(The Evening Before)
(Miranda Richmond, laden with parcels, is fighting her way out of the tram.)

MIRANDA: Oh, dear, it's simply impossible. People won't move. They seem to be hypnotized. Let me pass, please. Excuse me. I want to get out. Now, I dropped one; I knew I should.

(A young man picks it up. It is Andrew Gold, the artist.)
MIRANDA *(to herself)*: What a surprise! I never noticed him. *(Smiles sweetly.)* Thank you so much.
GOLD: I'm getting out, too. Don't worry. I'll give it to you when we're safe ashore.

(In the streets. The lamps are just lighted. A fine evening) (215)

Although this piece contains both dramatic elements and dialogue, it does not present as a playscript – the opening frame of a woman descending from a tram, laden with parcels, is pure early film, the cross-cut and close-up of the man picking up the parcel, the cut back to the smile, the rapid change of scene from the tram to the street and the change of light are all the stock-in-trade of movies.

Mansfield's deployment of filmic techniques in her narrative

Whether written in first or third person, Mansfield's early fiction from 1915 to mid-1917 demonstrates experimentation with film techniques. Stories like 'Something Childish But Very Natural', 'Spring Pictures', 'An Indiscreet Journey' and 'The Little Governess' are structured as episodic, filmic vignettes – the action moves forward in an often discontinuous manner, switching from one scene, time and place to another, with the added sensation of speed and movement, often by train, and the drama of darkness and light:

The train seemed glad to have left the station. With a long leap it sprang in to the dark. She rubbed a place in the window with her glove but she could see nothing – just a tree outspread like a black fan or a scatter of lights, or the line of a hill, solemn and huge. ('The Little Governess' 169)

The train had flung behind the roofs and chimneys. They were swinging into the country, past little black woods and fading fields and pools of water shining under an apricot sky. ('Something Childish But Very Natural' 153)

These stories contain teeming descriptions of the environment and deploy close-ups, cross-cuts, pan shots, long shots and a moving viewpoint, with the narrator as camera, capturing external detail in complex and rapid descriptions, which routinely alternate the focus:

A green room with a stove jutting out and tables on each side. On the counter, beautiful with coloured bottles, a woman leans, her breasts in her folded arms. Through an open door I can see a kitchen, and the cook in a white coat breaking eggs into a bowl and tossing the shells into a corner. The blue and red coats of the men who are eating hang upon the walls. Their short swords and belts are piled upon chairs. ('An Indiscreet Journey' 181)

The walls were covered with a creamy paper patterned all over with green and swollen trees – hundreds and hundreds of trees reared their mushroom heads to the ceiling. [...] On either side of the clock there hung a picture: one, a young gentleman in black tights wooing a pear-shaped lady in yellow over the back of a garden seat, *Premier Rencontre*; two, the black and yellow in amorous confusion. *Triomphe d'Amour*. ('An Indiscreet Journey' 186)

The writing typically contains filmic gestures like doors closing and the wringing of hands:

Across the river, on the narrow stone path that fringes the bank a woman is walking. [...] Now she has stopped. Now she has turned suddenly. She is leaning up against a tree, her hands over her face; she is crying. And now she is walking up and down wringing her hands ... ('Spring Pictures' 178–9)

There is no omniscient narrator, but gestures, costume and close-ups on symbolically significant details are consistently used as authorial devices, providing clues to the characters' nature or motivation, which is often shown to be at odds with the persona they present to themselves and to the world. This existential theme is also emphasized when characters like Ada Moss in 'Pictures' and the governess in 'The Little Governess' look at their reflections in the mirror and describe, camera-like, the external signs of their emotion:

> she caught sight of herself in the mirror, quite white, with big round eyes. She untied her 'motor veil' and unbuttoned her green cape. 'But it's all over now,' she said to the mirror face, feeling in some way that it was more frightened than she. (168)

But perhaps the most obvious example of cinematic aesthetics at play in Mansfield's early writing is at the end of 'The Wind Blows'. The central character spots a ship in the harbour, flashes forward to an imagined future when, with her brother, she stands on the deck of a ship putting out to sea, looks back at the town as it recedes and describes what she sees first in a long shot and then by picking out specific landmarks in close-up: 'Look, Bogey, there's the town. Doesn't it look small? There's the post office clock chiming for the last time. There's the esplanade where we walked that windy day. [...] Good-bye, little island, good-bye. . . . ' (194).

It was during this period from 1915 to 1917 that Mansfield's conception of fiction was radically revised as she grieved for her brother Leslie Beauchamp (killed in 1915 in Flanders), and as her own health failed (culminating in the confirmation of a tubercular spot on her lung in December 1917). Her response was to narrow her creative and artistic focus to her first calling of fiction, and it was in this fiction that she tried to find the form and technique to do justice to her people and her country in 'a kind of long elegy [...] in a kind of <u>special prose</u>', which would 'make our undiscovered country leap into the eyes of the Old World'.[22] These quotes from her journal entry of 1916 neatly describe the two most important innovations that she had mastered by 1917 and which she fused for the first time in her 'long elegy', 'Prelude': first, the 'special prose' of free indirect discourse, which plunges the reader into the inner mind of the character, and second, the filmic devices which move the reader discontinuously backwards and forwards, from one place or perspective to another, from the present to the past and the future, juxtaposed with minutely detailed descriptions of places and objects, with costume and gesture deployed as an authorial device. 'Prelude' is formed by the similarity or tension that exists between external and inner lives: the disordered, unpacked household and its inhabitants' similarly discordant dreams; the daughter and the grandmother, bathed in light from a dazzling full moon, contemplating the aloe together; Linda in turmoil, realizing in an epiphanic moment that she hated her husband as much as she loved him, contrasting bathetically with the old woman musing whether the currant bushes would yield enough fruit for jam.

Throughout Mansfield's work from this time there are examples of what she called the 'interrupted moment [...] like a cinema',[23] when an image is extracted from the flow, and flares into vision with an emotional intensity or sudden symbolic clarity of epiphanic importance within the narrative: for example, the aloe quite obviously, but also the pear tree in 'Bliss', the bunch of slightly soiled violets in 'Psychology', the tree in 'The Escape', the fur toque in 'Miss Brill', the eponymous fly, and the sun in the final section of 'The Daughters of the Late Colonel', to cite just a few examples.

This fusing of free indirect thought and cinematic techniques, first evident in 'Prelude', is central to the narrative power of her mature work; 'Bliss' has a dénouement that is pure film, Bertha's romantic illusions shattered as she witnesses her husband Harry passionately turning his lover towards him. 'Je ne parle pas français' is structured as a series of flashbacks, with a narrator – the writer Raoul Duquette – who is knowing enough to frame his story in metafictional and meta-filmic terms, consciously referring to the influence of 'the American cinema acting upon a weak mind' (278), but who is unwilling to confront and overcome his failings. 'Miss Brill' is structured as a harsh exposé of the sometimes brutal difference between an individual's inner life and the extrinsic life and how it is judged, with a cinematic final scene as Miss Brill herself scurries home, and in a symbolic gesture closes the lid on her fur toque. 'The Daughters of the Late Colonel' operates as a series of flashbacks, interspersed with the sisters' dreams and fears, with light playing a crucial role in the final section of the story. 'At the Bay' is framed by the movement of the sun over a single day, with sections that cross-cut between parallel stories and cross-cut between the characters' inner dreams and fears, and that short masterpiece 'The Fly' has as its climax the moment when – in almost microcinematographic detail – the boss deposits a fatal drop of ink on a struggling fly:

> The last blot fell on the soaked blotting-paper, and the draggled fly lay in it and did not stir. The back legs were stuck to the body; the front legs were not to be seen.
> 'Come on,' said the boss. 'Look sharp!' And he stirred it with his pen – in vain. Nothing happened or was likely to happen. The fly was dead. (533)

Mansfield's affection and respect for popular movies was unwavering. In the July 1920 leader for the *Athenaeum* she gives some insight into the psychological motivation for her and others' movie-going – describing it as an escapist narcotic – as well as making a prescient account of the modern allure of celebrity:

> People cannot keep their eyes on the agonies of Europe; it is too much to ask. Who shall blame them for seeking sensational distractions from the strain of living. But that this particular distraction should monopolise the hoardings; that there should be presumed an intimacy of affection for two cinematographic actors seldom felt for any man or woman within living memory – that gives us pause.
>
> Had it been Charlie Chaplin it would have been easier to understand, for within his province he is one of the first actors of the world; he has a universal significance. [...] But what do Douglas and Mary stand for? The one for adventure, the other for Sentiment? Together for Romance? To the people who exult and weep over them they must be symbols of something beyond themselves, something beyond the reality of themselves. [...] Would it not be nearer the truth to say that Mary and Douglas are worshipped because we have no Gods at all?[24]

In her 1926 book *Let's Go to the Pictures*[25] Iris Barry championed the idea of 'new women' like herself – not slaves to literary tradition, their modernity linked to their visual imagination and intelligence – writing for the cinema. Once she knew she was seriously ill, Mansfield put aside any ideas of earning a living from the movies – as either an actor or a writer – in order to focus on fiction, a genre in which she had a track record. Through her own writing she had developed literary contacts which meant that her work could be published, and she could make some money. But her love of film, the inspiration that she drew from it and the cinematic consciousness that is at play in her writing, mean that one can only agree with Vincent O'Sullivan who wrote in his 1985 preface to 'The Aloe' that 'A fair claim can be made that [Mansfield] was among the earliest writers to understand how the methods of film might be applied to prose.'[26]

Notes

1. C. A. Hankin (ed.) (1988) *Letters Between Katherine Mansfield and John Middleton Murry* (London: Virago Press), p. 11.
2. L. Marcus (2007) *The Tenth Muse: Writing About Cinema in the Modernist Period* (Oxford University Press), p. 243.

3. Marcus, p. 103. Quoted from W. K. L. Dickson and A. Dickson (1895) *History of the Kinetograph, Kinetoscope and Kineto-Phonograph*, facsimile edn (New York: The Museum of Modern Art, 2000).
4. D. H. Lawrence (1936) 'Pornography and Obscenity', in E. D. McDonald (ed.) (1936) *Phoenix: The Posthumous Papers of D. H. Lawrence* (London: Heinemann), p. 87.
5. *Letters* 1, p. 261.
6. Marcus, p. 5.
7. *Letters* 4, p. 333.
8. J. Middleton Murry (ed.) (1954) *Journal of Katherine Mansfield*, Definitive Edition (London: Constable), p. 63. (Hereafter referred to as *Journal*.) See also p. 95: 'I have put a table to-day in my room, facing a corner, but from where I sit I can see some top shoots of the almond-tree and the sea sounds loud.'
9. A. Alpers (ed.) (1984) *The Stories of Katherine Mansfield* (Oxford University Press), p. 192. All further references to Mansfield's stories are taken from this edition, and page numbers placed after any quotation.
10. *Letters* 5, p. 250.
11. B. J. Kirkpatrick (1989) *A Bibliography of Katherine Mansfield* (Oxford: Clarendon Press), p. 129.
12. T. Gunning (1989) 'The Cinema of Attractions: Early Film, its Spectator and the Avant-Garde', in T. Elsaesser (ed.) *The Cinema of Attractions: Early Film, Space, Frame, Narrative* (London: British Film Institute).
13. Reproduced in J. Donald, A. Friedberg and L. Marcus (eds) (1998) *Close Up 1927–1933: Cinema and Modernism* (Princeton University Press), p. 162.
14. *Ibid.*, p. 1.
15. *Letters* 1, p. 182.
16. *Ibid.*, pp. 293 and 294.
17. The other three are Brunel's *The Cost of a Kiss*, produced by Mirror and in production in January 1917; Frank G. Bayly's *One Summer's Day*, produced by the British Actor's Film Company with production completed by 18 January 1917, and Dave Aylott's *The Man Who Made Good*, produced by Zeitlin & Dewhurst and in production in January 1917.
18. Anon., *Picturegoer*, 3 February 1917, p. 409.
19. *Kine Weekly*, 25 January 1917, p. 2. The editor wrote of his visit the previous Wednesday, i.e. 17 January.
20. *Journal*, p. 69.
21. V. O'Sullivan (ed.) (1997) *Katherine Mansfield's New Zealand Stories* (Oxford University Press), p. 5.
22. *Journal*, p. 94.
23. *Letters* 1, p. 302.
24. 'The Stars in Their Courses', *Athenaeum*, 2 July 1920 (supplied by The British Library).
25. I. Barry (1926) *Let's Go to the Pictures* (London: Chatto & Windus).
26. V. O'Sullivan (ed.) (1983) *The Aloe with Prelude* (Wellington: Port Nicholson Press), p. xxii.

6

Katherine Mansfield and Music: Nineteenth-Century Echoes

Delia da Sousa Correa

In 1908, Katherine Mansfield brought with her to London a style that was, as Sydney Janet Kaplan so aptly puts it, 'already modern'.[1] At the same time, we know that nineteenth-century literature provided a wellspring of material which became transfigured in her modernist idiom. In this essay I propose that Mansfield's allusions to music are particularly informed by her nineteenth-century reading and listening, and that this played a crucial role in her development as a modernist writer.

Mansfield's stories invite musical analogy, and she wrote with music very consciously in mind. For her 1920 story 'Miss Brill', she recorded that 'I chose not only the length of every sentence, but even the sound of every sentence [...] I read it aloud [...] just as one would *play over* a musical composition.'[2] Mansfield rarely commented so directly on her writing and this statement provides an invaluable insight into her artistic methods. It also reflects the formal concerns of British aestheticism and French symbolist poetry, influences manifest throughout her writing and recorded in her early notebooks. Here, an entry on Pater falls alongside a transcription of Baudelaire's famous invocation of 'a poetic prose, musical without rhythm and without rhyme'.[3]

In a perceptive contemporary review of Mansfield's 1920 collection *Bliss and Other Stories*, Malcolm Cowley observed that her stories were sometimes structured around themes as well as around situations, commenting that her writing 'approaches here to the construction of music'.[4] Although he analysed 'Je ne parle pas français' as comprising an introduction, two reiterated themes and a final coda, he defined the musicality of Mansfield's prose as residing, not in 'an imitation of a sonata', but in the achievement, within a form that remains 'purely literary' of 'the suppleness and some of the abstractness of music'.[5]

In this essay, I begin with familiar examples of Mansfield's musical prose and then consider what might be the connections between this writing and some rather different invocations of music in her earlier novel-draft, 'Juliet'. Mansfield's musical modernism in its most developed form can be seen in her late New Zealand story 'At the Bay' (1921). This makes little direct reference to music, but is highly musical in its structure and language. Passages invoking the movement of sea and waves at dawn, noon and night punctuate the story's opening, middle and close, suggesting analogies with musical movements as well as with the textures and rhythms of music. In a calm opening *aubade*, land, sea, the sound and movements of a flock of sheep are woven together into a sinuous overture. A children's game of animal snap becomes a comic-macabre *scherzo*, a virtuoso performance where snippets of dialogue and description echo the slapping of cards on the table in a frenetic *crescendo*. This terminates in horrified silence when a face appears at the darkened window. Finally, in a lyrical coda, the 'deep, troubled' sound of the darkened sea fades into a 'vague murmur' before a final cadence, 'All was still.'[6] This is writing towards which Virginia Woolf seems quite specifically to gesture in her own musical stream-of-consciousness novels, especially *The Waves*.

The musicality of Mansfield's prose emerges in its lyricism and wealth of auditory allusion, and also in the highly comic sense of timing that structures her characteristic blend of dialogue and free indirect discourse. One of the early sections of 'At the Bay' portrays a rare sense of communion between the women of the Stanley Burnell household following his departure for the day:

> 'Gone?'
> 'Gone!'

Time expands for the women left behind:

> Their very voices were changed as they called to one another; they sounded warm and loving and as if they shared a secret. [....] the whole perfect day was theirs. (287)

The text takes up the rhythm of their exchange, 'Have another cup of tea, mother' one of them calls, as the grandmother tosses the baby upwards and the children run 'into the paddock like chickens let out of a coop' (287). The sequence peaks as Alice, the servant-girl, plunges the teapot under the water and holds it there 'even after it had stopped bubbling, as if it too was a man and drowning was too good for them' (288).

The epiphanic moment passes to leave us, as always in Mansfield, with a sharper sense of underlying realities, but a rhythmical disposition of language is fundamental to the way in which the inner and outer lives of characters in the story are caught up in a stream of consciousness, prefiguring techniques developed later at greater narrative length by Woolf.

Mansfield's musicalized prose needs to be seen in such contexts of wider modernist enterprise. Her 1918 story, 'Prelude', first published by the Woolfs' Hogarth Press, forms a musical companion name to *Rhythm*, the avant-garde journal for which several of her previous pieces of fiction had been written. But whilst an alignment of language with the non-discursive forms of music was obviously widespread amongst modernist writers, musical parallels had a greater specificity for Mansfield than for many of her contemporaries.[7] Mansfield's assured use of musical terminology is one of the many ways in which this is manifest: her aim for her writing was always to find 'the middle of the note'.[8]

Mansfield, after all, was a serious cellist who contemplated a musical career throughout her time at Queen's College from 1903 to 1906. A crucial set of friendships was that formed, while in New Zealand, with the musical Trowell family. The father taught her the cello; his twin sons were accomplished musicians who set off for careers in Europe in 1903. Mansfield herself arrived in London later that same year to enrol at Queen's. Of the two brothers, Mansfield was initially drawn to Arnold, also a cellist, although she subsequently fell in love with his violinist brother, Garnet. In Wellington, Mansfield had clearly regarded her cello as something of an escape from her irredeemably bourgeois family (notwithstanding that it was the bourgeois activity of her self-made bank-manager father that paid for her cello lessons and London education). In London, the avid joint consumption of music and literature was extremely important for her subsequent development as a writer.[9] Her friend Ida Baker photographed her practising her cello and later recalled her 'playing her heart out';[10] an incomplete poem of 1903 hailed her cello in lover-like terms: her 'beloved' her 'all in all'.[11]

Kaplan describes an early engrossment with musical practice as fundamental to the 'passion for technique' that Mansfield later identified in herself as a writer.[12] 'Out of technique is born real style, I believe,' she was to write, 'There are no short cuts.'[13] For Mansfield, music provided a practical correlative to a preoccupation with the sonic properties of language encountered in the symbolist poetry of Baudelaire and Mallarmé and with technique absorbed from English writing of the 1890s.[14] Moreover there are also affinities here with earlier decades of Victorian literature.

Mansfield's praise of 'the desire for technical knowledge' echoes George Eliot's comparison of musical and literary practice. In 1856, Eliot lamented that literature lacked the same 'positive difficulties of execution' that determined a realistic assessment of musical ability, for 'Every art which has its absolute *technique* is, to a certain extent, guarded from the intrusions of mere left-handed imbecility' (Eliot's italics).[15] That Mansfield's comments should prompt a comparison with George Eliot is but one indication of the close links that her writing, as well as that of other female modernists, maintains with Victorian literature.[16]

Given her date of birth, it follows that Mansfield also hatched her modernist sense of musical analogy in relation to a predominantly nineteenth-century musical repertoire. Indeed, this complements a sense of how strongly literary modernism has its roots in the nineteenth century. Mansfield lived in a London hostel for music students in 1908, a time by which, as Daniel Albright puts it, music had shed 'its belatedness' to become 'the vanguard medium of the Modernist aesthetic'.[17] Her letters of the time include comments on music from the period that Albright would define as modern – that is from 1890 onwards. Women in her hostel practising drums and trombone form 'a Strauss Tone Poem of Domestic Snoring'.[18] Sounds in a garden are invoked via an extended sonic metaphor: 'the sound of the falling leaves at our feet was like the sea breaking upon sand and shell', followed by a synaesthetic starlight, that for Mansfield, is 'almost like a Debussy theme'.[19] She frequently refers to the American composer Edward Alexander MacDowell (a pupil of the Venezuelan pianist and composer Teresa Carreno, whom Mansfield heard and met both in Wellington and in London), suggesting that Tom Trowell should set some lyrics that she has written 'with strange Macdowell, Debussy chords'.[20] In a vignette of the same period, a musician whistles 'the opening bars of Max Bruch's D Minor Concerto'.[21]

Although it is possible to ascertain some of the programmes of concerts that Mansfield attended in Wellington and subsequently in London, one of the tantalizing things about research for this essay is that the historical evidence of Mansfield's listening is patchy.[22] From the evidence of Mansfield's reading about music, it is clear that she was conscious of qualities that might define particular music as 'modern', a consciousness that I would trace, in major part, to her extensive reading of Arthur Symons through whom she encountered the aestheticist and symbolist models for her earliest writing. I have also been able to trace many of her comments about music to his early twentieth-century books on music and drama, which she clearly read with close attention. A 1908 notebook entry includes quotation and paraphrase of Symons's views on Wagner, Chopin, Strauss and Mozart. Strauss's music, Mansfield notes, is characterized by 'passion' and '[loneliness]' in contrast to the music of Mozart which is without desire and 'content with beauty'.[23] A letter of the same year echoes Symons's view (which itself may reflect the influence of Wagner and Baudelaire) that Beethoven manifested a

> sublime simplicity [...] not in accord with the spirit of our times. He loved the universe and God and love and virtue with a great, abiding natural love – never realised the subtle joy in pain – which is the supreme ecstacy of modern music.[24]

This phrase, so impeccably nineteenth-century in its pedigree, is one example of how Mansfield's letters of 1908 foreshadow issues that were to be crucial to her later fiction and criticism.

This comment on Beethoven appears in a letter to her lover Garnet Trowell, the violinist son of her former cello teacher in New Zealand. Not surprisingly, music figures significantly in letters to Trowell. These include reflections on the artistic calling, on composing song lyrics (which Mansfield did), on dance as abandon and numerous other topics.[25] Her musical letters, such as the invocation of Debussy quoted above, contain passages of impressionistic writing and internal monologue that prefigure the modernism of her fiction. Kaplan proposes that we can find every feature of Mansfield's modernist innovation 'remarkably prefigured' in her letters to Trowell.[26] At the same time, they show her connectedness to the literature of the past. One of these letters is an exercise in exorbitant late-romantic aesthetics. Writing in German, Mansfield describes a composition of Trowell's as 'so wunderbar schön – so träumerisch – und auch so sehnsuchtsvoll'.[27] Even in the clean modernist prose of her mature writing, where thematic allusions to music have generally been transposed into formal analogy, this transcendent romanticism retains a half-ironic presence, the legacy of a 'refashioning' in these letters 'of late romantic notions of art and the artist into a modernist idiom [...] through parody and self-reflexiveness'.[28]

Mansfield develops many of the stylistic features identified by Kaplan, 'ranging from extended metaphors to impressionistic descriptions to internal monologues verging on stream of consciousness' within her discussions of music in these letters to Trowell.[29] Together with her experimental prose-poems of this period, Mansfield's letters of 1908 can be seen as of decisive importance to her evolution of a modernist idiom.[30] The rhythmical prose and sense of dramatic timing characteristic of Mansfield's stories also exemplify, in the 'silent' medium of fiction, the continued interest in performance that she expresses when declaring to Trowell her plan to develop a new style of recitation: an interest fundamental to the innovative prose style that she developed for her fiction, where '[t]one should be my secret – each word a variety of tone'.[31]

The development of a distinctively musical prose is also acutely apparent in Mansfield's poems and prose-poem vignettes of 1907–8, many of which employ stream-of-consciousness techniques and are heavy with auditory allusion. They demonstrate an intensely inward Paterian vision, although without emulation of Pater's elaborate prose style, at work alongside the influence of the 'plotless' stories of *The Yellow Book* with their 'cult of London and its varied life from costers to courtesans'.[32] An example of this kind of writing is George Egerton's 'A Lost Masterpiece: A City Mood' for *The Yellow Book* of 1894, which features street musicians in an hallucinatory tour through the city.[33] In her own 'Trio' written in 1908, Mansfield similarly describes a group of three threadbare, staring individuals, two of whom sing a tuneless pastoral madrigal, savagely at odds with their condition and the quality of their musicianship.[34]

The 'cult of London' echoes in Mansfield's conjuring of the 'voice of London', heard in a thundering organ fugue in Westminster Cathedral,[35] and which becomes 'The drunken bestial, hiccoughing voice of London', as a barrel organ wheezes out a jarring burst of sound.[36] When November leaves fall in desolate silence 'the muttering murmur of London' percolates through the monstrous 'shuffling tread' of railway trains.[37] And a sensuous, personified London offers the 'intoxicating madness of night music [...] the sound of laughter, half sad, half joyous, yet fearful, dying away in a strange shudder of satisfaction', and 'the penetrating rhythm of the hansom cabs' as crowds flow out from the theatre.[38] Mansfield's vignettes have a concentrated lyricism, and feverish aestheticism animated by sound, to a degree not achieved by Pater's more static verbal portraits, in spite of his avowed aspiration to a condition of musicality in his prose.

'Juliet'

Although her letters and poetry foreshadow ways in which music was to be written into the form, fabric and movement of her stories, Mansfield's earliest attempts at fiction also included musical subject matter. Her unfinished novel, 'Juliet', written in 1906, features a cast of musical characters and numerous musical scenes.[39] The influence of Wilde's aestheticism and Mansfield's reading of 1890s fiction and criticism is apparent in the story's unorthodox artistic heroine and its depiction of a bohemian life in art. However, this also is a work which draws upon the musical tropes of mid-Victorian fiction, confirming that nineteenth-century novelists were as significant influences on Mansfield's work as the 'plotless' stories of *The Yellow Book*.[40] With its echoes of these earlier writers, the fragmented draft of 'Juliet' provides an interesting example of Mansfield making use of features encountered in more expansive literary forms as she worked her way towards the highly condensed medium of the short story.

Written while Mansfield was still at school, 'Juliet' draws on her own life for its characters and circumstances. Juliet is a heroine of trembling sensibility and extravagant temperament, albeit somewhat constrained by her bourgeois origins. The initial setting is in New Zealand, where Juliet meets David, a young cellist who is about to depart for a musical career in England. Juliet's powerful sensibility is established by her response to David's playing. Aestheticist and symbolist influences are very clearly at work in the languorous images of music and flowers that evoke the sensual delights of the night on which she first encounters David, when 'a faint, a very faint wave of Music was wafted to her'.[41] Similar imagery linking music and flowers is to be found in a quotation from Symons recorded in her notebook for 1908: 'He drew the melody from the violin as one draws the perfume from a flower, with a kind of slumberous ecstasy.'[42]

Although her musical responsiveness is conveyed in extravagantly aestheticized terms, Juliet also belongs to a lineage of musically vibrating heroines that reaches back to Maggie Tulliver in George Eliot's *The Mill on the Floss* and beyond. There is more than a faint echo of Maggie's conversations about music with Philip Wakem in Juliet's first encounter with David. In Eliot's novel, Wakem comments that 'Certain strains of music affect me so strangely – I can never hear them without their changing my whole attitude of mind for a time, and if the effect would last I might be capable of heroisms.'[43] Maggie agrees, '"At least", she added, in a saddened tone, "I used to feel so when I had any music."'[44] In 'Juliet', the following exchange arises after David praises the charms of night when the stars 'make me all music': '"Sometimes I think that if I could be alone long enough I should hear the Music of the Spheres". "I have heard so little music", said Juliet sadly. "There are so few opportunities. And a 'cello – I have never heard a 'cello."'[45] The very rhythms of George Eliot's prose are palpable here.

At the party where Juliet is to hear David play, a series of 'nondescript' performances offer shorthand references to satirical accounts of social music-making in nineteenth-century novels from Austen onwards. In this, as in other respects, these novels are a fertile source for the vein of satire that runs throughout Mansfield's fiction. As in many nineteenth-century novels also, the protagonist's musical sensitivity is contrasted with the less acute sensibilities of other characters. Until David plays, the evening party at Juliet's parents' house consists of 'the usual amount of very second rate singing concerning Swallows and "Had I known"' and 'several nondescript pieces on the piano'.[46]

Then David plays, and Juliet becomes an embodiment of musical response:

> Juliet watched him with great pleasure & curiosity. A bright spot came into her cheeks, her eyes wide opened – but when he drew his bow across the strings her whole soul woke and lived for the first time in her life. She became utterly absorbed in the music. The room faded, the people faded. She saw only his sensitive inspired face, felt only the rapture that held her fast, that clung to her and hid her in its folds, as impenetrable and pure as the mists from the sea – – –
>
> Suddenly the music ceased, the tears poured down her face & she came back to reality.[47]

Like her predecessor, Juliet is possessed; she becomes a musical instrument played upon by the bow that David draws across his strings, just as Maggie Tulliver becomes a vibrating Aeolian harp under the influence of Stephen Guest's singing. As in *The Mill on the Floss* also, music and sex are analogous. Given that Mansfield's early journals are full of Wildean celebrations of sensual experience, it is hardly surprising that she should use music to form a conspicuously sexualized language, nor that, as the story develops, music should also become associated, as it is in Wilde, Swinburne and Wagner, with destructive passion.[48] However, Mansfield's aestheticist association of music with fatal passionate abandon merges with a satirical stance that indicates the degree to which she is taking on board both her mid- and late Victorian feminist predecessors.

Juliet, like her author, follows her musical friend to London, where she aspires to become a writer. The MS includes an implicitly violent seduction scene, in which Rudolf, a fellow student of David, plays Wagner and Chopin at the piano, inflaming his passion for Juliet. Mansfield particularly calls upon the power of Wagner's music and the obvious thematic associations of many of his best-known leitmotivs: 'Rudolf tossed back his hair & opened the piano. He began playing the overture to Tannhäuser, heavily and magnificently.'[49] He goes on to play the 'Pilgrim's Song' and 'the Venus Motif' to communicate to Juliet that she is too conventional: 'He repeated the wonderful Venus call. "Ah, it is divine" he said. "That is what you should be, Juliet."'[50] Chopin also features here, and Mansfield would have been encouraged by Symons to regard him as a composer of peculiarly direct affective power.[51] '"Listen again" said Rudolf. It was a Chopin nocturne this time. "Live this life, Juliet. Did Chopin fear to satisfy the cravings of his nature, his natural desires."'[52]

Rudolf, who accuses Juliet of being blind and deaf to what is worth living for, has something of the magnetic gothic villain about him; his voice and eyes are 'abominable' reflects Juliet:

> The music was flooding Juliet's soul now. The room faded. She heard her hot heavy impassioned voice above the storm of emotion – – –
> 'Stop, stop' she said, feeling as though some spell was being cast over her. She shook from head to foot with anger & horror.[53]

Mesmerized by Rudolf's playing, Juliet succumbs to him. After she has fled the scene, David returns to find Rudolf composing at the piano in his pyjamas – intoxicated by his Wagnerian 'masterpiece'.[54] David comments that he has come from hearing Wagner at a concert to find 'Wagner incarnate' in the room.[55]

In fact, Mansfield admired Wagner, declaring in 1907 that on her longed-for return to London, she would 'live in a tent in Trafalgar Square – and only leave it for Bayreuth'.[56] It is also to Wagner's music that she turns to find an analogy for the experience of travelling through a stark area of recently cleared and fought-over New Zealand landscape. Against a lurid sunset and amidst the burnt remains of native bush, the travellers described in her notebook for this journey 'climb on to a great black rock & sit huddled up there alone – fiercely almost brutally thinking – like Wagner', above a river that is 'Savage, grey, fierce, rushing, tumbling, thrashing [?], sucking the life from the still placid flows of water behind – like waves of the sea, like fierce wolves'.[57] For Mansfield, Wagner embodied some of the raw, brutal energy that was to feature in stories about New Zealand written for the avant-garde journal *Rhythm*. 'The Woman at the Store', first published in *Rhythm* in 1912, went on to feature the same violated landscape associated here with Wagner, who clearly represents for Mansfield the revision of earlier romantic ideas about nature fundamental to her own apprehension of the New Zealand landscape. In 'The Woman at the Store', lark-song, an apparently innocent presence in her notebook entry, sounds, in a shrill parody of Shelley's romantic inspiration, like slate pencils scraping the surface of a slate-coloured sky: 'Hundreds of Larks shrilled – the sky was slate colour, and the sound of the larks reminded me of slate pencils scraping over its surface' (10).

So it is Wagner, rather than composers of the 1890s, who most seems to represent modernism in music for Mansfield. Despite the fact that Wagner died five years before Mansfield's birth, which might make him appear a curious representative of the modern, this still makes perfect sense within the context of Mansfield's literary mentor-influences. For Baudelaire, Wagner's combination of sensuality and mysticism, the 'passionate energy' of his music, had made him, in 1861, 'the truest representative [we now have of the nature ...] – of the modern'.[58] Jean-Jacques Nattiez finds a rich correspondence in the way in which Baudelaire, the 'inventor of the concept of "modernity"', makes Wagner 'the prototype of the modern artist',[59] and Albright upholds a view of Wagner, with his status as a politically rebellious public intellectual, ready to comment on all manner of subjects, as 'the clearest nineteenth-century prefiguration of the Modernist composer-intellectual'.[60] In Nattiez's view, Baudelaire's assessment of Wagner's modernism in 'The Painter of Modern Life' was based on Wagner's status as an innovative artist able to extract 'beauty and grandeur' from what is 'transitory and banal': 'Modernity is the ugliness of the present and the mediocrity of the human condition being transcended at the highest level by aesthetic representation.'[61] Mansfield herself was to make similar statements of the role of the artist: 'we single out, we bring into the light, we put up higher'.[62]

Mansfield would have gained a specific view of Wagner's proto-modernism from her reading of Symons. The selection of his comments on music that she noted 'for future reference' includes his celebration, clearly derived from Baudelaire, of Wagner's 'universality', and the vigour for which Symons celebrated Wagner 'alone among quite modern musicians'.[63] Mansfield's notebook entry closely echoes Symons's opinion when she records that, 'In the music of Wagner there is that breadth & universality by which emotion ceases to be personal & becomes elemental.'[64] 'The music of Wagner has human blood in it,' she continues. 'What Wagner tried to do is to unite mysticism and the senses, to render mysticism through the senses.'[65] These synthesizing qualities, so attractive to Baudelaire, were to be of vital importance to Mansfield's achievement in fusing symbolist and realist modes of writing in her fiction – as, for instance, in those slate-scraping skylarks.

But in 'Juliet', both the annihilating intensity of Wagner and aestheticist principles have to contend with Victorian realism. Rudolf's pronouncements to Juliet about risking a life in art and passion echo many that Mansfield herself made in her early journals and poetry, and Mansfield's style is emphatically not Victorian, for the scenes that follow Juliet's seduction develop into some of the most experimental stream-of-consciousness writing in the MS. However, within the extended structure required by narrative fiction, she generates a plot in which her artistic heroine's adventures lead to her death, and which evokes nineteenth-century dramatizations of creative aspiration and the perils of unguarded musical response.[66]

With Juliet's death, the aspiring writer becomes a silent muse – a very Victorian fate which lends 'Juliet', the story of a potential artist who fails, the status of a female *Bildungsroman*.[67] The satirical powers that were to feature so pervasively in Mansfield's later fiction come to the fore as her seducer Rudolf responds to news of her death by composing 'a very charming little morceau, "Souvenir de Juliet"'.[68] Juliet's previously bohemian friend Pearl and the cellist David marry and subside into insipid domesticity, described with the sharp ridicule that was to characterize her first collection of published stories: 'Pearl gave up smoking cigarettes & published a little volume which she called "Mother Thought".'[69] Early on, Juliet issues a musical condemnation of marriage: 'I loathe the very principle of matrimony,' she declares. 'It must end in failure & it is death to a woman's personality. She must drop the theme and begin to start playing the accompaniment.'[70] And here is yet another echo of George Eliot, this time of Armgart's scathing rebuttal, in her 1870 poem about a singer, of the notion that she might abandon her career and settle for singing to a husband as he reads the paper: 'What! leave the opera with my part ill-sung / While I was warbling in a drawing-room? / Sing in the chimney-corner to inspire / My husband reading news?'[71]

The links between Mansfield's writing and Victorian literature are clear, but precisely what connections should one propose between the thematic presence of music in 'Juliet', and later work where music becomes predominantly a source of metaphor and of analogy for writing itself? Only a small number of Mansfield's later stories are actually about musical topics, for there is little need for explicit allusion once music has become transposed from subject to structure and style. Undoubtedly musical technique informed Mansfield's evolution of a stream-of-consciousness style of writing. The MS for 'Juliet' moves from synaesthetic rhapsodizing on the effects of twilight[72] to feminist satire; its range of musical writing suggests that music was also fundamental to the integration of symbolism and realism that was to become as uniquely characteristic of her mature fiction as her employment of free indirect discourse.

In the concluding passage of her 1921 story, 'The Daughters of the Late Colonel', the recurrent sound of a hurdy-gurdy from the street outside is both realist and symbolic soundscape: 'A week since father died' it cries, as the daughters realize that they no longer have to run out to request silence, for their father's tyrannical stick-pounding summons 'never will thump again' (246–7). This musical intervention underpins the movement of Mansfield's prose, working alongside a transient burst of sunshine that fleetingly illuminates lost possibilities in the lives of two Edwardian women while a 'perfect fountain of bubbling notes shook from the barrel-organ, round, bright notes, carelessly scattered' (247). As in the story with which I began, Mansfield unites musicality and referential clarity to achieve an apparently effortless marriage of symbolism and realism. From her earliest writing, she enacts Pater's influential dictum that 'All art constantly aspires towards the condition of music' in a literary language that transforms her nineteenth-century inheritance: a prose style 'already modern' and intrinsically musical.[73]

Notes

1. S. J. Kaplan (1991) *Katherine Mansfield and the Origins of Modernist Fiction* (Ithaca: Cornell University Press), p. 61.
2. *Letters* 4, p. 165. For a reflection on some of the formal analogies suggested by Mansfield's comparison between the process of writing and musical composition see C. Hanson and A. Gurr (1981) *Katherine Mansfield* (London: Macmillan), p. 77.
3. C. Baudelaire, Preface to *Petits Poèmes en Prose*, A. Symons (trans.) (1905) *Poems in Prose from Charles Baudelaire* (London: Elkin Mathews). See also *Notebooks* 1, p. 160: 'reve le miracle d'une prose poétique musicale sans rhythme et sans rime'.
4. M. Cowley (1996 [1921]) '"Page Dr Blum!" *Bliss*', Review of *Bliss and Other Stories* [1920], *The Dial*, September, vol. 71, 365, repr. in J. Pilditch (ed.), *The Critical Response to Katherine Mansfield* (Westport, CT: Greenwood Press), pp. 5–6.
5. Cowley, p. 6.
6. A. Smith (ed.) (2002) *Selected Stories of Katherine Mansfield* (Oxford University Press), p. 314. All further references to Mansfield's stories refer to this edition and are placed directly in the text.
7. Recent criticism that explores the role of music in literary modernism includes work by S. Martin (1982) *Wagner to 'The Waste Land': A Study of Wagner in English Literature* (London: Macmillan); D. Albright (2000) *Untwisting the Serpent: Modernism in Music, Literature, and Other Arts* (University of Chicago Press); B. Bucknell (2002) *Literary Modernism and Musical Aesthetics: Pater, Pound, Joyce and Stein* (Cambridge University Press); M. Byron (2006) 'Musical Scores and Literary Form in Modernism: Ezra Pound's *Pisan Cantos* and Samuel Beckett's *Watt*', in D. da Sousa Correa (ed.) (2006) *Phrase and Subject: Studies in Literature and Music* (London: Legenda, MHRA/Maney Publishing).
8. *Notebooks* 2, p. 137; and see *Letters* 1, p. 205.
9. Claire Tomalin notes that in 1907 Mansfield set herself a schedule of six hours' cello practice each day and three hours' writing, evidence that 'she still thought of a musical career as a possibility'; see Tomalin (1988) *Katherine Mansfield: A Secret Life* (Harmondsworth: Penguin) p. 42.

10. I. Baker (1971) *Katherine Mansfield: The Memories of L. M.* (London: Taplinger), p. 31.
11. Mansfield, 'This is my World' [1903] in V. O'Sullivan (ed.) (1988) *Poems of Katherine Mansfield* (Oxford University Press), p. 1. 'And that is my 'cello, my all in all / Ah, my beloved, quiet you stand / – – – If I let the bow ever so softly fall / – – – The magic lies under my hand'.
12. 'Her emphasis on craft relates to her long-standing appreciation of technical perfection, beginning with her adolescent immersion in the study of music', Kaplan, p. 204. See *Letters* 4, p. 173.
13. *Ibid.*
14. For the influence of symbolist poetry on Mansfield's development see Hanson and Gurr, p. 23.
15. G. Eliot (1963 [1856]) 'Silly Novels by Lady Novelists', *Westminster Review*, repr. in T. Pinney (ed.) *Essays of George Eliot* (London: Routledge), pp. 300–24 (p. 324).
16. See Kaplan, p. 86.
17. D. Albright (ed.) (2004) *Modernism and Music: An Anthology of Sources* (University of Chicago Press), pp. 2, 1.
18. Strauss's *Symphonia Domestica* (composed 1903).
19. *Letters* 1, p. 66.
20. *Ibid.*, p. 80.
21. Mansfield, 'Through the Autumn Afternoon', *Poems*, p. 6.
22. The Alexander Turnbull Library in Wellington holds copies of the programme of the farewell concert given to sponsor the Trowell brothers' musical education in London and other concert programmes from the period when Mansfield lived in the New Zealand capital. I am grateful to Professor Vincent O'Sullivan for alerting me to the existence of this material and to the exceptionally helpful staff at the Turnbull, who enabled me to locate and examine the relevant files in their collection.
23. *Notebooks* 1, p. 214. Scott was unable to decipher one of the terms that Mansfield used to describe the music of Strauss. I suggest 'loneliness', as this is the term used by Symons from whom she is quoting. The source for the notes on Strauss and Mozart in this section of Mansfield's notebook can be found in A. Symons (1903) *Plays, Acting and Music* (London: Duckworth), pp. 80 and 191.
24. *Letters* 1, p. 59. See A. Symons (1906) *Studies in Seven Arts* (London: Constable), p. 24, which is the source for Mansfield's comment: 'to Beethoven nature was still healthy, and joy had not begun to be a subtle form of pain'. Symons apparently echoes both Wagner's view of Beethoven's naivety here and Baudelaire's view of Wagner's (thus modern music's) embracing of pain.
25. *Letters* 1, pp. 83–4, 61.
26. Kaplan, p. 206.
27. *Letters* 1, p. 39: 'so wonderfully beautiful – so dream-like – and so full of longing also' (my translation).
28. Kaplan, p. 207.
29. *Ibid.*
30. Kaplan reflects on the critical consequences of privileging 1908 in this way, pp. 206–7.
31. *Letters* 1, p. 84.

32. D. Stanford (ed.) (1968) *Short Stories of the 'Nineties: A Biographical Anthology* (London: John Baker), p. 16.

33. G. Egerton (1894) 'A Lost Masterpiece: A City Mood', *The Yellow Book: An Illustrated Quarterly*, vol. 1, April, 189–96. See also (1894) '"London" a story by John Davidson', *Yellow Book:* vol. 1, April, p. 233.

34. Mansfield, 'Trio' in *Poems*, pp. 23–4.

35. Mansfield, 'Westminster Cathedral', in *Poems*, pp. 11–12.

36. This is the conclusion of a poem composed to provide lyrics for song music by Tom Trowell, see *Letters* 1, pp. 83–4; *Poems*, pp. 19–20.

37. Mansfield, 'November', in *Poems*, p. 21.

38. Mansfield, 'Through the Autumn Afternoon', in *Poems*, p. 4.

39. See *Notebooks* 1, pp. 48–69.

40. 'How Pearl Button was Kidnapped', for example, recalls both Maggie Tulliver's 'escape' to the gypsies in chapter 11 of George Eliot's *The Mill on the Floss* and Dickens's counterpointing of the worlds of Gradgrind and the circus in *Hard Times*; Hanson and Gurr have noted that there are as many excerpts in Mansfield's notebooks from *Daniel Deronda* as there are from Wilde (p. 13).

41. *Notebooks* 1, p. 50.

42. *Ibid.*, p. 213. I have traced this quotation to Symons's description of the violinist Ysaye in *Plays, Acting and Music*, p. 6.

43. G. Eliot (1980 [1860]) *The Mill on the Floss*, G. S. Haight (ed.) (Oxford: Clarendon Press), p. 268.

44. *Ibid.*

45. *Notebooks* 1, p. 51.

46. *Ibid.*, p. 52.

47. *Ibid.*

48. See Martin, p. 59.

49. *Notebooks* 1, p. 61.

50. *Ibid.*

51. See Symons, *Plays, Acting and Music*, pp. 69–71, also p. 64.

52. *Notebooks* 1, p. 61.

53. *Ibid.*

54. *Ibid.*, p. 62.

55. *Ibid.*

56. *Letters* 1, p. 29. She also included Wagner in a list of ideal fireside companions: see *Letters* 1, p. 51, and was full of regret at not hearing *Die Meistersinger* in a production for which Garnet Trowell's touring orchestra played: *Letters* 1, p. 73.

57. *Notebooks* 1, p. 145.

58. Quoted in P. Dayan (2006) *Music Writing Literature, from Sand via Debussy to Derrida* (Aldershot: Ashgate), p. 29.

59. J.-J. Nattiez (2004) 'Tannhäuser through Baudelaire's Looking-glass: Modern or Postmodern?', in *The Battle of Chronos and Orpheus: Essays in Applied Musical Semiology*, J. Dunsby (trans.) (Oxford University Press), pp. 214–29 (p. 214).

60. Albright, *Modernism and Music*, p. 3.

61. Nattiez, p. 229.

62. *Notebooks* 2, p. 267.

63. Symons, *Plays, Acting and Music*, p. 16.

64. *Notebooks* 1, p. 214. See Symons, *Plays, Acting and Music*, p. 16: 'Wagner alone among quite modern musicians [...] has that breadth and universality by which emotion ceases to be merely personal and becomes elemental.'
65. *Notebooks* 1, p. 214. See Symons, *Plays, Acting and Music*, p. 66: 'This abstract music has human blood in it. What Wagner has tried to do is to unite mysticism and the senses, to render mysticism through the senses.'
66. For an account of which see my (2003) *George Eliot, Music and Victorian Culture* (Basingstoke: Palgrave).
67. See Kaplan, pp. 94–5. Kaplan also reads Mansfield's 1918 story 'Prelude' as a female *Bildungsroman*.
68. *Notebooks* 1, p. 59.
69. *Ibid.*
70. *Ibid.*, p. 58.
71. G. Eliot (1989 [1870]) 'Armgart', *Collected Poems*, L. Jenkins (ed.) (London: Skoob), p. 129.
72. *Notebooks* 1, p. 54.
73. W. Pater (1877) 'The School of Giorgione', in *The Renaissance: Studies in Art and Poetry*, 2nd edn, rev. (London: Macmillan), p. 140.

7
'Is this Play?': Katherine Mansfield's Play Frames

Janna K. Stotz

> John (my John) has given me an ivory shoe horn and
> a little ivory backed mirror . . . .
> > (Katherine Mansfield, Letter to Jeanne
> > Beauchamp, 11 October 1913)[1]

> Play is not the way to maintain a tightly controlled society
> or a clear definition of what is good, true, or beautiful.
> > (Stephen Nachmanovitch, *This is Play*)[2]

In the narrative of *Bliss and Other Stories*, Katherine Mansfield repeats objects that exist within a boundary or border, a frame. Mirrors, paintings and other framed objects form an intricate motif of binary relationships and codes to which the reader may or may not be attuned – creating a subtle form of communication that exists beyond the surface of the narrative. Modernist scholar Mary Ann Caws suggests that 'a framed object [...] may itself become the developing or revealing object for the import of the entire scene narrated, as it were, by condensation'.[3] While Caws's discussion centres on the novel, the same observation applies to Mansfield's short stories; framed or bounded objects communicate significant aspects of her entire narrative in focused moments. These either signal her characters' introspective epiphanies or hint at full narrative disclosure – moments Sarah Sandley has identified as 'the Mansfieldian glimpse'.[4] From their external vantage point, readers may anticipate that these multi-layered messages will ultimately explain a story's meaning. But the inherent remove between author and reader gives rise to varied interpretations or even miscommunication. When reader expectations are unsettled by discordant messages, Mansfield's apparent revelations may paradoxically seem disingenuous.[5]

To begin to understand this discord, readers must conceptualize the act of reading fiction as a form of communication circuit, a game based on perception. Mansfield as fiction writer and fiction readers as audience enter into a relationship and an agreement 'to play the same game'.[6] This 'game' functions if, and only if, the participants 'pretend together for the moment that what is denoted by some reference that they are making is exactly the same for both'.[7] As noted above, the distance between writer and reader flaws the agreement. The lack of 'direct interaction'[8] between them can necessarily render the 'reference' ambiguous.[9] This ambiguity thwarts readers' expectations that Mansfield's bounded objects will be fixed references in the communication circuit, further complicating the game built on mutual pretending. Though the meaning of these bounded objects is not anchored in common meaning, the game does not end. The momentary responses of readers to this unexpected turn perpetuate the repartee between participants, creating a series of new and different references.[10] Ambiguity, thus, becomes part of the game because '[i]n playing, we are fluidly changing definitions of things'.[11] This form of game is characteristic of intellectual communication in general.

In fact, this sort of evolving game exists in all kinds of sentient interaction. In his essay 'A Theory of Play and Fantasy', Gregory Bateson presents his theories on the fundamental concepts of communication among mammals. Mammalian play in various species rests on an agreement between participants that a game is at hand. Messages intrinsic to certain actions can be perceived by all and finessed and altered, based on various cues, changing the game. Because participants have physical contact with one another, non-verbal cues ensure adaptations of the message to newly agreed-upon goals. Nevertheless, the same communicative fundamentals apply to the relationship between writers and readers in the play of fiction.[12] Readers, on the contrary, cannot usually benefit from a live participation, making universally understood changes to the game impossible. Devoid of verbal, non-verbal and auditory cues, readers rely on perceptions of the written word as their only means to interpret messages of play.

While Bateson writes of face-to-face participants, the essential points of his communicative theory provide a way to examine Mansfield's use of bounded or framed objects, her characters' play behaviour and her objects of amusement. By choosing words that prevent readers from anchoring to an immovable meaning, Mansfield provokes shifts in readers' perceptions, perhaps foreseeing the ways in which people will perceive the words used. Imagining readers' perceptions raises the stakes of the game. Readers are left to wonder about the game at hand: 'Is this play?'[13] In 'Je ne parle pas français' and 'Bliss', I contend that Mansfield plays a communication game heightened by her subtle yet deliberate use of these elements.

A play frame

In most fiction, Mansfield's included, a frame signals a shared agreement in a narrative game and provides an initial understanding of how objects and terms should be understood. Bateson proposes that the establishment of this frame in turn provides the reader with a way to 'understand the messages included within the frame'.[14] But unlike physical play, the text is the only medium through which author and reader can communicate; Mansfield's reader, therefore, must interpret the messages contained in the narrative to complete the communication circuit on several abstract levels. Bateson generally identifies two such levels of playful communication as 'metacommunicative' and 'metalinguistic'.[15] Refining Bateson's terminology for use in interpreting fiction, Christine Knoop explains that '[m]etacommunicative remarks [...] happen when the characters or narrators show awareness of the fictional nature of the situation',[16] and that 'predetermined formal rules can evoke further metacommunication', 'such as recurring motifs'.[17] Knoop proposes that at the metalinguistic level in fiction 'the meanings we usually attribute to certain words may prove to be problematic during the reading of a text' because of differences in the 'word-concept relation'.[18] The metalinguistic level is particularly likely to cause miscommunication between an author and a reader.

During Mansfield's focused moments, communication may be muddled in various ways. A reader enters the game expecting that an epiphany will portray an individual's moment of sincere introspection or provide a potential resolution to the narrative. This is simply a rule presumed by the reader of the full import of events within a narrative. When Mansfield's moments fail to reassure the reader of his or her presumption it may seem as though a violation of 'predetermined formal rules'[19] occurs. At the metalinguistic level, ambiguity in the narrative surrounding these moments further confuses the reader's preconceived notions by preventing a concrete connection between word and concept. 'Such disappointment of seemingly pre-negotiated meanings', Knoop argues, 'can be seen as a strategy to (mis-)guide the reader and evoke surprises, discovery, shock, etc.'[20] Mansfield's use of bounded objects within the narrative further complicates the communication circuit even further. Each creates a doubled boundary; the play frame of her narrative encapsulates the objects within, paralleling the Batesonian notion of 'double framing'; successful communication 'need[s] an outer frame to delimit the ground against which the figures [inside a frame] are to be perceived' (for example, Duquette's café mirror and bedroom mirror; Bertha's parlour mirror and windowed garden pear tree).[21] In other words, the reader is now confused: is meaning to be derived from the initial frame or the secondary frame? Although the initial narrative frame has signalled to the reader that an agreement is in place and how to understand the contents of that frame, the reader's *external* positioning seems ultimately to provide the clear understanding of messages within Mansfield's narrative. By disrupting expected meanings and confusing perceived agreements, Mansfield perpetuates the game by depriving readers of certainty within the narrative. She carries the reader past the initial agreement to what Bateson sees as 'a more complex form of play; the game which is constructed not upon the premise "This is play" but rather around the question "Is this play?"'[22] The reader has entered the game with the understanding, or perhaps a predetermined assumption, that entails a shared control over the story's outcome. However, Mansfield has now changed the initial agreement in such a way that the reader begins to suspect that he or she is also being manipulated, leading the reader to ask: 'Is this play?'[23]

Mansfield seems to re-establish an equal agreement with the reader as participant. She accomplishes this by incorporating certain behaviours in her characters, which Bateson identifies as play behaviour – 'histrionics', 'deceit' and 'spectatorship'[24] – and figuring characters as objects of amusement. Mansfield invites the reader to accept the statement, 'This is play,' supported by these clearly delineated play behaviours and play objects, rather than allowing the reader to pose the question, 'Is this play?'[25] Without this question, the reader would not realize the manipulation at work, because of the assumption that he or she is an equal participant in the game. Mansfield adds to this endeavour by describing characters as non-human things: Duquette of 'Je ne parle pas français' as 'a little fox terrier'[26] and one of 'three little dice' (157), and Bertha's child in 'Bliss' as a 'fiddle' (176) and 'doll' (175). Reducing characters to these simple objects also reduces the surrounding action to make play clear. But Mansfield deliberately introduces this clarity in order to deceive. Each of these objects requires a human relationship to fulfil its role as an object of amusement, implying the reader's dominance within the agreed game and initiating the reader into a role as spectator; she perpetuates the illusion of control at the metalinguistic level. In situating the reader in a superior position, Mansfield seems to assure the reader of the certainty and fixed meaning of these objects, and thus of the message contained, yet these objects tend 'to suppress the ordinary meanings of the world'.[27] Her narratives, given Bateson's theories, become complex forms of communication – as play frames.[28]

'Right and wrong, pity and blame, she seems to say to us, are your affair. Mine is only to put the case to you'[29]

Mansfield's 'Je ne parle pas français' begins innocuously: 'I do not know why I have such a fancy for this little café' (142).[30] Mansfield's text teems with paradoxes, many emerging from the story's protagonist, Raoul Duquette, 'a Parisian, a true Parisian' (146), as she chronicles his relationship with Dick Harmon, an Englishman. After exploring Paris and their respective philosophies, Harmon abruptly severs their union to return to his home. Sometime later, Harmon pens a letter to Duquette imploring his aid in acquiring extended lodging for both himself and 'a woman friend' (153). Harmon, accompanied by his female companion, Mouse, arrives in Paris; yet they part company several hours later as Harmon unceremoniously flees from their lodgings, leaving behind a remorseful note disavowing his emotions for Mouse while proclaiming them for his mother, 'Not even for you. Not even for us' (164). Duquette is left to console the ill-prepared '*je ne parle pas français*' Mouse, reassuring her of Harmon's return and his continued comfort, but instead he 'never went near the place again' (166). Mansfield opens and closes this narrative with instances of metacommunicative and metalinguistic communication hinting at both play and a doubled narrative frame.

The Batesonian notion of 'double framing', or the creation of a double boundary, permeates this narrative in three different ways. Angela Smith uses the metaphor of a picture frame to illustrate this notion in that the initial frame, the frame created by the act of reading fiction, functions as the wall, while the painting within the picture frame corresponds to the narrative action in Paris; one narrative is embedded in another.[31] The wall is represented by Duquette sitting at the 'little café' (142), and the events that Duquette describes with Harmon and Mouse are within the picture frame. Mansfield's intentional use of bounded or framed objects within each of these levels – the narrative representing the wall and the narrative representing the painting – forms a complex of messages that the reader can interpret from their external vantage point, if and only if the reader perceives Mansfield's revision of the narrative agreement.

The beginning of this story suggests two distinct narrative levels. A level containing the initial frame and a framed or bounded object becomes apparent as Duquette sits at the deplorable café:

> Slowly I raised my head and saw myself in the mirror opposite. Yes, there I sat [. . .].

> I opened my eyes very wide. There I had been for all eternity, as it were, and now at last I was coming to life. . . . (144)

Duquette begins to describe the impetus for the story he is creating – the embedded narrative: 'I fell on to that stupid, stale little phrase: *Je ne parle pas français*' (145). Recognizing his own reflection in a bounded object, a mirror, implies Duquette's supposed awakening. However, his moment of revelation reflects a more sinister underpinning. Duquette's epiphany is not a self-referential moment within a mirror, but merely an inauthentic moment, a complication to the reader's perceived narrative agreement. It signals, also, a subtle change in the discourse at hand, shifting from one narrative level to another. Paradoxically, he is both creator and participant, and in a metacommunicative moment he admonishes the reader that he is 'master of the situation!' (143).

Although this glimpse of Duquette cannot reveal the full complexities of his character, deception is implied. Just as Bateson enumerates the kinds of behaviour that delineate a play frame, Duquette exhibits each – histrionics, deceit and spectatorship – throughout the narrative. Before yet another turn in front of the mirror, in a moment of remembrance, Duquette proclaims that 'I am going to make a name for myself as a writer about the submerged world. [...] from the inside' (148). And again, what frame bounds the narrative of 'the submerged world' which he implicitly infiltrates and writes 'from the inside'? Is this the same as the narrative of 'Je ne parle pas français' (the story we are reading), or is it a separate narrative altogether? Which of the narrative's messages should a reader consider more important? Deceit, by both Duquette and Mansfield, is at play.

Duquette's narration is replete with the accoutrements of dramatic performance in various moments of metacommunication. Prior to this shift in narrative discourse, the same language encircling Duquette's realization before the looking-glass is echoed within the story:

> Do you believe that every place has its hour of the day when it really does come alive? [...] There does seem to be a moment when you realize that, quite by accident, you happen to have come on to the stage at exactly the moment you were expected. (143)

On the metacommunicative level, this play within the story world creates a paradox between Duquette's levels of statements: what statement exists within the narrative that Mansfield is writing and what within the narrative that Duquette constructs? To whom is the question, 'Do you believe that every place has its hour of the day when it really does come alive?' (143) addressed? Theatrical notes implying spectatorship are inserted in the midst of discourse with Mouse: '(Soft music. Mouse gets up, walks the stage for a moment or so before she returns to her chair and pours him out ...)' (162). Play is obvious to the reader in these kinds of moments, a reaction Mansfield carefully creates.

Moreover, spectatorship permeates Duquette's characterization. From the start of the narrative Duquette interjects the idea of photography in several instances. But most notable, according to Smith, is the cinematic nature of Duquette's depictions, that 'he sometimes describes what he sees as if it were happening on a screen',[32] or through a camera, creating a bounded object, in literal frames of meaning. Duquette's cinematic description, playing dual roles as spectator and divine creator, is most markedly apparent as he travels by taxi with Harmon and Mouse: 'I had insisted on taking the flap seat facing them because I would not have missed for anything those occasional flashing glimpses I had as we broke through the white circles of lamplight' (158). Here spectatorship is most apparent in a playful turn of narrative embedding which 'often has the paradoxical effect not only of producing the illusion of a more profound realism or aesthetic unity [...] but also of undercutting that illusion at the same time'.[33] The cinema of Duquette's creation is contained within his memory of the event (the taxi ride) framed by his narration from the moment he saw or heard that 'stale little phrase' (145). Mansfield's play frames and her own playful notions of narrative embedding subvert the illusion of the assumed nature of Harmon and Mouse's relationship. The realism of the supposedly betrothed heterosexual couple, or two actors performing on screen, becomes the illusion that must be subverted. Much like Duquette's performance in front of his bedroom looking-glass, Harmon and Mouse must complete the aesthetic unity of heterosexuality and so replace the dissonance of homosexuality – between Harmon and Duquette – hinted at through much of the story.

Duquette, in a nod to his apparent sycophantic predictability, stands before his looking-glass, musing over Dick's initial departure and his sub-sequent 'charming' letter: 'I read it standing in front of the (unpaid for) wardrobe mirror. It was early morning. I wore a blue kimono [...] "Portrait of Madame Butterfly," said I, "on hearing of the arrival of *ce cher Pinkerton*"' (153). By fusing gender distinctions and gender expectations within his reflection, Duquette introduces a duality of self: his figure is simultaneously male and female, blurring the messages of the frame. Duquette's visage, in a literal bounded object, or frame, heralds a shift in the metalinguistic assumptions between narrative levels, confusing the 'code' for male and female.[34] The framed mirror prefigures his shifting sexuality within the embedded frames of the narrative itself, while 'Duquette's sexual orientation, as with much else about him, remains blurred despite the sharpness of the outline'.[35] In his feigned epiphany in front of the mirror, Duquette crosses the boundary of his own understanding including acceptance of his implied love for another man. This constitutes traversing the boundary of the male/female distinction.

Duquette's evocation of another double frame shifts the narrative to a second level. By adding another implied message to the nexus of interpretations, he intimates an assumption of play behaviour as well. His allusion to *Madame Butterfly* elicts an overly dramatized or operatic play frame. Dick Harmon is set to return to his love, much like Pinkerton of *Madame Butterfly*. Duquette's sexual ambiguity and homoerotic love are echoed as well. The plot of *Madame Butterfly* foreshadows Duquette's own relationship between the joyous returns of lovers and the mixed, culturally misinterpreted messages that follow. Not only does his commentary, standing at the frame, refer to the ambiguity of his sexual preference, but also to the ambiguity of his gender role.

Following Duquette's turn at the looking-glass, an overtly histrionic tone merges with elements of theatricality. Immediately following his kimono-wrapped performance in the looking-glass, Duquette imagines going to the window:

> According to the books I should have felt immensely relieved and delighted. '. . . Going to the window he drew apart the curtains and looked out at the Paris trees, just breaking into buds and green. . . . Dick! Dick! My English friend!' (153)

Although Bateson does not explicitly assign histrionics to a particular gender, sentimental tradition associates this kind of behaviour with the feminine. Duquette's 'I should have felt immensely relieved and delighted' (153) implies feminine behaviour, either imagined or performed in the narrative world. Duquette has consulted a book of relationships to reinforce his understanding of his own feminine role in a homosexual relationship. Thus, Duquette's momentary outburst substantiates Bateson's notions of play behaviour and further complicates the boundaries between male and female and their implied messages.

Objects symbolizing play project the inherent message of a game into Duquette's narrative. When his ambiguous sexual nature intersects with that of Harmon, Duquette calls himself 'a fox terrier', as in '(In my very worst moments my nose reminds me of a fox terrier's)' (152). Yet, this 'fox terrier' is connected with his thoughts and feelings within the narrative he has created and the Duquette sitting at the table penning his own existence. Smith interprets Duquette's 'fox terrier' as another evocation of his divine control of the narrative world, that 'Duquette is not a fawning dog who assists his master with the hunt; he is himself in control of the prey.'[36] And in a similar moment, Duquette depicts himself, Harmon and Mouse as 'three little dice that life had decided to have a fling with' (157). In Goffman's terms, by virtue of their use in the text, these objects of amusement imply a play frame throughout the scene. However, Mansfield's playfulness is not confined to this narrative.

In Mansfield's 'Bliss', a young woman prepares her home for a dinner party. As Bertha Young bustles about the family abode, she is 'overcome, suddenly, by a feeling of bliss – absolute bliss!' (174). She continues with the direction of domestic preparations, examining the fruits to be served and coddling her daughter under the nanny's watchful eye. She reflects on her and her husband Harry's anticipated guests and her special 'find', Pearl Fulton, whom she had encountered at the club: 'Bertha had fallen in love with her, as she always did fall in love with beautiful women' (177). The assorted dinner companions arrive, as does Miss Fulton. During their party's after-dinner banter, Bertha's bliss morphs into rapture at the thought of sexual congress with her husband. As their guests begin to leave, Bertha sees Harry with Miss Fulton, miming the words, '"I adore you."' Bertha returns to the drawing room and cries, '"Oh, what is going to happen now?"' (185).

Bertha's initial introspective glimpse begins the narrative when

> [s]he hardly dared to look into the cold mirror – but she did look, and it gave her back a woman, radiant, with smiling, trembling lips, with big, dark eyes and an air of listening, waiting for something . . . divine to happen . . . that she knew must happen . . . infallibly. (174)

Yet, there is a distinct disengagement in the language portraying Bertha's outward or perceived self and reality, an inauthentic moment. Bertha's outward appearance embodies blissful, childlike wonder: 'she wanted to run instead of walk, to take dancing steps on and off the pavement, to bowl a hoop' (174). This language of childlike astonishment at the narrative world continues as Bertha metaphorically consumes a portion of the sun and 'it burned in [her] bosom, sending out a little shower of sparks into every particle, into every finger and toe? ...' But, as she 'dared to look into the cold mirror', she is afraid of the visage that could be returned. Bertha, imbued with the 'late afternoon sun' (174), is thoroughly disconnected from the properties of her perceived self prior to looking in the mirror and her *real* self. The messages are discordant; identity is the game. Her visage portrays the liminality of Mansfield's boundaries. She tarries in front of the looking-glass waiting for it to 'bestow a sense of identity upon her'.[37] Mansfield's characters exhibit the same disconnected dualities between perception and reality; the framed mirror communicates opposing messages. 'Bertha', under Luce Irigaray's lens, as evoked by Moran, 'looks at herself as a man and what she sees is a woman the way a man would see her.'[38] Thus patriarchy imposes a dissonant message. However, Bertha elucidates another level to her character through interjecting awareness of such an imposition in a metalinguistic moment. As her maid inquires, '"Shall I turn on the light, M'm?"' Bertha, recognizing the implication, responds, '"No, thank you. I can see quite well"' (175).

Central to the exploration of 'Bliss' is the pear tree of Bertha's garden, framed within the drawing-room window: 'The windows of the drawing room opened on to a balcony overlooking the garden. At the far end, [...] there was a tall slender pear tree in fullest, richest bloom; it stood perfect, as though becalmed against the jade-green sky' (177). And later the tree is revealed for the second time in the story, as Bertha goes to the window with Miss Fulton:

> She crossed the room, pulled the curtains apart, and opened those long windows.
> 'There!' she breathed.
> And the two women stood side by side looking at the slender flowering tree'. (182)

Bertha's sexual revelation is prefigured by the framed pear tree. As her narratives create a boundary, so too the window frames the pear tree. The replication of seeing the pear tree and granting it symbolic significance renders each viewing of the tree as a voyeuristic exploration. Bertha's sexual awakening depends on her receipt of the messages communicated to her by the framed object, the pear tree. In viewing it with Miss Fulton, she is receiving incompatible messages. Much like Duquette's turn before his framed bedroom mirror, she is receiving the message of heterosexuality and that of homosexuality. Within the frame of the action outlined by the pear tree, Bertha demonstrates another of Bateson's behaviour cues, spectatorship. By repeatedly invoking the image, Bertha becomes voyeur to her own sexual symbol. And again, only the reader can see the entirety of the messages within the narrative completing the communication circuit.

Critically, the pear tree is presented as a monument to human sexuality, but the messages to be perceived within the frame are baffling. Moran confirms that

> [t]he pear tree functions [...] as a commonplace representation of the penis [...]. The doubled meaning of the pear tree [...] attests to Bertha's [...] bisexuality: at one point she identifies with Harry and desires Pearl, at another point she identifies with Pearl and desires Harry.[39]

Walter Anderson suggests that 'the flowering pear tree is a composite symbol representing in its tallness Bertha's homosexual aspirations and in its full, rich blossoms, her desire to be sexually used'.[40] Helen Nebeker, on the contrary, presents another interpretation, as she views the pear tree as an implication of 'sterility' and not fertility or 'flowering' within Mansfield's text.[41] She argues, from a botanical point of view, 'that sometimes in such a bi-sexual tree, a condition occurs wherein the male organ ripens before the stigma matures enough to receive the pollen'.[42] Thus, these perplexing interpretations of Bertha's sexuality, or lack thereof, through the framed pear tree, correspond to Bertha's entrance into a frame, or facet, of the male/female relationship she is ill-equipped to handle. Paradoxically, her own sexual stirrings should have allowed her to gain entrance into the play frame with an understanding of the game, but they did not. As she enters the realm of sexual desire, she crosses the boundary of the framed pear tree and its emblematic nature into sexual gamesmanship, a type of play of which she has neither prior experience nor understanding.

Bertha 'plays' with her own sexuality, losing herself at the confluence of sundry messages from society. One message seems to advocate repression of all sexual desire in women and another seems to advocate repression of her homosexual desire for Pearl, conflating the expected norms of gendered sexual roles, like her narrative counterpart Duquette. Bertha desires to be sexually used: 'Why be given a body if you have to keep it shut up in a case like a rare, rare fiddle?' (174). And, later, while standing before the piano, after she has imagined 'the dark room' that she could share with her husband she exclaims twice, 'What a pity someone does not play!' (184). But Bertha's yearning to be used in a sexual concert does not manifest itself. Reduced to an object of amusement, again, she does not understand the game in which she has entered. As Moran says, 'in assuming her husband's last name, Young, Bertha seems constrained by a childish role; indeed, with a cook, a maid, and a nanny, she plays at that most domestic of little girl's games, keeping house'.[43] The action of play is established in both Bertha's domestic realm and sexual realms. But Bertha misinterprets these messages of play and Mansfield causes confusion among readers.

Mansfield depicts Bertha as disengaged from the actions happening within her own household. This disconnect is most notable in a scene in the nursery between Bertha, her nanny and her small daughter. Bertha stands in front of her nanny and her daughter 'watching them, her hands by her side, like the poor little girl in front of the rich little girl with the doll' (175). The object of amusement is her daughter, but reinforcing the maternal relationship is yet another realm of which Bertha has inadequate knowledge. She is once again rendered as a spectator to a symbolic object, and this defines her as non-participant. She coddles her daughter, '"You're nice – you're very nice!" said she, kissing her warm baby. "I'm fond of you. I like you"' (176). Her lack of connection could be construed as evidence of an immaturity in the domestic sphere, as Moran affirms, as well as her inability to correctly interpret the inherent messages and expectations of domesticity and her own heterosexuality. Once again, Bertha is disengaged from the realm of play, from the 'game'[44] of the narrative; she cannot play with her daughter, 'the doll' (175). Bertha simultaneously confuses both the sexual messages from the framed pear tree and the messages of the domestic sphere.

Prior to her entrance into the nursery, Bertha exhibits one of Bateson's play behaviours: 'No, no. I'm getting hysterical' (175). Yet her histrionics result from the newly awakened sexual game and her ill-preparedness to participate in that play. 'Freud', as Chantal D'Arcy asserts, 'clearly states that the causes of hysterical disorders are to be found in the intimacies of the patient's psychosexual life, in their most secret and repressed sexual wishes.'[45] Ironically, Bertha's repression of both her lesbian affection for Pearl and her sexual desire for her husband could be the cause of her hysterics. She is incompatible with both forms of sexuality, as she does not accept the communications and messages of the game in which she is confined.

In each of the stories explored here, ordinary objects and common behaviours, interpreted through Bateson's notions of communication, form a more abstract plane on which to view Mansfield's work. However, recognition of this abstract plane, or abstract frames, does not lead readers to 'interpretive clarity'.[46] Any conclusion reached by examining Mansfield's work from this perspective would be as fragmented as portions of her narratives. Moreover, precise conclusions would reduce Mansfield's game play to an absolute. Play is an enduring amusement that challenges our perceptions. 'To play', as Stephen Nachmanovitch emphasizes, 'is to open our eyes to different possibilities.'[47] Mansfield enacts play; only the reader can cross the multiple frames completing her game. And, surely this is play?[48]

Notes

1. See *Letters* 1, p. 132.
2. S. Nachmanovitch (2009) 'This is Play', *New Literary History*, 40, 1–24 (p. 11).
3. M. A. Caws (1985) *Reading Frames in Modern Fiction* (Princeton University Press), p. 25.
4. S. Sandley (1994) 'The Middle of the Note: Katherine Mansfield's "Glimpses"', in R. Robinson (ed.) *Katherine Mansfield: In from the Margin* (Baton Rouge: Louisiana State University Press), pp. 70–89 (p. 71).
5. Neither Duquette of 'Je ne parle pas français' nor Bertha of 'Bliss' experience an authentic moment of realization in their encounters with Mansfield's framed objects. This dubious authenticity is suggested in Perry Meisel's essay, 'What the Reader Knows', in Robinson, pp. 112–18, in Angela Smith (2000) *Katherine Mansfield: A Literary Life* (Basingstoke: Palgrave), p. 19, and in S. Henstra (2000) 'Looking the Part: Performative Narration in Djuna Barnes's *Nightwood* and Katherine Mansfield's "Je ne parle pas français"', *Twentieth Century Literature*, 46, 125–49.
6. C. Bates (1999) *Play in a Godless World* (London: Open Gate Press), p. 73, cited in E. Wright (2008) 'Gregory Bateson: Epistemology, Language, Play and the Double Bind', *Anthropoetics*, 14: 1, 1–15 (p. 7). See also E. Wright (2005) *Narrative, Perception, Language, and Faith* (Basingstoke: Palgrave).
7. Wright, p. 7.
8. C. Knoop (2007) 'Fictional Communication: Developing Gregory Bateson's "Theory of Play and Fantasy"', *Kybernetes*, 36: 7–8, 1113–21 (p. 1114).
9. Wright, p. 7.
10. Nachmanovitch, p. 16.
11. *Ibid.*, p. 15.
12. The application of Bateson's premises presented in 'A Theory of Play and Fantasy' is mostly limited to the anthropological and linguistic. I have yet to find a focused application of Batesonian framing to literature. G. Bateson (2000) 'A Theory of Play and Fantasy', in *Steps to an Ecology of Mind* (University of Chicago Press), pp. 177–200.
13. *Ibid.*, p. 182.
14. *Ibid.*, p. 188. Portions of Bateson's essay, republished in *Steps to an Ecology of Mind* (1972 and 2000), were originally introduced in 1954.
15. *Ibid.*
16. Knoop, p. 1116.
17. *Ibid.*, p. 1117.
18. *Ibid.*, p. 1115.
19. *Ibid.*, p. 1117.
20. *Ibid.*
21. Bateson, p. 188.
22. *Ibid.*, p. 182.
23. *Ibid.*

24. *Ibid.*, pp. 181–2.
25. *Ibid.*, p. 182.
26. A. Smith (ed.) (2002) *Katherine Mansfield: Selected Stories* (Oxford University Press), p. 152. All textual references to 'Bliss' and 'Je ne parle pas français' are taken from this edition and noted parenthetically throughout the essay.
27. E. Goffman (1974) *Frame Analysis: An Essay on the Organization of Experience* (Boston: Northeastern University Press), p. 43.
28. Although Knoop clearly establishes a general connection between fictional texts and Batesonian play frames, my explication goes beyond this broader association with fiction to specifically interpret Mansfield's texts as intricate forms of playful communication.
29. H. Child (1920) 'Miss Mansfield's Stories', *The Times Literary Supplement*, 16 December, 855.
30. Meisel's essay is a precursor to my discussion here by proposing that Mansfield's 'writing of her real text [takes place] through the orchestrated play of her reader's moral assumptions' (p. 118).
31. Smith (2000), p. 16. See also Henstra, Meisel and W. H. New (1999) *Reading Mansfield and Metaphors of Form* (Montreal: McGill-Queen's University Press).
32. Smith (2000), p. 17. See also Sandley's discussion of Mansfield's cinematic influences, in Robinson, pp. 70–89.
33. W. Nelles (1997) *Frameworks: Narrative Levels and Embedded Narratives* (New York: Peter Lang), p. 149, cited in B. Clarke (2008) *Posthuman Metamorphosis: Narrative and Systems* (New York: Fordham University Press), p. 101.
34. Clarke, p. 102.
35. Smith (2000), p. 17.
36. *Ibid.*, p. 22.
37. P. Moran (1996) *Word of Mouth: Body Language in Katherine Mansfield and Virginia Woolf* (Charlottesville: University of Virginia Press), p. 56.
38. *Ibid.*, p. 57.
39. *Ibid.*, p. 42.
40. W. Anderson (1982) 'The Hidden Love Triangle in Mansfield's "Bliss"', *Twentieth Century Literature*, 28: 4, 397–404 (p. 400).
41. H. Nebeker (1990 [1973]) 'The Pear Tree: Sexual Implications in Katherine Mansfield's "Bliss"', in J. F. Kobler (ed.) *Katherine Mansfield: A Study of Short Fiction* (Boston: Twayne Publishers), pp. 151–8 (p. 152).
42. *Ibid.*
43. Moran, p. 50.
44. Bates, p. 73, cited in Wright, p. 7.
45. C. C.-G. D'Arcy (1999) 'Katherine Mansfield's "Bliss": "A Rare Fiddle" as Emblem of the Political and Sexual Alienation of Women', *PLL: Papers on Language and Literature*, 35: 3, 244–69 (p. 264).
46. Clarke, p. 104.
47. Nachmanovitch, p. 12.
48. I owe a tremendous debt of gratitude to many people but most notably: to Dr Bruce Clarke for his unwavering support of this work and for his willingness to share portions of his 'Posthuman Metamorphosis' manuscript with me during my initial stages; to Dr Sara Spurgeon for her invaluable suggestions; and to my colleagues Amanda Cooper, James Ola and Catherine Blackwell.

Part III
Psychoanalytical Readings

8
Katherine Mansfield's Uncanniness

Clare Hanson

> Who takes the trouble – or the joy – to make all these
> things that are wasted, wasted. . . . It was uncanny.[1]

This essay suggests that Katherine Mansfield's fiction, like that of her contemporary D. H. Lawrence, can productively be read in the light of and alongside Freud's 1919 essay 'The Uncanny'.[2] The uncanny is, by definition, resistant to definition, lying somewhere between a concept and a feeling, confounding attempts to distinguish between imagination and reality, self and other, the familiar and the strange. Its significance can be stretched so widely that it seems to encompass almost everything, as it does for example in Nicholas Royle's stimulating study, in which the uncanny is located in texts from the fourth century to the present and psychoanalysis itself is read as but one manifestation of it.[3] Freud certainly struggled to confine or tame what he had unleashed in his essay, which is of all his texts the one in which, as Robert Young points out, 'he most thoroughly finds himself caught up in the very processes he seeks to comprehend'.[4] Yet, despite its elusive character, it is possible to historicize and contextualize the cultural preoccupation with the uncanny which marked the years immediately following the First World War. Freud alludes to this context at several points in his essay, noting at the beginning that he has been unable to undertake 'a thorough survey of the literature' before writing his paper for reasons that are 'inherent in the times we live in' (124). The reference to wartime disruption and intellectual isolation is amplified when he writes of coming on a copy of the *Strand Magazine* 'during the isolation of the Great War'; here, among a number of 'fairly pointless contributions', he finds a story about the (apparent) invasion of a house in the London suburbs by a crocodile from New Guinea. It is not difficult to link his perception of the 'extraordinarily uncanny' nature of this story with the contemporary chaos in Europe and the destabilization caused by the movement of troops across the globe.[5] Moreover, towards the end of the essay Freud goes on to make a direct link between uncanniness and the aftershocks of war, writing of the contemporary preoccupation with the souls of the dead and of the '[p]lacards in our big cities [which] advertise lectures that are meant to instruct us in how to make contact with the souls of the departed' (148–9). As Hugh Haughton points out, this reminds us that

> although Freud's essay is not a contribution to the post-war vogue for the psychic, it is indirectly a commentary on it. For the uncanny is not only about the souls of the departed, but the departed, or departing, idea of souls, something that haunted all of Europe in these years.[6]

This was also the context in which Mansfield's major stories were written, from 'Prelude', first drafted early in 1915, to 'Bliss' and 'Je ne parle pas français', written in February 1918 in France before the Armistice, to 'At the Bay', 'The Garden Party' and 'The Fly', written in late 1921 and early 1922. Mansfield was directly affected by the war in a number of ways. Her brother died in a training accident in 1915 and her friends Frederick Goodyear, Rupert Brooke and Henri Gaudier-Brzeska were all killed in the war. She experienced first-hand conditions in France in early 1915, when she visited Francis Carco in the Allied war zone, and in 1918, on her way back from a winter spent in the south of France, she was trapped for three weeks in Paris while it was under bombardment. Although the impact of the war on Mansfield has been considered by several previous critics (and in C. K. Stead's novel *Mansfield*), what I want to pursue here is the particular thread in her work which links her with Freud, for both explore what Haughton calls a post-war 'psychic underworld' to conjure up 'a Gothic closet, an uncanny double, at the heart of modernity'.[7]

When 'The Uncanny' was written in 1919, Freud was also working on 'Beyond the Pleasure Principle' and the two essays are intimately linked. Famously, for Freud the uncanny (*das Unheimlich*) is something which is ghostly and alienating, but the effect of strangeness is produced by the mechanism of repression so that, as he writes, 'this uncanny element is actually nothing new or strange, but something that was long familiar to the psyche and was estranged from it only through being repressed' (148). Drawing attention to the double meaning of *heimlich* as that which is familiar and that which is concealed, Freud suggests that the uncanny is also something that was 'intended to remain secret, hidden away, and has come into the open', and that uncanny effects are produced 'either when repressed childhood complexes are revived by some impression, or when primitive beliefs that have been *surmounted* appear to be once again confirmed' (155, his emphasis). The main part of the essay is devoted to a discussion of the uncanny effects brought about by the revival of repressed complexes, in particular the Oedipus complex, which Freud explores in a virtuoso analysis of E. T. A. Hoffmann's story 'The Sandman'. For my purposes, however, his discussion of the revival of childhood beliefs is more significant. In relation to this theme, Freud returns to his theory that the development of childhood recapitulates the history of the species (ontogeny recapitulates phylogeny). Accordingly, the return of the primitive carries a doubly uncanny charge, as phenomena such as animistic thinking revive archaic structures at the level of both the individual and the species.

Freud singles out a number of tropes which reflect and release this double uncanniness. One is the automaton, the example Freud gives being that of Olimpia, the living doll in 'The Sandman'.[8] Such animistic fantasies have their origins in the sphere of infantile needs and wishes and in the 'primordial narcissism that dominates the mental life of both the child and primitive man' (142). Freud further pursues the question of childhood narcissism in relation to the image of the double, arguing that in primitive stages of life the fantasy of the double can act as a defence against death, but that once this phase has been surmounted 'the meaning of the "double" changes: having once been an assurance of immortality, it becomes the uncanny harbinger of death' (142). The double becomes an object of terror because it both reactivates archaic fantasies *and* recalls the later splitting of the ego and those repressed aspects of the self which had to be discarded because they were 'objectionable to self-criticism'. Freud then goes on to discuss the trope of unintended repetition, which represents for him a compulsion to repeat which is 'strong enough to override the pleasure principle' (145), before offering a brief discussion of a topic which itself seems to have been subject to some repression, as it is that with which, he acknowledges, he should have begun. It is the 'most potent' example of the uncanny, 'to many people the acme of the uncanny', and it is 'anything to do with death, dead bodies, revenants, spirits and ghosts' (148).

Freud develops the connection between the uncanny and 'things to do with death' in 'Beyond the Pleasure Principle', at the heart of which is the contention that the compulsion to repeat frequently involves the repetition of 'experiences which include no possibility of pleasure, and which can never, even long ago, have brought satisfaction even to instinctual impulses'.[9] Freud bases this claim on his analysis of the dreams of patients with traumatic neurosis and shell-shock, which were marked by an obscure, almost 'daemonic' compulsion to repeat the initial trauma. It is this drive towards the repetition of pain which leads Freud to suggest that *'an instinct is an urge inherent in organic life to restore an earlier state of things'* (308, his emphasis). Challenging the commonsense view of life as intrinsically creative and oriented towards the future, Freud argues that:

> It would be in contradiction to the conservative nature of the instincts if the goal of life were a state of things which had never yet been attained. On the contrary, it must be an *old* state of things, an initial state from which the living entity has at one time or other departed [...]. If [...] everything living dies for *internal* reasons [...] then we shall be compelled to say that *'the aim of all life is death'*. (310–11, his emphasis)

All organisms move with a 'vacillating rhythm', alternating between the pleasure principle, associated with creativity, sexual connection, reproduction and self-preservation, and the death drive, associated with repetition, aggression, compulsion and self-destruction. However, Freud's view is not straightforwardly dualistic, because in considering the mutual imbrication of the pleasure principle and the death drive he concludes that the latter has primacy over the former and that all drives, including the erotic, are ultimately subordinated to it. One of Mansfield's best-known statements on writing takes on a new and more sombre resonance when it is read in the light of this argument:

> Ive two 'kick offs' in the writing game. *One* is joy – real joy – the thing that made me write when we lived at Pauline, and that sort of writing I could only do in just that state of being in some perfectly blissful way *at peace*. Then something delicate and lovely seems to open before my eyes, like a flower without thought of a frost or a cold breath – knowing that all about it is warm and tender and 'steady'. And *that* I try, ever so humbly, to express.
>
>   The other 'kick off' is my old original one, and (had I not known love) it would have been my all. Not hate or destruction (both are beneath contempt as real motives) but an *extremely* deep sense of hopelessness – of everything doomed to disaster – almost wilfully, stupidly – like the almond tree and 'pas de nougat pour le noël' – There! as I took out a cigarette paper I got it exactly – *a cry against corruption*

that is *absolutely* the nail on the head. Not a protest – a *cry*, and I mean corruption in the widest sense of the word, of course –[10]

Mansfield here links joy conventionally enough with generation, with a flower unfolding ready to bear fruit. However, like Freud she also presents the experience of pleasure as always already inhabited by death: in this passage, the flower which opens in the first paragraph does not bear fruit in the second and the experience of 'peace' is destroyed by the 'wilful' and 'stupid' human urge to destruction. The connection between Mansfield's 'cry against corruption' and her perception of the horror of the war is implicit in the use of the word 'corruption', with its suggestion of fleshly as well as moral decay, and is made explicit when she goes on in the same letter to write that the war is 'never out of my mind & everything is poisoned by it. […] Its at the root of my homesickness & anxiety & panic.'[11]

When Mansfield writes of homesickness it is not easy to determine exactly where 'home' might be. Home is a shifting and unstable space which is rendered problematic by Mansfield's multiple cultural identities. As Bridget Orr points out, Mansfield's 'original' New Zealand identity was itself hybrid and conflicted: in the context of the white settler society of her childhood, Mansfield was ambivalently located somewhere between the 'imperial subject and the colonised other'.[12] Mansfield's identity as a colonial subject in Europe ('the little colonial walking in the London garden patch')[13] was similarly complicated, marked by shifting modalities of affiliation and estrangement from 'New Zealand' and 'English' identities. In the sense of national identity, home is thus *unheimlich* from the beginning in Mansfield's writing, undone by a colonial context in which its 'made-up' quality is foregrounded and it is disclosed as a copy without an original. But if home in this wider sense is *unheimlich*, so too is home in the familiar/familial sense.[14] Indeed, in this respect Mansfield's work seems particularly close to Freud's thinking about the uncanny. Freud locates the hidden forces which shape our individual and collective lives in the experiences of childhood, and seeks answers to such fundamental questions as 'why war?' in the desires and fears of early life: similarly, it is in representations of childhood and of domestic space that Mansfield evokes the uncanniness of both life and death.

*****

To return to Freud's instances of the uncanny, he chooses not to say a great deal about animism or automata, beyond making the point that their uncanniness derives from their connection with early stages in life; he also links animistic thinking with an 'excessive stress on psychical reality' (151). However, in Mansfield's fiction, the tropes of animism and the doll appear frequently, and to disturbing effect. For example, in the morning scene in 'Prelude', as Linda lies in bed, she feels that medicine bottles and bits and pieces of furniture are coming alive, turning into 'a row of little men with brown top-hats' or 'dancers with priests attending'. The inanimate world seems to 'swell out with some mysterious and important content', while, conversely, life drains out of her. Linda freezes and becomes inert: she 'could not lift a finger, could not even turn her eyes to left or right because THEY were there' (27). Linda's perception of the powerful life of things is associated with childhood because it is shared with her daughter; it is also linked with the fragmentation threatened by the mirror image (she always turns her head away as she passes the mirror). Yet something more, and other, is being staged in this encounter between Linda and the inanimate world: 'What Linda always felt was that THEY wanted something of her, and she knew that if she gave herself up and was quiet, *more than quiet, silent, motionless*, something would really happen' (28, my emphasis). Linda here fantasizes about a self-annihilation which would allow her to approach the impossible boundary between inside and outside, life and death. She is described as 'floating' in her bed 'scarcely breathing' (28) and in the terms of Freud's analysis in 'Beyond the Pleasure Principle' it could be argued that what is being staged here is a primary masochism linked with the desire to return once more to the inorganic.

Mansfield broaches similar issues in 'Miss Brill', which is, however, a darker, even a sinister, text. In it, the confusion between the animate and inanimate turns on Miss Brill's fantasy that the fur necklet which she brings out to wear each winter is a sweet little animal, both pet and projection of the self. Although she endows it with life, from the outset of the story an awareness of its lifelessness and imminent decay is forced on the reader and flickers on the margins of Miss Brill's consciousness:

> Dear little thing! It was nice to feel it again. She had taken it out of its box that afternoon, shaken out the moth-powder, given it a good brush, and rubbed the life back into the dim little eyes. 'What has been happening to me?' said the sad little eyes. Oh, how sweet it was to see them snap at her again from the red eiderdown! . . . But the nose, which was of some black composition, wasn't at all firm. It must have had a knock, somehow. Never mind – a little dab of black sealing-wax when the time came – when it was absolutely necessary. . . . Little rogue! (331)

Miss Brill's illusions about the value of her life are destroyed by the cruel remarks of two lovers: she goes home and puts the fur back in its box, but as she puts the lid on 'she thought she heard something crying' (336). Miss Brill has in effect buried the fur alive, and in one sense this is simply a reflection of her own state, as her home is coffin-like, no bigger than a cupboard. More harrowingly, however, the text suggests that this 'burial' may also offer a release for more obscure and painful feelings, for an impulse towards self-destruction (analogous to that of Linda in 'Prelude') is displaced onto an external object in the fantasy of killing the 'dear little thing'.[15]

The motif of the doll opens up similar aspects of experience. Reworking Freud's account of the *fort/da* game in 'Beyond the Pleasure Principle', D. W. Winnicott includes dolls among those 'transitional objects' which enable the child to overcome separation from the mother.[16] Such a separation is essential yet must involve the recognition at some point that the transitional object is indeed an object which cannot respond to the child's wishes and desires. It is in such a moment that we understand for the first time that the external world is indifferent to human need. Dolls and other toys which are supposed to support the child's identity thereby become, in Eva-Maria Simm's words, symbols of the 'silence and emptiness at the heart of our existence'.[17] Such feelings of 'futility and helplessness' are reactivated in one of Mansfield's most famous stories, 'The Doll's House'. In the opening description Mansfield foregrounds the fact that while the house itself, with its 'solid little chimneys' and 'real windows', is entirely realistic, or lifelike, the dolls that inhabit it are life*less*: 'The father and mother dolls, who sprawled very stiff as though they had fainted in the drawing-room, and their two little children asleep upstairs, were really too big for the doll's house. They didn't look as though they belonged' (394).

The dolls are *unheimlich*, representing not only the lifelessness of the universe but the potential lifelessness of human beings (the dolls in Mansfield's account are 'stiff' and corpse-like). In the inner logic of the story, they are linked with Aunt Beryl, herself 'too big' to be living in her sister's family home and caught up in sexual adventures which have led to threats of blackmail and exposure. Under the pressure of her fears, Beryl takes shelter in the psychic structures of childhood, converting her own terror into a sadistic attack on the Kelveys, the children of the washerwoman whom Kezia has invited in to see the doll's house. As soon as she has done this, she experiences a feeling of intense relief which is almost sexual pleasure: 'But now that she had frightened those little rats of Kelveys and given Kezia a good scolding, her heart felt lighter. That ghastly pressure was gone. She went back to the house humming' (401).

The relief is only temporary, however, as Beryl is caught up in the 'vacillating rhythm' described by Freud in which the 'true life instincts' are inextricably intertwined with the drive towards death.[18]

Mansfield frequently invokes exchanges with the inanimate world in which the boundaries between inside and outside, subject and object, are called into question, and the trope of the double creates similar instabilities. As we have seen, Freud associates the double with the return of repressed aspects of the self – either aspects of the self that have been rejected by the ego or more primitive selves constructed in childhood. He also associates the double with self-alienation, giving as an example an incident when he was travelling on a train and the toilet door of his compartment fell open: he was unable to identify himself as the befuddled elderly gentleman in a nightcap who appeared to be coming towards him in the mirror. In his rereading of 'The Uncanny' Mladen Dolar elaborates on this aspect of Freud's account to suggest that such alienating encounters represent a restaging of the *méconnaissance* of the Lacanian mirror stage, for in the gap between 'self' and image we are reminded of the fragile, indeed phantasmatic, nature of identity. Through (mis)recognizing ourselves in the mirror stage we acquire our imaginary identity, but at the cost of losing the immediate coincidence of self and being which Lacan calls the unsymbolizable 'object *a*'.[19] For Dolar, the uncanniness of the double derives precisely from the fact that it represents 'that mirror image in which the object *a* is included', in other words, it represents an undivided world, a world in which the imaginary coincides with the real. This coincidence shatters the distinctions which structure 'commonly accepted reality', creating a vertiginous anxiety.[20] Dolar invokes Lacan's concept of the extimate (*l'extimté*) to explain this collapsing of the boundaries between interior and exterior, writing that:

> [Extimacy] points neither to the interior nor to the exterior, but is located there where the most intimate interiority coincides with the exterior and becomes threatening, provoking horror and anxiety. The extimate is simultaneously the intimate kernel and the foreign body; in a word, it is *unheimlich*.

It has become a cliché to remark on Mansfield's belief in the multiplicity of the self, usually by making reference to the well-known notebook entry of 1920 in which she wrote of her 'hundreds of selves [...] what with complexes and suppressions, and reactions and vibrations and reflections – there are moments when I feel I am nothing but the small clerk of some hotel without a proprietor'.[21] Yet this, which has come to seem an emblematically modernist account of the self, does not quite capture the deeper doubleness – and uncanniness – of Mansfield's writing. Such doubleness which undoes the very logic of identity is at the heart of 'The Daughters of the Late Colonel', a story threaded through with uncanny motifs, including animism ('she [...] slapped down a white, terrified blancmange' [265]) and burial alive ('"Buried. You two girls had me *buried!*" She heard his stick thumping' [268–9]). Con and Jug's exploitative male relations are doubles in a social sense, inter-changeable in terms of their role, a fact emphasized in the image of a relay whereby the colonel's watch is transmitted down across the generations. More damaging is the emotional identification between the two sisters, which has undermined their identity to the extent that when a lover leaves a note they cannot establish which of them it is for. Pondering the question of identity, Con wonders if it would have been different if their mother had lived, and at this point Mansfield introduces the enigmatic image (so to speak) of the photograph:

> When it came to mother's photograph, the enlargement over the piano, [the sunlight] lingered as though puzzled to find so little remained of mother, except the ear-rings shaped like tiny pagodas and a black feather boa. Why did the photographs of dead people always fade so? wondered Josephine. As soon as a person was dead their photograph died too. But, of course, this one of mother was very old. It was thirty-five years old. (282–3)

In his analysis of the distinctive aesthetic effects of the photograph, Roland Barthes links it with two aspects of the uncanny. First, in an arresting account of the experience of being photographed, Barthes suggests that the photograph is 'spectral' because it both symbolizes and participates in the conversion of the subject into an object:

> [the photograph] represents that very subtle moment when, to tell the truth, I am neither subject nor object but a subject who feels he is becoming an object: I then experience a micro-version of death (of parenthesis): I am truly becoming a specter.[22]

In this sense, he argues, the photograph anticipates death and the return of the living subject to the inorganic world and offers an exemplary instance of the double as, in Freud's phrase, 'the harbinger of death' (142). At the same time, Barthes suggests that the photograph conveys, or embodies, something of the real because it collapses the distinction between signifier and referent. In the photograph, image and referent are, he writes, like a laminated object 'whose two leaves cannot be separated without destroying them both'. In its mute facticity, the photograph is thus uninterpretable, outside culture. It is: 'the absolute Particular, the sovereign Contingency, matte and somehow stupid, the *This* (this photograph and not Photography), in short, what Lacan calls the *Tuché*, the Occasion, the Encounter, the Real' (4). Barthes's account elucidates much of the haunting quality associated with the photograph in 'The Daughters of the Late Colonel' (and in many other stories by Mansfield). On the one hand, the photograph alludes to the way in which the girls' mother has been objectified by the 'late Colonel'; on the other, in detailing the 'puzzling' objects which survive her (ear-rings and feather boa), Mansfield invokes what Barthes terms the 'evidential force' of the photograph, its power to 'fill the sight by force', to overwhelm the onlooker with its record of the 'real encounters' of our existence (88–91).

Mansfield also writes a good deal about dead bodies, Freud's final 'instance' of the uncanny and one in relation to which, he argues, our thinking and feeling have changed little since primitive times, as 'our unconscious is still as unreceptive as ever to the idea of our own mortality' (148). This is a point he also makes in his 1915 essay, 'Thoughts on War and Death', in which he suggests that because our own death is strictly unimaginable, 'whenever we make the attempt to imagine it, we can perceive that we really survive as spectators'.[23] In the same essay, adverting to the theme of the primitive nature of our relation towards death, he emphasizes the ambivalence provoked by the corpse, which at some point in prehistory came to signify not just the death of another but the death of the self: 'when primitive man saw someone who belonged to him die [...] [t]hen, in his pain, he had to learn that one can indeed die oneself' (309). It is for this reason, Freud writes – in the midst of the First World War – that the corpse of a loved one, as well as that of an enemy, can be perceived as that of a stranger. Freud's analysis is particularly helpful for thinking about the complex ways in which the bodies of the dead are represented in post-war texts. Images of dead young men haunt the literature of this period, for example that of Gerald Crich in *Women in Love*, 'cold, mute, material', or that of Phlebas in *The Waste Land*, his bones picked over by the sea swell.[24] Mansfield's 'The Garden Party' is as much concerned with the war as these other texts: it is replete with war imagery (staves, tents, flags) and the title resonates with a comment she made in a book review that the war was 'the greatest garden party of them all'.[25] However, what distinguishes 'The Garden Party' is that in it death comes right into the home, specifically that of a young carter who has died in an industrial accident (his horse has shied at a traction engine, an emblem of industrial progress). His home is 'wretched', ill-lit, box-like, so small that once she is 'shut in the passage' there is nowhere for Laura to go, and nothing for her to see, but the widow and the dead man (260). Mansfield here dramatizes the traumatic intrusion of death into the space of the non-combatant who nonetheless, as Freud well understood, could suffer extreme mental distress in wartime. Here the trauma is deflected to some extent by Laura's self-protective adolescent imagination, as she converts the body of the dead man into a sleeping prince: 'He was wonderful, beautiful. While they were laughing and while the band was playing, this marvel had come to the lane' (261). Yet a sense of fear and unease is generated for the reader by the way in which Laura is drawn into viewing the body by Em's sister with her 'oily', 'sly' tones and her 'fond' packaging of the scene of death – ''e looks a picture. There's nothing to show. Come along, my dear' (261). There is a hint of necrophilia here, as though Em's sister is somehow taking pleasure in the death, rather than suffering from any form of what we would now call post-traumatic survivor guilt.

Mansfield takes up the complex questions of survival and guilt in a letter to Ottoline Morrell written at the time when preparations were being made to celebrate the Versailles Peace Treaty:

> When I read of the preparations that are being made in all the work-houses throughout the land – when I think of all these toothless old jaws guzzling for the day – and then of all that beautiful youth feed-ing the fields of France – Life is almost too ignoble to be borne.... I keep seeing all these horrors, bathing in them again & again (God knows I don't want to) and then my mind fills with the wretched little picture I have of my brother's grave.[26]

Arguably, Mansfield herself suffered from a degree of guilt in relation to the death of her brother in 1915. However, what she alludes to here and ruthlessly anatomizes in 'The Fly' is the obverse of such guilt, the disavowal and repression on which survival rests. As this would suggest, 'The Fly' is perhaps the most uncanny of Mansfield's stories and it is cer-tainly the one which engages most fully with the war. As in 'The Garden Party', the story dramatizes the incursion of death into the private sphere, here the 'snug', cosy office of a wealthy businessman ('the boss') which has recently been redecorated in sleek modernist style, with a 'bright red carpet with a pattern of large white rings' and electric heating ('five trans-parent, pearly sausages glowing so softly' [423]).[27] There is a discordant note in the scene, a photograph of the boss's son, 'a grave-looking boy in uniform standing in one of those spectral photographers' parks with photographers' storm-clouds behind him', but this uncanny image is something to which the boss does not draw attention. This well-ordered office space has its parallel in the war cemetery which the family of the boss's guest, old Mr Woodifield, has just been visiting. It too is wonderfully domesticated, 'beautifully looked after. [...] as neat as a garden' with 'nice broad paths' (424), which (almost) cover up its significance.

The motif of the double appears in this story in the relationship between the boss and Woodifield, and the boss and his son. In both cases, the boss seeks to deny the likeness between himself and the other man. He congratulates himself on his own energy whilst feeling extravagant pity for Woodifield (who is younger than him): 'Poor old chap, he's on his last pins, thought the boss' (423). In a more complex movement of feeling, he remembers his earlier pride in the son whom he thought of as just like himself, despite the fact that he now finds it hard to recognize him in his photograph: 'He decided to get up and have a look at the boy's photograph. But it wasn't a favourite photograph of his; the expression was unnatural. It was cold, even stern-looking. The boy had never looked like that' (426). The misrecognition stems from the fact that the son has become what Freud calls 'the enemy of the survivor' (159) and a harbinger of the boss's own dissolution. This is something he cannot afford to acknowledge, as Mansfield goes on to demonstrate in her dissection of the mechanism of repression. The boss sits down to concentrate on mourning his son, but is almost immediately distracted by a fly which has fallen into the inkpot (the ink constituting, perhaps, a self-referential allusion to the process of writing). He takes it out and then almost drowns it by deliberately dropping a heavy blob of ink on it, a process which is repeated twice before the fly finally dies. It seems that the boss has been seized by the compulsion to repeat which Freud links with the uncanny and which overrides the pleasure principle. Here the boss plays with death, keeps coming up to its frontier, re-enacting his son's death in ways which reflect his ambivalent feelings about it. He displaces his feelings about his son on to the fly, externalizing the conflict between identification with the victim ('He's a plucky little devil, thought the boss') and aggression ('there was something timid and weak about its efforts now' [427–8]). When the fly dies, he is seized by 'a grinding feeling of wretchedness', but after ringing the bell and asking for fresh blotting paper (a clean sheet) he has entirely forgotten 'what it was he had been thinking about before. [...] For the life of him he could not remember' (428). Repression and disavowal are complete.

In 'The Uncanny' and in other essays written during and just after the First World War, Freud argues that the edifice of civilization is founded on the repression of primal aggressive instincts. War is prompted by and allows for the release of such instincts and thus reveals, to some extent, that which had previously been hidden: it is in this sense that war itself can be said to be uncanny. Freud also suggests, however, that the unprecedented scale of death in the First World War had changed the relationship of humanity to death. Tom McCall summarizes Freud's argument in this way:

> Compared to their ancient counterparts, the relatively protected people of modern society had been in general less exposed to death, except during time of war and 'acts of God.' In World War 1, death became a weapon for timed delivery in paper bombs (newspapers, war reports, propaganda) aimed at non-combatant civilians who thus became a captive audience. It became less possible to deny death.[28]

Mansfield's fiction reflects a similar sense of an unsettling of the human relationship towards death. Not only had it become 'less possible to deny death', but it had become more difficult to disavow the complex, powerfully destructive instincts of human beings which could be directed not only towards others but also towards the self. Mansfield captures exactly this (uncanny) understanding in a letter to John Middleton Murry of November 1917. She is commenting on the failure of contemporary writers to 'face' the war:

> I cant imagine how after the war these men can pick up the old threads as tho' it never had been. Speaking to *you* Id say we have died and live again. How can that be the same life? It doesn't mean that Life is the less precious of [sic] that the 'common things of night and day' are gone. They are not gone, they are intensified, they are illumined. *Now we know ourselves for what we are. In a way its a tragic knowledge*. Its as though, even while we live again we face death. But *through Life*: thats the point. We see death in life as we see death in a flower that is fresh unfolded.[29]

There are several allusions to Wordsworth's 'Ode: Intimations of Immortality' in this letter but their overall effect is not to create a sense of continuity with the past but to sharpen the sense of an epistemological break between the Romantic period and the present. Mansfield calls not for the expression of a faith which sees 'through death', that is, beyond death, but invokes instead the ideal of a spectral, posthumous writing which would look back 'through life' to disclose that which, according to Freud, we have always already known ('the initial state from which the living entity has at one time or other departed and to which it is striving to return').[30] Reading Mansfield's writing through Lacan, who recast the Freudian death drive to link it with symbolic rather than organic death, it could alternatively be argued that Mansfield's writing inhabits what Lacan called the liminal 'space between two deaths' (symbolic death and natural death).[31] From either perspective, Mansfield's uncanniness can be understood as expressing what Dolar calls the *'specific dimension of the uncanny that emerges with modernity'* (his emphasis); still more specifically, that dimension of the uncanny associated with the social and historical rupture of the First World War.[32]

Notes

1. K. Mansfield (1945) *Collected Stories of Katherine Mansfield* (London: Constable), p. 221. All subsequent references are incorporated into the text.
2. S. Freud (2003 [1919]) *The Uncanny*, D. McLintock (trans.), H. Haughton (intro.) (London: Penguin), p. 124. All subsequent references are incorporated into the text.
3. See N. Royle (2003) *The Uncanny* (Manchester University Press). Royle links Freud's 'The Uncanny' and Mansfield's fiction in his *Telepathy and Literature: Essays on the Reading Mind* (Oxford: Blackwell, 1990); see also A. Bennett (2004) *Katherine Mansfield* (London: Northcote House) and A. Smith (1999) *Katherine Mansfield and Virginia Woolf: A Public of Two* (Oxford University Press).
4. Quoted in Royle, p. 8.
5. It is also relevant to note that Freud's homeland, Austria, was under pressure at this time and was compelled to give up the South Tyrol.
6. H. Haughton, 'Introduction' to *The Uncanny*, p. liii.
7. *Ibid.*, p. xlii.
8. The limitations of Freud's analysis of Olimpia have been discussed by Hélène Cixous and Sarah Kofman. For Cixous, what Freud fails to see in the figure of Olimpia is androgyny, or queerness; Kofman reads Olimpia in relation to male narcissism. See H. Cixous (1976) 'Fiction and its Phantoms: A Reading of Freud's *Das Unheimliche* (The "Uncanny")', R. Dennomé (trans.), *New Literary History*, 7: 3 (Spring), 525–48; S. Kofman (1991) *Freud and Fiction*, S. Wykes (trans.), (Cambridge: Polity Press), pp. 119–62.
9. S. Freud (1987 [1919]) 'Beyond the Pleasure Principle', J. Strachey (trans.), Pelican Freud Library, 11 (Harmondsworth: Penguin), p. 291. Subsequent references are incorporated into the text.
10. *Letters* 2, p. 54. Letter of 3 February 1918, Mansfield's emphasis.
11. *Ibid.*
12. B. Orr (1993) 'Reading with the Taint of the Pioneer: Katherine Mansfield and Settler Criticism', in R. B. Nathan (ed.) *Critical Essays on Katherine Mansfield* (New York: G. K. Hall), p. 53.

13. *Notebooks* 2, p. 166.
14. For a detailed discussion of the relationship between 'foreignness' and the Freudian uncanny see J. Kristeva (1991) *Strangers to Ourselves*, L. S. Roudiez (trans.), (New York and Chichester: Columbia University Press, 1991).
15. Such uncanny exchanges between the animate and inanimate are frequent in Mansfield's fiction, often associated with the experience of claustrophobic confinement. See, for example, this passage from 'The Wind Blows': 'It's frightening to be here in her room by herself. The bed, the mirror, the white jug and basin gleam like the sky outside. It's the bed that is frightening. There it lies, sound asleep. . . . Does Mother imagine for one moment that she is going to darn all those stockings knotted up on the quilt like a coil of snakes?' (109).
16. See D. W. Winnicott (1965) *The Family and Individual Development* (Harmondsworth: Penguin).
17. E.-M. Simms (1996) 'Uncanny Dolls: Images of Death in Rilke and Freud', *New Literary History*, 27: 4, 673.
18. The image of the doll recurs in 'Bliss' when Bertha's baby is compared to a doll, and more sinisterly in 'Revelations' as the protagonist pictures the dead child of her hairdresser: 'And all the way there she saw nothing but a tiny wax doll with a feather of gold hair, lying meek, its tiny hands and feet crossed' (196).
19. For an extended discussion of this concept see J. Lacan (1998) *The Four Fundamental Concepts of Psychoanalysis*, A. Sheridan (trans.), (New York: Norton, 1998).
20. M. Dolar (1991) '"I Shall Be with You on your Wedding-Night": Lacan and the Uncanny', *October*, 58 (Autumn), 6.
21. *Notebooks* 2, p. 204.
22. R. Barthes (1984) *Camera Lucida* (London: Flamingo), pp. 13–14. Subsequent references are incorporated into the text.
23. S. Freud (1950) 'Thoughts on War and Death', *Collected Papers*, vol. iv (London: The Hogarth Press and the Institute of Psychoanalysis), p. 305. Subsequent references are incorporated into the text.
24. See D. H. Lawrence (1969 [1921]) *Women in Love* (Harmondsworth: Penguin), p. 539 and T. S. Eliot (1974 [1963]) 'The Waste Land', IV, 15–16 in *Collected Poems 1909–1962* (London: Faber), p. 75.
25. In an acerbic review of W. B. Maxwell's *A Man and His Lesson*, first published in the *Athenaeum* on 26 September 1919, Mansfield describes the main character going off to war in this way: 'Off he goes to be honourably killed. Off he goes to the greatest of all garden parties.' See J. M. Murry (ed.) (1930) *Katherine Mansfield: Novels and Novelists* (New York: Alfred Knopf), p. 84.
26. *Letters* 2, p. 339.
27. Beneath the appearance of order, however, the metaphor of the 'five transparent, pearly sausages' invokes the burning flesh of the battlefield. There may also be a subliminal reference to the death of Mansfield's brother: the five fingers of his hand were 'blown to bits' in the training incident in which he died, when he was demonstrating how to throw a hand grenade. See A. Alpers (1980) *The Life of Katherine Mansfield* (London: Jonathan Cape), p. 183.
28. T. McCall (2006) 'Society – "A Gang of Murderers": Freud on Hostility and War', *Common Knowledge*, 12: 2, 262.

29. *Letters* 3, p. 97, my emphasis. There are several references to Wordsworth's poem in this letter. In this passage Mansfield converts the line 'And fade into the light of common day' into the 'common things of light and day'.
30. Freud, 'Beyond the Pleasure Principle', p. 310.
31. There is a striking parallel between Mansfield's description of spectral writing here and Lacan's description of Antigone in his *Ethics of Psychoanalysis*. Lacan writes of Antigone that she understands that 'life can only be approached, can only be lived or thought about, from the place of that limit where her life is already lost [...]. But from that place she can see it and live it in the form of something already lost.' See (1992) *The Seminar of Jacques Lacan, Book V11: The Ethics of Psychoanalysis 1959–1960*, D. Porter (trans.), (New York: Norton), p. 280. Antigone is excluded from the symbolic order by Creon and while she is buried alive is in Lacan's terms suspended between symbolic death and natural death.
32. Dolar, p. 7.

9

A Trickle of Voice: Katherine Mansfield and the Modernist Moment of Being

Josiane Paccaud-Huguet

As she was writing 'Prelude' in 1916, Katherine Mansfield spoke thus in her journal to her younger brother Leslie who had been recently killed in the war:

> Oh, I want for one moment to make our undiscovered country leap into the eyes of the Old World. It must be mysterious, as though floating. It must take the breath. [...] all must be told with a sense of mystery, a radiance, an afterglow because you, my little sun of it, are set. You have dropped over the dazzling brim of the world.[1]

The 'undiscovered country' here primarily refers to the pristine, radiant world of New Zealand; yet we cannot miss the echo of the 'undiscovered country from whose bourn no traveller returns' (*Hamlet*, III, i, 79–80), a literary topos for the Lacanian register of the Real as distinct from the Symbolic reality we live in.[2] It is in this realm beyond 'the dazzling brim of the world' that lies Mansfield's little *sun/son*, the irretrievable object to whom her writing is addressed: now she means to write a long elegy to him in a new poetic medium, a kind of 'special prose',[3] which is 'a hidden country still' to her.[4]

Like her fellow writer D. H. Lawrence, she often claimed her own passion for the real being of things – for the very 'duckness' of the duck,[5] for the 'seagull hovering at the stern'.[6] The natural world she depicts includes countless images of life swelling with a pure energetic drive, at times, however, permeated with uncanny malevolence: in 'Prelude', Linda Burnell always feels that there is an IT about the house. Things – a poppy in the wallpaper, a bird in the grass – seem to have a habit of listening and swelling 'with some mysterious important content' and to smile at her with their 'sly secret smile',[7] as if there were something vaguely threatening about the real thing beyond the thin veil of social semblances.

The Great War had indeed brought a radical change: 'We see death in life as we see death in a flower that is freshly unfolded,' writes Mansfield, who declares that she sees life now as 'darkly illumined' by this knowledge.[8] As argued by Pamela Dunbar, it would certainly be misleading to separate the lyrical from the radically subversive Mansfield who always takes us to the brim of the world we know, especially where gender issues are concerned.[9] She was not a mystic, but like Virginia Woolf she often refers in her non-fictional writings to a kind of secular mysticism, as in this dream where she feels her whole body breaking up:

> It broke up with a violent shock – an earthquake – and it broke like glass. A long terrible shiver [...] and the spinal cord and the bones and every bit and particle quaking. It sounded in my ears – a low, confused din, and there was a sense of flashing greenish brilliance, like broken glass.[10]

In order to render such borderline experiences of fragmentation involving a mode of *jouissance féminine* (feminine sensual pleasure) beyond the sex-gender system – such as that conceptualized by Jacques Lacan precisely in relation to the mystics[11] – 'new expressions new moulds for our new thoughts & feelings' will be needed.[12]

My argument is that the lyrical and the radical can be brought together if we pay attention to a certain economy of the voice beyond the personal/ impersonal polarities of social psychology: more precisely, of voice as *object*, that is, detached from subject and, as such, the privileged unconscious vehicle for affect and percept.[13]

What does a woman want?

Mansfield often confessed to some 'secret disruption' within,[14] a sense that what 'might be so divine is out of tune':

> There *is* no concert for us. Isn't there? Is it all over? Is our desire and longing and eagerness – quite all that's left? [...]
> Heavens! The hysterical joy with which Id greet the first faint squeakings of a tuning up – [...]. But no – I don't hear a sound –.[15]

'Is our desire [...] all that's left?' That is the question! It concerns desire in and for itself, the desire to desire or not to desire. Even though

Mansfield was wary of cheap psychoanalysis, she also credited Freud with a 'subconscious wisdom' which the artist cannot ignore.[16] The suspended form and metaphorical density of her stories make it clear that conscious psychological development is not really her point. In 'Psychology' one of the characters asks (and analyses) thus:

> 'How sure are you that psychology *qua* psychology has got anything to do with literature at all?
>
> [...] this generation is just wise enough to know that it is sick and to realise that its only chance of recovery is by going into its symptoms – making an exhaustive study of them – tracking them down – trying to get at the root of the trouble'. (159)

In order to get 'at the root', what is *radically* wanted is less a literature of fantasy than of the symptom, that which lies beneath the fantasy.[17] But what is a symptom? An enigmatic event or action that keeps repeating itself in our lives, 'a knot of enjoyment so resistant to the symbolic as to frustrate absolutely the attempt to interpret it'.[18] In this sense our symptoms are the most real thing about us, and they can have two faces according to what happens to the libidinal energy locked in them: either paralysis – like the Irish people's 'hemiplegia of the will' for Joyce[19] – or the creative use possibly derived from our intimate mode of enjoyment. When handled with care, the symptom may even become what Lacan has called *sinthom*,[20] a language formation loaded with affective intensities which is the result of a process of transfer: going into our symptoms means for Mansfield, among other things, that 'we must be sure of finding these central points of significance transferred to the endeavours and emotions of the human beings portrayed'.[21] It is less a matter of fear and disdain of the body than of acknowledging the subconscious wisdom, the aim of art being to tear the percept and the affect from individual perceptions and emotions, to extract 'un pur être de sensation' (a pure being of sensation) – in other words, to give body to the real of enjoyment.[22]

As to the prevailing symptomatic constellation in Mansfield's stories, it is of course hysteria which brings forth the question of 'woman' as not being duped by the scenarios explaining gender divisions. The hysterical subject, Sarah Kay explains, is 'preoccupied by her lack of some inner substance, and thus condemned to theatricality', she knows that 'there is no such thing as one's inner treasure, except as the object of one's desire'.[23] 'Bliss' boldly focuses on this issue: 'Why be given a body', Bertha Young wonders, 'if you have to keep it shut up in a case like a rare, rare fiddle?' (145); one may note in passing the ambivalence of 'shut up'.

Bertha feels her bosom as 'that bright glowing place' which makes her look radiant, 'with an air of listening, waiting for something :... divine to happen' (145), and she wonders what to do with this blissful gift (153). In other stories, the inner treasure is more impregnated by the sense of corruption and consumption. Ma Parker's breast in the eponymous story is inhabited by the voice of her grandson whose 'little box of a chest' harboured 'a great lump of something bubbling' (234) which did not bring bliss but death, indicating the closeness between feminine *jouissance* and the experience of the Real as mere dissolution of the body.

Mansfield's going 'through the symptom of our age' is also eminently political, as shown by the generation of feminist critics of her work. Her plots tend to shift women from object to subject position, the satirical elements of the stories serving as the ground to expose their discontent and a means of dislodging patriarchal codes of representation.[24] Bertha finds civilization perfectly idiotic in 'Bliss' (145). In 'The Garden Party', the absurdity of class distinctions is unbearable to Laura (288). But the stories move to more radical questionings as to what a woman wants, they take us beyond the fantasies generated by desire and lack, to foreground the enigmatic, invariant knot of the symptom: in the case of hysteria, conversion phenomena (like swelling body parts), mood swings, and a discursive mode which enjoys putting its finger on some soft spot, on the *'little pit of darkness'* (278, my italics) at the core of semblances. That this should pertain to the feminine is due to the fact that the Imaginary provides no image for the female sex 'hidden' within the body, given as an absence – another hidden country.

From the point of view of the unconscious which has nothing to say about sexual difference, the scenario of castration elaborated in the face of the impossibility of representing the female sex is but a useful fiction. Neither the Œdipal myth nor the family romance, it seems, will provide satisfactory answers to the question of what a woman really wants – Freud himself came to this conclusion at the end of his life. From the Lacanian perspective, castration, rather, is a *symbolic* operation which has a mortifying effect on both male and female subjects *qua* beings of language: we lose our being, our 'pur être de sensation', because we are never completely contained by the signifier representing us when it is exchanged for another signifier. But civilization, which needs images and representations to support its binary oppositions, tends to transform a structural absence into something that *shows* – and that shows best through scenarios of cutting and severing bodily parts, as an explanation of what differentiates a 'she' from a 'he': Mansfield's stories gently discard the explanatory power of such scenarios, by suggesting another one. In 'Prelude', the beheading of a duck which makes the little boys scream with joy does not mean much to little Kezia. She has received no answer to her question as to the difference between a ram and a sheep, and, as if in protest, she just wants the head to be put back (84), as if the neck could be whole again.

Many of the stories' female characters appear as objects exposed to the unrestrained greed of parental figures, the neck being the phantasmatic organ of the 'uncastrated' mother figure. In 'At the Bay', the flesh of Mrs Stubbs's neck takes on nightmarish hues for Alice, the kitchen maid, who has come to tea in the witch's den with her *perishall* in hand: 'What a neck she had! It was bright pink where it began and then it changed to warm apricot, and that faded to the colour of a brown egg and then to a deep creamy' (269). Mrs Stubbs's *imaginary* phallus never seems to fall or fade, and the threat of devouring orality is never very far away in a rather comic scene in which she looks greedily at Alice's mosquito bites (267). In 'Psychology' there is an obvious identification of the unnamed 'she' with the cookies she has made. And to her male companion, the cookies are simply something to be devoured: '"That shocks you, doesn't it?", he asks. "To the bone"', she replies (157) quite appropriately.

There are several escape strategies from these anguishing scenarios, according to the stories and their protagonists, one of which consists in deliberate exclusion from the game of gender relations. Sexual trios with a female character in a position of desiring, as it were, another woman's desire, are quite common. Not surprisingly, the body part invested with erotic value will be the neck, neither cut off nor outrageously swollen, but bending towards a silent voice that one might hear with one's eyes. In 'Bliss',[25] Bertha feels drawn to Miss Fulton for the way she bends her neck as though she 'lived by listening rather than by seeing' (151). As she watches her husband propose a date to the other woman, she sees a confirmation of this supposed feminine essence in the moonbeam fingers and eyelids saying 'yes' silently. 'Bliss' is mostly about a woman's 'dissident' desire for a logic other than the *off with its head* illustrated by the episode of the duck: at 33, Bertha still likes to dance *on and off* the pavement, just as Kezia likes to play with Pat the handyman's 'feminine' ear-rings, asking if they come on and off (106). One of the functions of the Mansfieldian moment is to reject the logic of *imaginary* castration, and to provide temporarily, in a flash, a different scenario.

Three epiphanic modes

Transferred to the textual body, the swing of the *on and off* mood which seems so characteristic of the cast of female characters will provide the very beat, the rhythm structuring the moment of vision enclosed by many stories, at the point of contact with the Real of enjoyment, pulsing with ungendered life. In its challenge to the social edifice, the moment holds out against pre-symbolic substance, in both senses of *against* (*in opposition to*, and *leaning against*): it reveals that the Thing itself is nothing, a negativity against which any odd object is likely to shine in a sublime flicker. The mysterious treasure turns out to be thin air, it falls in a voice effect, the *dying fall* which Raoul Duquette enjoys in 'Je ne parle pas français' – 'that bit about the Virgin [...] it has such a "dying fall"' (124).[26] Hence the two related affects which are only apparently contradictory: bliss in the presence of the epiphanized object swelling with life when the plug is on, and then a sense of lack when it is off. If the structure fundamentally remains the same, the moment falls into three distinctive modes according to where and when the point of contact with the Real is situated.

The first mode is the 'arboreal epiphany' where the viewer confronts a figure of the maternal object which appears infinitely desirable. The natural world brimming with life is the ideal setting for 'hallucinating' such a resplendent feminine essence. In 'Prelude' the swelling plant floating on an island of grass overwhelms Kezia with its 'thick, grey-green, thorny leaves' out of which springs a 'tall stout stem' (96) – another figure of the imaginary maternal phallus that seems to endow symbolic reality with transcendental significance and purpose.[27] As Linda and her own beautiful mother later step out on the moonlit veranda, the aloe seems to invite them to escape from the servitudes of womanhood. Then the mirage fades in a fall, marked by 'the special voice that women use at night to each other as though they spoke in their sleep or from some hollow cave' (110), as if the mysterious voice were tickling the nearby void from within. It is worth noting that such identifications tending to a *jouissance* radically alien to gendered identity do not necessarily involve a female gazer. In 'The Escape' a tame husband confronts another spectral plenitude beyond an immense tree with 'a round, thick silver stem' (188). As if listening to the ecstatic silence with his eyes, he hears the gentle sound of a woman's voice floating towards him; a strange conversion phenomenon then takes place as something dark, unbearable, stirs and pushes forth in his own bosom, shaping itself into a great floating weed that nearly stifles him. And then, the thing is over: he sinks into the silence, 'staring at the tree and waiting for the voice that came floating, falling, until he felt himself enfolded' (188). In the arboreal epiphany, then, it is the sense of oceanic plenitude that stands out, beyond male or female sexual identity.

Our second type is the *blank epiphany* which marks out 'the point at which the symbolic is out of kilter with the seeming wholeness of the imaginary order':[28] a word, a phrase, betrays an inconsistency, a point of silence as to what 'woman' is in her mirror. The narrative voice in 'A Cup of Tea' warns us that there are horrible moments in life when the semblances we live by collapse, when we emerge from shelter and are forced to look out. Instead of giving way to them, it is wiser to go home and have a very nice tea, the voice continues,[29] or to buy some expensive enamel box in an antique shop, like Rosemary Fell who knows that she is not exactly beautiful – but who wonders if she is at least pretty. 'Pretty?' the voice replies, 'Well, if you took her to pieces. . . . But why be so cruel as to take anyone to pieces?'[30] Just as Rosemary steps out of the shop, a voice breathes to her in a sob, and she sees a starving young woman whom she takes home and feeds with tea. Suddenly, the little captive she has netted blooms into that pure feminine essence – a creature who with 'tangled hair, dark lips, deep, lighted eyes, lay back in the big chair in a kind of sweet languor'.[31] When Rosemary's husband notices how pretty their strange guest looks, Rosemary presses his head against her bosom and asks him if she is *'pretty'*.[32] The story remains suspended here, but the answer has been given us from the start – only if she were taken to pieces: the signifier *pretty* is inadequate to define Rosemary as a whole, the symbolic is helpless to define the essence of femininity which may briefly appear in a poor beggarly figure.

Our third type is the *dark epiphany* which lays bare a kind of vacuum that dangerously threatens to suck other objects – including humans – into its place. In 'Psychology', a pool of silence falls between the two friends, a poetic evocation of the dark side of the world where Mansfield's little sun/son has dropped:

> ... into this unfamiliar pool the head of the little boy sleeping his time-less sleep dropped – and the ripples flowed away, away – boundlessly far – into deep glittering darkness. [...] Again they were conscious of the boundless, questioning dark. Again, there they were – two hunters, bending over their fire, but hearing suddenly from the jungle beyond a shake of wind and a loud, questioning cry [...] two grinning pup-pets jigging away in nothingness. (158–9)

Such threshold moments are very close to the Conradian 'flash of insight' that brings Marlow to the edge of the horror in *Heart of Darkness* or *Lord Jim*. Elsewhere the horror can be contiguous with a certain auratic beauty that is the signature of the sublime. In 'The Garden Party', Laura and Laurie enjoy prowling in the dark amongst the workmen's cottages in order to get the shudder of the real thing, however sordid – very much like Gudrun and Ursula in D. H. Lawrence's *Women in Love*. At the end of the day, Laura in her party dress takes a basket of sandwiches to the working-class family of a young man who has just died in an accident that broke his *neck*. As she realizes what a mistake it was to expose herself to the people's stare, Laura meets in the dead young man's figure something radically different, something like a gaze without a subject: there is no apparent wound, nothing to show on the body but a radiant absence, and a Buddha-like gaze as if turned inside:

> His head was sunk in the pillow, his eyes were closed; they were blind under the closed eyelids. [...] He was wonderful, beautiful. While they were laughing and while the band was playing, this marvel had come to the lane. (298)

Laura then records the overwhelming experience to her brother in a disconnected string of words: '"It was simply marvellous. But, Laurie –" She stopped, she looked at her brother. "Isn't life," she stammered, "isn't life –" But what life was she couldn't explain. No matter. He quite understood' (298). Is there a link to be drawn between the plenitude of the subjectless gaze and the holes in the spoken chain? Surely: the *aposiopeses* here signal the conversion of the epiphany into what we might call *apophany* that produces a textual blank, a hollow for the impalpable object in the very act of representation.

As will have clearly appeared from this set of examples, and even if the modalities vary, the aim of the Mansfieldian moment is both to hold at bay and to communicate something of the *jouissance féminine* which does not fit into class or gender patterns: but how to communicate something that does not show?

'Not a protest – a cry'

Mansfield's women often seem, like Miss Fulton, to *crane* their necks for something invisible. 'The Voyage' revolves around the verbal associations condensed in the word *crane* which is the story's subconscious, poetic kernel: it denotes a contrivance to lift things, and a water bird often sitting on one leg – the common semantic element being *suspension* in mid-air, the unorthodox signifier of femininity – reminiscent of the incongruously lifted foot of Jensen's Gradiva who was analysed by Freud. Little Fenella, whose mother has just died, goes for a boat trip with her grandmother, Mrs Crane, who carries a mysterious travelling piece, a swan-*necked* umbrella. As the old woman says her prayers in the upper berth she has taken for the night, Fenella sees a single grey foot hanging over her and hears a soft whisper – 'as though someone was gently, gently rustling among tissue paper to find something' (283), as if only the material envelope of the words – the signifier, rather than the signified – reached her.

Why should Mansfield's women be predominantly related to signifiers, and more particularly to *letters*? A letter is not simply the written translation of a sound, it is also the the the graphic 'envelope' of the linguistic sign, the 'litter' of meaning – with a precious little something in surplus: letters can be illuminated, they can flicker with a life of their own, independently of significance: in other words they can be the recipients for the real of enjoyment beyond the phallic order. 'An Indiscreet Journey' is a story that questions what a woman wants when she is out of the shelter of sociosymbolic patterns. With the help of a false letter, the heroine who wants to visit her 'little corporal' trespasses into the war zone. The true object of desire and the true revelation, however, is less a matter of encounter between the sexes than of letters; it bears the name, beautiful to look at, of a French liquor, *mirabelle*. The story's little arboreal epiphany occurs at the Café des Amis with its low room lit with a hanging lamp, and the shadow of the *plume*-like trees waving in the moonshine outside; and then the glass of *mirabelle* – the fruit of the plum tree – is produced:

> The faces lifted, listening. 'How beautiful they are!' I thought. 'They are like a family party having supper in the New Testament. . . .'
> [...] 'Ah, at last!' The blue-eyed soldier's happy voice trickled through the dark. 'What do you think? Isn't it just as I said? Hasn't it got a taste of excellent – *ex-cellent* whiskey?' (74–5)

Although the heroine has met her 'little corporal', the real point of the story is the brief, enigmatic moment of communion that celebrates in a trickle of voice, another dying fall, the glory of the *mirabelle* (a word which evokes admiration and beauty and could translate into something like 'admire the beautiful one').

Mansfield's stories are like those surprise matchboxes whose lid Kezia likes to flick on and off for the sake of her grandmother's joy, to show the fragments of a flower artistically arranged. Little Kezia has an eye for collecting such pieces of litter: when she wanders into the old home she is leaving she notices a blob of cotton wool in a pill box found in her parents' room, the bits of red stuff sticking to the carpet tacks after the covering has been removed. In 'Her First Ball', Leila feels a pang at seeing her cousin pulling away wisps of tissue paper from the fastening of his gloves (236). The wisp, the blob, a thread of the thing itself, are the very little somethings with which truly poetic writing is concerned. Like the *'little language'* made from the scraps of bright wool left by the mother in the nursery which Bernard looks for in Virginia Woolf's *The Waves*,[33] they are the precious remainders stored in our forgetful memories, permeated with some secret enjoyment which trickles in, in the aftermath of the secular epiphany.

'At the Bay' is another type of borderline story, suspended between the lifting of the curtain and the voices ebbing back into silence. Its energizing matrix is the trope of suspension, including its playful cross-genderism particularly evident in characters like Mrs Harry Kember or the feminine Jonathan Trout, who instead of swimming vigorously enjoys letting himself float on the waves like a seaweed. The story has a one-two beat which, I would suggest, is the narrative analogue of the epiphany. At night some big fish may be seen 'flicking in at the window and then gone again' (250) – on and off. In the moment poised between sleep and wakefulness, the human and the non-human, there is no confusion, simply a 'not-yet', including for the linguistic moment captured before the word-symbol is torn from the real. Mansfield playfully uses children's speech to break syntactic boundaries, to displace letters in order to suggest the stage when the borderlines of words are still uncertain: '"A bee's not an animal. It's a ninseck", somebody shouts in the washhouse' (269). When little Pip holds up a piece of glass looking like an emerald found on the beach, the focalized child-narrator of this section asserts: 'Aunt Beryl had a nemeral in a ring' (258), a symptomatic syntactic overlap if we bear in mind that an emerald is a *beryl*, and that Beryl herself constantly doubts her symbolic identity.

If Mansfield's 'special prose' enjoys the pleasures of suspension and generic overlap, to her the writing process is a game involving an ambivalent *jouissance* which she calls her two 'kick offs':

> *One* is joy – real joy – [...] something delicate and lovely seems to open before my eyes, like a flower without thought of a frost or a cold breath [...]. The other 'kick off' is my old original one, and (had I not known love) it would have been my all. Not hate or destruction [...] but an *extremely* deep sense of hopelessness – of everything doomed to disaster [...] like the almond tree and 'pas de nougat pour le noël [...] *a cry against corruption* [...]. Not a protest – a *cry*, and I mean corruption in the widest sense of the word, of course –.[34]

What is the difference between a protest and a cry? While the former lays emphasis on the signified (a protest against law, etc.), the latter is grounded in the signifier's acoustic substance (a cry may be addressed to no-one, it may only be the expression of bodily joy, pain or anguish). We are often made to hear such 'noises' in Mansfield's stories, at the very point at which the Imaginary and the Symbolic fail, where a wisp of silent knowledge oozes from the nearby void, like the little crying noise from within Josephine's bosom in 'The Daughters of the Late Colonel' – '*Yeep – eyeep – yeep*. Ah, what was it crying, so weak and forlorn?' (228) or the sob from the fur box in 'Miss Brill': in both cases it is as if the affect were transferred into a sob without a subject.

The *something crying* in the *apophanic* aftermath is what sings for the invisible feminine essence: it persists and remains in the *seaweedy* form of stories like 'At the Bay'. On the beach the children find a rusty button hook, a squashed boot; on the summer verandas strings of dresses hang 'as though they'd just been rescued from the sea' (267). There is no question of mourning weeds here, however. The bodies are gone, yet the envelope speaks for them: it is the purpose of elegy to sing with no other reward but its own song. A world of differences separates Mansfield's humans preoccupied with rewards for gold watches – 'LOST! HANSOME GOLE BROOCH / [...] / REWARD OFFERED' (267) –, from Mrs Crane's embroidered letters kept in a frame over her bed in 'The Voyage': 'Lost! One Golden Hour / [...] / *No* Reward Is Offered / For It Is GONE FOR EVER!' (286).

But all is not lost. In a flash and a dash, Mansfield's very special prose radically displaces the issue of the feminine beyond socially distributed modes of enjoyment. Last but not least, it offers a whisper from the primordial silence, a shred of voice in the place of the irretrievable object whose loss is the result of our entry in the world of language.

Notes

1. J. M. Murry (1954) *Journal of Katherine Mansfield 1904–1922*, Definitive Edition (London: Constable), p. 94.
2. In Jacques Lacan's conceptual trilogy Real/Symbolic/Imaginary, the Real designates the shapeless and nameless substance in which we are bathed before our entry into the world of symbolic relations. The Real, therefore, is the realm of pure speechless being which we have to abandon from the moment when we are given a place in language. In this sense it is distinct from the Imaginary (the world of binary oppositions which structure the reality we live in) and the Symbolic (the naming/connecting process, founded on the Saussurean principle of difference).
3. *Journal*, p. 94.
4. *Letters* 2, p. 343 (19 July 1919).
5. 'When I write about ducks I swear that I am a white duck with a round eye, floating on a pond fringed with yellow blobs [...]. In fact the whole process of becoming the duck [...] is so thrilling that I can hardly breathe, only to think about it. For although that is as far as most people can bet, it is really

only the "prelude". There follows the moment when you are more duck, more apple, or more Natasha than any of these objects could ever possibly be, and so you create them anew' (*Letters* 1, p. 330 [11 October 1917]).

6. *Letters* 4, p. 97 (3 November 1920).

7. V. O'Sullivan (ed.) (2006) *Katherine Mansfield's Selected Stories* (London: Norton Critical Edition), p. 91. All further references to this edition are placed directly in the text.

8. 'I can only think in terms like a "change of heart". [...] we have died and live again. How can that be the same life? It doesn't mean that Life is the less precious or that "the common things of light and day" are gone. They are not gone, they are intensified, they are illumined. [...] Its as though, even while we live again we face death. But *through Life*: that's the point' (*Letters* 3, p. 97 [16 November 1919]).

9. Dunbar suggests that beneath the safe lyrical surface of Mansfield's stories lies a radical questioning of the myths of 'personal and public life – the romance of marriage, family happiness, child purity, the grandeur of the artist's task, the coherence and integrity (in both senses) of the individual self, the immutable nature of sexual identity. [...] These two aspects of Mansfield's writing, the lyrical and the subversive, are in some of the best-known stories presented in a layered or contrapuntal manner.' P. Dunbar (1997) *Radical Mansfield: Double Discourse in Katherine Mansfield's Short Stories* (London: Macmillan), p. ix.

10. *Journal*, pp. 184–5.

11. In *Encore*, the seminar where he conceptualizes *jouissance féminine*, Lacan precisely refers to the case of the mystics whose writings convey such experiences of death in life (*Le Séminaire, Livre XX, Encore*, Paris: Seuil, Le Champ Freudien, 1971, pp. 63ff.).

12. *Letters* 3, p. 82 (10 November 1919).

13. This coincides with the modernist emphasis on art as an object with a power of its own. In relation to the new art of photography, Roland Barthes evokes the *punctum*, a little something in surplus which stands out of the *studium*, the depicted reality: like a pressure point lying at the core of the image, it may ravish or hurt you. The same applies to the written word as a manifestation of the object-voice, independently of meaning. See my essay (2008) 'A Remainder that Spoils the Ear: Voice as Love Object in Modernist Fiction', *English Text Construction*, John Benjamin Publishing Company, 1:1, 154–64.

14. 'I am a divided being with a bias towards what I wish to be, but no more. And this it seems I cannot improve. [...] So I am always conscious of this secret disruption in me [...]. It seems to me that in life as it is lived to-day the catastrophe is *imminent*; I feel this catastrophe in me. I want to be prepared for it, at least' (*Letters* 5, p. 304 [19 October 1922]).

15. *Letters* 2, p. 191 (24 May 1918).

16. Unlike cheap psychoanalysis which amounts to turning 'Life into a *case*', a good novel should 'be capable of being *proved* scientifically to be correct': 'With an artist – one has to allow – [...] for the subconscious element in his work. He writes he knows not what – hes *possessed*. [...] as a sort of divine flower to all his terrific hard gardening there comes this subconscious ... wisdom. Now these people who are nuts on analysis [...] write to *prove* – not to tell the truth' (*Letters* 4, p. 69 [13 October 1920]).

17. Symptoms being 'the virtual archives of voids – or, perhaps, better, defences against voids – that persist in historical experience' (S. Žižek [2001] *Enjoy Your Symptom* [London: Verso], p. 21).
18. S. Kay (2003) *Žižek: A Critical Introduction* (Cambridge: Polity Press), p. 65.
19. Joyce liked to explain to his brother Stanislaus that Dublin 'suffered from "hemiplegia of the will" with the corollary that all Europe suffered from an incurable contagion which he called "syphilitic" and would someday make public knowledge'. R. Ellman (1983) *James Joyce* (Oxford University Press), p. 140.
20. Lacan's reference to the Greek spelling *sinthoma* in relation to Joyce is the occasion for a pun on St Thomas Aquinas, the key reference of Joyce's aesthetics, on *sin* in the context of Catholic Ireland, and on the father's 'sin'. For a definition of symptom and *sinthom*, see Žižek, p. 199.
21. Mansfield writes this in a note on Vita Sackville West's novel, *Heritage* (1919). See J. M. Murry (ed.) (1930) *Novels and Novelists by Katherine Mansfield* (London: Constable), p. 29.
22. G. Deleuze and F. Guattari (2005) *Qu'est-ce que la philosophie* (Paris: Éditions de Minuit), p. 153.
23. Kay, p. 13. 'Woman' joins the hysteric in the challenge to the hegemony of the symbolic law. She is not convinced by the myth of castration nor persuaded that some phallus can fill the lack in the symbolic order. This capacity to conjure a relation 'beyond the phallus' constitutes *jouissance féminine*: 'a feminine relation to the real that, while unavoidably subject to the Œdipal order, is nevertheless aware of that order's deficiencies and its after-the-fact, fabricated character [...] "woman" provides the "answer of the real" to the deficiency of the symbolic order' (Kay, pp. 82–3).
24. P. Moran (1993) 'What does Bertha Want?: A Re-reading of Katherine Mansfield's "Bliss"', in R. Nathan (ed.) *Critical Essays on Katherine Mansfield* (New York: G. K. Hall), p. 21.
25. For Moran, 'a major text of revisionary female modernism, a story that creates and explores its own unmapped continent of female sexuality, a black hole where women have no story except for the story of how that absence came to be'. P. Moran (1996) *Word of Mouth: Body Language in Katherine Mansfield and Virginia Woolf* (Charlottesville: University of Virginia Press), p. 22.
26. This of course is a reference to *Twelfth Night* – 'If music be the food of love, play on; / Give me excess of it, that; surfeiting, / The appetite may sicken, and so die! / That strain again! It had a dying fall:' (I, i, 1–4).
27. 'the object whose position leads us to identify something as sublime. Any indifferent object can take on the arresting, captivating, fulfilling charm of the imaginary phallic object which seems to endow the symbolic with transcendental significance and purpose' (Kay, p. 56).
28. *Ibid.*, p. 55.
29. 'A Cup of Tea', in A. Smith (ed.) (2002) *Katherine Mansfield: Selected Stories* (Oxford University Press), p. 363.
30. *Ibid.*, p. 362.
31. *Ibid.*, p. 367.
32. *Ibid.*, p. 369.
33. V. Woolf (1995 [1931]) *The Waves* (London: Flamingo), p. 193.
34. *Letters* 2, p. 54 (3 February 1918).

10

'Ah, What is it? – that I Heard': The Sense of Wonder in Katherine Mansfield's Stories and Poems

Anne Mounic

In April 1920, Katherine Mansfield wrote to her husband John Middleton Murry: 'If you knew how full my mind is of Shakespeare! It's a perfect world – his pastoral world. I roam through the Forest of Arden & sit on the spiced Indian sands laughing with Titania.'[1] Everyone will recognize her allusion to *A Midsummer Night's Dream*: 'And in the spiced Indian air, by night, / Full often hath she gossip'd by my side' (II, i, 124–5). Mansfield's pastoral world is an enchanted world, a world of wonder since, as in Shakespeare's time, before the 'dissociation of sensibility' as T. S. Eliot called it, that occurred in the seventeenth century, there was between man and the world a sense of *participation*. This is Lucien Lévy-Bruhl's word for the intimate contact between man and reality, a metaphysical outlook, by contrast to the duality between subject and object required by modern science. From this perspective we could call Mansfield's work *transitive*; that is, her stories and poems set up a link, or even a communion, between the self and the world. The real things – trees and flowers, but also the lamp in 'The Doll's House' – that she uses as images of being, are not emptied of life as linguistic signs or even concepts, but are shown as things of wonder with a life of their own and an existential radiance that derives from this transitive quality. As Claude Vigée writes in *L'art et le démonique* (Art and the Demonic), quoting Goethe and Baudelaire, 'aesthetic expression is possible only when the subject-object network has taken some new solid unity, beyond its two original components'.[2] The world, therefore, is no longer lost to the poet who acknowledges, as Shakespeare did, the correspondences between man's soul and the outer reality of the world. The subject cannot be cut off from the world in which he or she is rooted and acts. This ethical move creates a new enchantment and a sense of wonder, based upon a full plenitude of being, that therefore creates one's own inner world.

A transitive outlook, or the 'fullness of time'

To describe this process in Mansfield's work we may use three words: love, distance and memory. The reality of love has to be recreated in the mind to become acceptable and full; she writes to 'dearest Bogey', her husband, in October 1922:

> But then I remember what we really felt there, the blanks, the silences, the anguish of continual misunderstanding. Were we positive, eager, real – alive? No, we were not. We were a nothingness shot with gleams of what might be. But no more.[3]

The process is akin to what Kierkegaard called 'repetition', as defined in *Fear and Trembling* (1843):

> For it is great to give up one's wish, but it is greater to keep a firm grip on it after having given it up; it is great to lay hold of the eternal, but it is greater to stick doggedly to the temporal after having given it up. – Then came the *fullness of time*.[4]

The Danish philosopher quotes Paul's Epistle to the Galatians (4.4), which refers to the coming of the Messiah and the Pauline view that in the process of recreating what has been lost we reach a new dimension in time, which we could call messianic[5] – an appropriation of time as experienced by the inner soul, by the subject, or the subjective time of creation. 'Only through time is time conquered,' T. S. Eliot put it.[6] In another letter to her husband in October 1920, Mansfield wrote:

> Looking back at our time in the Villa Pauline when the almond tree was in flower remembering how I saw you come out of the cave in your soft leather boots carrying logs of wood [...] it is all a dream.[7]

In her poem 'Villa Pauline' written in 1916 Mansfield speaks of 'Our childish happiness'.[8] Both love and memory involve the work of the imagination and this is indeed what she describes in 'Psychology'. The male character, 'He', says that everything in his life is of little interest to him except the studio of the female character, 'She'. He remembers the place and can even 'touch, very lightly, that marvel of a sleeping boy's head'.[9] In this remark, we find a striking combination of distance and closeness with reference to the hand touching the symbolic object while seeing it only in the mind's eye. Then the character says: 'I love that little boy.' What D. W. Winnicott calls 'potential' or 'transitional space'[10] is created between the two lovers with the 'little boy sleeping' as a transitional object both separating and uniting them. In Mansfield's writing, this ambivalence is symbolized by the numerous dashes and suspension points she uses. These punctuation marks also have a deeper poetic resonance as a manifestation of the radiating but inarticulate origin of poetry.

The medieval view of love, as described by the Italian philosopher Giorgio Agamben, is interesting to consider for a finer interpretation of the mystery of 'Psychology'. In *Stanze*,[11] Agamben explains that in the Middle Ages love was seen as the labour of the imagination. It was thought only possible to fall in love with an image recreated by memory. In 'Psychology', the male character's memory, and especially his reliance on the 'sleeping boy's head', provides such an image. From 'Psychology' we can deduce that, for Mansfield, as it used to be in the Middle Ages, the world of Eros is the world of the imagination, since the lover is in love with the image he has formed in his heart. This capacity to dream, Giorgio Agamben says in *Stanze*, finds its origin in the vital breath that animates both the whole universe and the individual soul in perfect unity of being. The imagination, made of memory and desire, is ambivalent; it looks back into the past to flourish into the future. The image it creates is an epiphany of this new dimension of time which Paul, in Galatians 4.4, refers to as 'fullness of time', as quoted above by Kierkegaard. This is the time that we experience inside, the subjective time of personal feelings, the time to which we give an outward form through a work of art. The subject converts the destructive time of outer loss into an inner feeling of life that is passing but which is also being constantly recreated, or renewed, and therefore deeply enjoyed. The enchantment lies in the awareness of such a full capacity of being, which compensates for the ever-impending threat of death. This involves a constant struggle with the negative, which the end of 'Psychology' illustrates: the female character recovers her joy, therefore her full capacity of being, by looking at the violets brought by the 'good friend' – some sort of 'transitional object' – 'Even the act of breathing was a joy' (118). With Mansfield, the notion of vital breath that animates the universe and the individual soul takes on a particular significance, and, knowing her life story, makes us aware of the crucial meaning of her reference to breathing. And that unity of memory and the imagination, as the past is converted into the future within the present moment of writing, becomes in fact the fullness of life, the fullness of time appropriated through the work of creation. The violets are a symbol of the present moment of the past's conversion into the future, of the unity of the universe and the soul – of the fullness of time.

Et in Arcadia ego ...

In Mansfield's work, the pastoral element keeps all its ambivalence, joy and anguish, life and death, and, given her special predicament, breathing and aching. In the *Notebooks*[12] she writes in December 1915 remembering her dead brother, '*Et in Arcadia ego.*' This phrase, reminiscent of Virgil's Arcadia, was the inscription on Poussin's painting (1638–40), *The Shepherds of Arcadia*, and was Walter Pater's epigraph to his chapter on Winckelmann in *The Renaissance* (1873). Her brother's death triggered Mansfield's process of remembering. In the last lines of the poem dedicated to him, 'To L. H. B. (1894–1915)', he becomes a mythic figure partaking of both Jesus and Osiris, and also of Hades:

> By the remembered stream my brother stands
> Waiting for me with berries in his hands ...
> 'These are my body. Sister, take and eat.'[13]

As some sort of Persephone, she is given the food of death in her dream, which she calls 'Dead Man's Bread'. Her brother calls for resurrection in her imagination, stories and poems. She has to convert the past into the future. Trees and flowers are the emblem of the wonder of this renewal. As such, they belong to the literary domain of the marvellous since they give a clear magic glimpse of the ambivalence of life, light and darkness enhancing each other in a fascinating paradoxical contrast – with no duality but a strong sense of presence emerging from two significant features: reciprocity and rhythm.

   'Ah, Jeanne,' she writes to her sister in 1921,[14] 'anyone who says to me "do you remember" simply has my heart. [...] I remember everything, and perhaps the great joy of Life to me is playing just that game, going back with someone into the past.' The words that I wish to emphasize here are 'with someone'. This conversion of memory into new food for the future implies sharing with someone in an *I and you* relationship – as is the case in the pear tree episode in the *Notebooks*.[15] The ambivalence of the imagination is stressed by the alternation of the dualistic third-person pronouns *he and she*, Brother and Sister (the third person means both distance and absence), and the subjective, intimate first- and second-person pair, *I and you*. In this recollection of October 1915 (her brother died on 7 October), we find the original pattern of her emblem of life and the self: a tree, the full moon, unity of being ('We were like one child'),[16] presence and reciprocity ('I feel that too'), past and future ('Where is it now. Do you think we shall be allowed to sit in it in Heaven'), eternity and the fleeting moment, light and darkness, and this recurrent leave-taking ('Darling goodbye – goodbye – – –') which we find in 'The Wind Blows', 'Psychology' and in the subject of 'The Canary' – this 'sadness' in life.

'Bliss' also uses the same image of the pear tree 'with its wide open blossoms as a symbol of her own life' (96). It seems to gather in one emblem her inner life, the fire burning in her heart, and her outer appearance as caught in a 'cold mirror' (92), her radiance and her sense of expectation: 'waiting for something ... divine to happen ... that she knew must happen ... infallibly'. The moment of writing is a critical one – a turning-point between past and future. It culminates in an instant of delusory communion: two women, Miss Fulton and Bertha, gaze at the tree in blossom 'like the flame of a candle' (102) under 'the round silver moon'. This moment is a revelation at the junction of the ephemeral and eternity ('For ever – for a moment?' [102]). It is an instant of conversion offering a glimpse of plenitude through the feeling of fullness provided by Bertha's assertion of her own inner creative powers. It combines certainty and questioning (Miss Fulton's first name is Pearl, a symbol of perfection and the Heavenly Jerusalem and, moreover, she has 'moonbeam fingers' [105]); it is a time of full participation in the world. Mansfield remembers Wordsworth: 'And she seemed to see on her eyelids the lovely pear tree' (96).

The aloe in 'Prelude' is another such emblem. It is a ship of life, riding through space and time, in 'bright moonlight' (53), and flowering. Linda feels it is coming towards her mother and herself. The experience is shared: 'And I am sure I shall remember it long after I've forgotten all the other things.' Memory opens the infinite beyond the circumscribed world of totality. The tree is a figure of the future in the past, a promise of survival in the imagination now – like love – and in recollection later. In so gaining life in the character's eyes, it might remind us of Hermione's statue recovering life at the end of *The Winter's Tale*, for the same type of wonder, linked with the enchantment of art, is at work. The aloe is a figure of presence and transience (it is moving fast), but also of permanence through the capacity of the mind to remain attentive. Its ambivalent feature is conveyed through the rhythm that we also find in the passages referred to in 'Bliss' and 'To L. H. B.' In the *Notebooks*, Mansfield writes: 'He puts his arm round her. They pace up and down.'[17] The blossoming pear tree in 'Bliss' 'quivers' (102). It does not move towards them but stretches up almost 'touching' the full moon. In the *Notebook* memory, the moon is also round, therefore full, as in 'Prelude' (52). The full moon means wholeness but also impending decay. It symbolizes a moment of perfected experience, a 'fullness of time'. The past and the future are suspended in reciprocal balance reinforced by a pulsating rhythm whether iambic or trochaic. The trochaic beat we find in 'Prelude' ('Now the oars fell striking quickly, quickly' or 'Faster! faster!') gives an idea of the struggle between the positive and the negative leading to a surge of ecstatic desire, symbolized by blossoming vegetable life. In the *Notebook* episode, the season is autumn, and Mansfield describes it with a Keatsian fullness in her letters:

> Its autumn. Now Jack brings home from his walks mushrooms and autumn crocuses. Little small girls knock at the door with pears to sell & blue black plums. The hives have been emptied; there's new honey and the stars look almost frosty.[18]

In 'Bliss' the season is spring, which means creation (it could be either spring or autumn, for both are seasons of passage, of blossoming or fruiting). Moreover the equinox is a balance of night and day, light and darkness. 'The light and the shadow whisper together,' she writes in 'A Little Girl's Prayer'.[19]

Therefore the vegetable emblem reveals the creative repetition of life in the mind's eye and this is best symbolized by the choice of the name Kezia for the author's *alter ego* in the New Zealand stories. Kezia is Job's second daughter once he has recovered all he has lost – Job, the 'man who holds a trump car such as a thunderstorm in his hand',[20] is the model for Kierkegaard's repetition. And Kezia is also the Hebrew name of an aromatic plant, a sort of cinnamon. Flowers, plants and trees are emblems of the soul's creative power – the unknown, invisible world of life and death made flesh, as Leslie, appearing in her sister's dream, invited her to do: 'These are my body. Sister, take and eat.' Vegetable life is subjected to the rhythm of life and death. So is the moon's waxing and waning. In each case, Mansfield chooses the moment when life is suspended between splendour and impending decay.

If I shut my eyes I can see this place down to every detail – every detail ... (114)

Through the image of the ship and the rhythm of the oars, an epic view of life is brought in. The marvellous is a distinctive feature of the epic, notably of the Christian epic, in which magic is linked with otherness and a glimpse of the *unheimlich*. The ambivalent aspect of awe and ecstasy, loss and adventure, transience and comfort, is suggested in the finest way in one of Mansfield's best stories, 'The Wind Blows'. The wind is the symbol of the oscillating rhythm of life and death, with an iambic leitmotiv throughout, iambic – 'The wind, the wind' (109) – and a dash appearing between the nouns in the motif's second occurrence.

The girl, who appears in the third person, wakes up with a sense of doom: 'Something dreadful has happened' (106). The impression remains vague ('Something') and the present-perfect is used. In the very first sentence, the adverb 'dreadfully' – a recurrent word and notion in Mansfield's whole work – appears between two dashes: 'Suddenly – dreadfully – she wakes up.' A moment of crisis thus occurs: she wakes up to a new awareness of the human plight – transience and the ephemeral, as symbolized by the violent wind, yet compensated for by the rhythm of music and the comfort that surrounds the piano teacher's character: 'But Mr. Bullen's drawing-room is as quiet as a cave' (107). 'But' opposes the day's turmoil and its suspension in the rhythmical balance of music, as suggested by the comparison 'as [...] as'. The word 'cave' opens a natural, mythic world. We may think of the Sibyl's cave and her oracular words and also of a Romantic setting for a Lorelei figure in the line of the Sublime. With 'the pale photograph of Rubinstein' ([107] – this is certainly Anton Rubinstein [1829–94, the pianist and composer]) and the description of 'Solitude' we are placed in a post-Romantic world. The painting itself recalls the Pre-Raphaelite imagination, for example Dante Gabriel Rossetti's *Beata Beatrix* (c. 1864–70) or any other of his female portraits.

For the young girl, life is 'revolting, simply revolting' (107), but music is comforting: '"Life is so dreadful", she murmurs, but she does not feel it's dreadful at all. He says something about "waiting" and "marking time" and "that rare thing, a woman", but she does not hear. It is so comfortable ... for ever ...' (109). The verbs 'waiting' and 'marking time' express the author's concern: music or poetic rhythm is time controlled, even if it is not vanquished. It is time made art. 'The wind – the wind!' The dreadful element becomes rhythm itself, which leads to the epiphany of the future in the past made present through writing.

> *They* are on board leaning over the rail arm in arm.
> '... Who are they?'
> '... Brother and sister'. (110)

The use of the third person in italics significantly reveals the slow estrangement of the self through time, already suggested in the echo: 'The wind – the wind!': 'Ah, they know those two in the glass. Good-bye, dears; we shall be back soon' (109). The looking-glass, revealing the outer appearance of the characters, reveals the distance indicated by the deictics: '*those* two'. And the passing of time widens the gap: 'They can't see those two anymore' (110). The rhythm is iambic again: 'Goodbye, goodbye'. In the centre, sheltered, the place of childhood is to be found, in a contrasting trochaic rhythm: 'Goodbye, little island, goodbye.' The little island then is a place comparable to Mr Bullen's 'cave' (107). 'Do you remember?' 'Don't forget.' The process of memory is a process of creation, of *re*-creation, which makes the individual real, and this is its enchantment, its magic. The dialectics is existential. 'Only through time is time conquered.' The present becomes the past that had been the future. Writing is a process of repetition, close to what Frances Yates called 'the art of memory', an art that attempts to arrange figures in a place, the theatre, through a rhythmical pattern of images – meaning not only the pulsation of sounds but also the syntax and the choice of words: *rhythm as the resonance of being*. The soul is made real through the tale, and this is its wonder. '*I want to be <u>real</u>,*' Mansfield wrote in 1922.[21]

Memory is connected with repetition not only in 'The Wind Blows' but also in 'Psychology': 'If I shut my eyes I can see this place down to every detail – every detail ...' (114). The male character describes a place with several things – the 'red chairs', the 'bowl of fruit on the black table' – and especially the figure of the sleeping boy, and a memory that individualizes '*every* detail'. Through memory, the individual grasps his or her own moment – his own place – in time. In the same way, in 'The Doll's House', the lamp is *real*. And the reality is defined in this manner: 'They [the dolls] didn't look as though they belonged. But the lamp was perfect. It seemed to smile at Kezia, to say, "I live here". The lamp was real' (384). Being real therefore means creating for oneself a place in time: the garden with the pear tree and the garden seat, near to heaven, the pear tree reaching for the full moon; the aloe transformed into a ship through an epic dream; Mr Bullen's drawing room as a 'cave'; the soul itself as a store of images and figures, the oracular soul converting the past into the future and vice versa.

The doll's house is such a place, endowed with an utmost energy of being: '"Oh-oh!" The Burnell children sounded as though they were in despair. It was too marvellous; it was too much for them' (384). And this existential quest of being opens the way to origins: 'Perhaps it is the way God opens houses at the dead of night when He is taking a quiet turn with an angel . . . . The present moment is linked with the eternal: 'But what Kezia liked more than anything, what she liked frightfully, was the lamp' (384). The lamp is opposed to the rest with 'But'. As a flash of the eternal through the present moment, it comes as a paradox. The words connected with the symbol of reality are ambivalent: 'frightfully', 'despair', 'marvellous'. They echo 'dreadfully', 'dreadful', 'awful', 'eager', 'quicker', 'do you remember' and 'don't forget'. The place – the doll's house – has a centre – a point where the positive and the negative have achieved a dialectical and critical moment of balance.

Its gift is balance[22]

A reader of Shakespeare and the Romantics, Mansfield was a modernist not because she broke with the past but because she aimed at creating herself as an individual through capturing figures of being in the flow of becoming; that is, she appropriated time as the inner pulsation of subjective achievement. She was also a reader of Proust, who was influenced by Bergson. Virginia Woolf also read Proust, and his influence is obvious in *Mrs Dalloway*, and especially in the short story sequence which is at the root of the novel: 'there is nothing to take the place of childhood. A leaf of mint brings it back: or a cup with a blue ring'.[23] In the novel, Virginia Woolf aims at creating a centre amidst the elusive multiplicity of life. The party is a metaphor for the novel itself, which brings together this multiplicity without denying it: 'and she felt if only they could be brought together; so she did it. And it was an offering; to combine, to create; but to whom?'[24]

Writing is at the same time a creation of the self:

> That was herself when some effort, some call on her to be herself, drew the parts together, she alone knew how different, how incompatible and composed so for the world only in one centre, one diamond, one woman who sat in her drawing-room and made a meeting-point, a radiancy no doubt in some dull lives, a refuge for the lonely to come to, perhaps.[25]

Yet this centre is no real 'fullness of time' since there is another centre in the novel, an empty tomb, the cenotaph[26] in Whitehall, erected in 1919–20 as a memorial of the Great War dead. The novel is based upon this duality, which is very different from Mansfield's ambivalent outlook, and is symbolized by the diverging fates of Septimus and Clarissa. 'Death was defiance. Death was an attempt to communicate, people feeling the impossibility of reaching the centre which, mystically, evaded them; closeness drew apart; rapture faded; one was alone. There was an embrace in death.'[27]

In this duality the marvellous has gone away through its dissociation. The sense of wonder is defeated. The subject himself is defeated in his enchanted act of creation:

> She had escaped. But that young man had killed himself.

Somehow it was her disaster – her disgrace. It was her punishment to see sink and disappear here a man, there a woman, in this profound darkness, and she forced to stand here in her evening dress. She had schemed; she had pilfered. She was never wholly admirable.[28]

Clarissa's happiness, her success, includes sacrifice, the other's tragedy, which is what Mansfield had imagined as a consequence of her own death in 'Et après', a poem written in December 1919:

> He retired
> And to the world's surprise
> Wrote those inspired, passion-fired
> Poems of Sacrifice![29]

Sacrifice should be considered as an aesthetic view of life's drama – or at least as an interpretation of it from outside, and therefore dualistic: a subject–object relationship, made of no communion but only distance, and even estrangement. Mansfield could have interpreted her brother's death as sacrifice but she never did so since death did not break the reciprocal quality of their relationship: 'These are my body. Sister, take and eat.' This is communion from subject to subject, and therefore participation, for there is no dissociation between subject and object.

With Clarissa Dalloway, the feeling of guilt tips the scales against the achievement of plenitude. Rezia's roses 'were almost dead already',[30] and they 'had been picked by him in the fields of Greece'. From *Kezia* to *Rezia*, short for Lucrezia, the raped wife who killed herself to save her honour, something has been lost, some gift of balance, or ambivalence.

'Fear not, fear not,' Woolf repeats throughout her novel, quoting Shakespeare's *Cymbeline* (IV, ii, 258–9): 'Fear no more the heat o' the sun / Nor the furious winter's rages'. But throughout she dissociates the fear from the ecstasy, while Mansfield constantly manages to keep the balance. At the end of 'Prelude', the calico cat topples the top of the cream jar which 'flew through the air and rolled like a penny in a round on the linoleum – and did not break' (60). Even if for Kezia 'it had broken the moment it flew through the air', for the writer of the story it has not. The fullness of the moment has been preserved. The balance has been saved. We find the same witty miracle at the end of 'Feuille d'Album': '"Excuse me, Mademoiselle, you dropped this." And he handed her an egg' (166).

The marvellous in Mansfield's stories and poems consists of a conversion of fear into joy. In Woolf's novel, we find the flowers, the tree of life (the 'flowering tree'[31] Rezia has become just before her husband's suicide), but never this gift of yielding to the wonder of experience and becoming – this ecstasy. In the end, terror and ecstasy are vivid in Peter's mind at the thought of Clarissa, and terror comes first.

Exile certainly makes a difference. Since it deprives the individual of any ingrained habits or conventional ties or limits, it is an incentive to self-creation through images borrowed from the outer world, and through memories, coinciding with the soul's deepest desires. Exile, which uproots certainties, creates the need for this inner theatre of memory in which the figures of bygone happiness find their eternity through being remembered in their ephemeral moment of being.

I think this is Mansfield's achievement: remembering the past, she does not set it in some sort of idealized eternity. This is certainly why she appeals to critics in Japan or China: she writes about the dialectics of becoming. There is always an opening in her stories and poems: to the lower social classes, as in 'The Doll's House' or 'The Garden Party'; to the world, with the presence of the sea in 'At the Bay', 'The Wind Blows', and with her strong feeling of empathy: 'I felt *just* like a bird,' she writes at the end of 'When I was a Bird';[32] to the flow of life's experience, and her own creative soul is the theatre in which the figures of memory are kept alive. The distance of space and memory, through exile, makes the 'little island' a closed, circumscribed place, comparable to the Biblical Creation, the Greek cosmos, or Hardy's Wessex – a stage for the human drama to be acted upon.

Like Abraham, as described by Kierkegaard in *Fear and Trembling* (1843), Mansfield goes beyond the universal, the ethical, the tragic. As an individual, she voices the particular and in so doing, 'stands in an absolute relation to the absolute'.[33] Her view of life is not dual. She assumes the ambivalence of feeling and experience and takes in fear and joy in the same surge of wonder, which also means an everlasting re-creation of the self. The negative becomes the very impulse for rebirth. Plants and flowers embody this ever-renewed surge of life while the sea is the deep breath of life radiating in the outer images of the inner soul:

Nature spoke.
'I am desire' said the sea, 'I crave all, insatiably I long, untiringly I hold.'
'I am breath' said the wind. 'I blow over all the waste places of the earth & make them filled with my voice'.[34]

Something dreadful has happened (106)

Mansfield's setting is the creation, the stage for the drama of being (see above), not the limited political and social world, as it is for Woolf. Participating in the world of things, she establishes a network of correspondences that lead her to find her particular voice, or way – to use a word reminiscent of the Tao – her particular rhythm. This is her response to the dark 'staring in, spying' (421) she describes in 'The Canary', her last completed story, which O'Sullivan regards as 'an elegiac farewell to a caged bird that is now silent'.[35] 'When I found him, lying on his back, with his eye dim and his claws wrung, when I realised that never again should I hear my darling sing, something seemed to die in me.' At the end of the story, she tells about the awful side of ambivalent wonder: 'It is there, deep down, deep down, part of one, like one's breathing. However hard I work and tire myself I have only to stop to know it is there, waiting' (422).

We move beyond the tragic through the individual's struggle to be.

Let us now come back to the present-perfect used at the beginning of 'The Wind Blows'. We may wonder why the future is not used, since in 'The Canary' the 'sadness' is 'waiting'. In 'Bliss', also, Bertha is 'waiting' for something. But in 'The Wind Blows' this sense of expectation becomes the experience of the immediate past.

Mansfield's writing is the work of an individual transcending the ethical, the universal, the tragic – what our plight is and can hardly be altered. Once we are alive, the dreadful thing has already happened, and it is bound to spill, or break. 'There are more things in heaven and earth, Horatio, / Than are dreamt of in our philosophy,' says Hamlet – in keeping with Ecclesiastes (8.17) – to his bosom friend (I, v, 174–5) who will eventually keep the memory of his 'wounded name' (V, ii, 297). What we cannot control or master is the origin of art, the source of creation, or how to overcome anguish. Hence the dashes and suspension points we find throughout her work. Kierkegaard states, in *The Sickness Unto Death* (1849): 'This then is the formula which describes the state of the self when despair is completely eradicated: in relating to itself and in wanting to be itself, the self is grounded transparently in the power that established it.'[36]

And this is the paradox – there is no justification for the individual's particular choice: 'But the one who gives up the universal in order to grasp something still higher that is not the universal, what does he do?'[37] This is exactly Mansfield's question at the end of 'The Canary': 'Ah, what is it? – that I heard?' (422). It is essential for a writer to acknowledge this sphere of unknowing, which is infinite and makes creation possible. 'The Fly' ends with the same type of questioning: 'What was it? It was. . . .' (418).

The individual goes beyond the limits of knowledge and opens the infinite. There is no empty centre, therefore, but profusion, abundance, a fountain of being in the breath of life. In 'The Wounded Bird', a poem that should be read with 'The Canary', she prays: 'O my wings – lift me – lift me / I am not dreadfully hurt!'[38] I think that her whole poetics is summed up in these words taken from 'Vignette' – 'I look out through the window':[39]

> The music, too is strangely restless . . . it is seeking something . . . .
> perhaps this mystic, green plant, so faintly touched with colour . . . . .
> . . . . . . I dream . . . And there is no plant, no music – only a restless,
> mysterious seeking a stretching upwards to the light – and outwards –
> a dream like movement.
> What is it?

Mansfield's entire work answers this question and puts it again at the same time. And this is the wonder – time being thus renewed in a world of proclaimed subjectivity, in a transitive mind transcending the terror of otherness, in a labour of love in spite of all the distance, and all the solitude.

Notes

1. *Letters* 3, p. 282.
2. C. Vigée (1978) *L'art et le démonique* (Paris: Flammarion), p. 250. My translation.
3. C. A. Hankin (ed.) (1991) *Letters Between Katherine Mansfield and John Middleton Murry* (New York: New Amsterdam Books), p. 371.
4. S. Kierkegaard (2006) *Fear and Trembling*, C. S. Evans and S. Walsh (eds) (Cambridge University Press), p. 15. My italics.
5. See G. Agamben (2004 [2000]) *Le temps qui reste* (Paris: Rivages Poche).
6. T. S. Eliot (1974) *Burnt Norton. Four Quartets. Collected Poems* (London: Faber), p. 192.
7. *Letters* 4, p. 65.
8. V. O'Sullivan (ed.) (1988) *The Poems of Katherine Mansfield* (Oxford University Press), p. 46. Hereafter referred to as *Poems*.
9. K. Mansfield (2001) *The Collected Stories* (London: Penguin), p. 114. Future page references to Mansfield's stories are placed parenthetically in the text.
10. D. W. Winnicott (1975 [1971]) *Jeu et réalité*, C. Monod and J. B. Pontalis (trans.) (Paris: Gallimard), pp. 25, 148.
11. G. Agamben (1998 [1981]) *Stanze*, Y. Hersant (trans.) (Paris: Rivages), pp. 136–7, 153.

12. *Notebooks* 2, p. 17.
13. *Poems*, p. 54.
14. *Letters* 4, p. 294.
15. *Notebooks* 2, pp. 14–15.
16. *Ibid.*
17. *Ibid.*
18. *Letters* 4, p. 275.
19. *Poems*, p. 73.
20. S. Kierkegaard (1983) *Repetition*, H. V. Hong and E. H. Hong (eds and trans.) (Princeton University Press), p. 216.
21. Hankin, p. 401.
22. V. O'Sullivan, 'The Professional', *Palms and Minarets* (Wellington: Victoria University Press, 1992), p. 111.
23. F. Prose (ed.) (2004) *Mrs. Dalloway's Party. The Mrs. Dalloway Reader* (New York: Harcourt), p. 15.
24. V. Woolf (1996 [1925]) *Mrs Dalloway* (London: Penguin), p. 135.
25. *Ibid.*, p. 42.
26. *Ibid.*, p. 57.
27. *Ibid.*, p. 202.
28. *Ibid.*, p. 203.
29. *Poems*, p. 78.
30. Woolf, *Mrs Dalloway*, p. 103.
31. *Ibid.*, p. 163.
32. *Poems*, p. 59.
33. S. Kierkegaard (2004) *The Sickness Unto Death*, A. Hannay (trans.) (London: Penguin), p. 48.
34. *Notebooks* 1, p. 224.
35. V. O'Sullivan, 'Katherine Mansfield's Canary: A "Wounded Bird"', *temporel* 2. http://temporel.fr (accessed 21 May 2010).
36. Kierkegaard, *The Sickness Unto Death*, p. 44.
37. Kierkegaard, *Fear and Trembling*, p. 53.
38. *Poems*, p. 82.
39. *Ibid.*, p. 25.

11
Cold Brains and Birthday Cake:
The Art of 'Je ne parle pas français'

Anna Smith

Setting the table

In 1951 there was a case of plagiarism reported in *Psychoanalytical Quarterly*.[1] The patient, a scientist with a respected scientific position, confessed that he sought treatment because he had a compulsion to plagiarize, and so had difficulty publishing. The man was on the verge of completing a major piece of research when he came to analyst Ernst Kris to report that he had found in the library a book published some time before, and which he had previously glanced at as he was doing his own research, but which he now felt contained the same thesis. On examining the book, Kris found that it supported his patient's thesis, but in no way reproduced it: 'The patient had made the author say what he wanted to say himself' (22). Further, Kris felt that the patient had frequently been under pressure to use the ideas of his close friend, a distinguished young scholar who occupied the office next door to his own. Kris concluded that it was the colleague, rather, who was taking the patient's ideas and dressing them up as his own without acknowledgement. 'The patient was under the impression he was hearing for the first time a productive idea without which he could not hope to master his own subject,' but an idea he could not claim because it belonged to someone else (22).

In imputing to others his own ideas the patient was behaving defensively, argued Kris. The fascination with others' ideas suggested that the scientist had made a negative identification with the figure of the plagiarist; out of anxiety he diagnosed himself as a plagiarist lest he actually become one. Having experienced a childhood in which he frequently engaged in petty theft, in order to defend himself against the possibility of continuing to steal things as an adult the scientist instead imagined himself to be a thief of ideas: 'Only the ideas of others were truly interesting, only ideas one could take' (23). As if in confirmation of Kris's diagnosis, the patient immediately began to tell him how, when he returned to his office from the analysis, he enjoyed walking down a street full of restaurants looking at menus in the windows until he found his favourite dish which, coincidentally, happened to be fresh brains. For Kris, the desire for brains was a metaphorical displacement of the notion that the man believed that he was stealing brains (that is, ideas) rather than childhood objects. Adding another twist, psychoanalyst Jacques Lacan argued that the real significance of the case lay in the fact that the man stole but he stole *nothing*, and he would continue to do so as long as he suffered from '*mental anorexia*', which Lacan explained as an aversion to one's thoughts.[2] 'It's his having an idea of his own that never occurs to him,' Lacan comments.[3]

Such a leap of interpretation could be explained by suggesting that it was not as a defence against stealing that made the patient identify with the thief, as Kris had argued, but the inverse possibility: the fact that he might have an idea of his own. According to Lacan, the patient pre-emptively identifies with the plagiarist simply because he doesn't want to acknowledge that he might be capable of offering an original argument himself.[4]

Earlier analysis had revealed that the patient's grandfather was an eminent scientist and well published. But his father, as even Kris notes, wasn't equally endowed and had 'failed to leave his mark in his field of endeavour' (23),[5] to which Lacan adds the following: 'Is it not that the grandfather, who was celebrated for his ideas, sickened him [the father] of them?'[6] The patient's refusal in turn suggests to Lacan an extended family rivalry which he, the grandson, wants nothing further to do with.

It is as if desire on which the idea lives has in the patient faded and become cheap – like green ink on a scrap of blotting paper in a café, to recall the words of Katherine Mansfield.[7] Mental anorexia, then, is a refusal, but it is still a desire: a desire for 'nothing'. In this case, it signifies its presence by the food fantasy for fresh brains which would compensate for the patient's intellectual inhibition. The fascination for others' ideas persists as an empty, unsatisfying gesture, for far from not eating he – the anorexic – is eating 'nothing'.

What can be extracted from this cryptic Lacanian vignette is the association of eating and its incorporation with plagiarism, and the idea of the false or fictional self. The man's favourite dish doesn't nourish him because he believes that these 'brains' belong to someone else. And because his ideas come to him from 'outside' as if they were stolen, he is left vulnerable to the very kind of extraction by other people that he fears he performs himself.

Object-relations theory, of which Donald W. Winnicott is the best-known exponent,[8] might claim that the problem with Kris's patient is that he has lost an authenticity of self, so that even when he is able to produce original work it still seems borrowed, a pastiche of quotations from others' writing. Treatment of the dilemma would involve helping the patient to build an interior life that could be recognized as personal experience rather than perceived as coming from the outside, as belonging to everyone and no-one. Thus experience, vividly felt, could be acknowledged as belonging to and legitimating the life of the self.

A rather different approach may agree with object relations that the patient needs help to construct an inner world of his own – an imaginary one – but may also see in the case a narrative about the split in the subject, or, as Julia Kristeva would say, 'The more I happen not to be, the more I reach being.'[9] In other words, this kind of reading may take the crisis in boundaries and make it an exemplary instance of our nature as speaking and writing beings who, in the manner of anorexics, bite on nothing. One of the tasks of literature, Kristeva maintains, is to bear witness to this appetite of the ego for disintegration through the former's disillusioning 'theatre of cruelty'.[10] Literature performs the tug of the fictional or false self precisely because it acts out a foundational truth of identity.

The menu

Mansfield's story 'Je ne parle pas français' illustrates some of these complexities. It is a brittle, self-reflexive piece of writing that explores precisely the opposition between authenticity and lies, between superficiality and depth, and between stealing and ownership, without rejecting either term. Unlike the earlier mental anorexic, however, its narrator Raoul Duquette insists that he is *not* a plagiarist in order to be one.

Duquette is a Frenchman making a study of English literature:

> The book that I shall bring out will simply stagger the critics. I am going to write about things that have never been touched before. I am going to make a name for myself as a writer about the submerged world. (147–8)

This then is to be a story about writing: about the author, Mansfield's writing; about the narrator's grandiose writing ambitions; but also about plagiarism and eating – and how the self is written, and written *out of* experience.

The story opens with Duquette sitting in a shabby café reflecting on the nature of the soul – or rather on the fact that the soul doesn't exist. In some respects, he sounds like the exemplary postmodern hero, shallow and without depth. Duquette may or may not be suffering from boredom. He may or may not be writing a story in which he is drawn into a strange ménage with an English couple, Dick Harmon and Mouse. (He had apparently met Harmon, arguably a mirror image of himself, when the Englishman was studying modern French literature at a salon in Paris, and they began an affair. But Harmon abruptly left for home, returning several months later with a woman. Eager to get even with Harmon, Duquette plays the part of the affable host and watches with delight as their relationship crumbles.)

Whatever the status of this Frenchman, Mansfield reveals him to be an impresario, a manipulator of other people's emotions and a poseur, whose life has evolved into a pastiche of literary quotations and forms.[11] The titles of his books: *False Coins, Wrong Doors, Left Umbrellas*, say it all. Nothing about Duquette is original or authentic; everything that happens to him confirms a view of life where genuine and spontaneous emotions and perceptions have no place. Literature caricatures what is real; reality caricatures literature. Interestingly, if caught cheating this plagiarist would not experience a sense of guilt. He has nothing to hide because there is nothing hidden in his life despite his claims to have access to a secret, submerged one. There is no difference, for instance, between Duquette's sexual life and the way he behaves in public – each identity is composed of a 'cascade' of images, borrowed words, borrowed ideas, borrowed emotions. Of this phenomenon, Kristeva observes that in some of her patients who have a fragile or non-existent self, rather than an '*unconscious*, it is an *unawareness* which speaks. Through a discourse without a subject.'[12]

It is hardly surprising when events in Duquette's life happen '*comme il faut*', a phrase that insists everywhere in the text.[13] Events contain a torpor and a predictability that perfectly enhance the effete picture the reader has of Duquette himself. Regularly seduced as a child by his family's African laundress, his childhood, as he so prettily puts it, was 'kissed away':

> I became very languid, very caressing, and greedy beyond measure. And so quickened, so sharpened, I seemed to understand everybody and be able to do what I liked with everybody.
>   I suppose I was in a state of more or less physical excitement, and that was what appealed to them. (147)

Thus the commercial exchange that transpires between the laundress and the young child comes to mark his future interactions with the world. Each seduction is accompanied by the gift of a little sugar cake. If Duquette trades his childhood to a devourer for a sugar cake, he in turn learns to devour, and what he devours (rather than material objects or rather than objects alone, because Mansfield describes him as 'plump') are the words of the other. There is a particularly telling example of the mark the laundress has left on her charge in his fascination with the way the Englishwoman Mouse asks for a cup of tea, raising her muff and beseeching the *garçon* to rescue her with the inevitable English comfort drink:

> This seemed to me so amazingly in the picture, so exactly the gesture and cry that one would expect [...] that I was almost tempted to hold up my hand and protest.
>
> 'No! No! Enough. Let us leave off there. At the word – tea. For really, really, you've filled your greediest subscriber so full that he will burst if he has to swallow another word.' (160)

Mansfield's character steals in order to devour, because someone once did the same to him, and the self he is left with is a conglomerate of repeated forms, half digested, illustrated in his passion for the stereotype. Where the scientist whom Kris analysed had a neurotic disorder, however, *imagining* that he was a thief, Duquette's disturbance appears to involve a literal extraction of the materiality of his acquaintances with a corresponding lack of knowledge of his own emptiness. His radical depletion of genuine inner life as an adult is a direct consequence of his childhood seduction. Russell Meares notes in *The Metaphor of Play* that when the child is too precociously attuned to the other, what is produced is what he calls a 'hypertrophy of a dialogue with the real', where the self grows as an extension of the impinging environment and where there is an elaboration of the shell rather than the core of the self.[14] The child, in other words, becomes entrapped in the world of stimuli. The field of play is broken when the child orients to the external world and the mother's gestures are substituted for the baby's own. This substitution extends as far as the use the child will make of language. Ironically, in explaining where he lives, Duquette uses the figure of the snail, which is itself a lifeless, borrowed expression; a stereotype: 'There I emerged, came out into the light and put out my two horns with a study and a bedroom and a kitchen on my back' (147).

What fascinates the reader about Duquette's personal narrative is that it is so contrived, so constructed around external images, so devoid of deep feeling, yet all the time the narrativist imagines himself a writer of deep intuitive powers attuned to the submerged world of seduction and suffering:

> But, wait! Isn't it strange I should have written all that about my body and so on? It's the result of my bad life, my submerged life. I am like a little woman in a café who has to introduce herself with a handful of photographs. 'Me in my chemise, coming out of an eggshell. . . . Me upside down in a swing, with a frilly behind like a cauliflower. . . .' You know the things. (148–9)

The inevitable accompaniment to appropriating images of the other is a hypertrophy of the observing self, the impresario. Duquette frequently confronts images of himself in the mirror that he senses only partly connect to his feelings. Even at the most intense moments when he is moved to tears, for instance, he is studying their aesthetic effect as they shine on his lashes, or inwardly applauding his apparently devoted efforts to show Mouse and Harmon Paris:

> Suddenly I realized that quite apart from myself, I was smiling. Slowly I raised my head and saw myself in the mirror opposite. Yes, there I sat, leaning on the table, smiling my deep, sly smile, the glass of coffee with its vague plume of steam before me. (144)

Equally, the impresario sees others as types too; as actors in a drama heard before. When he meets Mouse, he cannot help but see the Englishwoman as a type: 'She held out her hand in that strange boyish way Englishwomen do,' she greets him with the phrase, '*Je ne parle pas français*' (157), she orders tea, she wears a 'long dark cloak such as one sees in old-fashioned pictures of Englishwomen abroad' (158).

Kristeva has used the terms 'actor' and 'impresario' in order to understand what she calls the division in the speaking subject.[15] Her understanding of subjectivity is as a constant negotiation between stable and unstable and, more tellingly, between actor and observer. At once impresario (the stage manager, the commentator, the one like Hamlet who stands outside the drama) and at the same time actor, caught up on the stage in what happens, the human subject is perpetually subject to change. This division into actor and observer, apparently inherent to identity if one accepts a Kristevan reading of the subject-in-process, could be illustrated by the division between poetry and meta-language, or between involvement and disengagement. If doubling may be indicative of the position of all subjects, the borderline would be the person who never emerges from this state but habitually vacillates between the two positions.

The single-mindedness of psychoanalysis is ultimately limiting for reading literature. But there are moments when something from its intellectual constructions resonates productively with a piece of fiction. Mansfield's character brilliantly reflects a particular type of human experience – what has been termed the 'false self' – nearly four decades in advance of its having been brought to light, first by Winnicott, and then others.[16] The narrator in Mansfield's story who experiences doubling *without* resolution of the actor/impresario roles within the self, occupies the position of the borderline. Traditionally, this condition manifests itself as acting or seeming, where the sufferer both sees and presents him/herself through the use of masks. A borderline will frequently be obsessed by whether they are inside or outside. Duquette experiences something similar when on looking into the mirror he finds that he cannot distinguish between looking and being the part. Looking is being and being is looking, he finds, recording it in his notebook as if it had sprung new and fully formed from himself. The borderline's difficulty in finding a spontaneity and naturalness of expression without falling into dead phrases, finds a brilliant illustration in Duquette's reaction to this friends' misery on arriving in Paris:

> Ah, but how intriguing it was – how intriguing! Their excitement came nearer and nearer to me, while I ran out to meet it, bathed in it, flung myself far out of my depth, until at last I was as hard put to it to keep control as they.
> But what I wanted to do was to behave in the most extraordinary fashion – like a clown. To start singing, with large extravagant gestures, to point out of the window and cry: 'We are now passing, ladies and gentlemen, one of the sights for which *notre Paris* is justly famous'; to jump out of the taxi while it was going, climb over the roof and dive in by another door. (158)

The thrill of immersing himself in another's drama leads to ecstasy. But Duquette's pleasure goes beyond the delight in a loss of boundaries to include the necessity of remaining *foreign to the drama*, an impresario, that is, manager of his own and of others' emotions. For it is from the ultimately orchestrated nature of the drama and its manipulation of events which are excavated of their spontaneity, their strangeness, that he derives his identity. The clown mask worn by Duquette persists on the surface, then, as a mark of the loss of depth. Language disappears into the *comme il faut.* Parodying what 'one' does when 'one' comes to Paris the Frenchman discovers the only spontaneity possible consists in inhabiting the borrowed phrase, *le mot juste*. Superficiality is depth; meta-language, the drive for mastery and absolute knowledge, verges on psychosis.

Yet what is more remarkable than Mansfield's prescience in relation to modern psychoanalysis is her ability to knowingly, coldly, *play* with her creation's appetite for 'cold' or uncooked brains; that is, for the ideas and emotions of others. For there is a curious passage between items of food in the story, namely between the little French sugar cake and the English fish ball. Duquette fell in love with Dick Harmon when he heard the Englishman sing a song about a man who can't get anything to eat:

> Ah! how I loved that song, and how I loved the way he sang it, slowly, slowly, in a dark, soft voice
> There was a man
> Walked up and down
> To get a dinner in the town ...
> It seemed to hold, in its gravity and muffled measure, all those tall grey buildings, those fogs, those endless streets, those sharp shadows of policemen that mean England. [...]
> What more do you want? How profound those songs are! There is the whole psychology of a people; and how un-French – how un-French! (149–50)

By the end of the story, of course, he has himself come to inhabit the song when he leaves the café in which he has been writing without having dinner, as hungry and placeless as his English counterpart: the singer and the song become one. More telling is the way that the text signifies a deeper failure of appetite. In describing his writing to us, the narrator sets up a potential 'moment of being' only to deplete it of its extrinsic qualities:

> It was very quiet in the café. Outside, one could just see through the dusk that it had begun to snow. One could just see the shapes of horses and carts and people, soft and white, moving through the feathery air. The waiter disappeared and reappeared with an armful of straw. He strewed it over the floor from the door to the counter and round about the stove with humble, almost adoring gestures. One would not have been surprised if the door had opened and the Virgin Mary had come in, riding upon an ass, her meek hands folded over her big belly. . . .

> That's rather nice, don't you think, that bit about the Virgin? It comes from the pen so gently; it has such a 'dying fall'. (144)

In reverie, conversation is directed towards some shared play-space: a 'cinematic screen', to use another term from object relations.[17] Yet this reverential space is here continually interrupted by neurotic appeals to the reader. A scene is sketched into which we are drawn, but the reverie is immediately disturbed: Duquette's manipulativeness and refined self-consciousness persist in jarring the reader, hijacking that intimate indwelling of imagination projected in story. The passage above with its crucial scene recalling the nativity, only to be drained away in its ironic 'dying fall', surrounds the account of a moment of being experienced when Duquette finds what he names the 'stale little phrase' in the detritus of writing on the blotting paper; that is, *Je ne parle pas français*.

À la carte

The Frenchman is transfixed, ecstatic; he feels that he dissolves into water as he salvages those trite words, but consider what Mansfield does with his moment of ecstasy:

> If you think what I've written is merely superficial and impudent and cheap you're wrong. I'll admit it does sound so, but then it is not all. If it were, how could I have experienced what I did when I read that stale little phrase written in green ink, in the writing pad? That proves there's more in me and that I really am important, doesn't it? (149)

Duquette here stumbles and trips on his own irony. Writing therefore runs a risk. Perhaps 'Je ne parle pas français' is merely an impudent and cheap burlesque on bad writing. Curiously though, writing to Murry, Mansfield celebrates this as one of the first stories to make her feel an adult: 'I am in a way *grown up* as a writer – a sort of authority.' And: 'I *did* feel (I do) that this story is the real thing and that I did not once (as far as I know) shirk it.'[18] So what is it that makes her consider the story to be 'real' and, as she puts it to Murry, 'against corruption'? If writing's purpose is to refresh, how is one to bring to life the stale little phrase? Can Mansfield escape the trap she has laid for her gigolo – that is, by forcing him to show the reader his hand, can she escape the pastiche that entraps him, and arrive at the unusual?

Whatever else it does, 'Je ne parle pas français' functions as the mark of inauthenticity. The narrator is a Frenchman, and various

Frenchisms – islands of italic type in Mansfield's original published English version – float in the text like food that has been swallowed but not properly introjected. Even Mouse, who introduces herself to Duquette with those charged words of denial, turns out to speak French. Indeed, the writer herself is a New Zealander from England who speaks French. The phrase of the title, therefore, is a lie which in reverse obscures a truth: 'I am not what I say I am' stands as the key signifier of Duquette's duplicity. Equally, the stale little phrase is exactly what it purports to be – deposited by someone else and owned by no-one in particular, but claimed as the mark of originality by the most 'inauthentic' of writers. Needless to say, the reader can hardly escape the seductive complexities going on here. Mansfield eggs us on with her sugar cakes until we are as corrupted as Duquette.

That such a conventional man whose only access to truth is through over-conventionalized language should be the bearer of a very different, *literary* seduction illuminates the edge that Mansfield treads here. She sharpens the reader's receptiveness to the feints and interchanges between truth and lies, playing relentlessly on their capacity to be both apart from, yet always implicated in, plagiarism, the latter being what one might term the stealing of sad little phrases. According to this economy of Mansfield's, Duquette then becomes the false narrator who speaks truly; Mansfield herself, the true narrator who plays false. In fact, the by-now overused phrase *Je ne parle pas français* can be given a further twist where the language of its story begs to be read as that of a third impresario (or narrator) who speaks the truth unknowingly. For fiction above all is the unaware impresario of the drama of language, insisting everywhere its disingenuous 'little lies'.

Afters

Anorexia has been seen as a response on the part of the child to the mother who loves too much, alongside a hunger for meaning, summarized by Lacan in the following: 'It is the child one feeds with most love who refuses food and plays with his refusal as with a desire.'[19] In this connection, it seems appropriate to mention a slippage in Sheridan's translation of *Écrits*. The English version of the text renders 'fresh brains' as 'cold brains'. Curiously, it is only the English, Lacan maintains, 'with their cold objectivity', who have been able to recognize the 'want-to-be' at the heart of the subject.[20] It is the Anglo-Saxon lack of heat that has permitted them to discern the false warmth and allurements of interpersonal relationships, and to substitute for that sentimental truth a recognition that relation to the Other is founded on emptiness. Whether or not Lacan knowingly assumes the place of the man in Harmon's song (who on asking for food is contemptuously refused by the English waiter), nevertheless, both Duquette and Lacan identify with the one whose demand is refused. Such an identification leads the latter to attempt an interpretation of Freud's butcher's wife.[21]

The curvaceous butcher's wife dreams she cannot give a dinner party because she only has a thin slice of smoked salmon. Freud, on hearing that she foregoes what she craves, a daily caviar sandwich, while her thin friend craves smoked salmon which she wants in order to fatten herself up, tells the butcher's wife that her dream is a desire to keep her friend from her husband, who prefers more fleshy women. Lacan adds a new twist to what is by now a stale story: the butcher's wife, he says, really craves desire: she doesn't want her demand satisfied. The words of the other, the desire for the Other signalled for the butcher's wife by the salmon itself, come to us from elsewhere – they pre-exist as a kind of cultural detritus – on a blotter, perhaps, or as a plate of cold brains.

Naturally, Lacan's interpretation of the 'cold brain' case gave him the opportunity to talk about his own plagiarism. Kris, on meeting up with Lacan at the 14th International Psychoanalytical Conference at Marienbad in 1936, the latter having apparently taken the day off to see the Olympics in Berlin, said of his lack of seriousness, 'but that isn't done – *ça ne se fait pas!'*[22] Yet the defiles of the signifier are at work even here, because Lacan's account in *Écrits* appears to be at odds with the one offered by Elizabeth Roudinesco.[23] The comment was made, she said, the day after Lacan had been interrupted ten minutes into his controversial paper on the mirror stage by the conference chair, Ernest Jones. Lacan had left in a huff to watch the Olympics. Kris, by way of apology this reader infers, had merely been suggesting that the interruption was not professional. Typically, it appears that Lacan's account has been free with the words of the other; but Roudinesco also suggests that his interest in plagiarism and its relative qualities stems from his own work on the mirror stage, much of which he had borrowed without acknowledgement from psychologist and socialist philosopher Henri Wallon. It was Wallon who coined the concept of a literal mirror state as a Darwinian rite of passage to permit the child to procure for itself a unified ego; a social ego, rather than a psychic or linguistic one.[24] Wallon viewed the experience as a developmental stage, and so did Lacan, although his paper attempted to marry Wallon's 'historical' approach with a linguistic and libidinal reading of his own. It was not until the 1950s, much later in his career, that he translated the stage into a structure, a recurring, imaginary position. For his part at Marienbad, Lacan was quite happy to insinuate that his audience of analysts might filch this idea of the mirror stage from *him*.[25]

As every scholar knows, the theft of ideas is not merely the territory of neurotic or borderline patients in analysis. 'Plagiarism is relative to the practices operating in a given situation.'[26] What might this mean, then for the critic – and the writer, as plagiarist? Given that interpretation is only ever that, how might scholarship come to terms with stealing the ideas of the other?

A certain kind of mental anorexia and its corollary, an addiction to the words of the other, will always hang over criticism and writing. By its very nature, criticism appears to exist under the shadow of cold brains and a father not blessed with many ideas. Living on the cusp of borrowed texts as impresarios, readers of Katherine Mansfield inevitably bear witness to her perfidious enacting of the very corruption 'Je ne parle pas français' was designed to address. Even so, that literature is a borderline discourse and that, following Kristeva, every subject is an impresario may, after all, be insights too cheap, too easily won. Despite the secondary nature of all writing, some writerly gestures may still enhance the creative project – and the self – while others may result in an uncomfortable sense that the self is being falsified, a position that Mansfield brilliantly anticipated and playfully manipulated at least 35 years before its discovery. To put it another way: one person's meat – let us rename it birthday cake in this collection of essays celebrating the centenary of Mansfield's arrival in London to be a writer – is another's cold brains.

Notes

1. E. Kris (1951) 'Ego Psychology and the Interpretation in Psychoanalytic Therapy', *Psychoanalytical Quarterly*, 20: 1, 15–30. References in the text hereafter.
2. J. Lacan (1977 [1966]) 'The Directions of the Treatment and the Principles of its Power', in *Écrits: A Selection*, A. Sheridan (trans.) (New York: Norton), pp. 226–80. See especially pp. 238–44.
3. *Ibid.*, p. 239.
4. J. P. Muller and W. J. Richardson (eds) (1982) *Lacan and Language: A Reader's Guide to Écrits* (New York: International Universities Press), p. 271.
5. Kris further noted the fact that this was the patient's second analysis. In relation to his treatment, Kris commented how the new analysis owned the advantage of ego psychology, which the earlier analyst, a woman, had lacked. Lacan's reading of the same case can then be understood as the third instalment in a three-generational analysis of the intellectual expression and inhibitions of three generations of men. It may also go some way

towards illuminating the fact that anorexics, generally speaking, do not desire to 'chew the fat'. William Earnest gives the case a further turn. See 'Madness isn't the Only Option', his discussion of Slavoj Žižeck. http://www.ideologystop. net/Zizeckandnarcissismpage1.html (accessed 11 February 2010).

6. Lacan, 'The Directions of the Treatment', *Écrits*, p. 240.
7. 'Je ne parle pas français' (1918), in A. Smith (ed.) *Selected Stories of Katherine Mansfield* (Oxford University Press, 2002), p. 144. References in the text hereafter.
8. For a general and reasonably scholarly overview of object relations, consult the web-pages of psychology Professor Victor Daniels, Sonoma State University at: http://www.sonoma.edu/users/d/daniels/objectrelations.html (accessed 3 July 2009). Object-relations theory and authenticity is further explored in J. Mills (2004) 'A Phenomenology of Becoming: Reflections on Authenticity', in R. Frie (ed.) *Understanding Experience: Psychotherapy and Postmodernism* (New York: Routledge), pp. 116–36, but see especially pp. 123ff.
9. J. Kristeva (1984) *Revolution in Poetic Language*, M. Waller (trans.) (New York: Columbia University Press), p. 116.
10. See, for instance, her 'Word, Dialogue and Novel', in T. Moi (ed.) (1986) *The Kristeva Reader* (New York: Columbia University Press), p. 54 (pp. 34–61). (There are extended discussions of this question in *Revolution in Poetic Language*.)
11. Duquette's affection for pastiche is remarkably similar to that of Fredric Jameson's analysis of the postmodern waning of affect. See F. Jameson (1991) *Postmodernism, or the Cultural Logic of Late Capitalism* (Durham, NC: Duke University).
12. J. Kristeva (1996) 'Name of Death or of Life', in John Lechte (ed. and trans.) *Writing and Psychoanalysis: A Reader* (London and New York: Arnold), Section II, 6, p. 110.
13. Lacan also remarks on this overly dutiful habit in Ernst Kris's delivery of his paper on the nature of the ego. See 'The Directions of the Treatment', *Écrits*, p. 138.
14. R. Meares (2005) *The Metaphor of Play: Origin and Breakdown of Personal Being*, 3rd edn (London: Routledge), p. 99. The first text edition of *Play* published in 1993 bore the subtitle: *Disruption and Restoration in the Borderline Experience*.
15. Kristeva, 'Name of Death or of Life', pp. 103–16. Interestingly, elsewhere Lechte notes the connection of Kristeva's use of the impresario with the transcendent. See J. Lechte and M. Margaroni (2004) *Julia Kristeva: Live Theory* (London: Continuum), pp. 121–2. This suggestion certainly fits with Mansfield's granting to Duquette an 'epiphany' in the café.
16. See, for example, H. A. Bacal (1987) 'British Object-Relations Theorists and Self-Psychology: Some Critical Reflections', *International Journal of Psychoanalysis*, 6, 81–98. Otto Kernberg's 1983 paper on 'Object-Relations Theory and Character Analysis', *Journal of the American Psychoanalytic Association*, 31, 247–71, also contains useful summaries. The key text remains Winnicott's (1965 [1960]) 'Ego Distortion in Terms of True and False Self', in his *The Maturational Process and the Facilitating Environment: Studies in the Theory of Emotional Development* (London: Hogarth and Institute of Psychoanalysis), pp. 140–52.
17. R. Meares (1992) 'Transference and the Play-Space: Towards a New Basic Metaphor', *Contemporary Psychology*, 28, 32–49. It is certain that the notion of the screen was more loosely indebted to Freud. See S. Freud (1960 [1899])

'Screen Memories', in *Standard Edition*, vol. III (New York: Basic Books), pp. 47–69.

18. *Letters* 2, p. 66.
19. Lacan, 'The Directions of the Treatment', *Écrits*, p. 264.
20. J. Lacan (1977) *Four Fundamental Concepts of Psychoanalysis*, A Sheridan (trans.), J.-A. Miller (ed.) (London: Hogarth and Institute of Psychoanalysis), p. 29.
21. See Lacan, 'The Directions of the Treatment', *Écrits*, pp. 226–80. For a further helpful gloss, consult C. Clément (1983) 'No Caviar for the Butcher', in *The Lives and Legends of Jacques Lacan*, A. Goldhammer (trans.) (New York: Columbia University Press), pp. 103–48.
22. Lacan, 'The Directions of the Treatment', *Écrits*, p. 239.
23. E. Roudinesco (1997) *Jacques Lacan*, B. Bray (trans.) (New York: Columbia University Press). On Lacan, Wallon, Kris and plagiarism, see pp. 251–2; on Marienbad, see pp. 107–17. The context of Kris's remark to Lacan here is somewhat ambiguous. See also E. Roudinesco (1990) *Jacques Lacan and Co: A History of Psychoanalysis in France 1925–1983*, J. Mehlman (trans.) (University of Chicago Press), for an analysis of Wallon and Lacan's understanding of the mirror stage, especially pp. 68–71.
24. H. Wallon (1994 [1931]) 'How the Child Develops the Notion of his own Body', cited in M. Jay, *Downcast Eyes: The Denigration of Vision in Twentieth Century French Thought* (Berkeley: University of California Press), p. 2.
25. For an incisive critique of the accusations and counter-accusations of plagiarism, see Y. Stavrakakis (2007) 'Wallon, Lacan and the Lacanians', *Theory, Culture and Society*, 24: 4, 131–8. Not only does Stavrakakis refer to Lacan's 'complex citation practices', he also invites further discussion on the near-universal practices of 'intellectual debt and repression' by critics. Similarly, Richard Webster describes how G. de Clérambault charged Lacan with plagiarism after hearing his former pupil read 'Structures des psychoses paranoiaques'. http://www.richardwebster.net/Thecultoflacan.html (accessed 11 February 2010). M. Borch-Jacobsen's (1991) *Lacan: The Absolute Master* (Stanford University Press) has a helpful reference to Lacan's treatment of plagiarism: 'There is no such thing as symbolic private property', in his introduction, pp. 1–2. The original reference is from J. Lacan (1981) *Le Séminaire III: Les psychoses* (Paris: Seuil), p. 93.
26. Lacan, 'The Directions of the Treatment', *Écrits*, p. 240.

Part IV
Autobiography and Fiction

12
'Where is Katherine?': Longing and (Un)belonging in the Works of Katherine Mansfield

Janet Wilson

Mansfield, 'home' and longing

Recent revisions and reassessments of British literary modernism have focused on its metropolitanism, and its aesthetics of fragmentation, abstraction and artfulness.[1] Remappings which aim to situate modernism more fully within its socio-cultural matrix reconsider its transnationalism, such as the transformative cultural impact which occurred at the end of empire, due to the migration of colonial writers to England, many from non-elite communities, after the 1950s.[2] The geographical complexity of the movement, as current research on modernist little magazines shows, complicates the traditional metropolitan framings and opens up new perspectives on the contribution to modernism of earlier writers who were neither English nor American. Katherine Mansfield is traditionally celebrated as a modernist because of her formal experimentation, as well as her links with perceived avant-garde writers and artists such as John Middleton Murry, A. R. Orage, J. D. Fergusson and others. That she might be a more liminal writer, a 'colonial modernist' whose aesthetic and artistic orientations were shaped by her New Zealand origins, a view which hitherto has been little acknowledged, has recently begun to receive more critical attention.[3] Mansfield's colonial identity was both formative of her metropolitan modernism and marks her out as distinctive, in particular through her obsession with 'home', and with what Emma Neale describes as 'the fantasy of emotional settlement',[4] which inspired her great New Zealand stories like 'The Garden Party', 'At the Bay' and 'Prelude'.

The title of this essay alludes to the New Zealand writer Robin Hyde's *ubi sunt* lament about her famous predecessor, written soon after her death: 'Where is Katherine with weeds on her grave at Fontainebleau, when what she really wanted was the dark berry along our creeks?'[5] While Hyde's lament concludes with a hoped-for Arthurian-like 'return', this essay reflects on Mansfield's problematics of location, her ambivalence about home and her ontological state of '(un)belonging'.[6] It argues that her colonial modernism entailed a reconfiguring of the dialectic of home and away, due to an oscillation between belonging yet not belonging, because memory and longing led her to construct new images of locatedness in which degrees of belonging (or not) are accounted for.[7] This is evident not only in her last stories about New Zealand, written as forms of commemoration and memorial, but also in her earlier 'colonial' stories in which the white settler's deracination, sometimes manifested in terms of the uncanny, demonstrates an uneasy occupation of colonial territory.

For Mansfield, who often reacted to life's experiences in extreme terms, her mixed feelings about colonial New Zealand are central to her self-positioning in metropolitan Europe, beginning with the passionate desire to escape the home in Wellington to which she had returned after nearly four years' education at Queen's College in Harley Street, London (1903–6), and to rediscover the cultural capital of England. A premonition of the conflict this will entail is found in her unfinished novel 'Juliet', written in 1906, in which longing 'for fresh experiences, new places' carries the proviso 'but I shall miss the things that I love here'.[8] The effects of the loss of homeland and home, however, were more severe than her youthful rebellion could ever have anticipated. The tragic death of her brother, Leslie Heron Beauchamp, from a wartime training accident in October 1915 deeply traumatized her;[9] in 1917 came the knowledge of her tuberculosis, making a physical return unlikely; and the fantasies in her marriage with Middleton Murry of an idealized home were prevented from being realized by her illness. This loss and the desire for reconnection appear to have driven her to return to New Zealand through memory and imagination as her health declined. What Elizabeth Bowen calls 'the insatiable longing we call homesickness' inspired her finest stories. As Bowen says, 'her art grew not only from memory but from longing'.[10]

Mansfield's youthful reaction against her upbringing, family and nation, as well as her preoccupation with Oscar Wilde's celebration of the artificial in art, helped inform her self-presentation as colonial 'arriviste' upon her arrival in England in September 1908. Fluctuations of identity, manifested in performances of herself as the exotic other – Japanese or Maori – suggest the social distance she discovered there. Similarly, the experimentation with different versions of her name, the assuming of different names and her play with masks, all suggest that impersonation, supported by her gift for mimicry, became second nature for a while. Such exhibitionism provoked the derision of some literary contemporaries, who saw her as outlandish, a wild colonial, or, in the memorable words of Virginia Woolf, like 'a civet cat that had taken to street walking'.[11] Imitation and disguise may have been a form of bravado, inspired by a wish to shock and sometimes to go incognito, to adopt a form of anonymity given her relative obscurity at first in British society. The impulse very likely sprang from her infatuation with the nineteenth-century symbolists and decadents, Arthur Symons, Walter Pater and in particular Oscar Wilde. Wilde's emphasis on craft, artifice, immorality and the shaping of one's own life to that of being an artist encouraged her to experience life as intensely as possible. This *fin-de-siècle* aesthetic also catalysed her search for the unnatural within the familiar as well as the new or foreign; it included that feral, savage side of her being, symptomized by her restlessness, which she explored in early vignettes in relation to the Maori and the landscape, and identified with the savage spirit of the land in her story of raw New Zealand life, 'The Woman at the Store'.

Psychologically, however, Mansfield's impersonations were a response to her innate loneliness as much as to geographical dislocation. They dramatized and reflected her positioning between cultures, the consequence of being a white settler colonial subject in a metropolitan society. But, as I shall argue, the wearing of different identities and guises also points to her ability to absorb diverse artistic influences: of post-Impressionism, Expressionism, the Rhythmists. That her colonial identity had already undergone a metropolitan transformation during her education at Queen's College may explain Mansfield's predisposition to radical gestures such as imitation and experimentation upon relocation in a metropolitan milieu. Certainly her ability to locate the spaces between people and register the problems in crossing social distances – a feature of the late lyrical stories – might be traced to this to and fro movement between cultures. Her double expatriation, first at the age of 14, when the Beauchamps travelled to England in January 1903, and then her second return to the metropolitan homeland just before she turned 20 in 1908, entailed an unusually radical bifurcation and multiplication of identity.[12] As she wrote to S. S. Koteliansky in 1922, 'I am a divided being: I am always conscious of this secret disruption in me';[13] yet this internal splitting with its potential for accretions of identity seems to have made her adaptable, able to change roles, capable of cultural relativism and receptive to diverse experiences.

Colonial versus metropolitan influences

Mansfield's adolescent wish to distance herself from family and nation, then her later urge to recover belonging, are paradigmatic of subjects from the white settler colonies of New Zealand, Australia, South Africa and Canada. They can be read in terms of Homi Bhabha's argument that 'the colonial presence is always ambivalent, split between its appearance as original and authoritative and its articulation as repetition and difference'.[14] Bhabha, in talking of colonial imitation (of the metropolitan colonizer), argues that the excess or slippage produced by the ambivalence of mimicry (which embodies the desire for a 'recognizable Other, *as subject of difference which is almost the same but not quite'*) does not merely rupture colonial discourse, it becomes transformed into an uncertainty which fixes the colonial subject as a 'partial [that is, 'incomplete' and 'virtual'] presence'.[15] Critic Alan Lawson, in relating Bhabha's theories to the 'Second World' of the white settler invader colony, focuses on the inherent ambivalence of the white settler subject due to his/her in-between status, caused by two prior sources of cultural authority and authenticity: 'the originating world of Europe, [...] as source of the Second World's principal cultural authority; and that other First World, that of the First Nations, whose authority the settlers not only effaced and replaced but also desired'.[16] The settler's interstitial location between the European imperium and the indigene is at once colonizing – symbolically erasing and depriving the indigene of voice, partly assimilating him into the European self – and subject to imperializing by the centre. Lawson claims that the settler occupies 'not unbounded space but a place of negotiation', a 'neither/nor territory' where binaries such as self/other, here/there, colonizer/colonized are destabilized.[17] Any sense of belonging becomes problematic, even as this introduces tensions into hegemonic colonial discourse. Subjectively experienced, in-betweenness with 'its *internalization* of the self/other binary of colonialist relations', as Stephen Slemon puts it, and its reduced ability to resist any object or discursive structure positioned as purely external to the self, fragments identity into multiple selves and self-positionings; in short, the white settler manifests what Canadian writer Denis Lee calls 'alien inauthenticity'.[18] These complexities underpin Mansfield's construction of her own subjectivity and of settler life in her colonial stories.

Bhabha's theory about the incompleteness and partial presence of the colonial, Lawson's about the white settler's effacement and appropriation of indigenous authority and authenticity, and Slemon's about the settler's 'ambivalence of emplacement' between the 'First World/Third World, colonizer/colonized binary',[19] help contextualize Mansfield's propensity for impersonation and statements about her own plural subjectivity – 'True to oneself! Which self? Which of my many [...] hundreds of selves' – and her desire for 'our own particular self', the intimation of 'a mysterious belief in a self which is continuous and permanent'.[20] Crucially moulded by the disjunctures between the imperial and the colonial worlds, and the permanent dislocation caused by being between both but not fully belonging to either, Mansfield, even before she first left New Zealand in 1903, laid claim to the dual sources of the settler's authority and authenticity. On the one hand, she befriended the Trowells, the musical English family whose twin sons she fell in love with, becoming pregnant to one of them, Garnet Trowell, after her return to London in 1908. On the other, she was erotically attracted to her half-Maori schoolfriend, Martha Grace Mahupuku (called 'Maata'), from Miss Swainson's private school in Thorndon, writing of her in 1907: 'I want Maata. I want her as I have had her – terribly. This is unclean I know but true. What an extraordinary thing – I feel savagely crude, and almost powerfully enamoured of the child.'[21] Through her sensations of desire and longing – as in the relationships with Maata and Garnet Trowell – Mansfield mapped out her 'exotic' 'unbelonging', making a transition between erotic ties a way of focusing her colonial identity in her move from home into exile.

Mansfield saw herself as a hybrid, a metropolitan colonial or a New Zealand European, not a 'Pakeha' New Zealander.[22] This identity decision partly stemmed from her dissatisfaction with her 'vulgar' family and the primitiveness of New Zealand society. As she wrote in a letter to her sister in early 1908, 'I am ashamed of young New Zealand, but what is to be done.'[23] She was attracted to the Maori as the indigenous other, though, and the diary of her three-week camping trip into the Ureweras in late 1907 records encounters in terms drawn from European stereotypes of romantic impressionism and exotic indigeneity. Her intense, physical relationship with Maata Mahupuku, however, enabled her to internalize the indigenous presence, to attempt to incorporate it into her identity structures, and so distance herself further from her undesirable Pakeha-New Zealand identity. As Bridget Orr points out, 'in a settled colony with policies of racial assimilation, the other is with/in you'.[24] Although the Maori do not feature in her mature work as subjects in their own right, Maata is an exception. Journal entries and story fragments suggest Mansfield remained obsessed by this erotic, psychic involvement, and the interplay of their identities after their relationship ceased became subject matter for writing. A half-caste Maori called Maata is the heroine of a novel outlined in 1908, while an incomplete *Bildungsroman* of 1910 features a heroine called Maata who is based on Mansfield herself and incorporates elements of the Maata Mahupuku relationship.[25]

The vignette 'Summer Idylle' (1906), in which Mansfield reproduces the awakening of sexual desire between two women – one half-Maori, the other Pakeha – as a dialectic exploration of self and other, suggests that the relationship entailed a preoccupation with identity, distance and belonging. Marina, the half-Maori, is at home in the landscape, yet the Pakeha, Hinemoa, after her rhapsodic, semi-erotic awakening, becomes aware of her as exotic, foreign. The names and ethnicities are reversed (the Maori has an Anglo-Celtic name, the New Zealander a Maori name), so destabilizing ethnic stereotypes and Eurocentric colonial norms of self and other. Yet their maritime associations further suggest they represent interrelated parts of the one person, despite remaining culturally distinct: Hinemoa (the Mansfield surrogate) invokes the Hinemoa of Maori legend who swam out into a lake to join her lover on an island, because of adult prohibitions on their meeting, while the more sexually experienced Marina has a name which represents European classical nomenclature and legend.

The episode concerns the sexual arousal of the virginal Hinemoa, called 'Snow Maiden' by Marina, as symbolized by their dive into the sea's depths and swim to an island. This awakening comes with her appreciation of Marina's ethnic difference and her belonging:

> Hinemoa fell back a little to see Marina. She loved to watch her complete harmony – it increased her enjoyment.
>
> 'You are just where you ought to be' she said raising her voice. 'But I [am not like that]' said Hinemoa, shaking back her hair. 'I lack that congruity'.
>
> 'It is because you are so utterly the foreign element – – – you see?'[26]

The gendered and racial dimensions of the story pivot on tensions between the natural and the artificial or unnatural. The 'Other' is celebrated for her closeness to nature; Marina's 'congruity', her indigenous 'belonging' in the Pacific setting (which the European Hinemoa lacks), recalls Mansfield's description of a Maori girl in her Urewera notebook as the 'very incarnation of evening'.[27] Yet nature is also feral: Marina's hints of cruelty, saying of the fern trees which ensnare warriors, 'They are cruel even as I might wish to be to thee, little Hinemoa,' her savagery, 'half shut eyes, her upper lip drawn back showing her teeth', are marked out in terms of homoerotic, bisexual desire.[28] Being the 'foreign element' situates her as exotic, or as the other half of the divided self, as the foreign or stranger within; according to Kristeva this is the repressed side of the self that emerges to have a conscious mind.[29] In the final section cultural differences map onto ethnic divisions and specific practices are now registered as unnatural. Marina eats for breakfast the Polynesian delicacy, the 'unnatural' kumera (a root vegetable with a bluish tinge when cooked); Hinemoa, now dressed in virginal white, sensuously consumes a peach, letting the juice run through her fingers, and then breaks bread, evoking Christian ritual and atonement for guilt:

> Marina laughed. 'Hinemoa eat a koumara.'
> 'No, I don't like them. They're blue – they're too unnatural. Give me some bread.'
> Marina handed her a piece, then helped herself to a koumara, which she ate delicately, looking at Hinemoa with a strange half-smile expanding over her face.
> 'I eat it for that reason' she said. 'I eat it because it is blue.'
> 'Yes.' said Hinemoa, breaking the bread in her white fingers.[30]

This vignette exemplifies Mansfield's preoccupation with doubles and sexual transgressiveness, and a characteristic mode of narration in which gender and sexuality are organizing principles.[31] In its hints of the primitive, savage and exotic, the sketch is prescient of modernist appropriations of such images and discourses, as evidenced in Roger Fry's 1910 credo about post-Impressionist art, in the savagery embraced by the Rhythmists, or the barbarism of the Fauvists.[32] Primitivism would become a trademark of modernist experimentation, developed in order to counteract the staleness of modernity and the mechanization of civilization. Mansfield's attraction to the aims and ideals of the Expressionists evident in 'Ole Underwood', written just two years after the post-Impressionist exhibition in London, has been noted by Pamela Dunbar, while Angela Smith sees all three of Mansfield's early 'colonial' stories written in 1912–13 as 'impressive for their Fauvist vigour'.[33]

'Summer Idylle' shows Mansfield exploring mutually exclusive categories, the natural and the artificial, to show how the distance between them can be overcome by sexuality and the enactment of desire. The ethnic cross-over suggested by the characters' names, and the celebration of Marina as foreign, suggests that sexually transgressive behaviour as a form of youthful rebellion (as implied by the Hinemoa myth) is enjoyable, even thrilling, with its connotations of the unnatural (as symbolized by the unnatural blue of the kumera).[34] Similar play with these categories occurs in her 1907 vignette, 'In the Botanical Gardens', in which she describes the gardens as 'a subtle combination of the artificial and the natural'.[35] Kaplan draws attention to Mansfield's use of the Wildean aesthetic framework in her aim in 1908 to write 'a sketch' about the Maata/Mansfield pair, in which to 'fill it with climatic disturbance' (that is, nature) is likely to clash with 'the strange longing for the artificial'.[36] Mansfield at this stage emulated Wilde's critical attitude towards the natural, copying into her journal his quotation from *Dorian Gray*: 'Being natural is a pose and the most irritating pose I know.'[37] She projects the desired opposite vividly in 'Juliet', whose heroine's departure from her family in London and willed alienation brings about an enigmatic smile:

> She could be just as she liked – they had never known her before. O, what a comfort it was to know that every minute sent The Others further away from her! I suppose I am preposterously unnatural, she thought, & smiled.[38]

These early works show Mansfield interweaving images of the natural and of 'belonging' to nature, with those of the foreign, unnatural and artificial (with transgressive sexuality being a motivation and reward); and this exploration enabled her in later stories to use her European distance to recapture a more densely nuanced sense of belonging in memory and imagination.

White settler (un)belonging: the 'third rate article'

Mansfield's diary of her camping trip to the Ureweras records, in addition to her attraction to the Maori, her scepticism about the white settler subject – namely, her touring companions, the rural Pakeha they encountered and by extension Mansfield's bourgeois 'vulgar' family in Wellington. She comments dismissively: 'I am so tired and sick of the third rate article – give me the Maori and the [English] tourist but nothing between.'[39] Although this included herself, Mansfield's Eurocentric aspirations led her to ignore such interpellations and to resist incorporation into this colonial system of representation. In London, however, she saw herself as 'a stranger', as 'the little colonial', no doubt aware of the contradictions.[40] Although she separated herself from the deracinated Pakeha settler subjects of her 1912–13 colonial stories, she increasingly re-entered the same colonial space through memories of childhood, when life began to run out for her, developing what Edward Said calls 're-filiation', or in Lydia Wevers's terms, 'a new form of relationship which marks the transition from "nature" to "culture"'.[41] In her late stories, this terrain is inhabited by the Sheridan and Burnell families in Wellington.

Mansfield's capture of the 'alien inauthenticity' of the rural settler continues the paradigms established in 'Summer Idylle' and other early sketches, even though partly informed by the modernist valuing of alienation and artifice. It appears in three stories about the colonial out-back and colonial life, which were published in *Rhythm*: 'The Woman at the Store' (written 1911, published in 1912), 'Ole Underwood' (written 1912, published in January 1913) and 'Millie' (written 1913, published in *Rhythm*'s successor, the *Blue Review*, in June 1913). A fourth, 'Old Tar', written in 1913, is more a narrative of psychic encounter and indigeni-zation, touching on white settler guilt with its implications of injustice and the return of the repressed.[42] In turning to the savagery of nature and the cruelty of life in colonial New Zealand for her subject matter, Mansfield responded to *Rhythm*'s edict: 'Before art can be human it must learn to be brutal.'[43] The white settler's alienation and displacement are depicted in terms of murder and betrayal, delusion and madness. Colonial space, which Alan Lawson describes as 'outside discourse, a place of non-meaning, a place of chaos that threatens the coherence of the subject', she animates as a feral, hostile force in 'The Woman at the Store'.[44] The approach of evening is described as 'a curious half-hour when everything appears grotesque – it frightens – as though the savage spirit of the country walked abroad and sneered at what it saw'.[45] This recalls the narrator's troubled identification with primitive, primordial nature in 'In the Botanical Gardens': 'And, everywhere that strange, inde-finable scent. As I breathe it, it seems to absorb, to become part of me – and I am old with the age of centuries, strong with the strength of savagery.'[46] The savage is also associated with Mansfield's attraction to women and with feminocentric desire, as in her 'savagely crude' feelings of frustrated love for Maata, and the description in the Urewera diary of the young Maori girl as 'passionate, violent, crudely savage'.[47]

The various attributions that the concept of the savage came to have for Mansfield inform her representation of the white settler subject as isolated and asocial, whose disturbed psychology and radical alienation epitomize debasement of European enlightenment values. Extreme dislocation is epitomized in the violent, inarticulate figure of Ole Underwood, who has murdered a man, and just released from prison after 20 years and subject to fits of madness is about to murder again. The rhythms of insanity buzzing in his head are captured in the narrative voice. The female protagonists of 'Millie' and 'The Woman at the Store', victims of patriarchal, colonial structures, are reduced to primitive gestures representing severe psychological dysfunction. The woman at the store has been driven to murder her husband, it is suggested, by her extreme isolation and deprivation of any human kindness. Wevers in fact argues she has been taken over, appropriated, by the barbaric spirit of the country which the narrator perceives as wandering about at dusk.[48] A similar wandering spirit appears in 'Old Tar'. The protagonist is imaged in terms of fantasy and dream and these fairy-tale features are juxtaposed to the 'uncanny' revenge that is exacted: Old Tar, who has inherited land 'bought' from the Maori, tramples and gouges it while building his dream house, and is assailed by the spirits of place.

The story can be read as a critique of colonial ideology in that it dramatizes the white settler's insertion of himself into the physical and discursive space of the indigene. Young Tar (as he is at first), his chest straining against his Sunday clothes as he is told about his inheritance, is a symbolic reminder of the absent Maori, whom his ancestors have exploited and displaced, and of the falseness of the settler dream, shored up by religious convictions and the hubris of white heritage, which replaces indigenous ideas of ownership. Young Tar's father tells him:

> '– – yer know, boy, my Pap bought this from the Maoris – he did. Ye-es! Got it off Ole Puhi for a "suit of clothes an' a lookin'-glass of your Granmaw's." My stars! He had an eye! Larst thing the ole man says to me was – "James," 'e says, "don't you be muckin' about with that bit of land top of Makra Hill. Don't' you sell it. 'And it on," 'e says, "to you an' yours."' (299)

The patriarchal desire to ''and it on', suggests neglect, not just of Maori rights to the land that the settlers have wrongfully seized, but also of indigenous spirituality in relation to the land. But once the house has been completed, Old Tar's premonition of a Day of Judgement is borne out. As Lawson points out, the Other, being only displaced, not replaced, remains to confirm the boundary of the settler self's subjectivity; and like Freud's uncanny, it is always present.[49] The obliterated voices and repressed subjects whose land has been appropriated reappear as haunting disturbances in nature, another version of the savage spirit of the land:

> In the quiet he heard the sea beat, beat up, and then he heard the wind, very slow, snuffling round the house like a lonely dog. 'Ooh Hee! Oooh Hee!' it sounded. 'A rare, sad noise', thought Old Tar, shaking his head to it. 'Sounds as if it'd lost something an' couldn't find it again.' 'Lost for evermore,' and the sad words fell into his quiet heart and started strange uneasy ripples. (301)

Old Tar's disorientation and confusion are anticipated by the narrator's fears of reprisal in 'In the Botanical Gardens': 'Shall I, looking intently, see vague forms lurking in the shadow staring at me malevolently, wildly, the thief of their birthright?'[50] The later story illustrates that white settler unbelonging is caused by ignorance, predatory greed and transported puritanism: the white settler needs the presence of the Other to know himself, but with it comes the collapse of the dream of colonization. This moral fable, like other tales which deal with the capture of native spiritual rites associated with the land, such as James Fenimore Cooper's *Leatherstocking Tales*, concludes with Old Tar's dawning recognition, painful self-questioning and petition to his silent God: '"Wot's it doing there – wot's it for?"' and '"Oh Lord, wot 'ave I done – wot 'ave I done, Lord?"' (303). Mansfield's 'postcolonial' perspective appears in the way the lost voices and repressed presences return to haunt and disempower the settler who, following the dream of settlement, has been deluded by western notions of possession.

Mansfield as colonial-metropolitan modernist

It has been customary to see Mansfield's distance from New Zealand as crucial to her literary modernism, but for her modernism to be seen as Eurocentric, being that of an alienated metropolitan modernist.[51] The complexity of her colonialism, by contrast, has been argued by Emma Neale, Bridget Orr, Mark Williams, Angela Smith and Salkat Majumadar. Certainly, the internal ventriloquism, discontinuous narrative structures, and alienated states of being in her autobiographical fragments and stories, can be associated with the interstitial positioning of the colonial as well as with modernist practice. There is room, therefore, for further development of a critical practice in reassessments of modernism which challenges the colonial/metropolitan binary in order to reposition Mansfield more decisively as a liminal artist, a colonial-metropolitan modernist who is located outside as well as within the international establishment.

Mansfield consciously othered herself as a colonial in England. Although her fascination with Maata Mahupuku ceased after 1915, and she abandoned her plans to write the novel *Maata*, the relationship would have made her more than usually aware of the construction of the social outsider, the indigenous other, the in-between subject, and to register the gaps in consciousness created by the divisions of class, gender and ethnicity. Her embrace of the white settler's 'alien inauthenticity', combined with the Wildean emphasis on the artificial and unnatural, became counterpoints to her social exclusion from the British establishment. As Angela Smith points out, like the Scottish artist J. D. Fergusson, this predisposed her to follow the liberating manifestos of the post-Impressionists and Fauvists.[52] Certainly, as all attempts to write fiction at greater length led only towards thinly disguised autobiography or *Bildungsroman*, her confinement to the short story genre might be traced to her white settler identity structures. Arguably, however, in her short life there was no time to complete her rebellion against colonialism and develop a position that was sufficiently external to her origins from which to create an extended fictional narrative.

I would not wish to claim that this paradigm can be applied with equal value to all Mansfield's work, or argue that her colonial identity structures informed all her writing or were singularly responsible for her formal inventiveness. But I suggest that the foundation for her great stories was already there in her early vignettes and sketches, and the modernist experimentation to which she was open was just one new way in which to develop what she had already intuited from her ambivalent and multiple positionings as a white settler subject.

Notes

1. See P. Brooker, A. Gasiorek, D. Longworth and A. Thacker (eds) (2010) 'Introduction' to *The Oxford Handbook of Modernisms* (Oxford University Press), pp. 1–13; P. Brooker and A. Thacker (eds) (2009) *The Oxford Critical and Cultural History of Modernist Magazines*. Vol. 1, *Britain and Ireland 1880–1955* (Oxford University Press).
2. J. Esty (2004) *A Shrinking Island: Modernism and National Culture in England* (Princeton University Press), p. 200.
3. Most recent is Salkat Majumadar (Spring 2009) 'Katherine Mansfield and the Fragility of Pakeha Boredom', *Modern Fiction Studies*, 55: 1, 119–40 (p. 121) and Elleke Boehmer in this volume.

4. E. Neale (1999) '"Why Can't She Stay Home?" Expatriation and Back-Migration in the Work of Katherine Mansfield, Robin Hyde and Fleur Adcock', PhD thesis, University College London, p. 102.

5. R. Hyde (1970 [1938]) *The Godwits Fly*, G. Rawlinson (ed. and intro.) (Auckland University Press), pp. xx–xxi.

6. On the use of the term '(un)belonging' with reference to the second-generation Black British subject, see Vedrana Velickovic (2011) 'Melancholic Travellers and the Idea of (Un)belonging in Bernardine Evaristo's *Lara* and *Soul Tourists*', *Journal of Postcolonial Writing*, 47: 3.

7. M. Williams (2000) 'Mansfield in Maoriland: Biculturalism, Agency and Mis-reading', in Howard J. Booth and Nigel Rigby (eds) *Modernism and Empire* (Manchester University Press), pp. 249–74 (pp. 256–7).

8. *Notebooks* 1, p. 51.

9. Leslie's arrival in England in February 1915 is associated with a change of direction in her art. He and Mansfield shared memories of childhood and she composed the first draft of 'The Aloe' before he died. See the essays by C. K. Stead and J. Lawrence Mitchell in this volume.

10. E. Bowen (1996 [1956–57]) 'A Living Writer', in J. Pilditch (ed.) *The Critical Response to Katherine Mansfield* (Westport, CT: Greenwood Press), pp. 70–6 (p. 75); J. F. Kobler (ed.) (1990) *Katherine Mansfield: A Study of the Short Fiction* (Boston: Twayne), p. 142.

11. A. O. Bell and A. McNellie (eds) (1975–85) *The Diary of Virginia Woolf*, 5 vols (Harmondsworth: Penguin), vol. 1, p. 58 (11 October 1917).

12. On the consequences of double expatriation in the life of the New Zealand-born poet Fleur Adcock, see J. Wilson (2007) *Fleur Adcock* (Plymouth: British Council and Northcote House), p. 1.

13. *Letters* 5, p. 304.

14. H. K. Bhabha (1994) *The Location of Culture* (London and New York: Routledge), p. 107.

15. *Ibid.*, p. 86.

16. A. Lawson (1995) 'Postcolonial Theory and the "Settler" Subject', in D. Brydon (ed.) *Essays on Canadian Writing*, 56, 20–36 (p. 29).

17. *Ibid.*; see also S. Slemon (1997 [1990]) 'Unsettling the Empire: Resistance Theory for the Second World', in P. Mongia (ed.) *Contemporary Postcolonial Theory: A Reader* (London: Arnold), pp. 72–83 (p. 80).

18. Slemon, p. 81; D. Lee (1995) 'Writing in Colonial Space', in B. Ashcroft, G. Griffiths and H. Tiffin (eds) *The Post-Colonial Studies Reader* (London and New York: Routledge), pp. 397–401 (p. 400).

19. Bhabha, p. 86; Lawson, p. 26; Slemon, pp. 80, 79.

20. *Notebooks* 2, p. 204.

21. *Notebooks* 1, pp. 103–4.

22. For example, the title of the article by Vincent O'Sullivan (1994) '"Finding the Pattern: Solving the Problem": Katherine Mansfield the New Zealand European', in R. Robinson (ed.) *Katherine Mansfield: In from the Margin* (Baton Rouge and London: Louisiana State University Press), pp. 9–24 (p. 14); Pakeha is the Maori name for foreigner; that is, the European white settler.

23. *Letters* 1, p. 44.

24. Bridget Orr (December 1989) 'Reading with the Taint of the Pioneer: Katherine Mansfield and Settler Criticism', *Landfall*, 43: 4, 447–61 (p. 453).

25. *Notebooks* 1, pp. 112 and 237–61.
26. *Ibid.*, pp. 75–6. The emendation in square brackets is Scott's. The original entry reads: 'But I like not that'.
27. *Ibid.*, p. 149.
28. *Ibid.*, p. 76.
29. J. Kristeva (1991) *Strangers to Ourselves*, L. S. Roudiez (trans.) (London and New York: Harvester Wheatsheaf), p. 191.
30. *Notebooks* 1, p. 77.
31. See S. J. Kaplan (1991) *Katherine Mansfield and the Origins of Modernist Fiction* (Ithaca: Cornell University Press), p. 9.
32. A. Smith (2000) *Katherine Mansfield: A Literary Life* (Basingstoke: Palgrave), pp. 36–9, suggests that stereotypes of savagery in this story anticipate Mansfield's later engagement with Fauvism.
33. P. Dunbar (1997) *Radical Mansfield: Double Discourse in Katherine Mansfield's Short Stories* (London: Macmillan Press and New York: St Martin's Press), pp. 53–4; Smith, pp. 82–95.
34. Hinemoa may be the prototype of Hin, the sexually ambiguous character in 'The Woman at the Store', described as 'as white as a clown', a cross-over which accentuates the inauthenticity of gendered and racial identities in this story. See Dunbar, p. 47.
35. *Notebooks* 1, p. 170.
36. Kaplan, p. 55; *Notebooks* 1, p. 112.
37. *Notebooks* 1, p. 99.
38. *Ibid.*, p. 66.
39. *Ibid.*, p. 140.
40. *Notebooks* 2, p. 166.
41. L. Wevers (1995) '"The Sod Under my Feet": Katherine Mansfield', in M. Williams and M. Leggott (eds) *Opening the Book: New Essays on New Zealand Writing* (Auckland University Press), pp. 31–48 (p. 38); citing E. Said (1983) *The World, the Text and the Critic* (Cambridge, MA: Harvard University Press).
42. It was first published in 1974, in I. A. Gordon (ed.) *Katherine Mansfield: Undiscovered Country* (London: Longman), pp. 299–303. All future references are to this edition.
43. J. M. Murry, F. Goodyear and M. T. H. Sadler (eds) (1911) *Rhythm*, 1: 1, 36.
44. Lawson, p. 24.
45. K. Mansfield (1981) 'The Woman at the Store', in *The Collected Stories of Katherine Mansfield* (Harmondsworth: Penguin), p. 554.
46. *Notebooks* 1, p. 171.
47. *Ibid.*, pp. 104 and 148.
48. L. Wevers (1993) 'How Kathleen Beauchamp Was Kidnapped', in R. B. Nathan (ed.) *Critical Essays on Katherine Mansfield* (New York: Hall & Co.), pp. 37–47 (p. 44); see also Dunbar, p. 45.
49. Lawson, p. 28.
50. *Notebooks* 1, p. 171.
51. Orr, p. 451.
52. Smith, p. 22.

13
Mansfield and Dickens: 'I am not Reading Dickens *Idly*'

Angela Smith

It must seem a bizarre notion of mine to link Charles Dickens with Katherine Mansfield. If we accept that Gudrun Brangwen in *Women in Love* is partially modelled on Mansfield, we know that D. H. Lawrence saw her as a miniaturist, creating a 'savage carving' of 'odd small people' who 'have a sort of funniness that is quite unconscious and subtle'.[1] Most of Dickens's books were written, and published in serial parts, over 19 months; they were bursting with complicated plots and exuberant with characters, fitting Henry James's description of nineteenth-century novels as 'large loose baggy monsters'.[2] The delicate artistry of the avant-garde twentieth-century miniaturist and the broad brush-strokes of the sensationally popular Victorian novelist could not seem more different, yet Mansfield's passion for Dickens's fiction was a continuum in her short life. Why did she admire a writer whose fiction seems the antithesis of her own? I do not want to argue that Dickens's work influenced Mansfield's writing, but that her interaction with it provided a recurrent stimulus to her creativity. As she wrote to her husband, John Middleton Murry, from the south of France, 'When you feel you can afford it would you send me Nicholas Nickleby? (I am not reading Dickens *idly*).'[3] In her admiration for him, as I shall demonstrate, she was at odds with fashionable modernist opinion, which castigated Dickens's fiction as childish and vulgar. I shall begin by comparing her attitude to Dickens with that of some of her contemporaries, then focus on a six-week period in her life in 1918 to substantiate my argument about Dickens's work as a stimulus to her imagination and development.

When she was recreating her childhood in her notebooks in the process of writing the long story 'The Aloe', which was later transmuted into 'Prelude', Mansfield recalls that at Miss Swainson's private school, 'I could make the girls cry when I read Dickens in the sewing class.'[4] She seems to have reduced them to tears with the death of Paul in *Dombey and Son*, and when the headmistress read *David Copperfield* there was 'something so fascinating in her voice that I could listen for years & years'.[5] She sees the headmistress as being like one of the Phiz illustrations that are passed round in her class, 'so tiny, so spry'. Mansfield's letters and journals show that from her childhood on, Dickens's characters were part of the everyday texture of her experience;[6] in addition to this, when she was a child in Karori she and her family lived in a house rather forbiddingly named Chesney Wold, which was of course the ancestral seat of the hidebound Sir Leicester Dedlock in *Bleak House*.

In her adult life, in the draft of a letter to Frederick Goodyear, she impersonates Mrs Gamp from *Martin Chuzzlewit*: 'Never did cowcumber lie more heavy on a female's buzzum than your curdling effugion which I have read twice and wont again if horses drag me.'[7] As Ida Baker said of her, 'She was a born actress and mimic.'[8] In a letter to Dorothy Brett in 1922 she becomes Mr Toots when she writes, 'But it don't signify, Miss Dombey.'[9] In a very early vignette of 1908 she describes a gnome as leering 'in a Quilp-like manner',[10] and in the last year of her life she mocks herself, saying 'I hope I don't sound like Mrs Jellaby,'[11] the ruthless philanthropist in *Bleak House*. Other snippets referring to David, Dora and the Micawbers in *David Copperfield*, or to Podsnap in *Our Mutual Friend*, suggest that Dickens's characters people her imagination. Having read John Forster's *Life of Charles Dickens* Mansfield writes to Murry saying that 'we must have the books. We must have his complete works.'[12] The same letter, though it conflates various incidents, gives an insight into her delight in Dickens's capacity to entertain his own children, and to encourage them to put on plays:

> What will you do when you come to the description of how his little boy aged 4 plays the part of hero in a helmet & sword at their theatricals & having previously made the dragon drunk on sherry stabs him dead which he does in such a manner that Thackeray falls off his chair laughing & rolls on the floor.[13]

In a letter to Lady Ottoline Morrell Mansfield compares Dickens's writing with the work of her contemporaries: 'Yes – doesn't Charley D. make our little men smaller than ever – and such *pencil sharpeners*.'[14] We can speculate about what she means by this – it reminds me of her comment about E. M. Forster's fiction: 'E. M. Forster never gets any further than warming the teapot. He's a rare fine hand at that. Feel this teapot. Is it not beautifully warm? Yes, but there ain't going to be no tea.'[15] Her contemporaries sharpen their pencils or warm the teapot but Dickens delivers the goods.

It is probable that Virginia Woolf's attitude to Dickens was moulded by her father, Leslie Stephen; delivering the goods might be how Stephen saw Dickens, as a socially inferior literary tradesman. In his entry on Dickens in the *Dictionary of Literary Biography* in 1888 Stephen wrote: 'If literary fame could be safely measured by popularity with the half-educated, Dickens must claim the highest position among English novelists.'[16] Virginia Woolf, in her essay on *David Copperfield*, summarizes in 1925 what the fashionable attitude to Dickens's fiction is: 'The rumour about Dickens is to the effect that his sentiment is disgusting and his style commonplace; that in reading him every refinement must be hidden and every sensibility kept under glass.'[17] Though she does not entirely accept this patronizing perception, she goes on to write of Dickens's 'failure to think deeply, to describe beautifully. Of the men who go to make up the perfect novelist and should live in amity under his hat, two – the poet and the philosopher – failed to come when Dickens called them.'[18]

This is interestingly at odds with the view of her friend T. S. Eliot, expressed in an essay written in 1927 comparing Dickens and Wilkie Collins:

> In comparison with the characters of Dickens [Collins's characters] lack only that kind of reality which is almost supernatural, which hardly seems to belong to the character by natural right, but seems rather to descend upon him by a kind of inspiration or grace. Collins's best characters are fabricated, with consummate skill, before our eyes; in Dickens's greatest figures we see no process or calculation. Dickens's figures belong to poetry, like figures of Dante and Shakespeare, in that a single phrase, either by them or about them, may be enough to set them wholly before us. Collins has no phrases. Dickens can with a phrase make a character as real as flesh and blood.[19]

One might think of a phrase from *Our Mutual Friend* which Eliot thought of using as the title of what eventually became *The Waste Land*. The elderly widow Mrs Higden, who cannot read, praises the boy who turns the mangle for her, Sloppy: 'You mightn't think it, but Sloppy is a beautiful reader of a newspaper. He do the Police in different voices.'[20]

Sloppy's life and his relationship with the world are evoked in that short phrase, much as Laura's are in 'The Garden Party' when, alone with the carter's body, she says, 'Forgive my hat.'[21] Both phrases belong, in Eliot's words, to poetry, both are succinct but grow in the reader's imagination, making the character as real as flesh and blood. As she reads *Little Dorrit* in 1920, Mansfield recognizes what Eliot describes as 'a kind of inspiration or grace' in the book and records it in her journal:

> There are moments when Dickens is possessed by this power of writing – he is carried away – that is bliss. It certainly is <u>not</u> shared by writers today. For instance the death of Merdle – dawn fluttering upon the edge of night. One realises exactly the mood of the writer and how he wrote as it were for himself. It was not his will he <u>was</u> the fluttering dawn and he was Physician going to Bar.[22]

In the same year she tells Murry of her own comparable experience, this time of writing 'The Stranger': 'Ive been a seagull hovering at the stern and a hotel porter whistling through his teeth. It isn't as though one sits and watches the spectacle. That would be thrilling enough, God knows. But one IS the spectacle for the time.'[23]

Her consonance with Eliot's opinion of Dickens's fiction chimes with D. H. Lawrence's view of Dickens, but is at odds with those of other influential modernist editors, writers, publishers and critics. In *Aspects of the Novel* E. M. Forster writes magisterially that sometimes in Dickens's fiction 'the lively surface of [the] prose scratches like a cheap gramophone record, a certain poorness of quality appears [...] the world of beauty was largely closed to Dickens'.[24] Forster has a dilemma. In his categorization of characters in fiction, 'Dickens's people are nearly all flat (Pip and David Copperfield attempt round-ness, but so diffidently that they seem more like bubbles than solids). Nearly every one can be summed up in a sentence.'[25] On this analysis, as Forster says, Dickens 'ought to be bad',[26] but somehow he isn't, though he would be of course if Forster's assertion that his characters can be summed up in a sentence were sustainable. The American critic and journalist Edmund Wilson, writing in 1939, was scathing about what he saw as British intellectual snobbery with regard to Dickens:

> Dickens had no university education, and the literary men from Oxford and Cambridge, who have lately been sifting fastidiously so much of the English heritage, have rather snubbingly let him alone.

The Bloomsbury that talked of Dostoevsky ignored Dostoevsky's master, Dickens.[27]

As Wilson indicates, the irony of this is evident. Virginia Woolf, Ford Madox Ford and E. M. Forster extol the literary subtlety of Tolstoy, Turgenev and Dostoevsky and yet all three Russian writers acknowledge Dickens's fiction as formative. In *Dickens and His Readers*, George Ford writes:

> Turgenev's intelligence did not preclude his admiring Dickens more than any other nineteenth-century English author – a taste which must have been disconcerting to some of his disciples such as Ford Madox Ford in whose eyes Turgenev was greater than Shakespeare and Dickens a hack for children.[28]

Turgenev inscribed one of his novels to Dickens, from 'one of his greatest admirers, the author',[29] and Tolstoy declared that, 'If you sift the world's prose literature, Dickens will remain.'[30] Dickens's novels were translated early into Russian, and Dostoevsky responded to what he saw as their spiritual dimension: 'It is said that during his imprisonment, the only books he would read were *David Copperfield* and *Pickwick Papers*.'[31]

Though Mansfield read the fiction of Tolstoy, Dostoevsky and Turgenev, as well of course as Chekhov's work, from the time that she discussed Tolstoy with other pupils at Queen's College Harley Street this did not make her dismissive of Dickens. She even broke ranks, at least in her notebook in 1918, saying, 'I must admit the russians bore me – they are not couched enough in the bones of <u>Art</u>.'[32] Claire Tomalin remarks of a letter to Mansfield's lover written as early as 1908 that '[h]er writing is alive, her observation acute, and her imagination has a touch of nightmare intensity: Katherine's characteristic talent is already formed, and showing its affinity with Dickens'.[33] D. H. Lawrence made a similar comparison relating to Mansfield's intense perception, and ability to imbue what she perceives with an aura. In a letter to Murry, Frieda Lawrence wrote: 'Lawrence said Katherine had a lot in common with Dickens, you know when the kettle is so alive on the fire and things seem to take on such significance.'[34] We have descriptions of Dickens and Mansfield by other artists, commenting on their ruthless powers of observation. Henry James was intimidated when he met Dickens in America; James was confronted by a mask 'which met my dumb homage with a straight inscrutability, a merciless *military* eye, I might have pronounced it, an automatic hardness, in fine, which at once indicated to me, in the most interesting way in the world, a kind of economy of apprehension'.[35] Mansfield's eyes were seen as equally probing by her friend, the American painter Anne Estelle Rice, who painted her portrait and wrote this passage about her for an exhibition held in New Zealand House in 1958:

> The arresting feature was the beautiful, sombre, questioning eyes. They seemed to send out a penetrating beam into the crannies and recesses of one's nature and there was no escape from the searching scrutiny, often disconcerting and I'm sure not flattering.[36]

The six-week period in Mansfield's life that I want to focus on is from January to February 1918; I suggest that her reading of Dickens's *Our Mutual Friend* combines with events in her life to shift her writing onto a different plane. As I have indicated, there are ways in which their affinity was already obvious. Both are brilliant comic writers. In addition to this, Dame Jacqueline Wilson has spoken potently about the effect on her of Mansfield's ability to enter a child's consciousness; Dickens was of course the first British novelist to see the world through a child's eyes, most evidently in the opening chapters of *David Copperfield* and of *Great Expectations*. On a different tack, as a New Zealander who often felt alienated by life in London, Mansfield is likely to have relished Dickens's viciously satirical portrayal in *Our Mutual Friend* of Mr Podsnap, the embodiment of imperial bigotry. She mentions in a letter[37] the episode in which he plays host to an unfortunate foreigner at a dinner party:

> 'We Englishmen are Very Proud of our Constitution, Sir. It Was Bestowed Upon Us By Providence. No Other Country is so Favoured as This Country.'
> 'And ozer countries? –' the foreign gentleman was beginning, when Podsnap put him right again.
> 'We do not say Ozer; we say Other: the letters are "T" and "H"; you say Tay and Aish, You Know;' (still with clemency). 'The sound is "th" – "th!"'
> 'And o*ther* countries,' said the foreign gentleman. 'They do how?'
> 'They do, Sir,' returned Mr. Podsnap, gravely shaking his head; 'they do – I am sorry to be obliged to say it – *as* they do.'[38]

Though this kind of condescension was familiar to Mansfield it does not account for her claim that she was not reading Dickens idly. Let us move to the first two months of 1918. After an appalling wartime journey she had settled in Bandol, having been warned by her doctor that she should not winter in England. She writes to Murry in late January 1918 of her pleasure in reading *Our Mutual Friend* because 'the satire in it is first chop' and because 'I have a huge capacity for seeing "funny" people you know & Dickens does fill it at times quite amazingly.'[39] She asks Murry 'for another Dickens; if I read him in bed he diverts my mind',[40] but the comedy in *Our Mutual Friend* is mostly savagely dark and macabre, as in the scene where Silas Wegg's wooden leg rises in a quasi-erotic erection at the possibility of finding a miser's hoard, and then he falls into 'a kind of pecuniary swoon'.[41] As she read Dickens's novel, Mansfield began work on a new story, 'Je ne parle pas français'. In one of her rare comments on her own fiction she writes to Murry that she has two '"kick offs" in the writing game', one of them joy and the other

> an *extremely* deep sense of hopelessness – of everything doomed to disaster – almost wilfully, stupidly – [...] *a cry against corruption* that is *absolutely* the nail on the head. Not a protest – a *cry*, and I mean corruption in the widest sense of the word, of course –
>
> I am at present fully launched, right out in the deep sea with this second state.[42]

That is, on the writing of 'Je ne parle pas français'. *Our Mutual Friend* is surely Dickens's most probing and despondent cry against corruption, and it seems to have triggered a radical new development in Mansfield's writing. The corruption that surrounded her included the disease that was eating its way into her lungs; she sees the Great War as comparable with consumption when she writes that 'everything is poisoned by it. Its *here in* me the whole time, eating me away.'[43] Her sense of being eroded was intensified when her occasional companion Ida Baker threatened to arrive; Mansfield wrote protesting to Murry that 'Shes a revolting hysterical ghoul. Shes never content except when she can eat me.'[44] By the middle of February she had had her first experience of spitting bright red blood, and she knew that Keats, in the same situation, recognized it as his death warrant. No wonder that in another letter written in February she wrote that the 'english language is damned difficult but its also damned rich and so clear and bright that you can search out [...] the darkest places with it'.[45] She was excited and obsessed by her work but 'there is a great black bird flying over me and I am so frightened he'll settle'.[46]

Though Dickens was a phenomenally successful writer, by the 1860s he was bitterly disappointed that aristocratic patronage, amateurism and inertia had impeded the significant changes that he had championed in public health, the Civil Service, the franchise, the Poor Law and education. He wrote despondently in 1861 of the bishops that 'not a lawn sleeve fluttered when the poor law broke down in the frost and the people [...] were starving to death. The world moves very slowly, after all.'[47] In its dark places, there are aspects of *Our Mutual Friend* that chime thematically and aesthetically with 'Je ne parle pas français'. The book opens with the Thames portrayed as a source of carrion, with the carrion crow Gaffer Hexam trawling the water for corpses. Though some corpses are resurrected in the course of the novel, it is not depicted as a spiritually enriching, Lazarus-like, experience. Rogue Riderhood drowns and is resuscitated: 'And yet – like us all, when we swoon – like us all, every day of our lives when we wake – he is instinctively unwilling to be restored to the consciousness of this existence, and would be left dormant, if he could.'[48] The cynical narrator juxtaposes the squalid life of the scavengers on the river with, in the second chapter, the great and the good:

> The great looking-glass above the sideboard reflects the table and the company. Reflects the new Veneering crest, in gold and eke in silver, frosted and also thawed, a camel of all work. The Heralds' College found out a Crusading ancestor for Veneering who bore a camel on his shield (or might have done if he had thought of it) and a caravan of camels take charge of the fruits and flowers and candles, and kneel down to be loaded with the salt.[49]

The narrator's voice dominates the text, urbane and angry, exposing the hypocrisy of the society it depicts but showing the Veneerings and Podsnap still dominant at the end, unlike the hypocritical Pecksniff in the much earlier *Martin Chuzzlewit* who was unmasked and disempowered.

Greed permeates the world of the novel, and the most skilled performers acquire status and possessions. The Lammles, who make an unwise investment, or gamble, in marrying what each assumes mistakenly is a wealthy spouse, attempt to recoup their losses by playing roles which enable them to prey on their 'dear friends'. Macabre disguises and doublings perplex the reader and the characters; John Harmon dies but reappears first as Julius Handford, then as John Rokesmith, then as John Harmon again. The poor suffer and die from lack of medical help or because their terror of the workhouse drives them into exile, and those of their children who do go to school learn mechanically by rote. In a vivid moment of what Eliot might describe as 'inspiration or grace', Dickens encapsulates relationships in this society. The disabled

child, Jenny Wren, who makes dolls and their clothes, walks at night
with her friend Riah:

> Jenny twisted her venerable friend aside to a brilliantly-lighted toy-shop
> window, and said: 'Now look at 'em. All my work!'
> This referred to a dazzling semicircle of dolls in all the colours of
> the rainbow, who were dressed for presentation at court, for going to
> balls, for going out driving, for going out on horseback, for going out
> walking, for going to get married, for going to help other dolls to get
> married, for all the gay events of life.[50]

Just as Jenny makes the dolls, the glittering society of the Podsnaps and
Veneerings is all the work of others, their servants, tailors, tradespeople
and employees. The many voices of the text cover that spectrum,
from the inarticulacy of Rogue Riderhood to the sophisticated Eugene
Wrayburn. Mansfield compares herself to Dickens in relation to voice
in a letter to Ida Baker, suggesting that she hopes to give readings of her
work as Dickens did:

> I intend, next spring, to go to London, take the Bechstein Hall and
> give readings of my stories. Ive always wanted to do this and of course
> it would be a great advertisement. Dickens used to do it. He knew his
> people just as I know old Ma Parker's voice and the Ladies Maid.[51]

The voice of 'Je ne parle pas français' differs from anything that
Mansfield had previously written. As she wrote to Murry, using a metaphor related to consumption: 'I stand or fall by it. Its as far as I can get
at present and I have gone for it, bitten deeper & deeper & deeper than
ever I have before.'[52] Murry agrees, saying that this 'is the only writing of
yours I know that seems to be *dangerous*'.[53] The danger lies in the intimacy
of the narrator's delighted revelation of his own predatory powers, and
in the exposure of his society's hypocrisy. A different danger lurks in
the Englishman the narrator meets; in an echo of *Our Mutual Friend*, his
name is Dick Harmon. Totally unlike *Our Mutual Friend*, the plot is simple.
The Parisian narrator, Raoul Duquette, is a writer who ingratiates himself
with Harmon and is disappointed when Harmon returns to Britain.
Harmon comes back with a young unnamed woman known as Mouse who
is not his wife, and, oppressed by guilt about having deceived his mother,
abandons her without having occupied the hotel rooms that he had asked
Duquette to reserve for them. The narrator promises to return to help the
distressed woman, who does not speak French, but he too abandons her.

Though she paradoxically says in French that she cannot speak French, Mouse certainly cannot understand French mores, and is at the mercy of Duquette, who describes himself as a little fox-terrier, a breed designed to follow a fox down its hole. It is particularly sinister when the woman gets into a taxi: 'Mouse got in the black hole,'[54] followed by Duquette. He introduces himself to the reader in a workmen's café on a winter afternoon, and is immediately self-contradictory. He asserts that the clientele of the café does not sit down, and yet he sits gazing at himself in a mirror; he claims that it is a rule of his never to look back, yet the story is composed of his memories of Dick and Mouse. He is proud of himself as a performer, attractive to women although he describes his own appearance as feminine: 'without my clothes I am rather charming. Plump, almost like a girl, with smooth shoulders, and I wear a thin gold bracelet above my left elbow' (148). He compares himself to theatrical characters, for instance when he hears from Dick again: 'I wore a blue kimono embroidered with white birds and my hair was still wet; it lay on my forehead, wet and gleaming. "Portrait of Madame Butterfly," said I, "on hearing of the arrival of *ce cher Pinkerton*"' (153). His self-justification for writing about his own body is that he has lived a 'submerged' life, and he comments that his introduction of himself resembles the way in which a prostitute might offer pornographic photographs of herself. He seems indeed to be a bisexual prostitute and pimp who has no money but lives a comfortable life on credit and duplicity, though he keeps claiming that he is a serious young writer who is making a special study of English literature. The titles of the books he has published all evoke impressions of forgery or bedroom farce: *False Coins, Wrong Doors* and *Left Umbrellas*.

His dazzling narrative whirls through a series of clichéd images, juxtaposed against what is actually happening. His tawdry imagination conjures up a picture of the Virgin Mary on an ass and he asks: 'That's rather nice, don't you think, that bit about the Virgin? It comes from the pen so gently; it has such a "dying fall". I thought so at the time and decided to make a note of it' (144). Later, when Dick disappears, he imagines a melodramatic scene: 'Flash! went my mind. Dick has shot himself, and then a succession of flashes while I rushed in, saw the body, head unharmed, small blue hole over temple, roused hotel, arranged funeral, attended funeral, closed cab, new morning coat...' (163–4). Has this an echo of Mr Jingle in *Pickwick Papers*? Duquette knows that these distortions are the 'direct result of the American cinema acting upon a weak mind' (143), but at the same time he narrates vividly and cruelly the less frenzied and more poignant story of Harmon and Mouse. He leaves unexamined the bizarre doubling in his narrative, though the reader would not trust his interpretation anyway; his senses are superbly alert and his judgement is corrupt. When he first meets Dick he has a glimpse of a photograph of Dick's mother, '[d]ark, handsome, wild-looking, but so full in every line of a kind of haggard pride that even if Dick had not stretched out so quickly I wouldn't have looked longer'. Duquette is 'tempted to cross myself, just for fun' (152). To his horror, when Dick returns from Britain he has become his mother's vampiric double, looking equally haggard, wild and proud. So obsessed is Duquette with preying on Harmon, and with fanciful and clichéd gutter-press conclusions to Harmon's and Mouse's story, that he leaves the reader to draw what psychological implications there might be in the parallel images. His version of speaking French is revealed at the end of the story when he returns to the present and 'some dirty old gallant' comes to sit opposite him. He says, 'But I've got the little girl for you, *mon vieux*. So little... so tiny. And a virgin' (167). The theme of eating and being eaten, so evident in *Our Mutual Friend* in the comparison between the recurrent grand dinners and the emaciated poor, closes 'Je ne parle pas français', in a paragraph that was censored by Constable when the story appeared in book form:

> Madame knows me. 'You haven't dined yet?' she smiles.
> 'No, not yet, Madame.'
> I'd rather like to dine with her. Even to sleep with her afterwards. Would she be pale like that all over?
> But no. She'd have large moles. They go with that kind of skin. And I can't bear them. They remind me somehow, disgustingly, of mushrooms. (167)

In its ghastly way, this is surely an example of what Eliot identified as a phrase which makes a character as real as flesh and blood.

Like *Our Mutual Friend*, the story is unsparing in its insight into a predatory way of life which exploits women, which postures and poses, and is obsessed with material gain. Both texts concern child abuse, though in *Our Mutual Friend* the focus is on working children who support their dissolute parents whereas in 'Je ne parle pas français' the emphasis is on sexual exploitation; again, this is a passage that was censored by Constable. Duquette tells us that when he was ten, the family had an African laundress who took him into an outhouse and kissed him:

> And then with a soft growl she tore open her bodice and put me to her. When she set me down she took from her pocket a little round

fried cake covered with sugar and I reeled along the passage back to our door.

As this performance was repeated once a week it is no wonder that I remember it so vividly. Besides, from that very first afternoon, my childhood was, to put it prettily, 'kissed away'. I became very languid, very caressing, and greedy beyond measure. (147)

The reader is not, it seems to me, invited to pity Duquette but to perceive that the exploited African servant then exploits the child in her turn, who in his turn betrays and sells women. What I am suggesting is that the uncompromising vision of *Our Mutual Friend* elicited a similarly dangerous and disturbing imaginative leap in Mansfield when she wrote 'Je ne parle pas français'. Hers is a professional commitment to her art, knowing as she did that the story would be hard to publish. Dickens was similarly committed, writing of Thackeray: 'I thought that he too much feigned a want of earnestness, and that he made a pretence of under-valuing his art, which was not good for the art that he held in trust.'[55] Mansfield did not under-value Dickens's art or her own, and I hope I have shown that she did not read Dickens idly.

Notes

1. D. H. Lawrence (1995 [1920]) *Women in Love* (Harmondsworth: Penguin), p. 94, chapter 8.
2. H. James (1934) *The Art of the Novel* (New York: Charles Scribner's Sons), p. 84.
3. *Letters* 2, p. 52.
4. *Notebooks* 2, p. 24.
5. *Ibid.*, p. 26.
6. There is evidence in her letters and journals that she read *Nicholas Nickleby, The Old Curiosity Shop, Barnaby Rudge, Martin Chuzzlewit, Dombey and Son, David Copperfield, Bleak House, Little Dorrit, Our Mutual Friend* and *The Mystery of Edwin Drood*. She may well have read other novels, and she also read *Master Humphrey's Clock*.
7. *Notebooks* 2, pp. 60–1.
8. I. Baker (1972) *Katherine Mansfield: The Memories of LM* (New York: Taplinger), p. 233.
9. *Letters* 5, p. 203.
10. *Notebooks* 1, p. 111.
11. *Letters* 5, p. 267. The correct spelling is 'Jellyby'.
12. *Letters* 3, p. 229.
13. *Ibid.*, p. 229.
14. *Letters* 2, p. 274.
15. *Notebooks* 2, p. 93.
16. Quoted in P. Collins (1971) *Dickens: The Critical Heritage* (London: Routledge and Kegan Paul), p. 17.

17. L. Woolf (ed.) (1971 [1966]) *Virginia Woolf Collected Essays*, 4 vols (London: Hogarth), vol. 1, p. 191.
18. *Ibid.*, p. 193.
19. T. S. Eliot (1986 [1951]) *Selected Essays* (London: Faber and Faber), p. 462.
20. C. Dickens (1997 [1865]) *Our Mutual Friend* (Harmondsworth: Penguin), p. 198, Book 1, chapter 16.
21. A. Smith (ed.) (2002) *Katherine Mansfield Selected Stories* (Oxford University Press), p. 349.
22. *Notebooks* 2, p. 209.
23. *Letters* 4, p. 97.
24. E. M. Forster (1962 [1927]) *Aspects of the Novel* (Harmondsworth: Penguin), p. 24.
25. *Ibid.*, pp. 78–9.
26. *Ibid.*, p. 79.
27. E. Wilson (1961) *The Wound and the Bow* (London: Methuen), p. 1.
28. G. H. Ford (1965) *Dickens and His Readers* (New York: W. W. Norton), pp. 191–2.
29. *Ibid.*, p. 292.
30. Quoted in Collins, p. 242.
31. Ford, pp. 193–4.
32. *Notebooks* 2, p. 150.
33. C. Tomalin (1987) *Katherine Mansfield: A Secret Life* (London: Viking), p. 58.
34. Quoted in *ibid.*, p. 244.
35. Quoted in P. Ackroyd (1990) *Dickens* (London: Guild), p. 951.
36. *Katherine Mansfield in Her Letters and Works*. Exhibition catalogue, 25 April–16 May 1958, New Zealand House, London.
37. *Letters* 5, p. 257.
38. *Our Mutual Friend*, p. 137, Book 1, chapter 11.
39. *Letters* 2, pp. 45–6.
40. *Ibid.*, p. 55.
41. *Our Mutual Friend*, p. 477, Book 3, chapter 6.
42. *Letters* 2, p. 54.
43. *Ibid.*, p. 54.
44. *Ibid.*, p. 68.
45. *Ibid.*, p. 96.
46. *Ibid.*, p. 55.
47. M. House, G. Storey and K. Tillotson (eds) (1997) *The Letters of Charles Dickens* (Oxford: Clarendon Press), vol. 9, p. 389.
48. *Our Mutual Friend*, p. 440, Book 3, chapter 3.
49. *Ibid.*, pp. 20–1, Book 1, chapter 2.
50. *Ibid.*, p. 430, Book 3, chapter 2.
51. *Letters* 5, p. 160.
52. *Letters* 2, p. 56.
53. C. A. Hankin (ed.) (1983) *The Letters of John Middleton Murry to Katherine Mansfield* (London: Constable), p. 115.
54. Smith, p. 157. Further references are given in brackets in the text.
55. M. Slater (2009) *Charles Dickens* (New Haven and London: Yale University Press), p. 522.

14

'Not Always Swift and Breathless': Katherine Mansfield and the Familiar Letter

Anna Jackson

In a journal entry of 1908, Katherine Mansfield plans out a 'life' as she calls it, a work of fiction, about

> a girl in Wellington; the singular charm and barrenness of that place – with climatic effects – wind, rain, spring, night – the sea, the cloud pageantry. And then to leave the place and go to Europe. To live there a dual existence – to go back and be utterly disillusioned, to find out the truth of all – to return to London – to live there an existence so full and strange that life itself seemed to greet her – and ill to the point of death return to W. and die there. I should fill it with climatic disturbance – and also of the strange longing for the artificial.[1]

Sydney Janet Kaplan has noted the eerie prescience of this journal entry, written when Katherine Mansfield was about halfway through this 'life' as she had imagined it, before she became ill and before, on point of death, she did return to Wellington in a sense, through her stories 'Prelude' and 'At the Bay'.[2] It looks forward, too, to the way Mansfield has been read as an Impressionist writer, offering glimpses of strange and full moments of being, and as a writer whose self was always fictional, and whose life has been represented as a pageantry of pretence.[3]

An emphasis on the moment, and on the presentation of self, is what we look for in the genre of the letter. In a brilliant review of Elizabeth Bishop's collected letters, 'Writing to the Moment', Tom Paulin suggests a 'poetics of the familiar letter' might take as its starting point the 'spirit of newness and nowness' that he finds in Bishop's letters, the rejection of the written for the writing, and the rejection of the mind in rest for the mind in action.[4] I have found Paulin's work on letter poetics a useful starting point for developing a poetics of the diary, and particularly applicable to Mansfield's journal writing. The form of the diary is characterized by both continuity and fragmentation, with each daily entry having autonomy as a dated piece of writing, while at the same time having a place within a sequence. In Mansfield's case, since she didn't keep a 'diary' as such, but rather various notebooks containing autobiographical material ranging from notes on her surroundings to recipes and shopping lists, the 'moment of writing' of each entry is particularly important. The emphasis in her writing on visual details, climatic effects, glimpses and impressions, and the connections made through a date, or juxtaposition on a page, between plans for the evening, shopping lists, story ideas and her immediate surroundings, gives each entry a powerful immediacy, the 'spirit of newness and nowness' that Paulin sees as essential to the genre of the letter and which is equally essential in making a diary entry out of lines in a scrapbook.[5]

Given how useful I found Paulin's poetics of the familiar letter for a reading of Mansfield's journal writing, it seemed an obvious starting point for my reading of Mansfield's letters. Mansfield is as brilliant a letter writer as Elizabeth Bishop, and the qualities Paulin finds in Bishop's letters can be found in Mansfield's too. The spirit of newness and now-ness is present not only in the description of the moment of writing – the 'dirty egg-cup full of ink' in front of the piece of paper, 'my watch (an hour slow) [...] and two flies walking up and down [...] discussing the ratification of the Peace Treaty'[6] – but also in the exploration of ideas and opinions, the images she finds to describe her intentions as a writer, the attempts to describe people's characters and her own reactions to them. This is 'the mind in action' that Paulin celebrates,[7] the baroque details that he reads not as inconsequential decorativeness but as arising out of that distinction between the mind at rest and the mind in action, the written and writing. It might be supposed, even, that it is Mansfield's characteristic attentiveness to the moment of writing, and her ability to write in and of the present that accounts for how extraordinarily prolific she was as a letter writer.

Yet the more I read of the letters, the more I felt that the moment of writing was less important than the time before and after the moment of writing, the time remembered and the time spent waiting for a reply. Angela Smith argues against the common understanding of Mansfield as an Impressionist, emphasizing instead her connections with post-Impressionist art. Smith takes up Clare Hanson and Andrew Gurr's suggestion that an understanding of Mansfield's writing as post-Impressionist might be a useful starting point for a study of 'the solidity of the structure of her stories'.[8] She gives just such an analysis of the 'deep structures' of Mansfield's 1917 story 'Je ne parle pas français', noting Mansfield's own insistence on the story's 'outline', its 'sharp lines', and teasing out the patterns constructed through the shape of the sections and the recurrent images and motifs.[9] The letters offer further support for a reading of Mansfield as a post-Impressionist writer. Form doesn't have quite the same importance for the letters as it has for the stories, though the letters are often quite intricately structured. Where the letters go beyond Impressionism, and beyond Paulin's poetics of newness and nowness, is in their insistence on the importance of memory, and their insistence on the depth of the friendships they evoke and maintain.

Mansfield's poetics changed in the ten years after she planned that first 'life' in 1908. In January 1916, after the death of her brother, she was writing in her journal, 'the form that I would choose has changed utterly. I feel no longer concerned with the same appearance of things [...] The *plots* of my stories leave me perfectly cold.'[10] The form she looks for now is described in terms of surfaces and depths. One of the most well-known images for the kind of writing she wants to do is the description of the boats she sent to Middleton Murry, almost a year earlier – the spring image of the heavy boat, with the 'people rather dark and seen strangely as they move in the sharp light and shadow', accompanied by the sound of water.[11] That image has an echo in a note she added to a letter to Ottoline Morrell, in 1919. The letter itself is wonderful, full of news and descriptions, a page and a half printed, surely several pages of handwritten pages – so hardly a letter that needed apologizing for. But Mansfield scribbled on to the finished letter the quick apology, 'This is such a choppy letter, bumping over the waves. But *deep down* I am simply rejoicing & rejoicing because *we are friends* –.'[12]

This depth informs not only the content of the letters and the way Mansfield writes about her ideal of friendship, it informs the poetics of the letter as a genre Mansfield engages in. The 'newness and nowness' and the performance of a 'mind in action', while everywhere apparent and important, are strategies among others that serve the purpose of maintaining an ongoing friendship and relating the moment of writing to a correspondence that is insistently beyond temporal limits. Again and again, Mansfield makes it clear to her correspondents that the friendship that occasions the letter comes before and after the letter itself. In many of the letters, she apologizes for not having written sooner, or for longer, promising to write again soon, and insisting, as she did in a letter to Virginia Woolf in 1919, 'you would not believe me if you knew how often you are in my *heart* & *mind*'.[13] She wrote similarly to Dorothy Brett, in 1917:

> I have left your letter unanswered for more days than I could have wished. But don't think it was just because I am so careless and faithless. No, really not. I enjoyed keeping silent with the letter just as one enjoys walking about in silence with another until the moment comes when one turns and puts out a hand and speaks.[14]

These might seem like empty excuses, except that her letters do give such a good sense of how real to her the friendships were, even when she was too ill to write back with immediate responses. One of the most well-known passages from the letters is the passage, from the same 1917 letter to Brett, in which Mansfield declares, 'When I write about ducks I swear I am a white duck with a round eye.' This passage has been cited to support claims about Mansfield's multiple selves, or fragmented personality, and by Smith as an example of Mansfield's post-Impressionist emphasis on capturing not an impression but the essence of the subject – becoming, as Mansfield says, '*more* duck, *more* apple, or *more* Natasha' than the actual objects. It is indeed a wonderful passage, but the passage that comes just after it is perhaps even more characteristic of Mansfield's approach to letter writing, and is equally important in the way it shifts a reading of Mansfield away from the terms of Impressionism. In this section of the letter, Mansfield interrupts her own philosophizing to insert her friend's imagined reply: 'Brett (switching off the instrument): "Katherine I *beg* of you to stop. You must tell us all about it at the Brotherhood Church one Sunday evening."'[15] While passages such as that about the duck provide wittily phrased extracts that usefully present Mansfield's ideas about the self, it is passages such as her imagining Brett's reply that bring not only the letter itself alive but give a vivid sense of the friendship that exists beyond the confines of the correspondence. Mansfield shows herself fully aware that she is laying herself open to parody with her philosophizing, wittily pre-empting Brett's response with one she could hardly improve on. Even so, she clearly remains confident that Brett shares her interest in such matters as well as her alertness to tone, since in the very next paragraph she returns to the question of form, going on to write about 'the unpardonable unspeakable thrill of this art business'.

Even when Mansfield is writing about her immediate surroundings, when her writing belongs most to the moment, she often makes a point of including the person she is writing to, as someone who would appreciate the scene: so she writes to Koteliansky, 'I have taken this little villa for the winter, perhaps for longer. It is nice, Koteliansky; you would like it. It is on a wild hill slope, covered with olive and fig trees and long grasses and tall yellow flowers' and to Murry, she writes, 'You should have seen after the rain was over yesterday, little old men appeared from nowhere in peaked hats, crawling over the wild hill looking for snails.' When she observes that a large, fawn-coloured rat has just run past, she writes to Murry to tell their cat, Wing.[16] Describing how 'very lovely just now with every kind of little growing thing' the country is in a letter to Beatrice Campbell, she promises she will send her flowers as soon as she has a box other than an empty soap box in which she worries 'the violets would arrive in a lather'.[17]

For Paulin, this attention to the other person, the absent addressee, is a necessary part of a letter poetics based on newness and nowness, and these examples, especially the passing rat, support this connection between the immediacy of the letter form and its dialogic energy: he quotes Charles Lamb's description of letter writing as a 'grand solecism of *two presents*' where '*my Now*' collides with '*your Now*'.[18] But that present-tense collision only has any meaning because of the shared history between the letter writer and the letter reader. Mansfield constantly refers back to past occasions and shared memories. In a letter to Ottoline Morrell, she connects the importance of memory with a deeper sense of significance; even though the memories she selects are specific to that relationship, she says:

> there is something at the back of it all which if only I were great enough to understand would make *everything*, everything, indescribably beautiful. [...] Do you remember the day we cut the lavender? And do you remember when the Russian music sounded in that half-empty hall?[19]

The importance of memory to Mansfield makes sense of what might seem a contradiction in her fiction reviewing, when in reviews written in 1919 she criticizes Woolf twice for being too old-fashioned, yet is equally critical of Dorothy Richardson's experimentalism. She declares Woolf's 'Kew Gardens' to 'belong to another age',[20] and regards *Night and Day* so remote from current literary trends that 'we had thought never to look upon its like again'.[21] Yet while she criticizes *Night and Day* for being over-cultivated and controlled, she criticizes Richardson's *The Tunnel* for being 'composed of bits, fragments', and for the 'incredible rapidity' of its narrative, complaining that 'one cannot imagine her planning out her novel'.[22] She criticizes Woolf's focus on external objects and events, arguing that the surface realism is at the expense of 'the dream world', and yet she is equally critical of the psychological focus of *The Tunnel*, declaring that 'Miss Richardson has a passion for registering every single thing that happens in the clear, shadowless country of her mind.' Her objection to the egotism of this approach is, however, consistent with her criticism of Woolf's control over her characters, which is similarly represented as a kind of egotism. Woolf's characters, Mansfield suggests, only come alive when the author lets them move and speak but have no life beyond the page, where they are all the time overshadowed by the author, 'her personality, her point of view, and her control of the situation'. What is absent from both novels is memory. As Mansfield writes in her review of *The Tunnel*, 'There is one who could not live in so tempestuous an environment as her mind – and he is Memory. She has no memory. It is true that Life is sometimes very swift and breathless, but not always.' Mansfield sees both *Night and Day* and *The Tunnel* as too much restricted to the present, and in both cases she connects the absence of any sense of memory with egotism, and with a failure of form.

When Smith observes how post-Impressionist Mansfield's descriptions of places are in her letters – Menton for instance is described as 'a solid wall [...] of shapes and colours' – she explains what might seem simply a matter of style as, rather, expressing a post-Impressionist preoccupation with the 'link between the surface and the profound self'.[23] In the same letter, Mansfield's description of her own house builds up a pattern of shades of yellow and repeating forms that, Mansfield writes, 'belong to a picture or a story – I mean they are not remote from one's ideal – one's dream'. Here the link is clearly made between a formal patterning and an underlying idealism. It is interesting to note that 'Je ne parle pas francais', the story Smith selects for the solidity of its structure and its 'sharp lines', is described by Mansfield herself as an achievement because of its *depth*: 'I stand or fall by it [...] I have gone for it – bitten – deeper and deeper than ever I have before.'[24] Depth again is what she claims for 'Prelude', the story in which she aimed to 'bring the dead to life again', and, in going deep, to 'speak to the secret self we all have'.[25]

Mansfield looks for this 'secret self' in the work of other writers. Reading Emily Brontë's poetry, and reflecting on the experience in a letter to Ottoline Morrell in 1919, she wrote, 'the Beauty of it is contained in one's certainty that it is not Emily disguised – who writes – it is Emily [...] It *is* so tiring, isn't it, never to leave the Masked Ball – never – never.'

In the same letter, she wrote of 'One's own life – one's own secret private life – what a queer positive thing it is. Nobody knows where you are – nobody has the remotest idea *who* you are, even.'[26] Yet the letters allow for the sharing of this secret self, and even the letters that are unwritten are significant for this kind of idealized communion. By the time she makes the excuses for not having written, as in the letters to Woolf and Brett already referred to, she is of course writing an actual letter, but the significance she attaches to the time between receiving the letter and writing the reply reminds me of a line in a letter Emily Dickinson once wrote to a friend: 'I write you many letters with pens which are not seen. Do you receive them?'[27] Dickinson is alluding here to a passage in the Bible looking forward to a time when 'we look not at things that are seen, but the things that are not seen, for the things that are seen are temporal; but the things that are not seen are eternal'.[28] Mansfield's attention was more characteristically on what is seen than what is not seen, and her relationship to the eternal is ambivalent; nevertheless she similarly situates the moment of writing in the context of a more permanent, and idealized, friendship, which exists at its most real in the heart and mind.

Dickinson's eternity is wonderfully immaterial – in another letter she wrote: 'A letter always feels to me like immortality because it is the mind alone without corporeal friend'[29] – but Mansfield tended to imagine eternity more spatially, and not out of time but full of time. She imagines Ida Baker (L. M.) rattling around in eternity: 'it will be ideal for L. M. – time for everything, time to get to know everybody and to wonder about "this that and the other" to her heart's desire'.[30] She herself experiences a sense of eternity watching waves at a beach, and finding eternity within the moment: 'What is it that happens in that moment of suspension? It is timeless. In that moment (what *do* I mean?) the whole life of the soul is contained.'[31] She finds a kind of eternity, too, in relationships, and in the letters she shares: to Murry, she wrote (as her way of signing off): 'Your letters are HEAVEN and I fly about in them like a gold and silver … Wig.'[32]

Smith has observed Mansfield's tendency to use spatial metaphors particularly to describe the process of writing. In the letter which describes writing 'Prelude' in terms of going 'deep' and speaking 'to the secret self', she also describes how in writing the story 'Ive wandered about all sorts of places – in and out.'[33] Returning to the passage in the letter about Emily Brontë, and 'one's own secret private self', it is interesting to note that nobody knowing *who* you are comes after the more obvious point, to Mansfield, of nobody knowing *where* you are.

When literary works 'map out' a space, then, this can be read in terms of sharing these secret regions of the self. The trust, and the intimacy that this involves, come across in the metaphors Mansfield uses when writing about the literature that means most to her: describing herself as a reader, she often describes herself as a child, or as holding the hand of the writer. Reviewing Dostoevsky's collection of stories, *An Honest Thief*, she writes:

> Perhaps Dostoevsky more than any other writer sets up this mysterious relationship with the reader, this sense of *sharing*. We are never conscious that he is writing at us or for us. While we read, we are like children to whom one tells a tale; we seem in some strange way to half-know what is coming and yet we do not know; to have heard it all before, and yet our amazement is none the less, and when it is over, it has become ours.[34]

And concerning Knut Hamsun's *Growth of the Soil*, she writes, 'it is, indeed, very much as though we were allowed to hold him by the hand and go with him everywhere'.[35]

The image of holding hands is one that recurs again and again in the letters. It fits of course with Paulin's sense of 'nowness' as the essential quality of a poetics of the familiar letter, as an illustration of that moment of connection between two people. But, as we saw in the letter to Brett, in which Mansfield wrote of the silent companionship that comes before 'the moment one turns and puts out a hand and speaks', the moment of writing depends on a communion that extends beyond that momentary 'nowness'. A poem of Mansfield's, 'Pic-Nic', nicely illustrates the silent communion between friends, and how it depends on the withdrawal from the present and from physical presence to find, in solitude, the 'secret self' that makes the friendship meaningful:

> When the two women in white
> Came down to the lonely beach
> She threw away her paintbox
> And she threw away her notebook
> And down they sat on the sand
> The tide was low
> Before them the weedy rocks
> Were like some herd of shabby beasts
> Come down to the pool to drink
> And staying there – in a kind of stupor.

Then she went off and dabbled her legs in a pool
Thinking about the colour of flesh under water
And she crawled into a cave
And sat there thinking about her childhood
Then they came back to the beach
And flung themselves on their bellies
Hiding their heads in their arms
They looked like two swans.[36]

In its materiality, and in its silence, the friendship represented in the poem is quite unlike the incorporeal friendships maintained through language that Dickinson celebrates. Mansfield's letters, like Dickinson's, depend too on words, not silence, and sustain a friendship of the heart and mind in the absence of physical intimacy. Nevertheless, the image of the two women coming back together from the pool and from the cave captures something of the movement between past and present, ideal and reality, physical and intangible, that structures Mansfield's letters and that structures, too, the friendships that were so often conducted through the exchange of letters.

While the letters depend so much on an appeal to memory, they often look forward, too, to the future. When writing to Woolf, in particular, she often puts off mentioning literary matters, looking ahead instead till when they can talk: 'I positively must see you soon. I want to talk over so much,' she writes in April 1919, and in July 1918, less urgently, 'Your Pearl of a Letter made me realise what an infinite deal I want to talk about with you. But it will keep.'[37]

With Koteliansky, she imagines an idealized future, a future in which they build together a little house in the woods, or they ride in a closed cab to a house heated by a 'visionary caretaker', and she asks him if the detail of these imagined scenes seems to him, too, of infinite value, 'as though the Lord threw you into Eternity – into the very exact centre of eternity' (and then she imagines him laying the letter aside).[38] Writing to Murry, of course, she is often making quite specific arrangements for the next time they can be together, but for him, too, she will construct imaginary scenes of the future, and invite his participation, or imagine his response. Always, too, she is writing to solicit letters in return, from Brett, from Woolf, from Koteliansky and, most insistently, from Murry.

In Murry's first transcription of one of Mansfield's diary entries in 1927, he records what looks like a Freudian slip, where the word 'writing' takes the place of the expected word, 'waiting': 'I am writing for LM to come. She's very late. Everything is in a state of suspense – even birds and chimneys.'[39] In the 1954 edition of the journal the word is corrected to 'waiting', but there is a sense in which Mansfield might have been said to have been writing for LM to come. Many of the journal entries are written to fill in a time of waiting, and the letters too provide a way of waiting productively. The connection between writing and waiting is filled out further in a letter Mansfield wrote to Ottoline Morrell, describing an afternoon waiting for her father:

> Life is so strange. [...] Today this afternoon, waiting for my Father to come to tea – I felt I could have made – but only of that waiting – a whole book – I began thinking of all the time one has 'waited' for so many and strange people and things – the special quality it has – the *agony* of it and the strange sense that there is a second you who is outside yourself & does nothing – nothing but just listen – the other complicated you goes on – & then there is this keen – unsleeping creature – waiting to leap – It is like a dark beast – and he who comes is its prey – – – .[40]

This function of writing, 'writing for LM to come', transports even the 'nowness' that alternates in the letters with the appeals to memory and the anticipation of the future into this special space outside the everyday self and outside ordinary time. Mansfield describes her immediate surroundings in a letter to Koteliansky, and then has him striding in, interrupting the letter with lines she attributes to him. Even when she describes herself writing, as she often does in letters to Murry, it can be seen as a way of putting him in the frame, as observer. In a notebook entry written in 1920 when she and Murry were, as so often, apart, she wrote of her wish to have someone on the veranda with her, 'to *share* my vision with [...] Sitting out there in the sun – where is my *mate*.'[41] Describing scenery in letters to Murry is a way of sharing her vision with him, as if he were sitting there in the sun with her.

This is another way of understanding the recurrent imagery of holding hands, and if writing allows a connection that can be made outside space and outside ordinary time, it is a connection that takes on a special significance in relation to the dead. In her journals, Mansfield begins to use the holding hands imagery after the death of her brother Leslie, in writing about the composition of the New Zealand stories, and again in a passage remembering the baby sister who died at birth. She describes writing 'The Aloe' as if it were a way of holding hands with her brother as her imagined reader: 'Each time I take up my pen *you* are with me. [...] we shall range all over our country together.' But she is writing not only of the past but towards the future, too. The stories written in memory of the New Zealand childhood she and Leslie shared are written as letters: letters to her brother and letters to New Zealand: 'Oh I want this book to be written. [...] It must be bound and wrapped and sent to New Zealand.'[42]

Murry's letters in particular were so important to Mansfield that in one letter to him she suggests, 'when I die, just before the coffin is screwed up, pop a letter in. I shall jump up and out.'[43] If, in the early sketch towards a 'life', written in 1908, the young Mansfield looked forward to an early death, her focus on the moment complicated by a 'longing for the artificial', her later letters and journal writings reveal, in contrast, a longing for deeper truths, and a passionate resistance to death. The apparently impressionist term 'glimpse' is used again and again in her letters and journal entries to describe the perception of some kind of 'eternity', a moment 'in which the whole of life is contained'. It is this kind of moment which fills her stories, and this is the moment 'at the back of' the friendships she conducted through the familiar letter.

Notes

1. *Notebooks* 1, pp. 111–12.
2. S. J. Kaplan (1991) *Katherine Mansfield and the Origins of Modernist Fiction* (Ithaca and London: Cornell University Press), p. 53.
3. Vincent O'Sullivan, Kate Fullbrook and Sarah Sandley are critics cited by Angela Smith who read Mansfield as an Impressionist writer. See: A. Smith (2000) *Katherine Mansfield: A Literary Life* (Basingstoke: Palgrave), p. 8.
4. T. Paulin (1996) 'Writing to the Moment', in *Writing to the Moment: Selected Critical Essays 1980–1996* (London: Faber and Faber), pp. 215–39.
5. See A. Jackson (2010) *Diary Poetics* (London: Routledge).
6. *Letters* 3, p. 63.
7. Paulin, p. 229.
8. Smith, p. 9.
9. Smith, pp. 15, 23.
10. *Notebooks* 2, p. 32.
11. *Letters* 1, p. 168.
12. *Letters* 2, p. 330.
13. *Ibid.*, p. 347.
14. *Letters* 1, p. 330.
15. *Ibid.*
16. *Letters* 3, pp. 5, 24 and 27.
17. *Letters* 1, p. 260.
18. Paulin, p. 216.
19. *Letters* 2, p. 254.
20. J. M. Murry (ed.) (1930) *Katherine Mansfield: Novels and Novelists* (London: Constable), pp. 36–8.

21. *Ibid.*, pp. 107–11.
22. *Ibid.*, pp. 1–4.
23. Smith, p. 8.
24. *Ibid.*, p. 20.
25. *Ibid.*, p. 124.
26. *Letters 2*, p. 334.
27. W. M. Decker (1998) *Epistolary Practices: Letter Writing in America before Telecommunications* (Chapel Hill and London: University of North Carolina Press), p. 37.
28. 2 Corinthians 4.18.
29. Decker, p. 41.
30. *Letters 3*, p. 45.
31. J. M. Murry (ed.) (1954) *The Journal of Katherine Mansfield 1904–1922*. Definitive Edition (London: Constable), pp. 202–3. Hereafter referred to as *Journal*. It is interesting to note that she refers to this 'moment of suspension' as a 'glimpse', a word commonly associated with Impressionism, but used by Mansfield, here and elsewhere, to refer to the recognition of the timeless, a suspension, that takes the observer *beyond* surface impressions.
32. *Letters 2*, p. 58.
33. Smith, p. 124.
34. Murry, *Novels and Novelists*, p. 113.
35. *Ibid.*, p. 204.
36. V. O'Sullivan (ed.) (1988) *Poems of Katherine Mansfield* (Oxford University Press), p. 66.
37. *Letters 2*, pp. 311 and 258.
38. *Letters 1*, p. 192.
39. J. M. Murry (ed.) (1927) *The Journal of Katherine Mansfield* (London: Constable), p. 10.
40. *Letters 2*, p. 350.
41. *Notebooks 2*, p. 187.
42. *Journal*, pp. 96, 98.
43. *Letters 3*, p. 9.

15
Meetings with 'the Great Ghost'

C. K. Stead

My awareness of Katherine Mansfield began even before I'd read her. When I was at primary school during the Second World War there was a series of cards, 'Great New Zealanders', which came with the breakfast cereal, Weetbix, and I still remember some of them. The great New Zealand scientist was (of course) Rutherford, the great athlete was Jack Lovelock, the All Black George Nepia, the tennis player Anthony Wilding, the statesman 'King Dick' Seddon, the soldier 'Tiny' Freyberg, the opera singer Oscar Natzke, the Maori leader Sir Peter Buck and the writer Katherine Mansfield. There were others, but if my memory is right there was just one of each category. I'm sure Mansfield would have been chosen for one reason only – not because in New Zealand she was much read outside the literary community, but because she was known to have 'made it overseas'. These were still (though I would soon be resenting and rejecting the description) colonial times – but the Dominion (as it then was) was striving to shake itself loose, to see itself as an independent nation. What better measure (ordinary New Zealanders would have asked) that we were a nation in our own right than that some of ours could measure up against those of the homeland; could succeed and shine there?

Here, then, we have Mansfield figuring possibly as inspiration, possibly as burden; and the burden aspect, I'm sure, explains the irritation in the voice of Allen Curnow in the only spoken comment I recall him making on her. He and Denis Glover and I were on a literary panel in Auckland and her name came up. Curnow's response was to recall 'some fool' in the Christchurch of his youth writing that she was 'the only peacock in New Zealand's literary garden'. I interjected 'Peahen', which Denis capped with 'Piha'; and if more was said I've forgotten it.

The undertone of irritation with Mansfield around this time among New Zealand writers trying to establish an indigenous literature was quite strong. Curnow, dismissing what he calls the 'awful archness' of Robin Hyde's lines on Mansfield, adds a gratuitous footnote quoting Geoffrey de Montalk on the subject.[1] Denis Glover disparages her as 'prissy' and says he gave up reading her long ago.[2] And Frank Sargeson warns the young Vincent O'Sullivan not to 'spend his life on the dreams of a Karori schoolgirl'.[3]

For myself, reading Mansfield began at secondary school and university. It was random, intermittent, the stories only (no letters or journals), and quite unrelated to formal courses. She was not 'taught', nor was 'New Zealand literature', but I was very conscious of her, and admiring – especially of a quality I would much later describe as 'an indefinable, all-pervasive freshness in her writing, as if each sentence had been struck off first thing on a brilliant morning'.[4]

I think I was also soon aware that if you read more than a few stories you were likely to come upon some in which the wonderful sensibility deliquesced into mush, the sharp eye missed its target, the trick-cyclist fell off her bike. But these were only impressions, and I never gave Mansfield focused critical attention until 1972 when, at the age of 39, I was awarded the (as it then was) Winn-Manson Menton Fellowship – so named to commemorate its primary benefactor, Sheila Winn, its founders, Celia and Cecil Manson, and the French town that honoured Mansfield with a memorial. By that time I was Professor of English at Auckland, my special field being twentieth-century modernist poetry and criticism.

*****

Before I come to that, however, I want to say a word more about Mansfield's reputation in New Zealand when I was young. The two men who influenced me most, and encouraged me as a poet during my student years, were Frank Sargeson and Allen Curnow. Curnow was my teacher at the university, Sargeson my literary friend and mentor outside it. I never heard either of them say much about Mansfield. There was the irritable Curnow remark about the peacock in our literary garden; and I do remember Frank once, in conversation, saying of something of hers I had admired that, 'Yes, OK, it was good', but it was *the kind of thing women can do*. This rather odd idea (odd enough for the remark to stick in my memory) was one he had once tried to elevate into a critical principle, though I didn't know that until it appeared posthumously in a selection of his critical pieces.[5]

It was a radio talk he gave in 1948. His argument is that as a fiction writer Mansfield is 'in the *feminine* tradition'; and he hastens to add that this is not just another way of saying she's a woman. Others he lists as belonging to this tradition are Samuel Richardson, Jane Austen and E. M. Forster, all of whom he admires. But then he adds, seeming to contradict himself, that 'the feminine tradition is the *minor* tradition'. The tendency that characterizes it is concern 'with the part rather than the whole – in other words a tendency to make your story depend for its effectiveness on isolated details and moments of life'. A writer of Jane Austen's stature can get away with it; but fiction of this kind, when it fails, fails very badly, 'because everything is so very tenuous – everything is, as it were, hanging by the finest of threads'.[6]

He then offers two examples of Mansfield stories: one, 'The Voyage', which succeeds; another, 'Her First Ball', where those tenuous threads break and the story is a failure. I should think it's not difficult to agree that 'The Voyage' is a success and 'Her First Ball' possibly a failure. And other points he makes about her work, positive and negative, are plausible. But the larger point seems more than anything an indicator of an anxiety about Mansfield and a wish to place her safely inside a box; to label her '*minor*'; to contain her and put her away on a shelf.

That was Sargeson in 1948. Twenty years later, towards the end of his career, he found an entirely different way of dealing with her. In an interview published in 1970, he brings up something Winston Rhodes has reported of a girl student saying that there were two tragedies in New Zealand literature – one was Katherine Mansfield and the other Frank Sargeson. And he comments, 'This is a tremendous thing – I think it's very very good indeed – salutary, all sorts of things could be said about it.'

It becomes clear as the interview continues that Frank took this to mean that each of them, Mansfield and Sargeson, imposed a style which others felt it necessary to emulate. 'Mansfield, writing powerfully,' he says, 'imposed a pattern on our writing so that everybody was impressed and hosts of young women wrote Mansfield stories.'[7] And then he quotes something from Dennis McEldowney saying that when he (McEldowney) first read Sargeson he thought that *this* was New Zealand, and that Sargeson's was the only way to write about it.

There may be, or may have been, some broad truth in all this. But it strikes me, at this distance in time, as simultaneously a piece of self-promotion and of Mansfield-containment. It appears to be modest. 'Instead of opening something for New Zealand', he says, 'both Mansfield and myself have tended to be constricting influences.'[8] Modest, except that it puts him at a stroke alongside Mansfield, on a par with her. The twin tragedies of New Zealand Literature! She can come out of her box so long as he can sit at her right hand.

I stress that my view of all this is affectionate, even admiring, because I see strategies of that kind as an inevitable outcome of writers at that time struggling to be noticed in their own country, competing with the name that was big with the New Zealand public, not because they read her, but because they knew people 'overseas' did. Curnow's only serious comment on Mansfield is in the introduction to his 1960 *The Penguin Book of New Zealand Verse*. What appeals to him in the poem 'To Stanislaw Wyspianski' is the unambiguous self-identification as a New Zealander, couched in terms which are more negative than positive. What Curnow is weary of, clearly, is the false clamour of nationhood, the glamorizing of our collective identity, and the expectation that poetry should fly the flag. He lingers especially on the line 'I, a woman, with the taint of pioneer in my blood': 'the feeling', he comments, 'is something like shame for her country: for its childish clumsiness, its merely *physical* preoccupations [...], its ignorance of, or indifference to, "ghosts and unseen presences"'. And he goes on:

> Denial and acceptance are mixed in 'To Stanislaw Wyspianski', though the denial given to New Zealand is their argument. I think they express Katherine Mansfield's intuition that New Zealand's obstinate social hedonism, marching with the littleness and the isolation [...] stood between her and the knowledge of life (and death) she needed.[9]

This is among the clearest statements anywhere in the anthology's very long introduction of Curnow's own position – what might be called his 'negative nationalism'. Yes, the poets should speak for, as well as of, the nation; but they have a responsibility to represent the negatives as well as the positives; and in particular to articulate what he calls 'the New Zealand sadness (always there, however deeply buried)'.[10] The broader tradition Curnow is attaching himself to is the social realism of the 1930s that evolved partly out of the War poetry of 1914–18 and Wilfred Owen's dictum, 'The true Poets must be truthful.'[11] It's quite a weight for the young Mansfield's Whitmanesque windiness to carry; but he doesn't misrepresent her poem; and it does seem that, by 1960, he has grown beyond the resentment of her fame that was common two and three decades earlier, so that he can now call on the authority of her name to ratify something that for him is immensely important.

*****

I come back now to myself in 1972, the second writer to receive what's called these days the New Zealand Post Katherine Mansfield Menton Prize.[12]

In Menton I set about writing what Allan Phillipson has referred to as my 'difficult second novel'.[13] In that chilly little Memorial room under the Villa Isola Bella I worked very hard at the fiction; but the secondary task I set myself was to read everything of Mansfield's in print at that time, to read the biographies, and to form some sort of critical overview of her life and work.

My interest in her was still partly nationalistic – she was 'a New Zealand writer' and, whatever that means, so was I; and partly I saw reading her as a politeness, an acknowledgement of the fellowship that had brought me to the south of France. But neither of those motives would have kept me studying her for more than a few weeks if her work and her life had not engaged my mind and imagination as fully as they did. She was, quite simply, immensely rewarding; and it was in the course of that reading I conceived the idea of making a selection of her letters and journals which could be run together, arranged chronologically, with chapters and biographical notes.

I was in Menton for about eight months with my wife, Kay, and our children – then aged two, five and eight – after which we went on to London for the remaining five months of my sabbatical leave. There I put the letters and journals idea to Judith Burnley at Penguin/Allen Lane and received, in the right order, encouragement, the use of a Xerox machine and a contract.[14]

I knew there were problems with the correctness or otherwise of the published texts, and that I should check them where possible; so for those months I worked in the British Museum, reading Mansfield and Bloomsbury material, and reading relevant manuscripts held there, checking texts of letters I'd chosen, and now and then adding passages, or whole letters, omitted from the published editions. It was there I came on her letter from Cornwall describing Lawrence chasing Frieda and beating her, while Katherine and Jack sat transfixed at the supper table, embarrassed and uncertain what they should do. That letter was published for the first time in my selection; and years later I made it a scene in my novel about her.

Back in New Zealand I was on a committee that took me to Wellington from time to time, and I made each visit an opportunity to work on manuscripts in the Turnbull Library. The letters that went into my selection were checked against the manuscripts, which didn't mean there would be no mistakes (I'm a diligent, but also an impatient, scholar), but that there would be fewer.

But time was passing, and I knew to check the journal entries as well would try my publisher's patience. I had met Margaret Scott in

Wellington; and I remember she showed me her copies of the published editions of the *Journal* and the *Scrapbook* (as Murry called them), annotated with her corrections. That might have been a short-cut to more dependable texts; but I didn't like to ask, it wasn't offered, and if it had been, I would still have been dependent on someone else's transcriptions. So the texts derived from Murry's edition of the *Journal* were left uncorrected.

The edition was dedicated to Celia and Cecil Manson, the originators of the Menton fellowship. They deserved the acknowledgement and they were unambiguously pleased by it. A quarter of a century later, when the book had been reissued for the last time in the UK and was being taken up by Random House New Zealand, the Mansons were dead, and I dedicated the new edition to Margaret Scott – without, alas, first seeking her permission. Foolishly, I thought she would be pleased. She tried not to seem ungrateful; but she made it clear she was not happy to have her reputation for accuracy compromised by association with Murry's uncorrected journal texts. I'm glad to acknowledge here that the mistake was mine, and to apologize.

Of course this was never intended as an edition primarily for scholars; and one did, on the whole, get a very good sense of Mansfield from those early Murry transcriptions. Much of what he copied presented few problems; and where there were extreme difficulties (the *Urewera Notebook*, for example) no one was going to be infallible.

Sometime in the 1980s, after my selection was published, I spent a few days in the Turnbull Library doing a test transcription of some pages of the *Urewera Notebook* which I then compared with Ian Gordon's text, and have since compared with Margaret Scott's. I wanted to gauge how far the Murry text of her journal misrepresented her, and how much difference, if any, a further transcription would have made. Gordon's transcription is good, and Scott's, better; but neither can be called perfect, because in many instances it's impossible to be certain. Figure 1 shows two examples where, if you add mine to the others,[15] you get four different readings.

During the Rotorua visit Mansfield dashes down something which Murry transcribes (believing, apparently, that nga moni was a kind of sweet potato) as 'We pick nga-moni'. Gordon corrects this to 'We play nga maui', with a note explaining that 'nga maui' is a string game, otherwise known as cat's cradle. So Gordon's reading makes sense; but no-one, looking at the verb, could possibly read it as 'play'. This is a wishful reading. Scott corrects it to 'We pluck nga maui'. 'Pluck' is closer to the look of the word on the page, which undoubtedly begins with 'pl', but

220

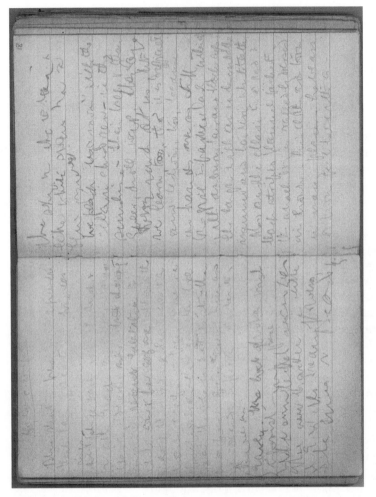

Figure 1 Transcriptions of a page of the *Urewera Notebook*. Alexander Turnbull Library, Wellington, New Zealand, John Middleton Murry collection, ref. no. qMS-1244

it only makes sense, if at all, with difficulty; and it's very difficult to see a 'u' in what Gordon saw as an 'a'. What it is, I think, is an 'e' and an 'a' pushed together, and the word, as I read it, is 'pleach' – 'we pleach nga maui'; unusual, but it has the double advantage of making sense,[16] and matching the look of the letters on her page. 'Pick', 'play', 'pluck', or 'pleach' – the difficulties of Mansfield transcription could hardly be better illustrated!

A little further on Murry transcribes 'That evening – horrid', and doesn't even try to copy the next phrase. Ian Gordon has 'that evening – horrid the purple bowl'. Scott has 'that evening – horrid – the people – bores [?]'. Gordon's 'bowl' is almost right but his 'purple' is clearly wrong. Scott's 'people' is right but her 'bores [?]' I think is wrong. My transcript reads, 'that evening – horrid – the people – bowls'. Since there was, even in 1907, a bowling green in those Rotorua gardens, and since people playing bowls are the kind the young Mansfield would very likely describe as 'horrid', I think my transcript is probably right.

So it is, up to a point, a game anyone can play; and no-one is going to score ten out of ten. But beyond question our chief debts are, first, to Murry, because he went first;[17] and second to Margaret Scott, because she has done the hard slog over so much material over so many years.

In my introduction to the selection I tried to do justice to Murry – not only as first transcriber of the manuscripts, but also as their preserver, and the one who kept the world interested in her and in them. Of course he profited by that. She had willed all her work to him, so that was his right. I was impatient with the view, quite widely encountered especially in the 1980s, and represented, for example, by that rather silly movie, *Leave All Fair*,[18] that Murry had sinned in not doing what she'd asked him to do; had not tidied up her 'camping ground' and '[left] all fair'. She had, I argued, given him impossible instructions: 'destroy all that you do not use', and 'destroy all [...] you do not wish to keep'.[19] The word 'use' surely suggests publication. And as to keeping or destroying: the same people who criticized him for preserving and publishing would have been merciless if he had destroyed so much as a single page.

My selection came out in hardcover from Allen Lane in September 1977, and simultaneously in the Penguin Modern Classics series, where it was reissued and remained in print for more than 20 years. Among other things, it was the initial trigger and provider of material for Cathy Downes's one-person show, *The Case of Katherine Mansfield*, which was also revived often over many years.

*****

Working with manuscripts, learning when and where they were written, produces a sense of closeness. Another source of that feeling is to meet survivors, as they seem, who were Katherine's friends. That happened to me only twice. The second and less significant occasion was in 1977 when A. S. Byatt suggested she and I should lunch with Claire Tomalin who was just beginning work on her Mansfield biography. I've forgotten where the lunch took place – somewhere in Bloomsbury – but a little old man who shuffled up to our table to greet Claire was introduced to me as Richard Murry, Jack's much younger brother. Katherine had been very fond of Richard, wrote him a number of good letters, and bequeathed him a pearl ring that he could give to his lover when he had one.

Much more significant was my meeting with Ida Baker in 1972.[20] I'd exchanged letters with her and she invited me to come to her cottage in the New Forest. It was a very amiable occasion, just the two of us; and I was surprised to find her quite a firm personality, not the dilly incompetent represented in Katherine's letters and notebooks – almost blind, but still able to cook lunch. And yet I could also see in her the quality of plodding, devoted literalness that Katherine had exploited while at the same time being driven mad by it – the 'ghoul' she dreamed of killing in Ospedaletti. And it seemed to me absolutely consistent with Katherine's portraits of Ida that she should explain to me that her door, opening not onto a road but what was hardly more than a track through the forest, had to be left open day and night because a bird (I think it was a swallow) was nesting in the beams of her ceiling and had to be free to come and go.[21]

A lot of what Ida Baker said had recently appeared in her book of memoirs – they were well-rehearsed stories, though better for being told in her own voice.[22] But now and then there were flashes which brought me suddenly closer to Mansfield's people – the slightly dreamy look when she said of Jack, 'Oh he was a *charming* boy'; and the sense of panic in her voice when she described Lawrence, with his flaming hair and beard, *pacing* up and down the room, hungry and impatient for the lunch it was her job to prepare.

By 1977 the selection was ready for publication and I was back in London as a visiting fellow in the English Department at UCL where I was part of Karl Miller's team teaching the twentieth-century moderns paper. I was now working on what was to be my second book on that subject, so I lectured on Yeats, Eliot and Auden; but I also included Mansfield in my part of the course, and an article based on my Mansfield lectures appeared that year in Ian Hamilton's *New Review*.

I was less inclined to be forgiving of Murry as Mansfield critic than I'd been of him as Mansfield editor. Murry had sentimentalized her and misrepresented her literary life, writing himself so determinedly into its centre that her fiction was shown as flowering when he and she were-together-and-in-accord, and failing, or turning dark, when they were apart in fact and/or in feeling.

Most of the first draft of 'The Aloe', for example, had been written, not during their idyll together at Bandol, as Murry asserted, but when she was alone in Paris living in the apartment of her French lover Francis Carco.[23] Further, I was able to cite a letter by Murry to Sydney Schiff, which I'd come across in 1972 in the British Museum, to show that 'A Married Man's Story' was written at the Chalet des Sapins in August 1921. This not only contradicted Murry's subsequent placing of that story (and consequently everyone else's) as coming from her stay in Cornwall in 1918; it showed again the inaccuracy and wishfulness of his positive/negative pattern for how, when and why her best work was done.[24]

*****

In my remaining years at the university my most serious academic work was completing my second book on Pound, Yeats and Eliot;[25] but in my New Zealand literature courses, Mansfield always had a place both at first year and MA levels, and from time to time I wrote about her work. I'd like to mention briefly now a mild spat that occurred in the early 1990s because I think it raises a question that still hangs over the figure of Mansfield.

In 1987 I reviewed Claire Tomalin's biography in the *London Review of Books*. It was a book I admired especially for its confronting the subject of Mansfield's health in a way that hadn't happened before. But in an otherwise entirely favourable notice, I objected to the description of Mansfield as 'sexually ambiguous, with a husband, a wife, and lovers of both sexes'. This was, at the time, a fashionable view, but it seemed to me imprecise to the brink of inaccuracy and untruthfulness, and I suggested the author was 'letting the times do her thinking for her'. Tomalin made no complaint; but four years later, when someone in the *TLS* quoted what I had said, she wrote objecting, and an exchange followed.

There is, of course, no doubt that in the hothouse atmosphere of Queen's College, where girls had crushes not only on their male teachers but on one another, Mansfield embraced the ideas of Oscar Wilde as exciting, liberating, avant-garde; and Vincent O'Sullivan has shown how these ideas led back to Pater as well,[26] and shaped some of her earliest and most enduring notions of the role of the artist, and of what constituted a work of art. No doubt either, that when she recorded in her notebooks her one or two immature homosexual experiences (if that's what they were), 'Oscar' was invoked – not the figure of delicate mockery he later became for her, but a serious intellectual influence. Whether, or in what way, lying all night in Edie Bendall's arms was sexual, can't be determined. In retrospect Edie was sure it was not; at the time, or for the purposes of her journal, Katie chose to give the impression it was, and that 'Oscar' would be pleased with her.

My point, in the exchange with Claire Tomalin, was that when Mansfield had emerged out of the turmoil and confusions of her teenage years into adulthood, it didn't seem to me that any significant shred of sexual ambiguity remained. She could love both males and females, as we all can – and from time to time her love was gushingly expressed. That was the manner of the time, and it suited her temperament. But sex for the adult Mansfield, as far as I have ever been able to discover, was something that happened with males – and, while her health held up, it happened quite often. This is also the view of Margaret Scott who, in transcribing the letters and complete notebooks, must have spent more time in Mansfield's company than anyone else alive. 'As a teenager,' Scott writes,

> [Mansfield] had crushes on one or two girls or women, as do many girls who are incarcerated in single-sex schools away from men. But in her adult life there is simply no evidence of her sexual interest in any woman, though plenty of her interest in men.[27]

Is this a question that matters? I think we all feel some responsibility to get these things right as far as possible; not to overstate for dramatic or fashionable effect; and not to insist where no-one can be sure. The writers we study, and whose work we teach, were people like ourselves, and would want us to be scrupulous. So when, for example, Tomalin says, 'None of her sexual relations with men appears to have given her happiness or even satisfaction,'[28] I ask myself what this means precisely, and how it can be known. Does 'satisfaction' there go together with 'sexual' in the same sentence? Sexual satisfaction? Pleasure? Orgasm? Or simply enjoyment, emotional fulfilment? In the journal entry about her brief affair with Francis Carco, she writes so simply about undressing and getting into bed with him, without trying to make any particular impression (unlike those overheated teenage entries) – just a truthful record:

> The act of love seemed somehow quite incidental, we talked so much. It was so warm & delicious, lying curled in each others arms, by the light of the tiny lamp […], only the clock & the fire to be heard. A whole life passed in the night: other people other things, but we lay like 2 old people coughing faintly under the eiderdown, and laughing at each other and away we went to India, to South America, to Marseilles in the white boat, and then we talked of Paris & sometimes I lost him in a crowd of people & it was dark & frightening, & then he was in my arms again, & we were kissing.[29]

No happiness? No satisfaction? The effect is of drifting in and out of sleep, uncertain which is which – and it sounds pretty enjoyable to me. And what of her relations with Jack? Of course (as most such relationships between talented and high-energy people are), it was turbulent and often negative; but by what right do you pass over all the evidence of the positives in it, including that late letter in which she says, 'I think no two lovers walked the earth more joyfully – in spite of all'?[30]

O'Sullivan also describes Mansfield as 'bisexual' (143), speaks more than once of her 'lesbianism' (144) and interprets 'Bertha's feeling for Pearl Fulton' in the story 'Bliss' as 'a lesbian one'. 'This may not be explicit,' he writes, 'but it would be an obtuse reading of the story which overlooked it.' This is not, as it happens, how I read the story; but more important, even if it were, I would not feel it meant the story's author was correctly described as 'lesbian'.

This is a large subject, and I touch on it only because the dispute was part of my ongoing engagement with Mansfield's life and work. It will at least explain why, when I represent her in my novel *Mansfield*, there is (or I hope there is) richness of personality, unpredictability, risk-taking, openness to whatever comes along; and she can *play the game* of bisexuality, as she does in one scene with Carrington at Garsington. But there is nothing to which the word 'lesbian' could properly attach itself.

*****

I come back to my title, which derives from Damien Wilkins's description of Mansfield as 'the great ghost in New Zealand's cultural life'.[31] She has certainly been a ghost in mine, but not a difficult or oppressive one; and I think this does mark an historical change from writers like

Curnow and Sargeson, born 20 and 30 years before me, for whom she was a decidedly mixed blessing and a problem requiring a strategy.

By 1972, my fortieth year, when I came to treat her work, not just as a reader but professionally, a lot had changed in the New Zealand literary scene, and those changes were continuing and accelerating. There was still (I detect, looking back) an element of slightly self-conscious nationalism in the way I went about my work; of 'laying claim' to her; but as a motivating factor that was insignificant, and soon absent altogether. What kept me at the task was the quality of mind, the superior literary intelligence and sensibility, and the way the letters and journals, together with unfinished, or finished yet imperfect, stories, opened the door on a writer's workshop. That Murry didn't 'leave all fair' was a great gift to modernist and postmodern generations, who valued the literary process as much as, and in some ways more than, the finished and perfect product. Mansfield was uneven (and how could it be otherwise? – she died at 34); but she was never boring. She loved the business of writing, loved to record it, reveal it, to be, and be seen to be, the writer at work.

But for myself a whole further aspect of my relationship with Mansfield was to develop, and I'll conclude by saying just a little about that. I finally left the university altogether in 1986, but soon found that I had taken Mansfield with me. She drifted in and out of my consciousness, first in poems and then, quite decisively, in my 1992 novel, *The End of the Century at the End of the World*.[32]

This is a novel in which the central character, Laura Barber, a 'mature student', is doing postgraduate work on a now-dead New Zealand writer, Hilda Tapler. Tapler has written, in the 1950s, a fictional account – or it has been assumed to be fiction – of meeting and interviewing Katherine Mansfield in Northland where she'd gone to live after faking her own death at the Gurdjieff Institute and taking the name of Katya Lawrence. Hilda Tapler's Mansfield fiction greatly interests Laura Barber, who begins to suspect, and even to find some evidence, that it might not be fiction at all.

This is metafiction of course, and by the end of the book the question of what happened 'really' and what is merely invented has become less important than, simply, the creation of a story: narrative as the structuring of experience necessary to the preservation of sanity; fiction as the recorder of social truths and human wisdom.

Nine years later Mansfield made another guest appearance, this time in my novel *The Secret History of Modernism*, where she's seen with T. S. Eliot, walking away from a dinner party in Hammersmith in 1917. That, in turn, gave me the idea of writing a whole novel about her;

and that novel, called *Mansfield* and published in 2004, opens with the same event (one which indeed happened) – Eliot and Mansfield walking along the towpath at Hammersmith, discussing the party they've just left where Robert Graves was still holding forth.

Mansfield came out of the recognition that here was a terrific story, full of incident and emotion, with an incomparably rich cast of ready-made characters, and that I might be as well qualified as anyone to write it. I decided to confine myself to three years of her life during the First World War, the period that would include her affair with Francis Carco, Leslie's death, the rediscovery of her New Zealand subject matter, the Bandol idyll with Murry, the Cornwall fiasco with the Lawrences, a glimpse of Garsington and Lady Ottoline, and only at the end the first unmistakeable intimation of tuberculosis. Much of what went into the novel was a filling in around, or building out beyond, what is already known.[33] But what you find when you write historical fiction is how huge the gaps are. The life we think we know so well is only a sketch. And the test is whether you can enter that sketch imaginatively, assume her voice and fill the gaps.

Notes

1. A. Curnow (ed.) (1960) *The Penguin Book of New Zealand Verse* (Auckland: Penguin), p. 57.
2. G. Ogilvie (1999) *Denis Glover: His Life* (Auckland: Godwit), pp. 413 and 381.
3. V. O'Sullivan (2008) 'Katherine Mansfield', *New Zealand Listener*, 5 July, p. 14.
4. C. K. Stead (1981) 'Katherine Mansfield: The Letters and Journals', in *In the Glass Case: Essays on New Zealand Literature* (Auckland University Press and Oxford University Press), pp. 20–8 (p. 27).
5. F. Sargeson (1983) 'Katherine Mansfield', in K. Cunningham (ed.) *Conversation on a Train and Other Critical Writing* (Auckland University Press and Oxford University Press), pp. 28–33 (pp. 29–30).
6. This is a line taken also by T. S. Eliot in his subsequently suppressed lecture series published in 1933 as *After Strange Gods: A Primer of Modern Heresy* (London: Faber and Faber) where he compares a Mansfield story with stories by Joyce and Lawrence, commends Mansfield's 'perfect [handling] of the *minimum* material', describes this as a 'feminine' quality and dismisses the story's 'moral implications' as 'negligible' (pp. 35–8).
7. 'Conversation with Frank Sargeson: An Interview with Michael Beveridge', in *Conversation in a Train*, pp. 147–85 (p. 153).
8. *Ibid.*, p. 154
9. Curnow, p. 40
10. *Ibid.*
11. E. Blunden (ed.) (1955) *The Poems of Wilfred Owen* (London: Chatto and Windus), p. 41.
12. The prize was worth, in 1972, NZ$1750; it is now worth NZ$100,000.

13. I'm referring to an abstract of one of Phillipson's papers, entitled 'Menton Blues: C. K. Stead and the Difficult Second Novel', presented at the New Zealand Studies Association conference in Florence, 'New Zealand and the Mediterranean' (2–4 July 2008).

14. Judith Burnley, herself a fiction writer, published two novels, *The Wife*, 1977, and *Unrepentant Woman*, 1982.

15. These are not in fact passages that occur in my Penguin selection.

16. 'Pleach – v. tr. To entwine or interlace (esp. branches to form a hedge)' (*Concise Oxford Dictionary*).

17. I'm speaking here of transcription and decipherment, not of editing and annotating of the kind done, most notably, by Vincent O'Sullivan.

18. *Leave All Fair* (1985), dir. John Reid. An interpretation of the life and relationships of Mansfield, starring John Gielgud, Jane Birkin, Feodor Atkine and Simon Ward.

19. *Letters* 5, pp. 234–5, 7 August 1922.

20. See 'Mansfield's F.O.' in my (2000) *The Writer at Work* (Dunedin: University of Otago Press), pp. 73–6.

21. Margaret Scott has many similar stories in (2001) *Recollecting Mansfield* (Auckland: Godwit).

22. I. Baker (1972) *Katherine Mansfield: The Memories of LM* (New York: Taplinger).

23. My 1977 *New Review* article can be found reprinted in (2002) *Kin of Place* (Auckland University Press), pp. 8–28. My correction to Murry's account of the writing of what became 'Prelude' was followed exactly by Vincent O'Sullivan in the introduction to his 1982 edition of *The Aloe with Prelude* (Wellington: Port Nicholson Press).

24. Antony Alpers rejects my dating of the story in a footnote on pp. 339–40 of his (1980) *The Life of Katherine Mansfield* (New York: The Viking Press), but in his collected edition (1984) *The Stories of Katherine Mansfield* (Oxford University Press), he dates it as I had done, citing the same letter as his evidence, but without referring either to my article or to his own footnote.

25. C. K. Stead (1986) *Pound, Yeats, Eliot and the Modernist Movement* (New Brunswick, NJ: Rutgers University Press).

26. V. O'Sullivan (1996) 'The Magnetic Chain: Notes and Approaches to K.M.', in *The Critical Response to Katherine Mansfield*, ed. J. Pilditch (Westport, CT: Greenwood Press), pp. 129–54. Further page references placed directly in the text.

27. Scott, p. 110.

28. C. Tomalin (1988) *Katherine Mansfield: A Secret Life* (London: Viking), p. 37.

29. *Notebooks* 2, p. 12.

30. *Letters* 5, pp. 234–5, 7 August 1922.

31. D. Wilkins (online article) 'Katherine Mansfield: Short Story Moderniser' http://www.nzedge.com/heroes/mansfield.html#GREATGHOST (accessed 11 July 2010).

32. C. K. Stead (1992) *The End of the Century at the End of the World* (London: Harvill).

33. The only really speculative thing I added, founded on known facts but going some significant way beyond them, was the brief affair with Frederick Goodyear.

Select Bibliography

Ackroyd, P. (1990) *Dickens* (London: Guild).

Albright, D. (ed.) (2004) *Modernism and Music: An Anthology of Sources* (University of Chicago Press).

Alpers, A. (1980) *The Life of Katherine Mansfield* (New York: The Viking Press).

—— (1984) *The Stories of Katherine Mansfield* (Oxford University Press).

Ashcroft, B., G. Griffiths and H. Tiffin (eds) *The Post-Colonial Studies Reader* (London and New York: Routledge).

Baker, I. (1972) *Katherine Mansfield: The Memories of LM* (New York: Taplinger).

Beauchamp, H. (1937) *Reminiscences and Recollections* (New Plymouth, New Zealand: Thomas Avery & Sons).

Begam, R. and M. Valdez Moses (eds) (2007) *Modernism and Colonialism* (Durham, NC and London: Duke University Press).

Bell, A. O. and A. McNellie (eds) (1975–85) *The Diary of Virginia Woolf*, 5 vols (Harmondsworth: Penguin).

Bennett, A. (2004) *Katherine Mansfield* (London: Northcote House).

Bhabha, H. (1995) *The Location of Culture* (London: Routledge).

Boehmer, E. (2002) *Empire, the National and the Postcolonial: Resistance in Interaction* (Oxford University Press).

—— (2005) *Colonial and Postcolonial Literature: Migrant Metaphors* (Oxford University Press).

Booth, H. and N. Rigby (eds) (2000) *Modernism and Empire* (Manchester University Press).

Brooker, P. and A. Thacker (eds) (2009) *The Oxford Critical and Cultural History of Modernist Magazines*. Vol. 1, *Britain and Ireland 1880–1955* (Oxford University Press).

Brooker, P., A. Gasiorek, D. Longworth and A. Thacker (eds) (2010) *The Oxford Handbook of Modernisms* (Oxford University Press).

Carswell, J. (1978) *Lives and Letters: A. R. Orage, Katherine Mansfield, Beatrice Hastings, John Middleton Murry, S. S. Koteliansky, 1906–1957* (London and Boston: Faber and Faber).

Caws, M. A. (1985) *Reading Frames in Modern Fiction* (Princeton University Press).

Collins, P. (1971) *Dickens: The Critical Heritage* (London: Routledge and Kegan Paul).

Cunningham, K. (ed.) *Conversation on a Train and Other Critical Writing* (Auckland University Press and Oxford University Press).

Curnow, A. (ed.) (1960) *The Penguin Book of New Zealand Verse* (Auckland: Penguin).

Da Sousa Correa, D. (ed.) (2006) *Phrase and Subject: Studies in Literature and Music* (London: Legenda, MHRA/Maney Publishing).

Dick, S. (ed.) (1985) *The Complete Shorter Fiction of Virginia Woolf* (San Diego: Harcourt Brace Jovanovich).

Dickens, C. (1997 [1865]) *Our Mutual Friend* (Harmondsworth: Penguin).

Donald, J., A. Friedberg and L. Marcus (eds) (1998) *Close Up 1927–1933: Cinema and Modernism* (Princeton University Press).

Doyle, L. and L. Finkiel (eds) (2005) *Geo-modernisms: Race, Modernism, Modernity* (Bloomington: Indiana University Press).

Dunbar, P. (1997) *Radical Mansfield: Double Discourse in Katherine Mansfield's Short Stories* (Basingstoke: Macmillan).

Eliot, T. S. (1986 [1951]) *Selected Essays* (London: Faber and Faber).

Elsaesser, T. (ed.) (1989) *The Cinema of Attractions: Early Film, Space, Frame, Narrative* (London: British Film Institute).

Esty, J. (2004) *A Shrinking Island: Modernism and National Culture in England* (Princeton University Press).

Ford, G. H. (1965) *Dickens and His Readers* (New York: W. W. Norton).

Forster, E. M. (1962 [1927]) *Aspects of the Novel* (Harmondsworth: Penguin).

Freud, S. (1985 [1915]) 'Thoughts for the Times on War and Death', J. Strachey (trans.), A. Dickson (ed.) in *Civilization, Society and Religion*, Pelican Freud Library, 12 (Harmondsworth: Penguin).

—— (1987 [1919]) 'Beyond the Pleasure Principle', J. Strachey (trans.), Pelican Freud Library, 11 (Harmondsworth: Penguin).

—— (2003 [1919]) *The Uncanny*, D. McLintock (trans.), H. Haughton (intro.) (London: Penguin).

Gordon, I. A. (ed.) (1974) *Katherine Mansfield: Undiscovered Country* (London: Longman).

Hankin, C. A. (1983) *Katherine Mansfield and her Confessional Stories* (London: Macmillan).

—— (ed.) (1983) *The Letters of John Middleton Murry to Katherine Mansfield* (London: Constable).

—— (ed.) (1988) *Letters Between Katherine Mansfield and John Middleton Murry* (London: Virago Press).

Hanson, C. (1985) *Short Stories and Short Fictions, 1880–1980* (London: Macmillan).

Hanson, C. and A. Gurr (1981) *Katherine Mansfield* (London: Macmillan).

Head, D. (1992) *The Modernist Short Story: A Study in Theory and Practice* (Cambridge University Press).

House, M., G. Storey and K. Tillotson (eds) (1997) *The Letters of Charles Dickens* (Oxford: Clarendon Press), vol. 9.

Kaplan, S. J. (1991) *Katherine Mansfield and the Origins of Modernist Fiction* (Ithaca and London: Cornell University Press).

Kierkegaard, S. (2006) *Fear and Trembling*, C. S. Evans and S. Walsh (eds) (Cambridge University Press).

Kimber, G. (2008) *Katherine Mansfield: The View from France* (Oxford: Peter Lang).

—— (2008) *A Literary Modernist: Katherine Mansfield and the Art of the Short Story* (London: Kakapo).

Kirkpatrick, B. J. (1989) *A Bibliography of Katherine Mansfield* (Oxford: Clarendon Press).

Kofman, S. (1991) *Freud and Fiction*, S. Wykes (trans.) (Cambridge: Polity Press).

Kristeva, J. (1984) *Revolution in Poetic Language*, M. Waller (trans.) (New York: Columbia University Press).

Lawrence, D. H. (1969 [1921]) *Women in Love* (Harmondsworth: Penguin).

Lea, F. A. (1960) *The Life of John Middleton Murry* (Oxford University Press).

Mansfield, K. (2007) *The Collected Stories* (London: Penguin).

Mantz, R. E. and J. M. Murry (1933) *The Life of Katherine Mansfield* (London: Constable).

Marcus, L. (2007) *The Tenth Muse: Writing About Cinema in the Modernist Period* (Oxford University Press).

Meyers, J. (1978) *Katherine Mansfield: A Biography* (New York: New Directions).

Moore, J. (1980) *Gurdjieff and Mansfield* (London: Routledge and Kegan Paul).

Moran, P. (1996) *Word of Mouth: Body Language in Katherine Mansfield and Virginia Woolf* (Charlottesville: University of Virginia Press).

Murry, J. M. (ed.) (1927) *The Journal of Katherine Mansfield* (London: Constable).

—— (ed.) (1930) *Katherine Mansfield: Novels and Novelists* (London: Constable).

—— (1935) *Between Two Worlds: An Autobiography* (London: Jonathan Cape).

—— (1954) *Journal of Katherine Mansfield 1904–1922*, Definitive Edition (London: Constable).

Nathan, R. B. (ed.) (1993) *Critical Essays on Katherine Mansfield* (New York: G. K. Hall).

New, W. H. (1999) *Reading Mansfield and Metaphors of Form* (Quebec: McGill-Queen's University Press).

Nicolson, N. with J. Trautmann (eds) (1976) *The Letters of Virginia Woolf* (New York: Harcourt), vol. 2.

O'Sullivan, V. (ed.) (1982) *The Aloe with Prelude* (Wellington: Port Nicholson Press).

—— (ed.) (1988) *Poems of Katherine Mansfield* (Oxford University Press).

—— (ed.) (1997) *Katherine Mansfield's New Zealand Stories* (Oxford University Press).

—— (ed.) (2006) *Katherine Mansfield's Selected Stories* (London: Norton Critical Edition).

O'Sullivan, V. and M. Scott (eds) (1984–2008) *The Collected Letters of Katherine Mansfield*, 5 vols (Oxford: Clarendon Press).

'Oxon, M. B.' (1921) *Cosmic Anatomy and the Structure of the Ego* (London: John M. Watkins).

Pilditch, J. (ed.) (1996) *The Critical Response to Katherine Mansfield* (Westport, CT: Greenwood Press).

Robinson, R. (ed.) *Katherine Mansfield: In from the Margin* (Baton Rouge: Louisiana State University Press).

Said, E. (1983) *The World, the Text and the Critic* (Cambridge, MA: Harvard University Press).

Scott, M. (ed.) (1997) *The Katherine Mansfield Notebooks*, 2 vols (Canterbury, New Zealand: Lincoln University Press and Daphne Brasell Associates).

—— (2001) *Recollecting Mansfield* (Auckland: Godwit).

Slater, M. (2009) *Charles Dickens* (New Haven and London: Yale University Press).

Smith, A. (1999) *Katherine Mansfield and Virginia Woolf: A Public of Two* (Oxford University Press).

—— (2000) *Katherine Mansfield: A Literary Life* (Basingstoke: Palgrave).

—— (ed.) (2002) *Selected Stories of Katherine Mansfield* (Oxford University Press).

Stead, C. K. (ed.) (1977) *Katherine Mansfield: Letters and Journals* (London: Penguin).

—— (1981) *In the Glass Case: Essays on New Zealand Literature* (Auckland University Press and Oxford University Press).

—— (1986) *Pound, Yeats, Eliot and the Modernist Movement* (New Brunswick, NJ: Rutgers University Press).

—— (1992) *The End of the Century at the End of the World* (London: Harvill).

—— (2000) *The Writer at Work* (Dunedin: University of Otago Press).

—— (2002) *Kin of Place* (Auckland University Press).

—— (2004) *Mansfield: A Novel* (London: Harvill Press).

Tomalin, C. (1987) *Katherine Mansfield: A Secret Life* (London: Viking).

Van Gunsteren, J. (1991) *Katherine Mansfield and Literary Impressionism* (Amsterdam and New York: Rodopi).

Webb, J. (1980) *The Harmonious Circle: The Lives and Work of G. I. Gurdjieff, P. D. Ouspensky, and their Followers* (London: Thames and Hudson).

Williams, M. and M. Leggott (eds) (1995) *Opening the Book: New Essays on New Zealand Writing* (Auckland University Press).

Wilson, E. (1961) *The Wound and the Bow* (London: Methuen).

Wilson, J. (2007) *Fleur Adcock* (Plymouth: British Council and Northcote House).

Wilson J., G. Kimber and S. Reid (eds) (2011) *Katherine Mansfield and Literary Modernism* (London: Continuum).

Woolf, L. (ed.) (1966) *Virginia Woolf Collected Essays*, 4 vols (London: Hogarth).

Woolf, V. (1996 [1925]) *Mrs Dalloway* (London: Penguin).

Index

Acacia Road, 32, 33, 35, 37, 40
Adcock, Fleur, 187, 232
Africa and African, 6, 47, 60, 61, 66,
68, 69, 70, 71, 161, 199, 200,
see also South Africa
Agamben, Giorgio, 146, 156
Albright, Daniel, 87, 93, 95, 96, 97,
229
Alcott, Louisa May, 37
Alpers, Antony, 24, 27, 31, 33, 36,
39–41, 47, 53–4, 83, 129, 228,
229
Anand, Mulk Raj, 58, 59, 60, 61
Anderson, Walter, 109, 112
animism, 117, 119, 120, 123
'Ark, The' (Gower Street), 42, 43, 77
Asquith, Herbert, 28
Athenaeum, 26, 74, 82, 83, 129
Auckland, 14, 214, 215
Auden, W. H., 222
Austen, Jane, 90, 216
automatism, *see* doll motif
avant-garde, 60, 70, 83, 86, 92, 175,
189, 223

Baker, Ida ['L. M.'], 43, 53, 86, 96,
190, 195, 197, 200, 208, 222,
228, 229
Bandol, 45, 195, 223, 227
Bannerman, Helen, 66, 71
Barry, Iris, 72, 83
Barthes, Roland, 7, 123, 124, 128, 141
Bateson, George, 6, 99–110 *passim*,
111, 112
Bateson, Gregory, 6, 100, 101, 102,
103, 104, 106, 108, 110, 111, 112
Baudelaire, Charles, 84, 86, 88, 93, 95,
96, 97, 144
Beauchamp, Annie, 33, 34, 39, 40, 73
Beauchamp, family, 8, 177
Beauchamp, Harold, 22, 28, 29, 30,
34, 38, 40, 86, 211, 229
Beauchamp, Jeanne, 29, 99, 147

Beauchamp, Kathleen Mansfield, 29,
31, 32, 33, 34, 37, 38, 73, 188,
see also Mansfield, Katherine (KM)
Beauchamp, Leslie Heron (*also*
'Chummie' or 'Bogey'), 5, 28–38
passim, 38–41, 80, 116, 125, 129,
131, 147, 153, 176, 182, 187, 204,
211, 212, 227
Beauchamp, Vera, 29, 36, 37
Beethoven, Ludwig van, 88, 96
Belgium, 33–4, 35–6, 38
Bell, James Mackintosh, 39
Bell, Vanessa, 54
Bendall, Edie, 224
Bergson, Henri, 19, 152
Bhabha, Homi, 58, 62, 70, 71, 178,
184, 187, 229
Bible, the, 13, 14, 146, 155, 196, 208
Bibliography of Katherine Mansfield, A
(Kirkpatrick, B. J., 1989), 83, 230
Bioscope, 77
Bishop, Elizabeth, 202, 203
Bloomsbury, 2, 193, 218, 222
Blue Review, 4, 36, 183
Boehmer, Elleke, 1, 4, 6, 8, 57, 70, 71,
186, 229
'Bogey', *see* Beauchamp, Leslie Heron;
Murry, John Middleton
Bowden, George, 74
Bowen, Elizabeth, 4, 10, 176, 187
Brady, E. J., 63
Brett, Dorothy, 22, 23, 42, 77, 190,
205, 208, 209, 210
Brontë, Emily, 207, 208
Brooke, Rupert, 116
Bruch, Max, 87
Buck, Peter, Sir, 214
Burgan, Mary, 3
Burnley, Judith, 218, 228
Byatt, A. S., 222

Campbell, Beatrice, 72, 206
Campbell, Gordon, 47